STAFF & CROWN

A Two Monarchies Novel

W.R. GINGELL

For all those readers who loved Melchior as much as I did.

Staff & Crown

Cover by Seedlings Design Studio

T hree years, thought Annabel, was a curious amount of time. It had seemed like a long time when she was looking at it from the beginning of those years, but now that she was nearly at the end of them, she didn't find them to have been very long at all.

Now it was more natural to think of it as *just three years*. Just three years ago, an enchanted castle had appeared to save Annabel and her best friend Peter from being killed by the rogue wizard Mordion. Just three years ago, her talking cat Blackfoot had led her a merry dance around that castle. And just three years ago, Annabel had been dismayed and surprised to discover that she had, in fact, passed a test designed by the ancient wizard Rorkin to select the next queen of New Civet. And then there was the fact that her cat Blackfoot turned out not to be a cat after all...

If it was unpleasant to be chased around an enchanted castle by a murderous wizard and led astray by the wiles of the castle itself, it was much worse to find out that she was the heir apparent to New Civet's throne. More importantly, when Annabel, Peter, and Blackfoot finally escaped castle, they had found themselves three years in the past, the castle gone again as mysteriously as it had come back.

Those three years before the castle returned and everyone found out that Annabel was the heir should have been a reprieve. A chance to learn things she desperately needed to learn, and for Blackfoot to make the kind of arrangements a spy-turned-cat-turned-man needed to make for the installation of a lost heir.

But if Annabel looked at it in another way—and these days, she found that she did look at it in another way—there was a distinct feeling of despondency to her thoughts. Part of that despondency could be put down to the fact that Annabel would be on her way to Trenthams' Finishing School within the week, and part of it could have been because that would mean not seeing Blackfoot and Peter for a whole half year. But the main cause of that despondency was almost certainly the fact that her three years were nearly up—and that, in less than half a year, the castle would return and Annabel would be officially recognised as the queen heir. She would actually be crowned within the year, when her time at Trenthams Finishing School was over. Nineteen years old was certainly too young to be crowned queen.

Annabel sighed. The only other occupant of the room, a slender, black-dressed individual who was reading over a letter and pretending not to notice anything but the letter, said without raising his head, "It's no use sighing at me. Your little friend can come back when he's learned some manners."

"I'm not sighing about that," said Annabel. She'd seen Peter just last month, if it came to that, but she wasn't about to tell Blackfoot—Melchior—that. Three months ago, Melchior had been annoyed enough to remove Peter from the house by his collar, an indignity that Peter could have obstructed with his very considerable magic powers if he'd chosen, but was too proud to do so. He was almost as tall as Melchior these days, and no doubt he would have liked to think he could best him in a scuffle.

Annabel found herself grinning and hastily stopped herself. She hadn't been best pleased with Melchior, either; Peter was a horrible little boy who said rude things that he shouldn't, but she and he had been best friends for too long to let that stand between them.

Melchior, on the other hand, had never been particularly good friends with Peter; and now that he had a human form instead of a cat one, he had made very obvious his refusal to allow Peter to speak to Annabel in the way he had been used to do. And despite the fact that Annabel missed Peter, she didn't think it a bad thing for him to be taught a few manners. It was high-handed of Melchior, but it was his manor after all. So she said, "I'm not sighing about that."

"Well, that makes a nice change, anyway," Melchior said. This time he looked up, and there was a glint to his eye that made Annabel think he knew more than she'd suspected. Confirming that, he added, "Did you have a pleasant heart-to-heart last month?"

Annabel blinked at him.

"Don't try that with me. It doesn't work. I saw Peter at the Terry party."

"He was invited."

"So was I, but I didn't climb through the window."

"I think he was sorry."

"For what? The way he speaks to you, or being thrown out of the manor? Or was it for bringing up his lofty assumption that you'll get married one day and telling you off for laughing with other boys?"

Annabel thought about that. "I don't know," she said at last. The Peter she'd seen at the party last month had been a rather raw and pale Peter. He had climbed through the window and dragged Annabel away from the other partygoers before anyone but Melchior had a chance to see him.

Annabel, rushed into the hall and rather more breathless than she would have preferred to be from a combination of too-tight lacing and a lack of exercise over the last few weeks, gasped out, "What? Peter, you horrible boy! What are you doing?"

"Ann," began Peter. He was frowning; and, most unlike himself, he looked as though he was having trouble finding the words to speak. Peter was more inclined to come out bluntly with the first, convenient words that sprang to mind, whether or not they were kind or helpful.

He looked...older? More worried? Annabel asked, "What's wrong?"

Peter laughed, then stopped. He dashed his fingers through his hair as she'd often seen him do. That was frustration and uncertainty. "There's—there's something I have to tell you," he said.

"Is that why you climbed through the window?" Annabel had

visions of Mordion come back to life, the castle torn apart by his escape, and Rorkin somewhere in the length and breadth of time, unable to assist.

"Yes. That's why I climbed through the window."

"What's wrong?" she asked again.

"I'm sorry."

Annabel blinked. "What?"

"All right, I know it's not like me," Peter said, with attempted dignity. "I'm *sorry*. Lately I've been—Actually, no; I've *always* been awful to you. I didn't know—Well, I suppose I knew, a bit. But you always just took it, and so I forgot to care about whether or not I was hurting your feelings. Anyway, I'm sorry."

"Is this because Melchior threw you out?"

"What? No. Well, maybe a bit. But someone told me—No, she showed me—"

"She?"

Peter flushed dull red. "Never mind. The point is that I didn't realise how awful I'd been to you, and I'm sorry."

It was only by a severe effort of self control that Annabel managed not to laugh. "Who is *she*?"

"Never mind about that," Peter said, this time setting his shoulders. "She's a quick-tempered madwoman, and I should have stayed away from her. Actually, no—That was my fault too, if it comes to that."

"I want to meet her."

There it was again. Annabel had spoken lightly, teasingly, but Peter's face was suddenly stiff and miserable.

"You can't," he said. "I did something—we did something—and you won't meet her for a bit."

"Peter," said Annabel suspiciously, "have you been playing with your tickerboxes again?"

"Anyway," Peter said, ignoring that completely, "I won't see you for a bit, either. I'm sorry about that. And—and about everything else. I didn't understand—I didn't know how it could affect you."

"What's wrong, Peter?" Annabel said sharply. "Really?"

"I don't have any time," Peter said. "And time is—Well, time is pretty important at the moment. I'm sorry, Ann."

He actually hugged her. It was the first time he had done so of his own volition, without being injured or sick, and he didn't let her go for quite some time.

That was the last Annabel had seen of him, and for the first few weeks afterward, she couldn't help feeling that he was avoiding her; whether from shame, embarrassment, or some other equally foreign emotion. Then it occurred to her that he had probably gone to visit his mother. The three years before the castle was due to return weren't quite up, but Annabel was quite sure he had visited his mother before then. She had left him to himself because she was quite sure if Peter knew anything, it was how careful he needed to be when it came to time.

Now, sitting across from Melchior, Annabel said, "I don't think we'll see him for a while yet."

Melchior looked at her sharply, and it occurred to her that he knew something when he said, "Ah. I see. Never mind, Nan; you'll see him again. Hopefully he'll be a bit better behaved by then."

Suspiciously now, Annabel demanded, "What do you know? Have you been talking to Rorkin? Where is he?"

Melchior grinned. "I haven't talked to Rorkin since the castle."

"What did he say *then*?"

"You're growing up to be a very suspicious young woman, Nan."

"Maybe I wouldn't have if you hadn't lied to me all the—"

"Don't start that again!" Melchior said hastily. "I managed to have a bit of a talk with Rorkin—actually, he managed to have one with me —and I was given the impression that your friend has something he needs to do somewhere else. But you know what Rorkin's like. It could have been what he wanted me to think."

"Yes," agreed Annabel. Talking with Rorkin was inclined to leave her a little bit dizzy and certain only that anything she thought she knew was likely to be something she was meant to think she knew, and not necessarily true. One thing Annabel was really very sure about, on the other hand, was that the letter at present forgotten between Melchior's fingers was from Mr. Pennicott, the driving force behind the group who had sent Melchior to find her so many years ago.

Three years ago, that thought would have prompted Annabel to thought but not to action. Today, she rose without a pang for her comfortable seat by the window and wandered behind Melchior's sofa, ostensibly to look at the books in the bookcase there. Lately Melchior, who had always curled up on her pillow and in her lap in his cat form, had taken to deliberately distancing himself. Sitting on the sofa opposite instead of the same one, for example, and chiding her when she tried to pat his head as she had used to do when he was Blackfoot the cat. Annabel was quite sure he was receiving more notes, too; and not all of them were from Mr. Pennicott, his employer.

Annabel leaned her forearms on the sofa back and looked over Melchior's shoulder, scruffing his hair by reflex. It was also three years since Melchior had been a cat, but the habit of patting his head and tickling his ears had stayed with her. Tugging on his short, dark hair as she'd used to tug on his ears, she said: "Is that from Mr. Pennicott? Do you have to go away again?"

"Don't do that, Nan," he said, batting her hand away. The letter vanished at the same time, though Annabel wasn't sure if it was purposely or simply a result of fending her off.

"Why?" she demanded, evading his swipes and ruffling his hair even more vigorously, this time with both hands. "I *like* patting your head."

This time, Melchior moved away entirely, twitching around to look at her. "I'm not your cat any more, Nan."

"Yes, you are," Annabel said. "You're mine, my cat. You should purr like you used to."

"Then it seems rather awkward to mention at this stage that I am, in fact, a man," remarked Melchior. His thin lips had a rather curious curl to them. "Have you never noticed?"

"Of course I have," said Annabel. "You take up a lot more space and you're not as furry. But it's still nice to pat you on the head."

"Nice it may be," Melchior retorted. "It's certainly not proper, however. And for that matter, neither is leaning over the backs of sofas and whispering in gentlemen's ears."

"I wasn't whispering in gentlemen's ears!" Annabel protested. "I was talking, and it's *your* ear! You were muttering in the back of my mind for five years, so I don't see why I shouldn't pat you on the head and talk in your ear now and then."

Melchior's hazel eyes gazed at her for quite some time before he said pleasantly: "I feel I should mention once again that I am no longer a cat."

"But I can see that!"

"I don't think you do."

Annabel, crossly, said, "I wish you'd speak in proper sentences. You're as bad as Rorkin."

"Now there's an idea," said Melchior to himself, even more maddeningly incomprehensible. "You've always liked cat-me better than human-me, haven't you?"

"You *are* cat-you."

"That's not what you said three years ago," Melchior said. He was looking very thoughtful, and Annabel wasn't sure that was a good thing. "Maybe I should have bitten you once or twice."

"You did," remarked Annabel, circling to the front of the sofa and sitting at the other end of it.

"I can't imagine why you liked me."

"Neither can I," Annabel said, but she couldn't help grinning. That wasn't strictly true. "Anyway, I know you're you. It was just that at the start—Well, everything was changing, and you know I don't like change."

"I know," Melchior said, crossing one ankle over the other and leaning against the other sofa arm. "I'm not sure I appreciated how very much you disliked it until lately, however."

"Anyway, I got used to human-you."

Melchior's brows rose. "I'll beg to differ on that head. You've never gotten used to me; you've simply treated me like a cat ever since you got over being angry at me."

"You are a cat," said Annabel again. "My cat. Anyway, I haven't been angry at you for a very long time—and that was just because I wasn't used to you looking like this and it was hard to think of you as the same person."

"Now there's another idea," murmured Melchior.

"What idea?" demanded Annabel. She wasn't sure she was ready for more of Melchior's ideas. They usually involved a lot of work from her, and even if she was beginning to bestir herself more than she had done in the past, it was still a conscious effort to do so.

"Never you mind."

Annabel made a small *pft* noise at him. If there was anything more annoying than Melchior talking in riddles and coming up with ideas, it was Melchior talking in riddles and refusing to explain his ideas. Still, she'd been around him long enough to know it wouldn't do any good to pester him for explanations, so she went to her room instead. Sometimes it was easier to deal with Melchior if you came back to him in the morning when he wasn't feeling so facetious or pernickety.

In the morning, however, it was painfully obvious that Melchior was not inclined to be either less facetious *or* pernickety. He didn't come to breakfast, and when Annabel looked for him to find out why, he was stalking around his private wing of the manor, trying to fix a top hat spell.

"Why don't you just buy one?" she asked, leaning in the doorway to watch.

Melchior's eyes flicked over to her and away again. "You're not supposed to be in this part of the manor."

"You said that last time, too," pointed out Annabel. "Anyone would think you're hiding bodies here."

"You can't come into a gentleman's wing." Melchior narrowed his eyes at the top hat and very cautiously curled the brim just a little more. Annabel might have thought it was part of the spell if she didn't know exactly how stylish human Melchior liked to be as opposed to cat Melchior. "It's not polite. What if I was getting dressed?"

"Then it would serve you right," Annabel said. "You shouldn't be dressing with your doors wide open. I don't bellow at you every time you wander into *my* hallway and tap on the door."

"I should hope not!" Melchior said, turning his head to one side and adjusting the other side of the hat brim minutely. "This is my manor. I refuse to be bellowed at on my own grounds."

"Actually," said Annabel, who was feeling argumentative, "if I'm the queen heir of New Civet, doesn't all this belong to me by sovereign right? You're the one who taught me that. So I'm allowed to bellow at you in the manor if I want—it's *my* manor. Sovereignly. And if I want to bellow at you in a sovereignly manner, I will."

Melchior squinted at his hat. "I thought you were boasting that you'd *refrained* from bellowing."

"I was," Annabel said, grinning in spite of herself. "I got confused. What I meant to say was that we've lived together for years in one way or another, and there's no need for us to be standing on ceremony when we're so comfortable with each other."

"I'm beginning to think, Nan," said Melchior, "that there is such a thing as being *too* comfortable."

"I don't think there is, you know," Annabel argued. "When Peter and I—"

"I have absolutely no intention of being comfortable with you in the same manner that Peter was."

"I don't see why not," protested Annabel, feeling slightly hurt. "I'm nothing like as difficult to get along with as Peter!"

"I don't believe I said you were," Melchior said, touching one long finger to the crown of his top hat and crouching to observe the effect of his magic, so utterly invisible to Annabel. "However, *I* have every intention of being very difficult."

"Yes, and speaking of Peter—!"

"I don't want to speak of Peter. As a matter of fact, we weren't speaking of Peter. I was warning you that I intend to be very difficult to get along with. I find I don't approve of too much comfort."

"That—" Annabel paused for breath, and said plaintively, "That makes no sense!"

"I really don't think I could make myself any clearer," said Melchior, straightening. "But perhaps I should try a different way."

He turned toward the doorway, and for the first time Annabel noticed that he was smiling. She hadn't seen him smile in just such a way before, and she found it distinctly off-putting.

Annabel took one step backward and said uncertainly, "What—"

"Huh," said a voice in her ear. "Here you both are."

Annabel jumped and squeaked, then glared at the interloper. He was a dishevelled, dark-haired man, and the look of faint absent-mindedness he wore was as familiar to Annabel as his mud-splattered overcoat. After leaving the enchanted castle, but before she and Peter managed to wriggle themselves into Melchior's , they had both lived with Luck and his wife, Poly. Annabel adored Poly but she found Luck, with his habit of appearing and disappearing and doing exactly what he felt like, as annoying as Melchior found Peter.

"Luck!" she said, catching her breath. "What are you doing here? Is it something to do with why Peter has disappeared?"

"Thought you weren't going to tell her about that?" Luck said mildly, to Melchior.

Melchior, looking significantly more annoyed than Annabel was used to seeing him with anyone other than Peter, said, "I hadn't. You just did."

"Oh," said Luck. "Whoops." He disappeared.

"I *knew* there was more to it!" Annabel said accusingly. "I want to know—wait! Where are you going?"

"To find Luck and throttle him," said Melchior, in a particularly grim tone of voice. "I've never found his timing particularly wonderful, but it has reached its peak maladroitness today!"

"But Peter—"

"I've always found Peter less than congenial company," Melchior said even more grimly, "but allow me to tell you, Nan, that today I find him completely insupportable."

And Annabel, open-mouthed, couldn't gather her wits quickly enough to protest before Melchior opened one of his odd little tunnels and vanished into it as thoroughly as Luck had vanished. She was left alone in the hallway to the indignant thought that Luck and Melchior were sure to be talking secrets, and that both of them knew more about Peter than they were telling.

"Just wait until I'm queen!" she told the wall into which Melchior had vanished. "*Won't* I make you run around!"

She resented the fact that when Luck appeared at the manor, Melchior was missing more often than he was around; and in this case, it was even more annoying. There was obviously something going on and Annabel was, just as obviously, excluded. Much of her annoyance could have been mitigated had Poly arrived along with Luck, but when Annabel went down hopefully to the horseless carriage in which Luck generally travelled, it was empty of anything except a small crab. That small crab was trying to climb onto the seat by pinching the passenger strap in its pincers, but its eyes swivelled hopefully when Annabel opened the carriage door.

"What?" Annabel said irritably to those hopeful eyes; but she lifted it up on the seat anyway. Serve Luck right if he came back to find his carriage seat torn to pieces by tiny pincers. It was at times like these that she resented her complete lack of magic. There was, of course, the royal staff she had originally found in the castle when it was still a ruin—even if, at present, it was in the form of a small, well-bitten pencil—but it wasn't the sort of thing Annabel liked to use, willy-nilly. If she had had her own magic, however, she could have gone off to visit Poly in Luck's horseless carriage, leaving Melchior and Luck to talk secrets all they wanted. During the two and a half years Annabel had spent at Poly and Luck's house, she had come to learn that Poly was the one who knew all the interesting things, anyway.

It wouldn't have been so bad, thought Annabel, trudging back to the manor, if only she wasn't off to Trenthams at the end of the week. If she'd had longer than a few days, she would have been able to bother and tease Melchior until he answered her questions. As it was, there were only a few short days before she was supposed to begin her year at finishing school, and while Luck was around there wasn't the slightest chance she would get enough time with Melchior to do more than ask him if he wanted butter for his toast. And if Melchior continued not coming to breakfast, she wouldn't even get that much in the way of conversation.

Much to Annabel's relief, Luck's visit didn't outlast the day. Shortly before nightfall he came striding around the outside of the manor toward his carriage; and Annabel, who had been waiting for just such a thing to occur, caught him at the gate.

"What about Peter?" she demanded.

"What about my crab?" demanded Luck in return. "You didn't let it out, did you?"

"It's sitting on the seat," Annabel said. "Luck, about Peter—"

"Oh, good," said Luck. "It's driving. Poly says hello. Goodbye."

"Luck!" snapped Annabel, but Luck only darted into his carriage.

Either he or the crab set it bowling forward jerkily before she could say anything else, and it swept out the gate while she glared at it.

"I hope you get sick," she muttered, to its swiftly-departing backboards.

She was inclined to forgive him, however, when he leant out the window as he passed the wall on the other side of the garden and called out, "The brat is safe—Well, safe-ish. He's got something to do. Wouldn't go looking for him if I was you—you'll be busy enough without that."

That comforted Annabel somewhat—Poly might know all the more interesting things, but Luck tended to be right about the things he did know; or at least, the things he chose to *share*. She went back into the manor with the lightened feeling that now she could go off to Trenthams without worrying too much.

Unfortunately, Melchior's absence did outlast the day, and Annabel was left to eat by herself at all three meals the next day. She might have felt less worried about Peter, but she didn't find that she felt any more cheerful in general, and when Melchior failed to show up again for breakfast the morning after that, Annabel briefly considered drawing him in with the pencil staff. She didn't do it; she was grown up, after all, and even if she was childish enough to stomp grimly around the manor in search of Melchior, she was adult enough to know she was being silly. He didn't seem to be in the manor at all. Annabel, who had grown used to always having him with her from the time when he was a cat to the last three years as a human, found herself indignant. Didn't he care that he wouldn't see her for months?

"Rude," she muttered.

Then, because she felt dismal and in need of cheering up, Annabel went up to her suite and drew in her sketchbook until night fell, surrounded by boxes and trunks. She would have stayed there all night if she hadn't heard the butler opening the front door, and his faint voice welcoming *Master Melchior* home. She rather expected Melchior to come up and walk her down to dinner, but he didn't do that, either. She wasn't sure when he'd started doing it, or when it had become so familiar that she didn't even think about it any longer, but it was conspicuous in its absence tonight.

That was silly, Annabel told herself severely; and sillier to be annoyed by it. Melchior didn't have to walk her to dinner every night like she was a fine lady. But she was still annoyed to find Melchior already seated and eating when she arrived in the dining room.

He made a small bow at her over the table—was there an edge of mockery to it? a hint of challenge? Annabel thought so—but only said, "Cook mentioned that you wouldn't be down to dinner."

"I wasn't going to," Annabel said, "but I heard you arrive."

Melchior's hand paused above the soup ladle. "Oh? Did you want to see me particularly, Nan?"

"No," said Annabel, helping herself to the beans. She didn't like soup very much. "I just thought you should know that I'm leaving for Trenthams tomorrow."

"I remember," Melchior said, and filled his soup bowl, smiling faintly.

"Do you?" Annabel was aware that her voice sounded sour. "I thought you must have forgotten. Were you out doing something for Mr. Pennicott?"

"No," Melchior replied, so easily and comfortably that she knew he was telling the truth. "I thought it was time I cut my hair. I went to the barber."

"You were away at the *barber*?"

"You don't expect me to cut my own hair, surely, Nan?"

His hair had been cut, Annabel noticed belatedly. She must have seen it when she entered the room, but she didn't remember taking note of it especially. Her temper slipped just a little more. If he had been away for two days right before she was to leave, she had expected that it would be on account of Mr. Pennicott; and that Melchior would at least have been careful about any answers he gave, even if he didn't outright admit the fact.

"I could have cut it for you," she said, and ate her beans gloomily.

"Good heavens." Melchior looked startled. "No, I think not."

"Rude," said Annabel. "You don't know I'd do a bad job. I haven't tried to cut hair before."

"Exactly my point."

"Is that all you were doing? Getting your hair cut?"

"I bought some new clothes as well," said Melchior.

Annabel let her face settle into the familiar, blank expression with which she found it easiest to mask her feelings. "You bought new clothes?"

"While some people—" began Melchior, "mentioning no names, of course—while some people are content to grub around the manor in clothing either too large or favourites long since grown out of, I prefer—"

"Yes, yes, you like to look dashing and debonair at every moment," Annabel said.

"—I prefer," continued Melchior, very firmly, "to be ready to meet my future wife at a moment's notice."

"Oh," said Annabel. Her face felt slightly stiff. She was obviously out of practise with her blank face. "Are you planning on getting married?"

"I imagine it will be easier when I'm not looking after a rather badly dressed future queen all the time," Melchior said, as if she hadn't said anything.

Annabel, who didn't care for his tone of voice—it could have been Melchior addressing Peter instead of Melchior addressing herself—lost a little more of her temper and said, "You should have said so a fortnight ago, then. I would have introduced you to the girls in my circle who were staring at you all night. Some of them were even better dressed than you."

"Whatever you may think, Nan, I don't propose to consult you on the matter of my future bride. I've already made up my mind."

"Lucky woman," Annabel said, with a hefty dose of her own kind of sarcasm. "I'm sure she'll be very grateful for the benefit of your fashion advice."

"No doubt," said Melchior coldly. "Are you prepared for tomorrow?"

Annabel pushed at her beans and decided that she wasn't hungry after all. She put her fork down. "Yes."

"I won't bring you anything you've forgotten," he warned.

"It doesn't matter if I've forgotten anything," Annabel told him, without blinking. "They'll just get me a new one of whatever it is."

"Getting very used to your new consequence, aren't you?" said Melchior, an edge of sarcasm to his smooth voice. "Very well. Just don't expect me to be making tunnels into the dormitories to bring you things. I've warned you."

"I don't expect anything!" snapped Annabel, and went upstairs in a temper.

❧ 2 ❧

If Annabel had expected anything the next morning, it would have been that Melchior, failing to turn up to breakfast yet again, would show up before the carriage was actually at the door to take her to Trenthams. He did not. Shortly after breakfast, however, which Annabel ate with the despairing malaise of the soon-to-be-executed, three visitors arrived directly in the breakfast room without the aid of a carriage. One of them then proceeded to throw up in the chafing dish lid while another patted him consolingly on the back; and the third, a young boy of roughly ten years old, threw himself across the room at Annabel, howling in his joy.

"Use your words, Onepiece," said the female briskly, still patting away cheerfully on the other's back.

"*Hooray for me!*"

"Not...much better," croaked the one who was throwing up, between paroxysms.

"Hallo, Poly," Annabel said, with the feeling that sanity had arrived in the manor, despite appearances to the contrary. Between Melchior and Peter, she was always glad to feel the peaceful warmth that was Poly. She was never sure if it was an actual warmth, or if she only imagined it, but she had lived with Poly long enough to be fairly certain that it was as much of an extension of Poly's self as her magic was. Annabel looked cautiously at Poly's companion and said guardedly, "Luck."

Luck hiccoughed at her.

"What are you doing back here so soon?"

Luck stared at her across the chafing dish lid, made a noise that could have been a belch or a hiccough, and threw up again.

"What Luck means to say is that we came to see you off." Poly stopped patting Luck on the back and began to do something to the air around him instead. Her voice took on a thoughtful lilt as she added, "And if he had been so thoughtful as to take Onepiece and me with him when he took off in the carriage the other day, he wouldn't be feeling so sick from having to use shifting magic *now*. We would have already been here."

Annabel, feeling several degrees more cheerful, watched as Luck also began to look several more degrees cheerful. She said, "I'd call Melchior to say hello, but he's vanished ever since Luck came to see us."

"Ah," said Poly. "I thought you—well, I thought the place looked a bit more lonely than usual."

"He's keeping secrets again," Annabel said gloomily. She threw a look of dislike at Luck and added, "He and Luck snuck out of the manor to talk secrets the other day."

"*So* insulting," Poly said at once.

Indignant in her turn, Annabel exclaimed, "Yes! It's not as though I've got any magic to be able to eavesdrop on them anyway!"

Luck gave her a particularly glassy look. "You wouldn't need magic to eavesdrop on Melchior; you're a hardy, determined blob of no-magic. Reminds me of someone."

Poly grinned.

Onepiece said reproachfully, "*Sausage*, Nanabel! I have starved and *starved*."

"And now I don't even know where he is." Annabel stifled a sigh and gave the rest of her sausage to Onepiece, who took it with a delighted chuckle and nearly choked in his eagerness to eat it.

"Dear me," said Poly. She looked vexed, though not as vexed as

Annabel felt. "I really don't know. *No*, Onepiece! One sausage at a time!"

Annabel didn't ask what Poly *really didn't know*, but she didn't think it was anything to do with where Melchior was keeping himself.

"I know," said Luck.

They both looked at him, Annabel half-suspicion and half-hope, Poly all suspicion.

"What have you and Melchior been up to?" Poly demanded. "And why wasn't I included?"

"I did nothing," Luck said, swaying.

"All right," said Annabel. "What did Melchior do, then?"

"Can't tell you," said Luck. "Sorry."

But he didn't *sound* sorry, and since he steadfastly refused to answer further questions directed at him—either Poly's or Annabel's—in any comprehensible manner, Annabel concluded that he had mentioned it only with the idea of annoying her. Luck quite often did so, though Annabel had never been able to decide if he did so because he liked her, or because he didn't.

Since she still wasn't sure either way, Annabel soon ceased to ask questions and merely patted Onepiece's head by way of consolation. It wasn't quite the same as patting Blackfoot—Melchior's—head, but it did away with some of her annoyance. It was difficult to be annoyed at a man-turned-cat-turned-man when a puppy-turned-boy was making visible magic in front of her. Polly didn't look as though she was prepared to give up so quickly, but since she was far too nice to give Luck a decent dressing down in front of anyone else, it wasn't likely that Annabel would find out what Poly discovered until far later.

By way of retaliation, Annabel said, "Have a sausage," at Luck in a friendly sort of manner.

Luck went slightly green again. Poly didn't grin but Annabel was fairly certain her eyes were brighter when she passed Luck the toast rack and the butter dish.

"*I* am sausage," said Onepiece.

"You're not a sausage, you *want* a sausage," Annabel said, and passed him the bottom part of the dish that was still filled with too many sausages. Luck looked ill as it came within sniffing distance of him, but that could have been because the top half of the dish still contained what must have been his breakfast earlier.

"Yes," said Onepiece, very precisely. "I am *sausage*. Most cer-*tain*-ly I am sausage. With beans."

"All right, you're a sausage," Annabel said good-naturedly. Onepiece had been working hard at being a boy instead of a dog. When Annabel had first met him, he communicated in short bursts of three or four words, and made up the difference in a kind of mental communication that made her head buzz. Nowadays he was more inclined to speak in full sentences, even if those sentences weren't always quite right.

"Luck is sausage and should eat," said Onepiece, and stuffed a sausage in the general direction of Luck's ear.

"It's a conspiracy," said Luck, removing the sausage from his ear with the wearied look of one who has had the need, habitually, to remove sausages from his ears. "That's all right. *You* eat it."

"Don't want it," Onepiece complained. "Was in Luck's ear. Yuck."

Luck looked at him bemusedly. "Huh. That's what I thought. I don't want marmalade in my ear, either."

Onepiece, looking disappointed, put the spoon back in the marmalade. "I want magic," he said.

"I want magic, *please*," Poly reminded him.

"*Luck* doesn't please," complained Onepiece. "Why am I pleasing if Luck is not pleasing?"

"Please pass the tea," Luck said to Annabel, smiling amiably at her.

Annabel did so, but she would have snorted if Onepiece hadn't been there. It was the first time she'd heard Luck say please, and if Onepiece's open mouth was anything to go by, he hadn't ever heard Luck say it either. Still, it was enough to make him say "Perlease the magic," at which Luck gave him something Annabel couldn't see.

"Why does he want Luck's magic when he's got his own?" she asked. Magic was another one of those things that, like being the queen heir, made her feel entirely separate from the rest of New Civet in general. It was no good people even trying to explain it to her, because she couldn't see it, couldn't experience it, couldn't understand it.

"Luck's magic is *prettiest*," Onepiece said happily, and sat back in Annabel's lap to make more magic that she couldn't see.

As usually happened when Annabel ate breakfast with Luck and Onepiece, she found herself occasionally annoyed, but never bored; and she was surprised to find that it was time for her to leave before she was ready to get up from the table.

When she heard the crunch of gravel that meant the carriage was pulling around to the front steps, she sighed. "I suppose you're not going to see Melchior this time."

"I didn't come to see Melchior," Poly said.

"Just as well," said Annabel, who was still sulking just a little bit, though she couldn't help smiling, too. "Since he's not here."

"Do you have to leave now?"

"Yes," Annabel said glumly. "The carriage is packed and ready now. What about you? Melchior won't mind if you stay for a while until Luck's better."

Poly hesitated. "Well, we might. The carriage is coming, but it'll take a little while yet and I don't think Luck is ready for another Shift right now."

"Anyway, Melchior will probably reappear the moment I leave."

"When you get back on holidays, I think we'll have a talk," Poly said thoughtfully. "What a shame I wasn't able to come with Luck last time!"

"Talk about what?"

"There's been too much talking already," Luck opined, and stood up. "I'm going to look for Melchior."

Annabel rather expected him to disappear again, but his stomach must still have been uneasy, because he simply wandered through the door and into the main hall, his hands in his pockets and a faintly hopeful look to his face.

"I think I'll have to have a talk with Luck as well," said Poly, looking even more thoughtful. "He and Melchior have been getting on much better than usual lately, and I'm not sure I approve."

"Why?"

There was a brief pause before Poly said, "Well, I don't know. If it's for the reason I think, I could be swayed; but if it's for Black Velvet business I'm not so sure."

"Yes!" Annabel said, with heartfelt agreement. "Because they won't *share!*"

ANNABEL WAS HEARTILY SICK OF HER CARRIAGE BY THE TIME SHE stopped for lunch. If she'd had Peter to squabble with or Melchior to talk to, it might not have been so bad, but by herself there was no escaping the fact that she was only about a fifth of the way to Trenthams. Melchior wasn't a good enough magic user to have a specialised travel spell on hand, and Annabel had learned, much to her surprise, that the laws of New Civet prohibited any potential heirs to the throne from traveling via magic.

"Makes you wonder what happened to one of them," she muttered to herself, when the door shut behind the servant who showed her to her own private parlour. Thankfully, Melchior seemed to have taken care of her meals along the road, even if he hadn't bothered to see her off himself.

Annabel reached up to take off her hat in front of the mirror. As she did so, she turned just enough to catch sight of something blue and elegant reflected from behind her. There was a girl there, leaning comfortably into the wall as if she'd been there all along—and she might have been, for all Annabel knew.

Who was that? Annabel wondered in annoyance. This was meant to be a private parlour. Now she would have to be polite to someone who had probably sneaked in for a quick look at the future queen. She didn't like having to be polite; despite what Melchior said, Annabel found that she preferred to be able to be decently rude than politely rude with sharp edges and insincere smiles.

"So you're it, are you?" said the mirrored vision in blue, catching her eye. "The queen heir, I mean. How—well, I can't say 'how fortuitous', considering I was waiting for you. What shall I say? Ah yes! What I meant to say is *how expedient!*"

Annabel let her face slip into the familiar, heavy lines of stupidity, and turned to face the girl.

The other girl said, "That's really very impressive! Do you do that often? It must be terribly useful!"

"Oh," said Annabel, taking in red hair and the intelligent sparkle of those grey eyes. "You must be Isabella."

Isabella grinned at her. "I suppose you've already heard about me. We were supposed to meet a long time ago."

"Yes," Annabel said. "Nearly three years ago, actually."

She hadn't meant to feel slighted, but somehow she *did* feel slighted. Annabel had heard so much about Isabella from Poly and Melchior that there had burned in her a deep desire to meet the other girl. It had seemed natural that the feeling would be mutual, and Isabella had been expected every few months for the first year—until it finally occurred to Annabel that she was not to meet Isabella. Or perhaps that Isabella was determined not to meet Annabel.

"Ah," said Isabella, and she sounded pensive. "That was very rude of me, I'm afraid. The thing is that there have been problems along the border of New Civet and Broma—my little Papa was all alone and he's not really very good at the organisation side of being an ambassador. I've not even been able to spend a whole year together at Trenthams; I've been arranging parties and soothing hurt feelings for the last two years."

"Isn't the Bromian and New Civetan border the Great Escarpment?"

"Bromians," said Isabella earnestly, "are *very good* at climbing ice cliffs. I think it's all the skating and ice-fishing they do."

Annabel, who still wasn't sure if she should be offended or forgiving, asked, "What are the parties like?"

"Ugh." Isabella shuddered. "So beautiful, and *so* cold! You have no idea! But really, I was *pining* to see you; Poly's told me such an awful lot about you, you see."

That was unlikely to be strictly true, Annabel considered; there was so little really interesting about her if you didn't consider the fact that she was to be the next queen of New Civet. But that fact was usually quite enough for people to find her *very* interesting. Annabel's heart hardened just a little bit more.

"When exactly did Poly—?"

"Oh, Poly has a way of being able to talk to you even if she isn't exactly *there*," said Isabella. "Don't ask me how; I have no idea how things like that work. I have the tiniest bit of magic, and all that's good for is unlocking things and making a nuisance of myself."

"Is that why—"

"Exactly," nodded Isabella. "I've never met anyone with as little magic as me—you're the first. Besides, I thought we might be able to Treat."

"Really?" Annabel looked at her expressionlessly. "I thought you were going to say that we should be friends."

Isabella looked knowing. "Ah. You've had a few of those, have you?"

"Nobody is supposed to know about it—" began Annabel, before she could stop herself.

"But somehow someone always does," agreed Isabella. "Yes. You'd best be prepared for a lot of that at Trenthams too. I can think of at least three or four girls whose families will have 'specially prepared them. They'll be very friendly and very useful, and very, *very* careful about what they say to you."

"What about you?"

"Well, I'll at least be honest about it," Isabella said cheerfully. "I *do* want something from you. I want something very much, as a matter of fact. I'm proposing that we form an Accord where each of us will agree to terms and provide certain benefits."

"What about your father? Doesn't he need you any more?"

"Oh, Papa has been recalled," said Isabella. "Actually, everyone has. That's why so many people are starting to realise what is happening."

"Oh." Annabel grimaced, and caught the sympathetic look that passed across Isabella's mobile face. "That's annoying."

"Yes, I'm afraid it's going to be very tiresome for you," said the other girl. "That's perhaps where I can help a little. I'm very good at mitigating things."

"All right," Annabel said, interested and even amused. If she hadn't been so suspicious, she probably would have been more amused; Poly had said she would like Isabella. "What terms, and what benefits?"

"How lovely!" said Isabella. "You're decisive and to the point.

They'll praise you for that. I'm decisive and to the point too, but since I'm not going to be queen I'm only said to be stubborn."

"Melchior says I need to learn how to say things in a more delicate manner."

Isabella's head tilted. "I'm always inclined to think that Melchior is in the right, but in this case I should think he's only about half right."

"Which half?"

"I think it's important for you to learn how to dance rings when you're talking. I think it's more important to know when *not* to dance verbal rings—and just as important to know when someone else is talking you in a circle."

"Oh," said Annabel. "Like now, you mean?"

The other girl gave a delighted chuckle. "Exactly so! I think it's important to know a lot of things that aren't necessary to use at every opportunity. The point is to be able to use them when you need to use them. People do so love to harp on ignorance in New Civet; such a high brow lot! If you know when to use your skills, people get the idea that you're not ignorant even when you don't use those particular skills. You begin to have a reputation as an honest and a strong ruler."

"I'd rather not be any sort of ruler," Annabel said. She hadn't said that to anyone outside her small circle, and for a moment she was very startled to find she'd said it to Isabella.

"Oh, me too!" said Isabella. "Good heavens, being stuck inside all the time, and surrounded by courtiers? No thank you! Mind you, I think you'll be very good at it. You know, as much as *anyone* is exactly good at being a ruler. And luckily for you, you've got a face that's pretty hard to read, so if you keep practising that blank look of yours and speak more bluntly than prettily, I think you'll grow a very nice reputation as a solid, fair queen."

"I don't want to just gain a *reputation* for—"

"Of course you don't," said Isabella. "That's one of the things that makes me think you'll be a good queen. And—if you'll pardon me cleverly turning the conversation back to the important point—one of the reasons I'll be so invaluable to you. Me and my little Papa, of course."

"What are your terms, exactly?"

"They are very simple," Isabella said. "I want a position in your cabinet."

"You want to serve——"

"Not me; my little Papa. I want to make sure you'll keep him on as New Civet's Ambassador when you form your own cabinet. And I'd like to be made a viscountess in my own right—my mother was Lady Farrah and I've a mind to be Lady Farrah, too."

"What else?"

"That's all," Isabella said. "It's not a bad exchange, you know; my little Papa is a very good ambassador. He's been doing the job since before it was a paid position, back when it was still dangerous to poke your nose over the Lacunan border."

"I thought it was still dangerous to poke your nose over the Lacunan border," remarked Annabel.

"Perhaps it is," said Isabella. "But at least now the Emperor publicly frowns upon plots to attack ambassadorial staff."

"That must be a big help."

"Oh well, it's leverage of a kind," Isabella said cheerfully. "*If* you know how to use it."

"Don't you have any brothers or sisters?" Annabel, whose scant experience with persons approaching to treat with her was one of carefully hidden requests and outright demands for favour, both personal and familiar.

"Kit knows how to look after himself and Susan is too young to need more than a horse and something to do out of doors. No, my little Papa is the one who needs attention right now. He'll be very happy to stay in the same position—he hasn't said anything, but his bald patch has grown over the last few months."

"What about you?"

"In return for that," Isabella said, blithely taking her own meaning from Annabel's question, "I engage to guide you through your year at Trenthams, entire. We'll room together, eat together, and walk around arm in arm together. I'll tell you who is who, what families are inclined to fall under each particular political persuasion, and how to engage with any and all comers."

"Weren't you supposed to do that, anyway?" asked Annabel, who had more than a shrewd idea of exactly why Melchior had been so keen for herself and Isabella to meet.

"Yes, and I would have been paid very well for it," Isabella said, wrinkling her nose. "I dislike being paid to have fun."

"But—"

"On the other hand, I adore making bargains. Now, in addition to your instruction in everything social, I'll also engage to help with your dressing—"

"Wait," said Annabel, sensing a familiar and unwelcome theme. "What's wrong with the way I'm dressed?"

"Good heavens!" Isabella said. "It's worse than I thought. You should have asked me what *isn't* wrong with it."

Annabel blinked, stared; grinned.

"Oh, good!" said Isabella frankly. "I thought I'd gone a bit too far!"

Amused in a way that she wouldn't have been if it had been Melchior or Peter saying the same thing, Annabel suggested, "Don't you think you should be more polite when you want something?"

"Nonsense. I'm delightfully direct. And *while* I'm being direct, I'm afraid that the current style for bustles is decidedly not the best style for you. We'll change that."

"How can I change?" demanded Annabel, with a resurgence of the irritation she had felt when she first saw Isabella. She had lost a lot of weight in the passing of three years, but she had the feeling that her current size was as small as anything was going to get. If it came to that, it was as small as she wanted to get. She was healthy and comfortable, and had no intention of being as skinny and elegant as Isabella.

"Goodness, no!" Isabella said. "We're not going to change *you*. We're going to change the fashion."

For the first time, Annabel stared at the other girl with unqualified respect. "You can do that?"

"Certainly I can! Aren't you glad you've got me?"

"Yes," said Annabel, with absolute truthfulness. "Wait—but aren't you older than me?"

"That depends," Isabella said. "For another year, yes. When I turn twenty there will no admission of age at all. Why?"

"Won't the other girls think it odd—us rooming together, I mean? Aren't there dormitories?"

"Not for you," Isabella said decidedly. "The others, yes. And I'm certain that Melchior has already arranged for us to room together. We won't need to say anything."

"Are you on your way to Trenthams, too?"

"Of course!" Isabella nodded. "Now, if you look at it in one way, it was awfully rude of me to sneak into your private parlour to make sure I had the first word with you. If you look at it in another, it was a very clever ruse to get myself invited along in your carriage."

Annabel wasn't certain whether to be irritated at Isabella's scheme or amused that the other girl had admitted it so readily. In genuine curiosity, she asked, "What if I don't invite you along?"

"Then I hint, very delicately."

"What if I'm not very good at taking hints?"

"I hint more broadly."

"Actually," said Annabel, her face flat and expressionless again, "I'm very good at ignoring broad hints, too."

Isabella chuckled suddenly. "That's going to be very useful for you," she said.

"I thought so." Annabel considered for a brief moment and came to a conclusion that surprised herself. She said, "You might as well come along with me."

"How lovely! I've already sent my carriage ahead, you see. There was no room for me in it; it's packed to the roof with clothes. Now that I think of it, the roof is piled high, too."

"You have a *whole carriage full* of clothes?"

"Of course not!" Isabella assured her. "I have two. The carriage has already been and come back with one lot of baggage."

"It'd serve you right if I made you walk," said Annabel, grinning in spite of herself. "Anyway, how did you get here? I didn't hear a carriage pull up."

"Oh, it was dreadfully uncomfortable! I was perched on top, you know! With the driver! I had to sit on two of my cases, and they *would* keep moving. I fell off just before we got to the turn in, and after that it seemed easier to walk the rest of the way."

"I should think so," said Annabel, who had had more than one accident when it came to a certain horseless carriage owned by a certain enchanter. Belatedly, it came to her attention that Isabella was carrying a rather large parcel. It looked a bit battered around the edges, even if Isabella herself didn't, which leant a certain amount of credence to the idea that it at least had had an accident on the way to this way stop. "Is that all you've got with you?"

"Yes," said Isabella seriously. "I brought with me only the necessities. Also, I have two hidden pockets and a very useful garter, so I don't have to carry much."

Annabel would have asked exactly what a very useful garter did apart from the obvious very useful job, but the girl who had shown her into the room now returned to bring in lunch. Isabella proved to be just as interested in that fact as Annabel was, and they sat down by tacit agreement and discussed nothing else until they had made decent inroads on the spread. There would be time enough for discussion on the road over the next two days.

THERE WAS NO ROOM RESERVED FOR ANNABEL WHEN SHE WOULD have stopped for lunch again the next day. Fortunately, Isabella's haughty nose tilt and sudden alarmingly stiff bearing got them a private room and an offer of ices placatingly made, where Annabel was convinced that her own, less than commanding presence would only have gotten her a scowling face and a begrudging acknowledgement that if someone *cared* to share their parlour with her she might think herself fortunate.

Feeling annoyed and hurt, and just a little bit on her dignity, Annabel retreated into the blank, silent front she had used for so many years with such success, and brooded on Melchior's many evils. If it had been Poly or Onepiece in the coach with her, she would have made the effort to bestir herself to civility, but Isabella could have been said to have foisted herself on Annabel—*had*, now that Annabel thought about it, foisted herself on her—and she was fully prepared to take advantage of the fact that Isabella wasn't a friend who, like Peter, could be expected to tell her to stop sulking.

And Isabella didn't tell her to stop sulking. She did, however, after a thoughtful hour in her corner of the coach, ask very directly, "Did I offend you by taking charge at the inn? Only I'm so bossy that I sometimes forget, and if you don't tell me to stop it straight away, I'm likely to keep going on like that."

Annabel blinked. It hadn't occurred to her that her sulking could be interpreted in that way. What a bother. Now she would have to be more thoughtful.

"You didn't offend me," she said. "I just—well, I suppose I expected Melchior to make sure there were rooms and lunches all the way along the road. I don't know why, since he didn't even trouble himself to see me off."

"He didn't see you off?" Isabella's eyes narrowed. "Really? I wonder why?"

"That's what I'm wondering, too," Annabel said resentfully. "He threw Peter out and now I have no one but him, so why should he disappear for most of last week? And why shouldn't he be there to see me off? Oh well, I suppose I'm sulking. Sorry."

"Don't let me interrupt," said Isabella, who was finally unwrapping that rather battered box she'd arrived with, "only I'm about to open this very big box of chocolates and it would be such a waste to eat them all by myself."

Annabel looked at her suspiciously.

"No, no!" Isabella assured her. "This wasn't part of a clever plan; it's just that I *adore* chocolates. Here, have one of these—I like them best, so there's lots. Why is Melchior playing least in sight?"

"It doesn't matter," Annabel muttered, but she took the chocolate. "It's not as though he *had* to come out and say goodbye."

"What nonsense! Of course he had to! It's not as though you're only the queen heir, after all, and Poly says—that is, he's clearly being rude."

"He's been like that for the last few weeks, actually," Annabel said gloomily. "He's always been sarcastic, but mostly he's sarcastic at Peter. Now he keeps saying things at me in that needling voice of his."

"Very curious," said Isabella. "I wonder why? What is he up to, do you think?"

Annabel blinked. There *had* been that letter she thought might be from Mr. Pennicott; Melchior had very carefully refrained from either confirming or denying it came from Mr. Pennicott. And of course there was Luck, but Melchior couldn't have been avoiding her because of that, could he? She was used to him vanishing every now and then, but this was a new development. "Oh. I didn't think of that. I should have thought of that."

Isabella put another chocolate in her mouth, her grey eyes light and bright. "Really? What did you think?"

"I don't know. He's been in an especially bad mood this week," Annabel said, accepting the chocolates that Isabella pushed toward her. "I don't know why. And he's been away more often, too. That's the most annoying thing, because he won't tell me what he's up to."

"I see," said Isabella, in a pondering way that made Annabel think she really did see. "Now, going back to Melchior needling you—what happened before he started being so annoying?"

Confused, Annabel asked, "Happened? Nothing happened."

"It was probably small and innocent and—wait, that friend of yours, the rude one. Where is he?"

Annabel found herself grinning again. "Most of my friends are rude," she said, "but I suppose you mean Peter."

"Yes. Peter."

"How do you know about Peter? Oh—Poly."

"Exactly so! I got the impression she might have given him a clip over the ears every so often."

"Something like that," Annabel said, still grinning. Poly's effortless magic—not to mention her rather frightening *un*magic, and the swirl of antimagic that curled up one arm—had woken in Peter a vast respect that even Rorkin hadn't. Poly hadn't been equally impressed with Peter, and from Peter's expression every so often, Annabel was quite sure that a magical reprimand or three had happened under her nose. It hadn't deterred Peter in the least, though whether that was because he chose to regard Poly in the light of the mother he was missing, or because he was aware that he deserved a lot more in the way of punishment than he actually received, Annabel wasn't sure. It had certainly made him better behaved, though Annabel was reasonably certain that it wasn't possible to rub away all of Peter's sharp edges. He simply didn't notice them on himself unless they were pointed out with a cudgel.

And that reminded her. "Actually," she said, frowning, "actually, Peter disappeared a few months ago. He was being rude as usual—something about me going around laughing with other boys when I was supposed to marry him, or something like that—and Melchior threw him out. I thought he'd gone to see his mother, but I don't think so any more."

She looked up to find Isabella's eyes on her in a thoughtful, steady sort of way. "Now *that* is interesting."

"Yes, but he showed up again a little while ago. I think he's done something, or someone's done something to him, but Melchior and Luck won't tell me—"

"Not Peter," Isabella said decisively. "No, I meant that—"

A sudden crack of sound echoed through the open carriage windows and hung in the air. Annabel blinked a little more slowly than usual, too startled to jump.

"Was that—"

"A pistol shot? I think so."

There was a particularly sick-making lurch, and the countryside seemed to blur just a little bit faster.

"Ugh," said Annabel. The chocolates she had eaten were sloshing around her stomach in a decidedly dubious manner. "I think we've sped up. Oh, and there are people on horseback galloping up beside us."

"Good heavens," said Isabella thoughtfully. "I think we're being held up."

❧ 3 ❧

Annabel looked out the window again, gloomily. "Probably. It's just that sort of day. Well, if they jostle me too much, they'll have to deal with all the half-digested chocolate I've eaten."

Isabella eyed her with some respect. "I would never have thought of that! I was just going to poke a few of them with my parasol."

"You might have to do that anyway," Annabel said, a little grimly. She could feel the staff in her pocket beneath her travelling cape; it was still in its pencil form, though Melchior insisted that wasn't its real form. She wasn't supposed to use it for another few weeks yet—until the three years were fully up and she and Peter came back into synch with the castle, and the castle came back into synch with real time. Still, if it came right down to it, wasn't using the staff preferable to being captured by footpads?

Another shot sounded and there was a distinct lurch as their carriage pulled up in more haste than style, catapulting Isabella over to Annabel's side.

"I shouldn't wonder if this is why Melchior didn't travel with us," remarked Isabella, straightening her hat. She didn't sound annoyed, but she was rather anxiously feeling the front brim of that hat to make sure it wasn't damaged.

"Too bad," Annabel said, grinning. "It's bent up at the front."

"Very well," said Isabella, wrathful in the blink of an eye. "Just you *wait* until I get hold of them!"

Horses pulled up in a thundering of hooves and a clouding of dust on either side of the coach. Above their heads, there was the distinct sound of Annabel's coachman promising not to move an inch and volunteering the gasped information that *'er 'ighness was inside and fer pity's sake not to shoot!*

"I don't think much of your coachman," remarked Isabella.

"It's not his fault," Annabel protested. She knew what it was like to be so frightened that you said or did anything to make things less frightening. "He just doesn't want to be shot."

Isabella sounded slightly waspish. "I don't want to be shot either, but I'm not going to be declaring to all and sundry that the queen heir is in the coach."

"You don't have to," said Annabel, and her own voice held just a touch more vinegar, too. "The coachman's already done it."

Isabella giggled suddenly. "He has, hasn't he? Oh dear, and I was so determined to be less bossy and more conciliating this year! There—I apologise for criticising your man!"

"I don't think that's important right now," Annabel said in slight exasperation. "I'm more worried about the highwaymen, actually."

"Apologising is *always* important—dear me! I'm being bossy and forthright again. Perhaps we should back away from the window; it looks like that one is going to come in."

"Out you get," said one of their attackers, tapping on the window frame with his pistol barrel.

"No," Annabel said.

That made him look at her blankly. "What?"

"I don't want to."

"You don't—Don't *want*—? Get out!"

"It's muddy out there," said Isabella, who had been doing something very light fingered to the end of the pistol barrel while the highwayman was busy talking to Annabel. "Why should we get out in all that? You've already done dreadful things to my hat. Who's going to pay for that, I should like to know?"

"Last chance," the highwayman said, and levelled the barrel of his pistol at Annabel.

"Whoops!" said Isabella, and put up her parasol.

There was a very loud explosion that ended, not with the tearing pain of a bullet in Annabel's heart, but a soft snick as Isabella shut her parasol again. The window of the carriage was empty.

"I do apologise," said Isabella. "I really thought he'd shoot my way first. He must be labouring under a misapprehension."

"What—?"

"He shot himself. Isn't that convenient?"

"Is that what you did to the barrel?"

"Oh, bother," Isabella said. "Here come more of them. If I look after this side, do you think you can look after that?"

"Yes," said Annabel.

"Dear me, what a salutary lesson for me!"

Annabel was conscious of the warring of exasperation and hilarity within her. "What?"

"I'm about to do what I just told you I wouldn't in any case do," Isabella said cheerfully. In a clear, carrying voice, she added, "Do be careful, your highness! We can't have you being shot now, can we?"

Annabel would have stopped and stared, but the two men on her side of the carriage had already put away their pistols. Had they first thought that Isabella was the queen heir? Probably. They certainly didn't think so any longer. Would the three on Isabella's side put up their weapons too, or would they risk shooting Annabel through Isabella? Annabel was less sure of that; and if she was not sure, Isabella was certain to be feeling exposed, too.

Unfortunately, the closest footpad chose that moment to wrench on the coach door. The action catapulted Annabel, who had been wedging her foot against the door, out onto the road in a tumble that was neither graceful nor queenly. In the coach, Isabella sat down backwards rather suddenly on the carriage floor.

Annabel scrambled to her feet, dimly conscious of pain in one of her palms, and called back to Isabella, "Are you all right?"

"Perfectly fine!" called Isabella. "After all, what else are bustles good for but protecting one's rear end in the event of sudden collapse?"

"Up you get," said one of the footpads unnecessarily.

"I'm already up, actually," Annabel said, dusting off her hands and finding that she was smearing blood on her clothes. "*Now* look what you made me do!"

"Don't forget my hat," Isabella reminded her, leaping lightly down into the road. "Somebody is going to pay for my hat as well. Who shall it be?"

The footpad grinned at her. "And who is going to make us pay, missy?"

"If you're very lucky," said Annabel, scowling at him, "it'll be Belle."

"Pointed shoes are not only fashionable but useful," Isabella said sweetly to the dumbstruck footpad, displaying one dangerously shod foot.

Around them, the other footpads began to gather, grinning. Heartened by this, the first footpad enquired, "And if I'm unlucky?"

"If you're *very* unlucky," Annabel said, the pencil staff balanced lightly and dangerously between the first two fingers of her bloody hand, "I'll deal with you myself."

"How delightful!" said Isabella irrepressibly. "*Fair gave me the shivers*, as cook says! I'd listen to her, you know; she may be small, but she's quite reasonably grumpy and I really don't know what she's capable of."

Annabel sniffed. "Thank you." She caught a flicker of movement and colour between the trees behind the assembled footpads and felt an easing of her stiff shoulders. Were those New Civetan colours? She was reasonably sure of it. "Also, you might all wish to know that there's a regiment of New Civetan Guardsmen in the forest behind you. I don't think they're very happy."

"H'ain't no use saying things like that, missy," said the footpad reprovingly. "We scouted you out well in advance."

"You know best, I'm sure," said Isabella, even more sweetly than before. "But when you're addressing the prospective queen of the land, I really do think it's politic to address her as *your highness*, don't you?"

"Well now, that's a matter h'of opinion, ain't it? We ain't got anything against her little missness, but the man who hired us don't seem to like her much. And a queen ain't queen until she's crowned, like."

"Oh well, it's not like he's actually wrong," said Annabel, tucking her pencil staff away. "Belle, I think we'd probably better duck now."

She dragged Isabella down with her as she said *now*, and a sudden stillness fell around them as each and every foodpad froze in place with similarly surprised expressions.

"Good heavens!" said Isabella. "There really is a regiment of New Civetan Guardsmen?"

"I hope so," Annabel said. "Otherwise, we're about to be held up again. And these ones have magic, too."

Isabella looked at her admiringly. "And I thought it was merely a particularly good bluff of yours! You do keep a nice cool head, don't you? Didn't I say we were going to get along well?"

"You've said it more than once," Annabel said expressionlessly, her eyes on the six Guardsmen who were approaching. "And I still think it's suspicious."

"Didn't I tell you from the start that I wanted—" Isabella stopped. "Good heavens! You're teasing me! What an amazingly straight face you have! Raoul, you *might* have got here a bit sooner, I think!"

Since this last sentence was addressed to the tall, broad-shouldered First Guardsman who was currently attempting to bow with all the solemnity and dignity of his office, Annabel only grinned at his discomfiture. The Guardsman, on the other hand, shot Isabella a look of annoyance and tried very hard to otherwise ignore her as he said to Annabel, "Our apologies for seeming to be late to the rescue, your highness; once you were out of the coach we couldn't be sure we wouldn't hit you if we targeted the kidnappers."

"Oh, you saw that?" Annabel said gloomily.

Another of the guardsmen—the medical officer, said the part of Annabel's brain that had been very busy memorising insignias and coats of arms over the last three years—a stocky, blond boy who was a thought shorter even than Annabel herself, added, "We're very grateful you were observant enough to duck right when you did, your highness. We'd just come to the conclusion that we'd have to knock you out as well."

"Thank you, I'm sure!" said Isabella, making the medical officer's cheeks turn pink.

"I've got a field kit, your highness," he said to Annabel, who didn't realise what he meant until he held up a roll of bandage. "It's not much, and none of us have more than the minimum level of magic, but it'll stop you bleeding for the rest of the journey. I daren't try to fix it with magic in case I hurt you."

"Thanks," she said, and held out the hand. Melchior would have fixed it up with a touch of magic, but Melchior wasn't here. Startling the young medical officer considerably, she said indignantly, "Just you wait!"

He dropped the bandages. "Your highness?"

"Not you," Annabel said. "Sorry. I was thinking about someone else. Who arranged for you to shadow us, anyway?"

"Well—"

Isabella gave Raoul a sharp look. "What? Not allowed to tell us?"

Raoul tried to look dignified. "It's not that. It's just that—well, we don't know ourselves, if you must know, Belle! The Head Guardsman gave the orders, but no one seems to know where *he* got the orders."

"Just as I thought!" Isabella said triumphantly.

"Don't try and pretend you know everything," Raoul said at once, and Annabel grinned.

"Are they always like this?" she asked the medical officer, tilting her head in their direction.

The medical officer went pink again. "Yes. They get along very well, your highness; I don't want you to think they don't."

"Oh no, I can see that," Annabel said easily. "Sorry for the trouble, by the way."

"No, no, it's a pleasure!" he blurted, and then blushed fierily. "I mean—it's not a pleasure that you've hurt yourself—it's—"

"Actually, it's mostly embarrassing," said Annabel. Good grief, he went *very* red. "I was hoping not to fall over in front of people after my training."

"Did you fall over often before it?" asked the medical officer, as if he couldn't help himself. He blushed again, more painfully.

"Lots!" Annabel said frankly. "That'll teach me to be so confident. What's your name?"

"Good heavens, I think you've broken him," said Isabella, as the medical officer opened and closed his mouth without a sound.

"His name is Dannick," said Raoul.

"Yes, Dannick," said Dannick.

"And he's not used to dealing with royalty."

"Or being asked his name," Isabella remarked irrepressibly. "Otherwise he might have had it on his tongue more readily."

"I've finished, your highness," Dannick said hastily, and darted away to the back of the group. He came back a moment later, even more flustered; bowed his respects, and darted away again.

Was it the queen-to-be who had so thrown Dannick out of his stride, or Annabel herself? wondered Annabel. She wasn't used to producing such an effect. She repressed a sigh, and found herself thinking about Peter again. They'd promised they would marry each other when they got older. It would have made things a lot easier if she'd kept that bargain. No need to try and decipher who was caught with the Queen and who was caught with Annabel—Peter had absolutely no interest in being King Consort, and if he wasn't always kind or pleasant, at least he was familiar. It was stupid to think about that, however; she'd already told Peter that she wasn't going to marry him, and now he'd disappeared, to boot.

"Come along, Nan," said Isabella, pinching at her sleeve. "We'd best start off again; we'll need to make up a bit of ground before we stop for the night. There's nothing worse than arriving at Trenthams half way through the first free day; all the other girls arrive then, too."

"You're being a bit familiar, aren't you, Belle?" demanded Raoul. Despite the tone, he lifted Isabella over the muddy patch at the door of the coach and put her carefully in the coach. "Her highness won't understand your—actually, it's just plain cheek! Please excuse her, your highness."

"I was familiar first," Annabel said cheerfully. "And after we've fought off footpads together, it's a bit silly to be 'your highness'ing and 'Miss Farrah'ing each other. "Anyway, it's what Melchior calls me, too."

"Lucky, Belle!" said Raoul, lifting Annabel in as well. His tone sounded more warning than congratulatory.

Isabella *poohpooed* at him. "Watch your own luck, thank you, Raoul! And next time, make a showing before my hat is ruined!"

"What a shame," said Annabel, grinning. She picked up the ruined hat and examined the brim. "You didn't get a chance to take vengeance for your hat!"

"Oh, I don't know," said Isabella, more cheerfully. She was watching the Guardsmen bundle up the frozen footpads with a professional kind of interest. "I managed to poke one or two of the ones nearest the door with my parasol. And it's not a complete loss, after all; I can use a few pieces from this one on a new hat or two."

"Yes," agreed Annabel, eyeing Isabella in fascination. She had absolutely no idea how a person was supposed to take pieces of an old hat to make a new one, but she was inclined to think that if anyone could do so, it would be Isabella. "Do you often make your own hats?"

Isabella nodded and said confidingly, "Of course. You can always get a beautiful hat from a good milliner, but a really *useful* hat can only be made at home."

"What do you keep in these useful hats of yours?"

Isabella gave a surprised giggle. "I keep forgetting how quick in the uptake you are! It's that face of yours!"

"Rude," said Annabel, as the coach gave a lurch forward again. She wondered where the guardsmen had put the footpads—on the back of the coach, or on one or two of their horses? The coach certainly felt heavier.

"If you must know, it depends upon the hat. The smaller brims, you know, are for later afternoon and evening—they have a smaller crown, too, so it's harder to hide things in them, but during the evening I would only usually need my lockpicking things and perhaps a little grease."

"You need *grease* in the evenings?"

"Well, in the evenings it's usually things like opening doors and drawers and making sure hinges don't make too much noise. Not that I sneak around *every* evening, of course!"

"Of course!" echoed Annabel. "What sort of things do you keep in your other hats?"

"One of them has some lovely little knives," said Isabella. She sounded regretful as she said, "They don't really come in useful for me, you understand; I just like to take them with me sometimes, anyway."

"I'm not surprised," Annabel said. "I suppose you talk your way out of everything."

"Pretty nearly!" Isabella said, not at all offended. "And I've been known to run for it once or twice. You have no idea how difficult it is to keep to a trot in corsets, Nan!"

"Well—"

"You have? Of course you have! Dear me! Why am I blathering away about hats when I haven't even asked about the castle yet?"

"I'm not supposed to talk about the castle," said Annabel.

"Of course not!" agreed Isabella. "But the journey is long and I'm awfully inquisitive—not to mention very hard to put off—so you might as well begin now. I think there are still some chocolates that weren't lost in the upheaval, by the by."

"Yes," said Annabel. "You sat on one, actually. The rest are mostly in the box, but I think there's a bit of grass in there, too."

"Oh well, a bit of grass won't hurt us," Isabella said, dubiously examining the chocolate smear on the skirt of her blue overcoat. "What a good thing I wore my blue duster today! I'll have to have it cleaned, but at least I can take it off when we get to school so that I don't disgrace myself."

She sat back down with perfect goodwill and offered the grassy chocolate box to Annabel as a small lurch forward announced the continuance of their journey. And Annabel, who hadn't intended on saying any such thing, took a chocolate and said, "It was a ruin at first. Peter and I always played there when we were kids..."

It wasn't until they got to their next stop that Annabel realised she'd been talking nearly the whole afternoon and well into the evening. For a person who talked as much as she did, Isabella was a surprisingly good listener. That was another thing about her, thought Annabel gloomily as she climbed out of the coach, that was decidedly suspicious. If Isabella's father was anything like Isabella, the ambassadorial affairs must have been going along swimmingly these last few years.

There was no dinner or room arranged for her at that stop, either, and the only significant amount of talking Isabella did was to arrange rooms—and when that proved too difficult to accommodate, *a* room —and dinner for them both. Annabel, who was much more used to thinking than speaking, thought that this was by far the most dangerous quality that Isabella had thus far displayed. It would prob-ably be wise to stop talking so much, especially since it was so easy to trust the other girl. Annabel preferred to be more careful about how much she said in public places.

She stopped talking in the face of Isabella's encouraging silences, and soon Isabella, with perfect politeness, took up the burden of conversation once again. Since she did that by asking cheerfully, "Rethinking your decision that I'm to be trusted?" Annabel was able to withstand feeling grateful to her.

"No," she said, looking pointedly around the room. "But I'm not supposed to talk about this sort of thing. Where other people can hear, I mean."

"Oh!" Isabella looked genuinely surprised. "How lovely! I merely thought you didn't trust me. Well, that's good policy, after all."

Annabel couldn't help grinning. "You look so surprised! Do people usually not trust you?"

"Not at all," said Isabella. "I'm very trust-inducing. It's just that you're a little more discerning than the average person I meet with, and I'm suffering from the odd circumstance of being wrong. It's very unusual."

Annabel, with a slight edge of sarcasm, said, "I suppose you're always right."

"Generally speaking, yes!" Isabella said frankly. "Well, not *always*; but often enough to trust my intuition most of the time. People are people no matter where you go, I find; in any one place you'll find all the people you met at the last place. It's rather depressing."

"That is depressing," agreed Annabel. "Fancy thinking there might be more than one Luck in the world!"

Isabella gave vent to a surprised giggle. "Oh well, so long as there are enough Polys to deal with them!"

BY THE TIME THEY ARRIVED AT TRENTHAMS, THE CHOCOLATES WERE well and truly gone. They would have arrived at Trenthams, in fact, an entire day before they did, if Isabella hadn't insisted that it was impossible to travel any further without more chocolates. Annabel, who only found out the next day that Trenthams was a bare twenty minute journey from the village where they spent the vast portion of the previous afternoon and night, had no fault to find with Isabella's insistence. The closer they got to Trenthams, the gloomier she became, and she fully approved of Isabella's love for chocolate, though she wished it would show as little on her own figure as it did on Isabella's slender one.

Still, she couldn't help sending an accusatory look in Isabella's direction when the carriage, with its Guardsman escort, pulled up at a pair of impressively curly gates that said *Trenthams School for Elegant Young Ladies* amidst its curls.

"Don't be like that, Nan."

"I feel ridiculous," said Annabel, beginning to laugh. "I was prepared for another full day's journey!"

"Well, aren't you glad it isn't?"

"Yes, but why didn't we come last night?"

"*Nobody* arrives on the first day!" Isabella said, earnestly. "Really, Nan! And considering who you are, we really should be setting a fashionable way of things from the start."

"Won't it be awfully crowded today?"

"Perhaps a little," agreed Isabella. "But that's the joy of it! We can be important with very little trouble—all we have to do is meet with the headmistress and go to our room, and *everyone* will see you."

"I don't particularly want everyone to see me."

"Would you prefer them all to be lined up outside our room later on?"

Annabel looked at her in horror as the carriage pulled up outside a vast blockwork building with reinforced, double doors. "Would they?"

"Quite a lot of them will still do so, but the ones who are only curious should be content to see you in the corridors and the dining hall." Isabella tilted her head carefully, her new hat just clearing the window frame, and looked around with a sparkling alertness. That new hat was another thing she had found it necessary to purchase in the village, though the fact that it was new hadn't stopped her from tearing it nearly to pieces and making it up differently again. "Ah, yes —there are already faces in the windows. Don't fall over this time, will you, Nan?"

"I'll do my best," said Annabel, repressing the urge to remark that she hadn't exactly done it on purpose last time.

Isabella left the carriage first, new hat foremost, and stood in front of the carriage steps for just a little too long. Annabel would have been annoyed by it if it hadn't occurred to her that Isabella was providing a shoulder for Annabel to steady herself by if she tripped again.

Annabel took her time following, her face settling comfortably into a familiar, flat gaze. Falling over in front of brigands and guardsmen was bad enough; she didn't think she could bear to fall over in front of the assembled face of Trenthams as well. She didn't need Isabella's shoulder, and that shoulder moved forward smoothly as soon as she was safely on the gravel, tilting just a little bit for its owner to direct a smile over it at Raoul, who had opened the door for them.

"Now this is arriving in style!" Isabella murmured.

Annabel looked up at the windows for one brief, sick moment, and away just as quickly. "Where do we go now?"

"It's not a matter of where we should be going, it's more a matter of who should be here to meet you," said Isabella. "Now, this is a little odd; the headmistresses should really be here to meet you."

"No one is supposed to know I'm the queen heir."

"Of course not; but you can't expect them to lose their chance to ingratiate themselves with royalty, can you? Only see how desperate I

was! I threw myself into your carriage, flailing and throwing chocolates at you."

Annabel gave a small giggle. "Is that what you were? Desperate?"

Isabella turned a sparkling look on her. "Of course! We shall walk,
Nan; very slowly. Just a few steps forward, because the front doors are
beginning to open."

The doors *were* beginning to open. As Annabel took those few,
slow steps forward, keeping pace with Isabella, a twin pair of shadows
darkened the stairs and moved forward gracefully. They were taller
than Isabella, taller even than Raoul; a pair of well-dressed, well-
coiffed women who looked as though they had just that moment
stepped from their boudoirs.

"The Awesome Aunts," murmured Isabella. "Try not to look so
overawed, Nan! They're not so fearsome so long as you don't break
too many rules in too short a time."

"You know that by experience, I suppose," said Annabel.

"How else?" Isabella said lightly, and moved forward again. "Good
day ma'am; ma'am!"

"Miss Farrah," said both women at once, and bowed very slightly.
Enough to acknowledge, but not to concede. One of them—how was
she supposed to tell them apart? Annabel wondered—added, "I see
you have brought another student with you."

"I have," agreed Isabella. "Although you might say that she brought
me, since the carriage is hers, after all. This is Annabel—I suppose
you were expecting her. If you weren't, I've brought her to the wrong
school."

"Miss Farrah, you are pert. You must not suppose that your work
with your father over the last two years pre-empts you from abiding
by the rules of this school. You have only been back at the school for
six months and have much to learn."

"Not at all," Isabella said politely. "I should never suppose that two
years as an ambassadorial adjunct would be of any use whatsoever
when it comes to learning how to behave in polite society. I look
forward to learning a great deal now that I'm back to stay."

"Yes," said one of the Awesome Aunts. She sounded doubtful
about that, but, to Annabel's bemusement, didn't seem to find

anything dubious about the rest of Isabella's reply. The Awesome Aunts, she was beginning to think, only *looked* awesome; she had the feeling that they might even be the slightest bit...well, slow.

"We will show you to your room," said the other Awesome Aunt. This one was wearing a lavender cameo pin; the other wore a yellow pin.

Annabel, in relief, seized upon this single method of differentiation, and said, "Thank you. We appreciate it."

"We consider it good manners to show a new student to her room," said the Yellow Aunt, impressively. "We shall be family, and it is imperative that things Get Off to a Good Start."

"Oh," said Annabel. "Yes, of course."

"The men will take your bags," said the Lavender Aunt.

To Annabel that seemed hard on the guardsmen, who were there to guard her and not to carry her bags, but Raoul was already loosening the knots that held her baggage in place.

The Lavender Aunt added, "Do follow me, my lady, Miss Farrah."

Annabel didn't miss the quick look that Isabella flicked at her. So they were calling her 'my lady', were they? That was a nice way of pretending they didn't know she was the queen heir; they could still show deference without being too noticeable about it.

"Lights out and curfew are strictly enforced," said the Yellow Aunt, as she led the way into the school. "As likewise are boundaries. You will be provided with a list of school rules, and if you possess anything of magical origin, you are requested to leave it with us until the end of term."

Since she ceased her majestic glide to turn expectantly to Annabel and Isabella, it was rather obvious that she expected an answer to her statement.

With a hand in her pocket that was wrapped tightly around a pencil most definitely of magical origin, Annabel very carefully said, "I don't have anything to declare. Belle?"

"I have no magical abilities," said Isabella. "I don't make spells or work magic." Her tone was blithe, but Annabel was quite sure she had worded her sentence as carefully as Annabel had worded her own. It wouldn't surprise her to find that Isabella had also brought in something that wasn't strictly allowed.

"Very well, said the Yellow Aunt, and resumed her glide. "The corridors are routinely monitored by magical means after curfew, the doors and windows by the same means, and any infractions will be punished swiftly. It is not presumed—*not* presumed, my lady—that you will engage in any nefarious practices, but girls have been known to break curfew for any number of reasons. We should prefer to be Absolutely Clear about our rules to discourage any Unfortunate Occurrences."

Annabel almost expected the Yellow Aunt to direct her *have been known to break curfew* at Isabella—*Have been known, Miss Farrah! To break curfew*—and caught the look brimful of mischief that Isabella threw her.

"Don't worry; I'll be sure to show Annabel exactly how she ought to go on," Isabella assured the Aunts.

The Aunts exchanged a vaguely worried look and said together, "Yes, of course. This way, young ladies."

It wasn't until they reached the third floor of the school that the Aunts slowed, and finally stopped outside a door. To Annabel's surprise, the usually surefooted Isabella's foot faltered just one more step forward before she stopped behind the Aunts. Her eyes were quite wide and just a bit watchful. Annabel wondered exactly what it was that had surprised her, and looked curiously around the hall. There was nothing there beyond the guardsmen murmuring politely as they passed the group to add Annabel's luggage to the mountainous pile inside that was Isabella's luggage.

Obeying the encouraging gesture that both Aunts gave her, Annabel stepped through the doorway and into their suite. Isabella followed her, a bright, inquisitive look to her face.

"We will leave you," said the Lavender Aunt from the doorway, "to unpack your night things. A maid will be along shortly to assist you in your unpacking. Do bear in mind that lunch will be served promptly at noon, and dinner at seven. You may ring for tea and light refreshments at any time."

Both the Aunts bowed again, not too deep and not too shallow.

Annabel gave the very calculated head bob that Melchior had taught her several years ago, and Isabella made a flourishing curtsey that made the Aunts look uneasy again as they glided away.

"Thank goodness!" said Isabella, and shut the door behind the guardsmen. She came back into the centre of the room, her eyes very sharp, and gazed around the room. Pensively, she said, "It's all very odd."

"What's all very odd?" The room looked perfectly normal, if somewhat larger than Annabel had expected at school.

"They were just a smidgen too late meeting you, did you notice?" Isabella nodded to herself. "Yes, and they walked us to our room."

"Is that odd?"

"Not at all. The least they should do is walk the future queen to her room. That's perfectly normal."

"Then what exactly is it you're suspicious of?" demanded Annabel, in some exasperation.

"I don't know, exactly," said Isabella darkly. "Just small, irritating things that might not mean anything. But it's all very odd."

❧ 4 ☙

"This is all very odd," said Isabella.

"You've said that," Annabel muttered. In fact, Isabella had said it about three or four times now, and it was very annoying to be told several times that something was odd without the person expanding on the subject.

"Four times," agreed Isabella cheerfully. Annabel didn't know whether the other girl's cheerfulness was because she was aware of Annabel's annoyance, or because she was *not*. Having seen a little of Isabella, she was inclined to think it was because she did. And Annabel was also inclined to resent that.

"All right, but *why* is it all very odd?" she demanded. "As far as I can see, it's a room! Well, just a suite, anyway."

"Exactly. It's just a suite. No, no, no, this will never do! What were they thinking?"

"You expected a different suite!" realised Annabel. "Is that why you wanted to room with me?"

"Dear me, what a suspicious thing you are!" said Isabella. "As a matter of fact, yes; it does happen to be one of the reasons I wanted to room with you. The one I expected is much larger than this—it's a proper suite, not this little pretend thing. It's a perfectly lovely suite with a perfectly lovely view, and a perfectly lovely little balcony simply *made* for sneaking out of the school."

"That's probably why they didn't give it to us," remarked Annabel. Anyone with brains would have taken Isabella's measure very early in the piece and made an effort to keep her in check.

Isabella gurgled with laughter. "That's something to think about! Goodness, could the Awesome Aunts be aware of the full extent of my activities? No, I'm sure they're not! There must be another reason, and it's—"

"—all very odd," agreed Annabel gloomily. "But what can we do about it, anyway? Nothing."

"That's what people always say, and they're almost always wrong."

That, Annabel agreed with. She wasn't sure that she would consider the size of a suite something worth fighting for, however.

"You're probably thinking," Isabella said accurately, "that this is something so small as to not be worth bothering about."

"Actually," said Annabel, annoyed to be caught in the very thought, "I was wondering when we're going to start unpacking our things."

Isabella shot her a keen, grey-eyed look. "Were you?"

"Yes," Annabel said firmly. "Look, it's no use fussing about whether it's the right suite or not—it's the one we've got. You'll just have to manage to sneak out another way."

Isabella sighed. "Oh, well; I suppose it's good practise, after all!"

"I don't think your little Papa can be as good of an ambassador as all that if you've got to practise sneaking about."

"My little Papa," said Isabella, quite stiffly, "is a *wonderful* ambassador! And all I can say is that if you fancy sneaking about to be of little use—well, no, I won't say it. I've already been rude enough today and it's probably because I haven't had a cup of tea yet."

"I want a cup of tea!" instantly said Annabel. "All right, I'm sorry. I was being rude first."

"Do you know," said Isabella unexpectedly, "I've got the feeling we're going to be very good friends. We might as well go and get ourselves a mediocre cup of tea from the afternoon parlour—we won't get any decent stuff in our room until I can smuggle in a few things. Anyway, we should go to the nurse and get your hand seen to properly;

the maids will take care of the unpacking for us. They like sneaking a look at our things, anyway."

Annabel wasn't so sure, but she cautiously said, "All right," and followed Isabella down the hall, wondering exactly what Isabella felt she *needed* to smuggle into their room other than the obvious tea. Her musings on the subject were cut short by a rising babble that met them in the next passage; a shifting crowd of mingled uniformed and ununiformed Trenthams girls were milling in the passage, cooing and squealing and generally blocking the way forward.

Annabel sighed and concentrated on trying not to step on any of the older girls' longer skirts, but Isabella stopped altogether.

"Good heavens," she said, in a thoughtful voice. Since she had used just that tone and that expression when their carriage was held up, Annabel looked up in some dismay.

The first thing she saw beyond the throng of schoolgirls was a pair of hazel eyes glinting above a mouth that was smiling, to her eyes, in a decidedly sarcastic manner.

It was Melchior. What was Melchior doing at Trenthams? Why, if it came to that, was Melchior surrounded by a group of giggling girls who were obviously vying for his attention?

"Ladies!" fluted a voice. "Ladies, really! Please comport yourselves in a...*ahem*...seemly fashion!"

"Good heavens!" said Isabella's voice again, somewhere above Annabel's ear. "I'm afraid Miss Cornett will be fighting a losing battle with this lot. How lovely! This week keeps getting more and more enjoyable!"

Annabel would have asked if Isabella was referring to the footpads as part of that enjoyment, but since she was more than slightly certain Isabella *was*, she merely said, "That must be why he said he wouldn't bring anything if I forgot it."

"This is all very interesting," Isabella said.

Annabel looked up at her and found that Isabella wasn't looking at her. Instead, she was looking at Melchior, her eyes very narrow and sparkling.

"Don't tell me you're going to moon over him as well?" she said crossly.

Isabella might be occasionally irritating, but she hadn't seemed like the sort of girl to make a fool of herself over Melchior. Annabel had had her fill of that type of girl in the last few months of parties with Melchior.

"No," said Isabella slowly, looking down at Annabel and then back at Melchior. "I rather think not. Melchior and I are old friends, that's all."

Unreasonably more cheerful, Annabel turned her eyes back on Melchior and found that he was still watching her, one eyebrow raised. She made a face at him and said to Isabella, "Aren't we going to get a cup of tea?"

Isabella blinked, then her teeth sparkled in a small, mischievous grin. "Really? I approve, I really do! You'll have to excuse me while I use my elbows to make a path for us—*what* a shame I don't have my parasol! Even a hairpin would do at a pinch."

Still, Annabel didn't notice any lack of efficacy to Isabella's elbows, and they were soon well into the crush. It was more difficult to move right where Melchior was, but Annabel might still have at least given a nod or a smile in passing, if he hadn't quite deliberately winked at her as they passed shoulder to shoulder. She scowled at him instead, which reaction seemed to delight him, because his hazel eyes danced at her above the heads of the other girls.

"Oh, just you wait!" she muttered, pinching the fabric at Isabella's elbow just a little too tightly.

"Nan," Isabella said plaintively, "I really do understand the urge to destroy, but *must* you destroy this dress? It's one of my favourites and I have nothing to replace it at this moment."

"Oh, sorry," said Annabel. She added, with some asperity, "I know you said that people are people wherever you go, and that you meet all the same people every place you go, but I didn't know you meant it literally!"

"Goodness, I had nothing to do with this! I'm just as surprised as you are! Well, maybe not *quite* so surprised—it was quite evident that he was up to something."

"Yes," Annabel agreed darkly. "I didn't expect this, though! What do you suppose he's doing here?"

"I think we can assume that something has happened," Isabella said seriously. "Something Melchior hasn't told you about."

"Rude!" said Annabel. "If it concerns me, I ought to know!"

"Didn't you say Luck came to see Melchior before you left?"

"Yes, and they were behaving suspiciously." Annabel thought about that and added, "*More* suspiciously. Perhaps there have been threats."

"Perhaps. And we can't forget that someone knew your route and tried to attack us on the way here. They're bound to be connected. Oh! Raoul! Quick! We'd better go after him!"

"What?" Annabel dashed after Isabella. "Why are we in such a hurry? Won't the Guardsmen stay the night?"

"No," Isabella tossed over her shoulder. "Raoul *knows* me! Oh, what a sneak! He only answered the questions we asked!"

"People usually only answer the questions you ask," said Annabel, who was very familiar with the concept of very carefully answering questions and avoiding the inception of others. Blackfoot—no, Melchior, had been *very* good at that. "I should have known to ask more questions."

"We have been very remiss, Nan," said Isabella, prodding at a panel in the hallway. "We didn't ask questions we should have asked—with all the information we had, too!"

"Shouldn't we be going down to the stables?" suggested Annabel.

"Oh! There it is!" Isabella said triumphantly. Something gave a faint click, and a portion of the wall swung inwards. "No, we're not allowed to travel the hall that leads to the stables. There are Men there, or so Miss Cornett says. I'm not sure it's not just a rumour."

"If we're not going to the stables—"

"No, no; we are going to the stables," Isabella assured her, pulling her into the wall. "We're simply taking another route. Going by the main way has the unfortunate result of getting one caught, and it's a little too early in the term to be getting caught by the staff just yet."

Annabel watched the panel close again behind them and said, "Do they know the school is riddled with passageways?"

"Of course!" Isabella said. "Unfortunately—*most* unfortunately—they don't know where the passageways are. It's a running battle between the school officials and the students as to which ones are discovered and which ones are still safe."

"It's more likely to be a battle between the school officials and you," Annabel muttered. "I haven't seen a single other girl creeping about."

"If she's good, you shouldn't," pointed out Isabella. "Well, perhaps I've had more than my share of close calls, but I tend to think of it as part of the education system here. This way, Nan. Be careful of the beams, they're rather low."

"So that's what it is," Annabel said, shivering in the darkness. Inside the walls of Trenthams Academy for Young Ladies wasn't so very different from the wandering, shifting, deadly maze that had been the castle three years ago. She hadn't expected to feel quite so claustrophobic. "You're making sure you take full advantage of all the learning opportunities the school offers."

"Exactly so," said Isabella.

"Belle?"

"Right through here."

"Are we nearly out?"

There was a flash of pale skin as Isabella's head turned to look at her and then back to the front. "Very nearly. Are you all right?"

"Yes," said Annabel. "But I'd like to be out soon."

"Through here, and *duck*—ow! Who put that there?"

"Teachers, probably," Annabel said, darting out into the open without injury. They were across from the stables, in the carriageway and well shielded from the windows of the school above by the carriageway roof. "All right, Belle?"

"It'll only bruise," Isabella said, feeling the spot carefully. "I wonder if the teachers have found this one? That's new since last I was here. Oh, look! We're in luck!"

Annabel, who had already seen Guardsman Raoul walk around the corner and stop in dismay, started forward again.

Raoul said, "You're not supposed to—" and stopped abruptly, presumably because he remembered he was talking to the future monarch as well as his friend.

"Actually," said Annabel, who had not read the rules the Aunts gave her—nor listened to Isabella—in vain, "we're allowed to be in the stables. We're just not allowed to enter the stables from the main passage. The rules are very specific."

"Of course they are," Raoul said, throwing a look of some dislike at Isabella. "And where exactly did you happen upon a copy of Trenthams rules and regulations this early in the term, if I may ask, your highness?"

"It's very important to know the rules," Annabel said seriously.

"So important!" said Isabella. "One needs to know how one can wriggle around them if need be."

"Exactly," agreed Annabel. "And it was the Aunts who gave it to me. Also, we aren't here to discuss the rules with you—no matter *how* curious we are about how you know that particular rule so well."

Raoul went faintly pink, and Isabella said in well-feigned outrage, "Raoul! Well, I never!"

"*You* never!" spluttered Raoul. "*You* never? You're probably the only one in the school who sneaks in and out enough to know every passageway in the place!"

"We'll talk about this later," Isabella promised, her eyes bright and dancing. "Nan's right. We aren't here to talk about how *very* well you seem to know the rules at Trenthams. We want to know why you didn't tell us that Melchior was coming here."

"You didn't ask about it, and we weren't supposed to tell," Raoul said, with some attempt at regaining his dignity.

"Did you speak with Melchior before you accompanied us?" asked Annabel.

"We were told to get our final orders from him," said Raoul, with the air of one who has given up the attempt at secrecy in disgust. "I'm surprised you didn't know that, Belle, since you always know everything!"

"When did you come to the manor?"

"I didn't go to the manor," Raoul said, with a more professional air. "I was told to meet Melchior in the village. We met a day or two before you were due to leave, at the posting stop."

"That settles it!" said Annabel, to Isabella. "It does have something to do with Luck!"

Raoul looked alarmed. "Why would it have anything to do with the Enchanter? Can't Melchior be here just to make sure you're taken care of?"

"Why would you answer Nan with a question?" instantly asked Isabella.

"Two," Annabel reminded her. "It's suspicious."

"*Very* suspicious," agreed Isabella. "Raoul, what do you know about Luck and Melchior's plotting?"

"Oh, look!" Annabel said. "He's sweating! That's pretty useful, actually."

"I've always thought so," Isabella said, observing Raoul with an assessing eye. "I keep telling him he'll have to get out of that habit if he wants to be a diplomat."

"I don't want to be a diplomat!"

"That's probably a good idea," Annabel said. "You'd never make it. As a Guardsman, you're very good."

Raoul looked flustered. "Thank you, your highness!"

"But don't you think it's a good idea to be *very truthful* with your future monarch?"

"I don't—I didn't—Yes, your highness."

"All right, then. When you met with Melchior—wait a minute. *Was* Luck there, too?"

Raoul gave up all pretence of a straight face, and closed his eyes for a pained moment. "Yes, your highness. It was like this: I was told to meet with Luck and Melchior to arrange for a guard for your carriage. They were already talking when I got there; something about a couple of Old Parrasian threats that had been left at the manor and in the post tubes. Melchior said that he had already arranged to be at the school when you got there. He mentioned they were in need of a master, but he was grinning, so I got the idea that—Well, that's only surmise on my part, your highness."

"You think he created the vacancy," nodded Isabella. She looked amused. "That doesn't surprise me. I've seen how Melchior works before: he's rather ruthless."

"Old Parrasians?" Annabel frowned. "They're those ones who picket the streets and carry signs about *Parras for Parrasians* and *No queen, No problem*, aren't they? The ones they call anti-Royalist nowadays."

"Exactly," said Isabella. "Awful people! They're worse than the Royalists, and the Royalists are pretty annoying."

"So it was Old Parrasians who attacked us on the road?"

"I don't know," said Raoul. He looked rather relieved to be able to say so truthfully. "We suspect so, but I don't know for sure. I'll have to speak with Melchior about it when we meet to—"

"Oh, how interesting!" Isabella said instantly. "You're still going to be keeping in touch with Melchior, then?"

Raoul made a small, inarticulate sound of annoyance.

Annabel grinned at him. "What are you going to be, a stable boy?"

"I'm going to be a footman at the local inn, thank you very much!" said Raoul, forgetting himself. "A stable boy inde—er, I mean, I'll be posted at the local inn, your highness."

Isabella tutted at him. "The cheek of some people! Give them a drop, Nan, and they'll take a bucket!"

"Speaking of drops, and buckets—!" said Raoul, with a meaningful look at the heavily laden bucket nearby that was buzzing with flies. "I'd be a bit more careful if I were you, Belle!"

"Threats and insults," Isabella said confidingly to Annabel. "That's where it starts, Nan! You'll have to keep your eye on this one."

"So there have been threats I knew nothing about, and warnings— about which I also knew nothing," Annabel said thoughtfully, ignoring both Isabella's arch look and Raoul's protests. "Not to mention a guard that I knew nothing about, and now two spies at my school."

"That you knew nothing about," added Isabella. "It strikes me as unfair, Nan!"

"Yes," Annabel said shortly. "That's how it strikes me, too. Moreover, it strikes me that I'm not being taken very seriously, and that's annoying. We should do something about that."

"If it helps, your highness," said Raoul; "I take you very seriously indeed!"

BY THE TIME THEY WENT BACK TO THEIR SUITE, THE CROWD IN THE

lower corridor had well and truly cleared, though enough of the girls still loitered hopefully to make Annabel think that Melchior had been roomed very close to the spot they'd last seen him. Unfortunately, the same couldn't be said for their own corridor and their own suite; the hall was full of girls. None of them quite looked at Annabel or Isabella, as if they were there simply on the way to their own rooms, but the few around the door had the determined air of girls about to begin an all day social assault. Annabel was very familiar with that look; she'd seen it often enough through the window when people began to call at Melchior's manor to meet her. These girls wanted to meet the future queen—and unlike Isabella, it seemed as though they weren't planning on being open about it.

"Good heavens," said Isabella lightly. "It's a little busy this afternoon, isn't it?"

She didn't seem to expect a reply, which was just as well, because Annabel was too busy taking in the reactions of the girls around her to do so. Some of them looked slightly sheepish, some faintly amused, and some downright poisonous. Isabella ignored all of the looks, poisonous or otherwise, and towed Annabel safely through the press to their door.

The girl closest to the door said in a friendly fashion, "We came to call on you both."

"Isn't that nice, Nan?"

"Very nice," said Annabel glumly. She didn't feel like being polite, but she knew she would have to be whether or not she wanted to be. It was probably very good for her, but it didn't make her appreciate it any the more. "I suppose you'd better come in."

The girl looked uncertain. "What, *all* of us?"

"Good heavens, no!" said Isabella briskly, much to Annabel's disappointment. She would have preferred to get all of the visiting over in one fell swoop. "A new rule popped up in the list this year; very odd! Trenthams prefers student meetings to be kept to an attendance of fifteen or less students when the meetings occur in private rooms."

"What about our clubs?" indignantly said one of the girls in the hallway.

"Don't meet in a private room and you're free to do as you like."

"Funny timing," said Annabel, in an undertone. "A new rule appearing just when you're due to come back after an absence of two years?"

"I'm sure I don't know what you mean," Isabella said. "Is it reasonable, Nan, I ask you, to link the circumstance of my having precipitated a small—a *very* small—riot the day before I left—"

"Precipitated or orchestrated?" Annabel asked, grinning. The girls in the hall were, variously, listening avidly or open-mouthed in shock.

Isabella continued serenely "—to the circumstance of there being one or two new rules in the official charter this year?"

"I'm surprised there aren't more new rules," said a small, plump, dusky haired girl, "after the things that happened two years ago. They want to get a running start this time, I should think. They couldn't pin a single thing on you because there were no rules against any of the things that happened. You'll have to take us in lots of ten or fifteen, your—er—"

Annabel might have let her flounder for a little bit longer, but the girl hadn't done anything really wrong. It wasn't her fault that Annabel didn't want to entertain. She said, "If we're being polite, you can call me Miss Ammett."

A ripple of change ran through the crowd of girls—a changing of expression, or perhaps just a murmur of surprise.

One of the other girls said, "Just *Miss?*"

Another one said, "And what if we're being friendly?"

"Come along, Nan," said Isabella. Annabel wasn't sure if she said it to make a point, but the girl who had asked about being friendly went a little bit pink. "We'll do what Delysia says. Ten at a time, and you can decide between yourselves which ten should come first. Just don't cause a riot, or the Awesome Aunts might blame it on me."

Annabel found herself swept away through the door to the rising babble of roughly fifty girls each trying to press her superior claim to going first. She shut the door behind herself and Isabella with some thankfulness.

"That'll give us a bit of respite," Isabella said. "Not much, but enough to settle a few things."

"What things?"

"Most importantly, tea."

"Oh *good*!"

"Not as much as you might think," Isabella warned. "You won't get a chance to drink much; you'll be too busy answering questions and giving out tea. The problem is that we aren't allowed to have magical means of warming, and if we keep calling up for trays of tea the kitchen will eventually rebel. So we'll have to make do with our fireplace and the hob, and that's bound to be a nuisance. At least it's not the good stuff—I hate having to give out the good stuff."

Annabel grinned. If there was anything she knew how to do after a childhood spent with Grenna the witch, it was making a fire. "Don't worry," she said. "I'll take care of that."

"Good heavens, can you light a fire?"

"Officially, no," Annabel said. "Melchior says it isn't a really queenly thing to know how to do. But since I've spent most of my life *not* being a queen, it didn't occur to me not to learn how."

"I wish I knew how to light a fire!" Isabella said enviously. "I've tried, but I really can't make it work! Even if I get a spark, it never will catch! You wouldn't believe how lowering it is to try and coax a flame that won't be coaxed, Nan!"

"If you could *talk* it into being—" said Annabel, before she could stop herself.

Isabella began to laugh, but smothered it quickly. "The *other* things are just a warning or two. Don't let any of the girls get too friendly unless you plan on having them as friends for life. If once they begin calling you Nan, you'll have to put up with impertinences for the rest of your rule, and oblique references to marrying off your children."

"*Children*? Isn't that looking a bit too far into the future?"

"Not for them," Isabella said firmly. "If there's anything you can say about the girls who come to school here, it's that they always have an eye to the future."

"If I let them call me Nan they'll expect our children to marry? What about *our* children?"

"Good heavens, no!" said Isabella. "It's extremely unlikely that I'll ever marry. I'll leave that up to Kit and Susan; I'll be much too busy with my little Papa's ambassadorial business to be playing those sort of games. And I can't ask you for anything else other than what I've already put in our agreement, so you've no need to worry that I'll hang on your sleeve all my life. Well, I *can't*; I'll be out of New Civet for most of the time."

"All right, I won't get too friendly," said Annabel, feeling at the same time relieved and a little disappointed. "What else? Melchior already taught me how to pass the tea things."

"The other thing...Now, don't be offended, Nan—"

"What now?" demanded Annabel. This time it was her turn to stifle laughter. "I suppose I'm not fashionable enough to be receiving visitors."

"Your clothes are very fashionable," Isabella said, with an edge of disapproval, "but they don't at all suit you. More importantly, for an afternoon visit at school you should be casually elegant. Better take off your overdress."

"I can't go around in my underdress!"

"Of course you can! It's the height of fashion to take afternoon callers in your underdress, provided that you wear an afternoon or evening wrapper. Something to show how elegant and at ease you are, you see. Sheer sleeves and floating overskirts are the thing; I'll have to see if I don't have something for you."

"But the girls—"

"They'll still be waiting in twenty minutes," said Isabella, without baulking. "As a matter of fact, I'm certain they'd still be waiting tomorrow morning if you chose to make them wait. This is a matter of great importance."

"What about the kettle?"

"I'll look after the kettle. Take care of your overdress, Nan."

Annabel grumbled, but did as she was told. By the time she unbuttoned herself and struggled out of the dark blue overdress she'd been wearing since the morning, not only was the kettle over the hob and beginning to sound like it was boiling, but Isabella had already changed her own overdress for a gauzy, floating thing and was looking thoughtfully between another two she had laid out on the bed.

"Yellow or blue?" she asked.

"Yellow," said Annabel, who always did like a brighter colour if possible.

"Yes, I thought so," said Isabella, throwing the yellow one back on the bed. "Not at all suitable. I wondered if we could get away with it, but I think not. Blue it is."

"Rude!" said Annabel, but she caught the blue wrapper Isabella threw to her despite that. It was too pretty to fall on the floor, and it wasn't that she was opposed to blue, after all. She just liked bright colours when she could have them. She slipped her arms carefully into the sheer sleeves, wary about catching her nails in the fine fabric, and buttoned herself up at the front.

"Oh, how lovely! How did they make it so fine?"

"Magic-made," Isabella said. "Perfectly lovely, isn't it? Ah, and that reminds me. You can't do magic."

"Not a speck," Annabel agreed. "Why? Do I need to?"

"Well..." Isabella hesitated. "The thing is, I'm a dreadful magic user, and I won't be able to tell if any of the girls tries to start up a spell this afternoon."

"I thought the Aunts said magic was strictly prohibited!" protested Annabel, her fingers automatically seeking the pencil staff. She had a moment's panic before she remembered it was in the pocket of the overdress she'd just taken off. "If they can't get spells in—!"

"Nan, I really worry about you! Of course it's prohibited! That is *not* to say, however, that none of the girls will have smuggled something in. Well! Only look at me! You have no conception of the amount of things I've already smuggled into the school, and it's only the first day!"

"Smu—what have you smuggled in? You only had a box of chocolates!"

Isabella sent her a demure look. "But only think of all the time I had in the village! Allow me to demonstrate."

To Annabel's astonishment, the other girl swept up her skirts at the front until the whole of her stocking and garter on the left leg were shamelessly displayed to the room.

"This, Nan," said Isabella, with the air of one giving vital instruction, "is a smuggling garter. You'll notice the small pockets, the useful loops, and the reinforced nature of its construction."

"The reinfo—is that a bottle of lilly-pilly oil?"

"Of course! There are times when other people should be usefully asleep."

"How much have you *got* there?"

"About as much as I have on the other," Isabella said cheerfully. "Most of it was already there when I met you, but I had to restock with Verisimilitude pills at the apothecary in the village. One trusts that they are the true thing and not a fake, since one does not have the magical aptitude to test them."

"Oh, does one! What if the Aunts caught you?"

"The Aunts catch me from time to time," Isabella agreed. "It's good for them, poor ducks. If they don't catch me once or twice a semester, they begin to think that I'm completely out of their control and talk about sending me away for the good of the school. Honestly, I think they might have been glad I was gone for two years."

"Did you really start a riot before you left last time?"

"Riot is a bit strong," protested Isabella. "If it comes to that, did you really bring the castle back and make it swallow Mordion?"

"It wasn't exactly me," Annabel muttered.

"Exactly. These things happen from time to time, and who can say who is at fault?"

"The girls seemed pretty sure."

"Sheer jealousy, Nan; sheer jealousy. By the way, are we advertising your relationship to Melchior?"

"Good grief, no!" said Annabel. Melchior might be up to something that he hadn't seen fit to tell her about, but although Annabel was prepared to be annoyed about that, she wasn't prepared to ruin his game. "There's no need for them to know who my guardian is."

"Exactly my thoughts," agreed Isabella. "We should strive to preserve some mystery, after all. Are you ready?"

"No," Annabel said gloomily.

It was too late, of course; Isabella was already opening the door. Annabel went to check on the simmering kettle, amused in spite of herself, and wondered exactly how Isabella was planning on running this afternoon.

The first ten girls came in with the air of an expedition to see the local faire animals, while Isabella closed the door firmly behind them and went to attend to the tea making. Annabel, who might once have been annoyed at their attitude, now looked across at Isabella and tried not to grin. Isabella was preparing the tea, but there was a certain sparkle in her grey eyes that Annabel recognised. Isabella was having fun. It was surprising how much better that made Annabel feel. If Isabella was enjoying herself, then there was no reason for Annabel not to enjoy herself, too.

Perhaps just a *touch* of her cow-face, enough to make her more expressionless than usual without making her look actually stupid— that was it! thought Annabel, catching sight of herself in the over-mantle glass. Let them try to get an expression out of her by surprise now.

The other girls looked around at each other uneasily, and it was left to the girl who appeared to be the leader—the one who had asked about being friendly—to sigh impatiently and make introductions.

"I'm Lady Caroline Boyyd-Smyth," she said. "I know everyone here at Trenthams, Miss Ammett, so if you would like a more *ahem*," she glanced delicately toward Isabella, who was making tea with shadowed, dancing eyes, "up-to-date knowledge of who it is good to know at school." She sent another delicate, faintly disturbed look around the room, as if to imply that the entire room didn't quite hold up to that standard, and added confidentially, "You can always speak to me in my rooms, Miss Ammett."

"Thanks," said Annabel. "Who's everyone else?"

The dark-haired girl who had spoken outside the door—Delysia, had Isabella said?—giggled into her handkerchief.

Lady Caroline very carefully took no notice. "Allow me to present the Lady Gwyn—" this, at a thin, golden girl with a high nose bridge and aristocratic nostrils, "and Lady Janna. From your left are Miss Pinet, Miss Charlotte, and Miss Danners. From your right, Miss Channing, Miss Tournet, and Miss Emily."

"Charmed," said Annabel, more cheerfully. Melchior had told her she was allowed to be short, so long as she was polite, and it was amusing to see Lady Caroline looking for words. She wondered why Lady Caroline didn't see fit to fill the silence with an introduction of the last two girls in the room, but the lady's lips only pinched together for a moment.

She opened them to speak again, leaving Annabel to speculate whether she was about to be delicately rude at the expense of the other girls again, or at Annabel's expense, but she was too late.

"I'm Delysia," said Delysia, when it became obvious that no one was going to introduce her. "My sister is Miss Matcham, but I don't see why I can't be a Miss Matcham here at Trenthams. Dolly will get married soon, anyway. You can call me Delysia if you like, but you don't have to. Oh, and this is Miss Almina; she's in from Broma."

The Bromian girl bowed, swift and short, her brown eyes bright. Annabel couldn't tell whether the girl was interested or mocking. And if the expression *was* mocking, was it at Annabel herself, or the order that had been so well established in the room by Caroline? Obviously, Annabel was supposed to give first importance to the Ladies and then to the misses—and finally, to the Bromian girl and the Delysia girl. That much was very clear. The problem was, Annabel knew far too many ways of getting around the things she was supposed to do.

She settled her blank expression a little more carefully on her face, and said to Delysia, "Do tell me about your sisters!"

5

The tea bell rang before the crowd of girls at the door had more than half dissipated.

"Tea!" said Isabella brightly. "Well, that's good for a rest break, after all! They won't all stay, but they'll all go. They'll want to know who has come back for the year, but once that's out of the way, they'll be back."

As if belying her words, there came a knock at the door.

"What now?" wailed Annabel, but when Isabella opened the door, one of the teachers stood there.

She was the same, thin, fluting teacher who had been trying to bring order to the girls swarming Melchior earlier—Miss Cornett, was it?

Isabella curtseyed and stepped back from the door, and Annabel wondered if it was her imagination, or if the whole bearing of the other girl displayed amusement.

"*Such* an instructive day for me!"

"I beg your pardon, Miss Farrah?"

"Nothing at all, Miss Cornett. I was merely remarking that this day has been a day of surprises for me. Can we offer you a cup of tea?"

Miss Cornett's head twitched forward on her thin neck as if to say *yes, she really quite would,* but her foot hesitated on the threshold. "I shouldn't like to inconvenience you on your first day here."

"You might as well come in," said Annabel, amused in spite of herself. "Everybody else has already been in."

"Yes, I suppose you've been quite busy—only to be expected—but one shouldn't *ahem*, say so."

"Shouldn't one?" asked Isabella. "I'm sure you're right, but I quite like being busy."

"Do sit down," said Annabel, since it seemed that Isabella was in a mood for laughter. "Do you take sugar?"

"Just a little!" Miss Cornett said. "Five lumps, thank you."

Isabella blinked a little and dropped five lumps into the tiny teacup, one after the other. "I thought you would be busy today, Miss Cornett."

"No, no—well, that is, yes a little! Still, one should be polite, and..."

"Goodness!" said Isabella. "When you said that you were a little busy, I didn't realise you were going to visit all the new girls. That *is* polite of you!"

"Oh! Well! Perhaps not all of them...that is, I thought since Miss Ammett is so *ahem*, new, and since it's your first term back again..."

"Ah," nodded Isabella. "You came to share your wisdom. We appreciate that very much, don't we, Nan?"

"Very much," agreed Annabel. Miss Cornett was looking more flustered, and Annabel wasn't sure whether to feel satisfied or sorry for her. "Biscuit, Miss Cornett?"

"Oh! No, thank you. I shouldn't really stay."

"Oh, but we're waiting for your wisdom, Miss Cornett!" protested Isabella. "Just think how long I've been out of the fold, and how much Nan has to learn!"

"It's nothing really," Miss Cornett said, a touch of pink in either cheek. "I simply wanted you to know that if you need anything, you need only ask. My door isn't always *ahem*, open, as such, but I am quite often there between classes."

"Oh," said Annabel. She glanced up at Isabella and caught the other girl looking distinctly sardonic. Was Miss Cornett not to be trusted either, then? "Thank you. I'll remember that."

"Then I'll take my leave," said Miss Cornett. "Miss Ammett, Miss Farrah."

They both curtseyed, Isabella with elegance and Annabel with relief.

"Do remember," said Miss Cornett, pausing at the door, "that curfew begins in half an hour. Any girl caught out in the hallways after curfew will be punished regardless of her standing in the school."

Annabel and Isabella looked at each other; said in tandem, "*Yes*, Miss Cornett," properly.

When Miss Cornett closed the door behind herself, Annabel said, "Do you know, Belle, I get the feeling they don't trust you."

"We should go out," said Isabella decidedly.

"Didn't Miss Cornett *just* say—"

"Of course she did; she says the same thing every year. I suppose it's up to you, after all—do you want to stay here and receive visitors every few minutes for the next half hour, or—?"

"We should go out," Annabel said hastily. "Where are we going, by the way?"

"That depends," said Isabella. "Is there something you want to know? For instance, *I* want to know why we weren't given the suite we ought to have been given."

Annabel thought about it and came to the conclusion that there was, in fact, something she wanted to know. "I want to know why Melchior is here. Really. Of course he's here because there have been threats, but I'm sure there's more to it."

"Oh, good!" Isabella said, in a pleased voice. "I was beginning to wonder if you were a curious sort of person—I always get along better with curious people."

Annabel gave a smothered giggle. "I don't think you should be calling your future monarch a curious person!"

"You'll just have to have me beheaded when you're sworn in," said Isabella. "That will teach me! Shall we really see what Melchior's up to? I'm sure we can sneak into the school office and see if he's on the teacher's schedule if we're very careful about it."

"Are you?" said Annabel doubtfully. She was less sure. "Won't the office have a lock?"

"Of course! Isn't it lucky that I can pick locks?"

"Lucky?"

"Well, I did work very hard at it," confided Isabella. "There was this man who kept breaking into the Imperial Palace when I was in Lacuna with my little Papa, you see. He didn't want to kill anyone or steal anything, he just wanted to get *in*. You know, and have people *know* he'd been there. Anyway, there was this man, sneaking in; and there was I, sneaking about..."

It was fortunate, thought Annabel, fifteen minutes later, that not a soul was about the halls, since Isabella's idea of sneaking about seemed to be to stroll down those hallways without a care in the world. When Annabel protested this, all Isabella said was, "Oh no! There are magical curfew keepers, but they don't start for another hour, and they'll only stop us if we're being furtive. They're built to allow the teachers through, you understand. Everything is perfectly fine, so long as one doesn't panic. Besides, everyone else is either at tea or too scared to be out here, so who is there to see us? The teachers will be having their first night meet and greet—*especially* with Melchior here now. There are at least two female, unmarried teachers. Oh, look! Here we are!"

"The office?" It didn't look much like an office, and they'd been walking down a particularly luxurious hallway on what Annabel was sure was the highest floor.

Isabella gave her a sparkling, mischievous look. "No! The suite! Feast your eyes, Nan!"

Annabel wasn't sure how she did it, but she was fairly certain Isabella picked the lock with a thumbtack and something equally small and unlikely. She did it very quickly, too; the door was open before Annabel had a chance to protest that she had thought they were going to the office first.

The protest died away as she gazed into that room. "Oh," she said. "Oh. It's rather big, isn't it?"

"Not big," said Isabella, her eyes bright; "*Magnificent!* And it should have been ours. Do you know what is the most irritating thing about this whole situation, however?"

Annabel didn't know, but she was quite sure Isabella was about to tell her whether or not she wanted to know, so she merely wandered further into the room.

"The most irritating thing," continued Isabella, not at all put off, "is that we can't even ask why, because this room isn't actually part of the dormitories. Technically, it's only ever supposed to be given to visiting dignitaries, and you can be sure that's exactly the answer they'll give us if we ask. But just the same, every year the head girl or the richest girl at Trenthams rooms here. It's *understood*."

"Perhaps they were doing it up," suggested Annabel, who could smell the familiar scent of newly dried wall spackle. No one ever thought their rooms were good enough for the future queen, and no matter where she had visited in the last three years, she had smelled that smell.

"Ye-es," Isabella agreed doubtfully. "I suppose it could be as simple as that. But they would have done it much earlier, if that was the case —or put us in here after airing the place out for a while."

"I can still smell the spackle," Annabel said.

"Oh, is *that* what it is? Well then!"

"It does," Annabel said reluctantly, "look as though they're nearly finished preparing it. And I suppose if they're preparing it, they must be preparing it for *someone*."

"Very odd," said Isabella. Annabel had expected her to bristle at the suggestion, but Isabella only looked interested. "And that's just a little bit too late as well. What a nice little puzzle for us. We might even be able to dig up something about this in the office, too. Shall we?"

"All right," agreed Annabel, already moving toward the door. The room was grand and its surrounding suite was really very lovely, but it wasn't to her taste.

Isabella hesitated, pouted a little, and said, "Go ahead, Nan. I want to revel a little bit before we go."

Annabel left her to revel and stepped quietly into the hall. Was she imagining things, or had a shadow passed the door just as she turned? Her right hand automatically sought the pencil staff in her pocket, but she didn't get the chance to pull it out. Someone grabbed her around the waist and pulled her into the shadowy hall with one hand against her mouth.

Annabel's shoulders met the wall. She would have struggled but she already knew who had snatched her away, and she had a rather good idea of why.

"There you are!" hissed Melchior's voice, as the hand was removed. "Nan, you were supposed to come and see me!"

Annabel glared at him. "You didn't say so. You didn't say anything, actually; you just disappeared and didn't see me off. Why should I come and see you just because you're sneaking into the school?"

"I didn't sneak in," said Melchior. He grinned, eyes glowing in the shadows. "I'm one of the masters. Didn't you know?"

"I didn't ask," Annabel said, putting her nose up and hoping it looked as elegant on her as it did on Isabella. "And if you're a master, I'm not allowed to consort with you, anyway."

Both of Melchior's brows went up. "Consort? We're doing nothing of the kind! Don't look down your nose at me, Nan; you're too short and you'll make yourself cross-eyed."

"I have to be in my room by the time they snuff the hall lights," Annabel said in annoyance. She wondered when it was that she'd begun to find it hard to keep her blank expression in front of Melchior. "I can't stop and talk."

"Now that's very interesting," said Melchior. It wasn't until he took a step closer that Annabel realised he still had one arm around her waist. "Because the lights are already snuffed and you're still out. What are you up to?"

"Good heavens!" said Isabella's voice before Annabel had a chance to discover why she was feeling so very startled. "An interlude! Shall I close my eyes?"

"Whatever for?" Annabel said crossly. "And I think it's pretty rich of you to be asking what we're up to, Melchior! You're sneaking around as well!"

"I was looking for you," Melchior said, stepping back unhurriedly until he was in the dim light of the only remaining hall lamp. "What else would I be doing? You weren't in your room. Hallo, Firebrand. I trust you're not leading Nan astray?"

"I'm reliably informed," said Isabella, very sweetly, "that only a very select few students are allowed to bring their pets with them to Trenthams. I'm glad to see that you're in their number, Nan."

Melchior's eyes narrowed. "Nan, I won't have you telling people that I'm your cat!"

"You are my cat," said Annabel.

"Do you fancy there's room to keep him in our suite, though, Nan?"

"I have my own room, thank you very much," said Melchior. "And speaking of which, perhaps we could take this conversation there instead of remaining here to be seen by every other schoolgirl who wants to sneak out tonight."

"No one else will be sneaking out tonight," Isabella said tranquilly, but she followed when Annabel went after Melchior. "No one sneaks out on the first night."

Melchior's lip curled slightly. "Evidently."

"What better night to sneak out than a night when no one would be stupid enough to sneak out?" protested Isabella.

"It's what you thought yourself," Annabel said to Melchior. Isabella and Melchior were very similar in some ways. "And it's no good both of you glaring at me; you're like peas in a pod."

"I'm offended," Melchior said. "Nan, I'll have you know that—"

"*You're* offended!" gasped Isabella. "Well, I never! Nan, I'm at least twice as elegant as Melchior!"

"No one is as elegant as I am."

"I would like to remind you, Melchior, that I am fully aware of how long you spent as a cat, and if *that* is your idea of elegance—"

Melchior grinned and opened the closest door along the hall. "Next time come and see me alone, Nan," he said, to Annabel. "I refuse to be bested in my own room."

"Oh! Is this your room? Why couldn't we have this one! This one is nicer!"

Isabella gazed at her in wonder, then around the small, crimson and teak room. "Nan, you have the *oddest* taste!"

"I like comfortable rooms," Annabel said, refusing to feel defensive. "Look at how warm and cosy it looks! And there's a skylight—Melchior, did you choose this room so that you could sneak out when you needed to?"

"I warned you, Firebrand!" said Melchior wrathfully, pushing them both through the door and closing it. "I won't have you being a bad influence on Nan! I disapprove of this friendship utterly!"

"That means yes," Annabel said, in a loud aside.

"Now *there's* an idea!" Isabella said, her eyes kindling. "I think our suite might have a skylight somewhere, too!"

Melchior, grinning reluctantly, said, "Oh, sit down, the pair of you! There's a kettle here somewhere. We'll have a cup of tea."

"*Bless* you!" said Isabella earnestly. "We've been fetching tea for other girls all afternoon!"

"It's all right to say you won't have Isabella being a bad influence on me," began Annabel, who was just as eager for tea but didn't see why she had to let Melchior off the hook just for that, "but you weren't the one who made a footpad shoot himself when our carriage was held up. That was Belle!"

A kettle lid clanged loudly against something wooden. "*What* happened?"

"Oh, didn't you know?" Isabella asked innocently. "I thought that's why you came separately. The carriage was attacked by footpads: we were almost killed!"

Melchior, very pale, said, "There was meant to be a guard—"

"There was," said Annabel. "And Belle hit one or two of the footpads with her parasol, so it was—"

"Were you hurt?"

"Of course not," said Annabel loftily, ignoring Melchior's searching look. "We can take care of ourselves."

"Nan hurt her hand," Isabella offered. She smiled sweetly at Annabel's look of reproach and added in Melchior's general direction, "You should probably look at it. I think the medical officer who bandaged it was too overcome by devotion to do a proper job."

"Overcome by—" Melchior raised one brow at Isabella and retrieved the kettle lid. Slowly, he hung the kettle on the fireless hob and snapped his fingers. Annabel couldn't see the magic it made, but the air in the room felt warmer at once.

"Oh yes! You shouldn't send young, impressionable guards along to guard female royalty."

"I'll remember that," Melchior said, leaving the kettle to boil, and Annabel to wonder if he knew he'd just confirmed what had only previously been a suspicion in Isabella's fertile mind.

Raoul might not know exactly who had sent the orders, but it was obvious it had been Melchior himself. And if that was the case, it was likely that there was more in the wind than a few threats.

Melchior sat down next to Annabel by the simple expedient of removing Isabella by her collar as if she'd been Peter, and taking her place. Ignoring Annabel's protests, he picked at the binding around her hand. His face looked particularly grim, though Annabel wasn't sure whether that was because of the footpads or because there was blood beginning to seep through the first layers of the bandage he'd uncovered.

"He wasn't overcome," she protested. "He was just a bit nervous."

"Well, *I've* never seen any of Raoul's regiment trip over his own feet before."

"Why didn't you get this seen to by the nurse?"

"That's your fault," Annabel said, surprising Melchior into a grin.

"I might have known. How exactly am I to blame this time?"

"We were on our way to do something about it," began Annabel, not entirely mendaciously, "when we were interrupted by a riot in the hallway. We tried to push our way through and there you were. Miss Cornett isn't at all pleased with you, you know."

"We'll see about that!" Melchior replied outrageously. "No, hold still, Nan! I'm not very good at this and I don't want to do it badly."

"There's a comfort," murmured Isabella. "Nan, perhaps we should call for the little medical officer again—what was his name?"

"Dannick," said Annabel, to the crown of Melchior's head. Isabella wasn't the sort to forget names—was she trying to needle Melchior? And if so, how? Perhaps she was teasing Annabel instead. "He said he can't do much in the way of healing, and he was afraid of making it worse. That's why he bandaged it."

"Is it?" Isabella sounded innocently surprised. "And here I thought it was merely in order to have an excuse to hold your hand. By the way, Melchior, you might find it harder than you think to sweet talk Miss Cornett into forgetting a Scene. Mr. Turner is a lovely little man and she withered him earlier just for leaving a smudge of mud in the entry way."

"I would like to know," said Melchior, sounding particularly annoyed, "how it is that there are so many men in this supposedly reputable all female school!"

"Miss Cornett wonders the same thing often," said Isabella helpfully. "Perhaps they'll get along better than we think, Nan!"

Annabel scowled down at her bandages, and looked up to find Melchior watching her. "Aren't you finished yet?"

Melchior's eyes flicked back to her hand. "Not quite yet, no. If you would be good enough not to wriggle so much, Nan—!"

"It tickles!"

"Firebrand, would you kindly make tea?"

"If one must, one must," said Isabella. She said it very innocently, which made Annabel gaze after her in astonishment. What was she laughing at this time?

"Nan," said Melchior, rewrapping the bandage around a hand that was, Annabel now realised, gazing down at it, pinkishly scarred instead of red and puckered, "it is commonly thought a bad idea for the future monarch to be upon too good of terms with her soldiery."

"Is it?" Annabel thought about that, and said, "Yes, but how can they be expected to fight for her if they're not on good terms with her?"

"Pure altruism, one suspects," said Isabella. "A better breed of man entirely!"

"You should be more careful, Belle," Annabel said, grinning. "That sounded a bit too much like sarcasm."

Isabella sighed. "Perhaps I'm losing my touch? I like to leave people in *some* kind of suspense, after all!"

"Oh!" said Annabel, remembering, "and at least the soldiery remembers to make sure we eat, unlike some cats I know of!"

Melchior frowned and put Annabel's re-bandaged hand in her lap. "What nonsense is this? I arranged for your meals along the way."

"You arranged for one meal," said Annabel. "And if you meant it for a prod at me—"

"What prod?" demanded Melchior blankly. "I refuse to be sniffed at for things I haven't done!"

"Well, even if you forgot," said Annabel, slightly mollified, "I don't think it's very good of you!"

"I arranged for a midday meal each day, and for dinner and breakfast at the two overnight stops," Melchior said firmly. "I've a good mind to—Just a moment! When did the highwaymen show up?"

"Ah," said Isabella. "Now *there's* a thing to think about."

Annabel blinked. "They didn't want anyone to be expecting me, but they weren't quite sure when they would be attacking, either, so they went along telling all the stops to cancel dinners and lunches."

Melchior sat up very straight, his eyes gleaming. "Careless of 'em!"

"On the contrary," said Isabella. "If we hadn't got away, it probably wouldn't have occurred to you to check on the meals you'd arranged. And none of the inns knew they were expecting the queen heir, so they wouldn't have confided the information."

"Very useful for me."

"Useful for *us*," Annabel corrected.

"Nonsense," Melchior said. "You're not allowed to leave the school grounds except on half days. You'll be confined to your rooms for a week."

"Only if we're caught."

"Firebrand, what did I tell you about being a bad influence? There's no need for either of you to leave the school grounds—as a matter of fact, I'd far prefer that you remain here. At least there's some safety here. I can do all the outside investigating that's necessary."

Annabel made a disgusted noise and muttered, "Typical!"

"I'm sorry, did you mutter?" One of Melchior's brows was up. "One would think, Nan, that you enjoyed being in peril."

"I don't," said Annabel bluntly. "But I like to be able to know for myself that something nasty isn't about to drop on me. And after all the years you spent murmuring in my ear about stirring myself and doing things, I think it's a bit much for you to be discouraging me from doing things now!"

"If I remember rightly, you were very nearly killed by Mordion several times."

"If *I* remember rightly—"

"Good heavens, it's like a play!" said Isabella, looking avidly from one to the other. "Have some tea, Nan. If you feel that you simply must hurl it in his face, do wait for a few minutes until it cools."

"Throw it in his—"

"Of course, you could always slap him."

"Oh, shut up!" Annabel said, grinning. "Drink your tea and stop needling people. You were bad enough with Miss Cornett."

"That's because I was annoyed," Isabella said. "If people are going to hang on your sleeve, they should at least be honest about it!"

"I don't understand how you can be useful to your little—I mean to your papa at all. You always tell people the truth!"

"Yes, and very useful I've found it," agreed Isabella. "Half the time people don't believe me, you know."

"That doesn't surprise me," said Annabel. "I've never met someone as dishonestly honest as you."

"I'm one of a kind," Isabella said simply. "Aren't you glad you met me?"

Annabel looked at Melchior over the rim of her teacup. "You should learn from Isabella. *She's* always honest."

"Always—What exactly is it, Nan, that you suspect I'm not telling you?"

"If I knew that, I wouldn't be asking, would I? Stop answering questions with questions."

Melchior's brow rose. "If I haven't told you something, it's for a very good reason."

"I want to know why you've snuck into my school," Annabel said. "And if you don't tell me why I'm going to be very queenly and annoyed with you."

"You're not queen yet," said Melchior, crossing one leg over the other and leaning back at his ease. He sipped his tea and smiled insincerely at Annabel.

Annabel allowed her face to become just a little bit blanker. "There's also the question," she added, "of what you and Luck were talking about in the village that day."

"I like queenly you," said Isabella, taking two biscuits at once with an even more innocent air than usual. "It's a bit like normal you, but more beef in the gravy."

Annabel spluttered a laugh that ruined her blank face.

"There are times, Nan," said Melchior, "when it is not expedient to tell the queen everything. And before you're queen, there are more of those times."

"I see!" said Annabel, more stiffly. She stood up. "Well, if that's the case, I don't see why we should sit here drinking tea, Belle! We might as well keep going on with our own investigations."

"And if it comes to that," said Melchior, rising along with her, "*I* would like to know how you knew about my meeting with Luck."

"There are times—" began Annabel. "Oh, never mind! It's none of your business anyway! Come on, Belle! We'll go back to what we were doing when Melchior interrupted."

"I don't think so," Melchior said. "There's no reason for either of you to be wandering around the school at this time of day."

"It's none of your business if we're wandering the school!" Annabel said indignantly.

"I hate to remind you, Nan—"

"Oh, do you."

"I hate to remind you, but I am, in fact, a master here." Melchior smiled gently at them both. "Wouldn't it be a shame if I had to report two students for sneaking out on their first night?"

"Well!" said Isabella. "Nan, I do think your taste in pets could be better!"

"He's just getting old and pernickety," Annabel snapped. "Let's go back to our suite."

Melchior, smiling faintly in a way that made Annabel want to hit him, followed them to the door and said, "Allow me to accompany you."

Annabel looked at him resentfully. "We don't need your company."

"I hesitate to annoy you, Nan," said Melchior, "but I really must insist."

"Oh, do you," muttered Annabel again. "Belle, let's go."

"Very well," said Isabella. "But if your pet is going to follow us all the way to our suite, shouldn't we give it something to eat before we put it out?"

"It can fend for itself," Annabel said, marching on ahead of the faintly smirking Melchior.

Melchior continued to follow them until they reached the door to their suite. He didn't leave—and neither, Annabel noted sourly, did his smirk—until they had opened the door and closed it behind them.

"It's no use trying to go out later, either," Annabel grumbled. "He'll just loiter in the hall until he thinks it's safe."

She glanced at Isabella, aware of a distinct lack of expected outrage from her general vicinity, and saw a thoughtful expression on her face.

"Belle?"

"Dear me!" said Isabella slowly, looking around the room. "How very odd!"

"What's odd?"

"Oh, well; I suppose it's not *that* odd," admitted Isabella. "Only I didn't expect it so very soon. I hope that you didn't leave anything important in our suite, Nan; I very much fear that someone has been digging through our things."

Annabel frowned and gazed around the main room. "I don't have anything important except the staff, and I always have that with me. What makes you say th—oh, never mind."

Isabella blinked twice, rapidly. "I've a feeling we're not talking about the same thing," she said. "What makes you think someone has been in the room, Nan?"

"Well!" said Annabel in surprise. "The maids have already been, haven't they?"

"Indeed."

"Then why is our coal scuttle messy again? It was clean before.

Someone has jostled it." Annabel gazed at it suspiciously, then frowned. "Why? What did you notice?"

"It's not so much what I noticed as the fact that a trap I set has been sprung."

"A trap? You set a trap?"

"I always leave a feather in the doorjamb before I leave the room," said Isabella. "Actually, it's more of a habit than anything, so I didn't really think about it."

"What does a feather—" began Annabel; and then she remembered the tiny blue feather that had caught up in the hallway carpet a few feet away from the door. "Oh! That's very clever!"

"I thought so," agreed Isabella. "I learnt some form of that one rather a long time ago, and sometimes when I'm travelling with Papa there are places that don't have magical security, so..."

"You'll have to teach me things like that," said Annabel. "It's no use learning how to speak and negotiate and plan if people can sneak into my rooms whenever they want to. And magical security is no good for me, anyway."

Isabella, who was sorting very slowly through the hat-making things she'd left out on her bureau top, turned one hat over and sighed. "It's not the sort of thing you expect to happen at a place like Trenthams," she said, shaking her head sadly. "They've gone through our things as well, Nan."

"Rude!" said Annabel, but she couldn't help feeling a kind of respect as well. "Who do you think is bold enough to go through someone else's room on the first day of the term?"

"Off hand, I'd say there are about three in the school," Isabella said. Her grey eyes were very narrow.

"That's all very well," Annabel said, "but what if it's someone not in the school?"

Isabella shook her head. "Unlikely. The security here is really very good, if you don't consider how ridiculously trusting they are with their students and teachers, and—"

"Ah," said Annabel.

Isabella, in quite a different voice, said, "Oh."

"I think we can assume that Melchior isn't the only interloper, then," Annabel said. "Are there other new teachers this term?"

"I must confess my ignorance, Nan," said Isabella. "How very annoying! I knew that there would be some inconveniences to coming back after two years, but I didn't consider this particular one. Three of the teachers are new to me, but they may well have been here for the last two years. I shall make enquiries."

"I'd also like to know how many of the other girls have something like smuggling garters," Annabel added.

"Not to mention how many of them are good enough magic users to be able to bypass the magic sensors and bring something wickedly dangerous into Trenthams."

Annabel hesitated. "Are any of them really ruthless enough to really try and hurt me, though? They're all awfully young!"

"And how young were you when you disposed of Mordion?" Isabella reminded her.

Annabel looked around, frowning. Another question had occurred to her. "What do you think they were looking for, anyway?"

"That's a good point." Isabella looked around, too; her eyes catalogued everything in a brief moment, and came back to rest on Annabel. "They've been careful not to make a mess, so I think we can assume they don't want us to know they've been in here."

Annabel grinned. "It's a bit insulting, isn't it?"

"My feelings exactly. Imagine thinking we wouldn't notice!"

"Maybe they wanted the staff?"

"Perhaps," Isabella said slowly. "But if so, why? It's a curious thing for someone to try and steal—especially when they could simply try to kill you again. Even a staff wielding queen can be taken by surprise if you've got enough money for a really good assassin."

"And if they're good enough to slip into our room without anyone catching them, why not just leave a useful assassin here?" agreed Annabel.

Isabella giggled suddenly. "Oh, well! An assassins is a useful thing to have around the place, after all! So long as it matches the décor!"

6

The first official day of school at Trenthams didn't occur, much to Annabel's surprise, until all the girls had been there for two days.

"They like to give us a chance to settle in," said Isabella, at breakfast that morning. "Not to mention a chance to find all the right classrooms. For example, we will begin our day with Advanced Polite Conversation, move from there to Carriage on Horseback, which is a bit of a bother, but what else can we do?"

Annabel put down her biscuit and said with more than a little suspicion, "All right, what else *can* we do?"

"The question was rhetorical, Nan."

"*Was* it."

"Goodness me, when you do that with your voice, it's absolutely *squashing*," said Isabella said, without sounding squashed. "Just like what you do with your face. I say that it's a rhetorical question because I've already done something about it. I abhor horses and I refuse to Improve my Carriage on one."

"You already—What did you do?"

"The good thing about the lessons here at Trenthams," Isabella said complacently, "is that there are two of each for every year level. They do it to add to the feeling of exclusivity at the school—smaller classes, you understand—while still making *very* good money taking in a decent amount of students. Girls are assigned to one or the other, and if there are two teachers for each particular version of the class, they always hate each other."

"Why? Oh. They each want to have the best class."

"That, or the most socially sparkling," nodded Isabella.

"Do you mean that you just don't go to either? Won't one of them notice when you don't show up?"

"Oh no," said Isabella. "I simply make sure that each of the teachers thinks I'm on the other one's schedule by erasing my name altogether. Provided it's not the same teacher doing both classes, it's beautifully complete."

"You—"

"I erased your name, too. Aren't you thankful to me, Nan?"

"Very!" Annabel said, without any attempt at concealing the relief in her voice. "I don't like horses much, either."

"You're fortunate," Isabella assured her. "Horses don't like me, and I can assure you that that is far worse."

"Oh well, I suppose there has to be something you can't charm," Annabel said, grinning.

Isabella grinned, but said, "I am also unable to charm the entirety of the third floor. I think they view me in a worse light even than horses do."

Annabel was quite sure that the entire third floor hated Isabella purely for the circumstance that she was rooming with Annabel, and that Isabella didn't care enough about them to make the effort to charm them.

"Wait!" she said suddenly. "I didn't think to ask which lesson Melchior takes!"

"Oh yes," Isabella said. "I checked that, too. Look, I got us both a schedule."

Annabel gazed at her in open-mouthed surprise and took the card-stock schedule. "*When*? When did you do all of this?"

"When I was in the office earlier this morning. I was called in for something small and irrelevant; a button missing on my cuff, I believe. You were still sleeping."

"*You* had a button off your cuff?"

"I needed a reason to get in the office," Isabella said reasonably. "And it only cost me a single Disorderly Mark, too! I find that a real bargain, Nan."

Annabel frowned down at her teacup. If she remembered rightly, the main office on the first floor was mostly a single room with just a small dispensary accessed through a locked door. "Did you fix all that while the teacher was in the room?"

"Of course not," Isabella said. "I waited until she went into the dispensary to fetch thread and needle."

"You—Did you lock her into the dispensary?"

"Who can say how these things happen? The hinges are quite loose, I believe; the door swung shut behind the teacher, and it took me quite some time to hear her calling."

"Thick door, is it?" Annabel said.

"Very! Such a large room, too. And then when I did hear her, it took me *such* a long time to find where the spare key was kept! You wouldn't believe it, Nan!"

"I believe it," said Annabel, giving up the attempt not to grin into her tea. "What is Melchior teaching, by the way?"

"Elegant Elementaries of Ensorcellment."

"Good grief, what a mouthful."

"Very select, I believe."

"Probably because no one can say it," opined Annabel. "Oh well, there's a relief, anyway. We won't be attending that class."

"Think again."

"Wait!" Annabel protested, searching her schedule with disbelieving eyes. There it was: *Elegant Elementaries of Ensorcellment*, fifth on her schedule for the day. "Neither of us can do ensorcellments, elegant or otherwise!"

"I can," said Isabella. "Not *well*, mind you, but I can do them. It's the area in which I receive the lowest marks. I would have taken us both off his class schedule, but I'm fairly certain he'd notice straight away."

"He's probably the one who put us there," Annabel said. "What rubbish, putting me in an ensorcellment class!"

"I thought," said Isabella thoughtfully, "that he would find something less...well, *confining* to do. Like patrolling the halls or presiding over meals—something to keep him around if someone tried to kidnap you. I mean, really, the only effort he's gone to in order to keep you in sight is making you take his class. I wonder why that is."

"If he's only here because of threats against me, you mean?" Annabel thought about that, and nodded. "And it's an odd class for him to take, besides. We've got any number of classes in here that he could have taken—" she shook her class schedule at Isabella "—and he picks the one he's least qualified to teach."

"I thought Melchior was quite good with magic."

"He is," said Annabel. "*If* you want tunnels forming in things, and *if* you want to turn into a cat. Actually, any animal, and he's really very good; but you can't really call either of those elegant. He knows all the theory, but he's very specialised when it comes to practical."

"Then there are Things To Consider," said Isabella impressively. "One: Why has Melchior taken the class he has taken? Two: Why are we both forced to take that particular class? Three: why have we been ejected from our rightful suite to—"

"We weren't ejected," interrupted Annabel. "We were never there in the first place. *Three*: who was it that searched our room on the first night? Four—oh, there's Melchior after all. It looks like he *is* presiding over meals. I thought there was a Matron for that."

"There is," said Isabella. "But they like to have one of the teachers here at each main meal, too. They take it in turns. Well, then. I think we can surmise that there have at least been further threats. It still doesn't answer the question of why he took that particular class, but it does bear out the fact that the attacks on you will probably increase."

"Maybe if we're Advanced and Polite enough in our Conversation, we can converse our way out of danger," suggested Annabel. After the ordeal in the castle that had turned her into the queen heir, none of the threats she had received over the last three years had been enough to do more than irritate her. It was difficult to be frightened of a group of old-fashioned and backward Old Parrasians when she had once been threatened by a wizard who had stripped enchanters and enchantresses of their power over the years and used it to sustain himself. Of course, she'd been lucky then; the same staff that declared her queen had saved her. If she'd been left to her own devices she would have been dead very quickly.

"Anyway," she added, "I've got the staff. I'd like to see 'em try and hurt me while I've got that."

"Does it stop you from being hit on the head from behind?"

"Not really," Annabel said reluctantly. In truth, the staff did very little in the way of passive protection—it was all active unmagic, that mysterious power that turned any magic around it to its own ends. The staff did nothing Annabel didn't make it do, and of the things she did with it, all of those were concerned with drawing. That was the main problem with an unmagic staff that preferred to express itself as a pencil—it was beautifully portable, but it did tend to mean that a person did a lot of drawing. And while Annabel loved to draw, she felt that the staff could have been a little more impressive in the way it worked.

"You'll have to explain the staff to me one of these days," Isabella said, unblinkingly sneaking the last muffin off the plate before Annabel could get to it. "Not here, of course; we might have got the only table that seats two, but you can depend on it that the ones who can lip read are trying to figure out the best angle to see us talk."

"Some of them can lip read?"

"Of course," nodded Isabella. "There was a class a few years ago. Very useful, of course, but one suspects that the pupils may have learned a little too well for comfort."

Annabel thought about it, and came to the conclusion that it was extremely unlikely Trenthams itself had ever countenanced such a class. "You ran it, didn't you?" she said. "An underground class on lip reading."

Isabella gave a surprised chuckle. "Of course!" she said. "And some of the little horrors learned *amazingly* well! Better than I did, to be strictly honest."

"What other classes did you have?"

"Amateur Fainting, Elementary Lockpicking, and a rather short lived course on Explosives," said Isabella promptly. "Well, but Nan! If we're expected to go out into society with only the classes that Trenthams teaches, we'll be woefully unprepared!"

"How does knowing about explosives help you in society?" protested Annabel.

"I might once have asked that question," Isabella said solemnly, "if it had not been for the circumstance—"

"Someone probably tried to blow you up," Annabel said. "I don't blame them. You were probably poking your nose into their business."

"In my defence, it was a *very boring* party, and they were silly enough to try and pass as guests when not one of them knew how to tie a Bromian Ceremonial knot," Isabella said. "At any rate, if I'd been well taught in explosives prior to that point in my life, a few people might have had fewer grey hairs. A class is absolutely essential."

"Don't tell me you taught that one, too!"

"Not at all," said Isabella. "I smuggled in a teacher. It was a dreadful bore, because she was far too large to fit in my smuggling garters."

Annabel coughed into her toast.

"As a matter of fact, she may still live in the village. Perhaps we should see about starting classes again."

"Only if we can have a class on lock picking again, too," said Annabel. "And one on untying knots. I don't care about the Amateur Fainting, but I would very much like to know how to pick locks and untie knots."

"Those aren't skills you should need, are they?" Isabella sounded surprised. "Melchior can make tunnels through nearly everything, and if you've got the staff—"

"Sometimes people are so focused on the magical defences that they don't look at the ordinary ones," said Annabel. As someone without even the slightest bit of magic to her, she was extremely conscious of it. "There have been a few times when Melchior and I were shut up somewhere we couldn't get through with magic, but the lock was ordinary. They thought that so long as we couldn't get out via magic, a normal lock was good enough for the door."

"Was it?" Isabella watched her, fascinated. "I can't imagine it was, with how determined you are. Fancy! Melchior hasn't told me any of this, and I highly resent that!"

Annabel grinned. "One time, the hinge pins were on the inside. All we had to do was lever them out. We got back to the manor before the ransom message did."

"That strikes me as very unprofessional," Isabella said disapprovingly. "Never mind—perhaps it was their first kidnapping attempt. They might well learn better as they go on."

"Anyway," said Annabel. "I want to learn how to pick locks and untie knots. I can't use the staff if my hands are tied up, can I?"

"Very well. Do bear in mind that I'm only a beginner myself, Nan, and that I'll only be able to teach the very basics. Lockpicking, I can also begin until a better teacher is found."

"That will do to go on with," Annabel said, very well pleased with herself. "Maybe we can smuggle in a lock picking teacher later on."

"If the teacher is any good, we won't have to," Isabella pointed out.

"If Melchior had thought to get a teacher in before now, we wouldn't have to do it ourselves. What an annoyance he is!"

"He seems to be winking at you, Nan."

"He's been doing that for the last five minutes whenever he thinks no one is looking," Annabel said crossly. "He's probably been up to something; he looks awfully smug."

"It didn't strike me as smug winking," Isabella said. "As such. However, I dare say you're right. That's right. Look down at your class schedule and ignore him completely."

Annabel did so, annoyed by the faint gleam of mockery she could see in Melchior's eyes. He had certainly been up to something, and whatever it was, it was obvious that it would annoy her as much as his walking them back to their room the other night had done.

"Oh, what a bore, Nan!" Isabella said, likewise studying her schedule. "We're stuck in Elegant Elementaries of Ensorcellment with Melchior while the class on Tea Crafting is going on. What a shame! It's the only class that doesn't have two sessions, and there are some really very useful people there."

"Do we need to know how to craft tea?"

"Well, properly speaking, no! If you employ the right kind of people, your tea will always be perfectly crafted for you; and for myself, I've already attended the class. However, I am *extremely* fond of tea, and I find the different scents soothing. It would have been a balm to my soul."

"Why do you need a balm for your soul?"

"Perhaps I should have said it's a balm for everyone else's soul," said Isabella, grinning. "It's the only class in which I happen to be entirely peaceful and disinclined to cause disruption. Although, if it comes to that, I should like to point out that I don't *set out* to cause disruption—it finds *me*."

"Maybe a bit of disruption will come and find you during Advanced Polite Conversation," Annabel said gloomily. She had already had as much Polite Conversation on the way to breakfast as she wanted for the day. "We can only hope!"

ADVANCED POLITE CONVERSATION DID NOT, AS ANNABEL HAD secretly hoped it would, provide her with any of the skills Isabella had mentioned when they first met. Instead, it seemed to consist of talking a great deal without saying anything much, which didn't interest her until she remembered that Isabella was also very good at saying quite a lot without giving away very much. When it occurred to her that the class could at least be useful, if not interesting, Annabel begrudgingly gave it her full attention, which pleased Miss Cornett very greatly. She didn't say so, but Annabel saw her eyes brighten, and a few of the girls who had been practising their own conversation skills *sotto voce* at the back of the class, began to pay more attention. Isabella didn't pay much attention, but she at least appeared to be doing so, despite the fact that she was busily doing something else below the desk. She knew how to comport herself when called upon to answer questions or give examples, too, Annabel noticed; though she also noticed that Miss Cornett didn't often call upon Isabella. Was that because she didn't expect Isabella to know the answers due to her two years' absence, or because she *did* expect it?

Annabel was still trying to decide that when the class ended. She would have stood up straight away, glad to be gone, but Isabella was still doing something with her hands beneath the desk, her back impossibly straight and her face impossibly innocent.

Annabel sat back again and hissed, "What are you doing?"

"Nothing. Nothing at all."

"You said that you're *always* up to—"

"Well, nothing anyone will be able to prove, anyway," Isabella corrected herself. "Nan, if I were to affix something to the outside of the classroom door—hypothetically, of course—do you think you could loiter for a moment or two to hide that fact?"

"Will I be hypothetically loitering, or do you want the real thing?"

Isabella made a tiny choke of laughter and stood up. "I leave that entirely up to your good judgement."

"All right," agreed Annabel, and followed her out. Miss Cornett was preparing for the next class, and they were the last two students to leave, so they wouldn't have to worry about anyone else coming out while they were busy. That was probably why Isabella had taken a little longer, if it came to that.

The hallway was busy outside, but Annabel wasn't called upon to do as much loitering as she expected; Isabella was swift and unnoticeable, her back to the door as she greeted one of the younger girls who was walking past. Annabel had barely closed the door when Isabella turned with a smile and said, "Off we go, Nan! Carriage on Horseback!"

In an undertone, Annabel protested, "I thought we weren't going to that!"

"Exactly so," agreed Isabella, drawing her away from the door and the swelling tide of other girls who seemed to be torn between following the future queen and getting to their own next lesson. "We're not going, so we'd best find somewhere useful to be instead."

"Does it *have* to be useful?" Annabel was aware that her voice sounded plaintive. "Can't it just be nice?"

"Of course! But think how pleasant it would be if it was both nice *and* useful."

"What is useful to us at the moment?"

"I suppose it depends on what we want to find out," Isabella said. "But I'm not really sure where we should start."

"That's all right," said Annabel. She had found that a bit of not-quite-aimless wandering produced good results. "We'll have a stroll, shall we? There are girls with free periods now, aren't there?"

"Other than us? Of course—the entire third year will have their first free period in order to collect all their furbishments for their next class. Hat making, I believe."

"They teach us how to *make hats* here?"

"Not us, you understand," said Isabella. "We're superior young ladies. Well, you are, and I already took the class when I was here before. No, no; we'll be learning things that the idle rich don't learn."

"Just not Carriage on Horseback," grinned Annabel.

"Exactly so. Nan, where *are* you taking us?"

"Don't know," said Annabel, tugging at Isabella's arm just enough to turn them both down a staircase that was narrow enough to be somewhere interesting and potentially disallowed. "I haven't been here before. This is a nice staircase, so I thought we'd go down here."

"Oh well, I suppose I've heard stupider reasons," allowed Isabella. "I think this is one of the older stairways. Not a servants' stairway, fortunately: I've nothing against the servants here, but if the security magic doesn't catch one on the servants' stairs, the servants give one away. Very bad, I think. If one can't trust the servants, who can one trust?"

"It's probably because you call them *the servants*," said Annabel. In her experience, people who referred to servants as *the servants* were drawing a very definite line between *us* and *them*.

"Oh, that's a good point," Isabella said thoughtfully. "I forgot that you'd been a ser—hmm, it's possibly a good idea to mind my tongue until we're somewhere we can't be overheard."

"Does Trenthams have trouble with people listening to other people's conversations?" Annabel asked, much astonished. She'd already been surprised about the lipreading.

"Trenthams is populated by the very rich, the very important, and the very clever," Isabella said. "Of course it has trouble with secrets being kept and conversations remaining private. The young ones might be wonderfully clever at learning to lip read and improving their skills, but the older ones are usually very good at using that to their own advantage."

"That's probably your fault," Annabel said. "You turned half the school into regular little spies and now everyone can have their own without any trouble."

"Supply and demand, Nan," said Isabella, opening a door on her side of the hallway and gazing into it without either embarrassment or reserve. "Supply and demand. And be that as it may, we should try to find ourselves a nice little place to sit out of sight for a little while. Especially if we're going to talk."

"Somewhere like this?" suggested Annabel. The door she had opened was a small, unassuming one in peeling yellow paint. A door, in fact, that looked as though it might open to a painting supply cupboard or a forgotten storage area. It opened to neither of those things; instead, it opened into a small library that was panelled half way to the ceiling in light wood with the occasional dark grain to it. The bookcases were made of the same wood, and here and there around the room were plump red chairs that had enough dust on them to make Annabel think that this library hadn't been much used lately.

She wandered into the room, looking around in interest. It wasn't large, but it had a lot of books—and some of them, she noticed, with kindling interest, were novels. She hadn't had the chance to read many novels over the last three years. There were too many fat, awful, mind-numbing books on statecraft, politics, and economics to read instead, and Annabel had felt her misfortune.

A few dust motes floated in the air on a beam of sunshine that came through the high window. That window looked out on the grounds outside, and it wasn't until Annabel saw a skirt rustle past, blocking the sunshine for a brief moment, that she realised they had gone lower in the school than she realised.

"Goodness!" said Isabella, following her in. "Fancy this being here! Evidently I've been away for far too long. Well, well, well! This will be quite useful, I think."

"And comfortable," Annabel said, plopping herself down on a sofa. "Oh, lovely!"

"Quite central, too," agreed Isabella. "We can make a quick dash to the classrooms if needed, we can stay quietly indoors in inclement weather, and if we *really* must, I daresay we could just get to the ground level from here."

"Not in a bustle, we couldn't," Annabel said frankly. "And I'd be lucky to squeeze out of *that* window even without one!"

"Nonsense!" said Isabella, and briskly began to strip off her overskirt.

"What are you doing?"

"What do you suppose? I'm going to see if I can get through comfortably. The room is only half as useful to us if we can't climb out the window. Look after my bustle, won't you?"

"I'm not trying that," Annabel warned her, but she got up from the sofa in spite of that, measuring the width and height of the window with a closer eye. It was possible—though not probable—that Annabel could get through there too, but she would very much prefer not to have to do so. The thought of getting stuck and having a grinning Melchior come to help her out wasn't one she could entertain without shuddering.

Isabella, a thin, wriggling length of white muslin, had already jumped herself up to the window by way of a sofa arm and was now halfway through, her palms resting against the grass outside and her legs kicking enthusiastically.

"I'm *definitely* not doing that," said Annabel as Isabella's red-stockinged legs gave one last kick and folded through the window.

There was a final flash of red and white before Isabella's bright face appeared at the window. "Easily done, Nan!" she said. "Oh, isn't this lucky! This little library is *beautifully* located—better than our suite, if it comes to that. My only astonishment is that no one else has claimed it. Shall we make it our headquarters?"

"Do we *need* a headquarters?" Annabel asked doubtfully.

"Certainly! Especially now that all the girls feel themselves free to call."

"I thought we had to see them!" protested Annabel. "Shouldn't we have refused to see them if the idea was to stop them coming to see us?"

"Certainly not," said Isabella decisively, and began to wriggle back through the window. "That leads to speculation and an air of injury. It's important to give the impression that you're available to see without wearing you out by actually *seeing* people all the time. How clever of you to find this place!"

"Is it all right for us to just take it over?"

Isabella dropped down onto the sofa and shut the window again securely. "Of course! We were here first, after all! We will need to make sure this room is safe to speak in before we become too dreadfully comfortable, however. Do you think Melchior would make us a security spell or two if you asked him?"

"Probably," said Annabel. It wasn't a thing he would ask too many questions about, either, since it would fit his ideas of safety and security very well. "I just won't mention what we're trying to secure. Oh! What about asking Raoul for another one?"

Isabella looked at her admiringly. "Goodness! I didn't think of that! Naturally, Melchior will exclude himself from any security spell he gives us, and we can plug that particular hole with a security spell from Raoul. There's no need to let Melchior get more comfortable than he has to be, after all. I applaud your reserve, Nan."

"You don't suppose someone—" Annabel stopped, frowning, and asked, "You don't suppose there's already something in our room? I was looking to see what might have been taken or disturbed, but I didn't think to check if anything else had been put *in*."

Isabella made a small sound of irritation. "How clumsy of me! I didn't think of that! Perhaps Melchior will check the suite for us. He was winking at you before—he probably wants you to meet him."

"Yes, that's what I thought," Annabel said. "It would serve him right if I didn't go, but if we need him, I suppose I might as well. Is he allowed in our suite?"

"Absolutely not," Isabella said promptly. "If we're caught, Melchior will be let go and we'll be severely punished. If it comes to that, a male in the suite would probably be enough for them to send me home. Do you know, Nan, I'm surprised someone hasn't tried to have me sent home that way already. I'm inclined to think the girls of Trenthams lack imagination."

Annabel grinned. "What, because they haven't put a man in your suite? Maybe they're too big to smuggle in as well."

"And that reminds me," Isabella said, her eyes widening. "There's a competition every year about who can smuggle in the largest thing to the school. It has to be smuggled right into the halls, not just the grounds, and there's no magic allowed. We'll have to think about that later, after we've nosed out what Melchior is up to."

"Nothing less than an elephant," Annabel said, with her best expressionless face. "Otherwise it's not worth the bother."

"Naturally," Isabella said. "Although, I suppose we could argue that we smuggled a teacher in, at a pinch. Melchior certainly came here because of you, so it's technically true."

"I wonder if Melchior can change into an elephant?" wondered Annabel, becoming side-tracked. "I'll have to ask him when I see him after class. Will you come?"

Isabella's grey eyes widened a little in surprise. "You want me to come along as well? I think it likely that Melchior would prefer to see you alone, Nan."

"Melchior won't mind if you're there, too," Annabel said in surprise. "We're room mates after all, and he was the one who arranged for us to go together."

"Ye-es," said Isabella slowly. "Be that as it may, Nan, I believe I'll stay in our suite tonight. I'd like to make absolutely sure nothing was taken the other night. Do bring Melchior back with you if you can manage not to get caught, however. I do think it would be just as well to check our suite as soon as possible."

"All right," agreed Annabel. "How long do we have before we have to go to Statecraft?"

"A good hour yet," Isabella said. "That's another reason why Carriage on Horseback is a good class to skip; it's far too long. Honestly, I don't know why they've put you in Statecraft, either; you're bound to have covered all that with Melchior anyway. I can't see there being any new information there for you."

"Are you in Statecraft too?"

"Naturally," said Isabella. "It wouldn't do for the teachers to think they have nothing to teach me. They get discouraged, poor things.

Besides, it's a good place to make connections; all the girls from important families are there. Some of them are even pleasant girls."

"How many of them did I meet on the first day?" Annabel asked gloomily, remembering the constant stream of visitors.

"All of them, of course," Isabella said. "They study Statecraft, Nan. One of the first lessons is the importance of making good connections. I suppose it's a mercy they put us in the advanced class, at least. A sop to both of us, I should think."

"Oh," said Annabel. "Now I'm hungry. Why did you have to mention sops?"

"That's another thing," said Isabella, with great seriousness. "We'll have to establish a Stash somewhere. Perhaps we can make a hollow behind some of the books."

"A *stash?*"

"Of food, naturally! It's no use smuggling in all the best chocolates and other goodies if the maids find them in our room and report us. Not to mention the distinct possibility that an intruder might decide to munch on them. I may not be able to prevent ruffians from breaking into our suite, Nan, but I absolutely refuse to feed them my favourite things as well."

"What if other girls find them in here? Won't they eat them?"

"Certainly not! A food stash is a clear indicator that the room is spoken for. They will politely leave."

Annabel, who had seen some of the younger girls freely pilfering what they liked best from the plates of their fellows, said doubtfully, "I suppose you know what you're talking about."

"Very rarely," Isabella assured her. "But at least I sound sure of myself, Nan! Never mind, if we're very clear on the fact that this room is taken, none of the girls should go so far as to wander in without permission—especially if they know it's been taken by seniors."

"How do we make that clear?"

"Ah," said Isabella, tying her bustle and then rotating it into its rightful position. "Well, if you'll be so kind as to help me back into my skirt, Nan, I'll initiate you in the art of bagsing a room!"

❧ 7 ❧

Annabel had not been to school for several years. When she had gone, that school was a small building with a single room where all the children were taught by one teacher. The sheer bustle and busyness of Trenthams, therefore, with its changing classes and seemingly random free periods, was an entirely new kind of experience. She sat quietly through a Statecraft class, where the teacher seemed afraid to call on her to answer questions and the other students looked covertly at her from behind books, and walked stiffly through the Deportment class, where the teacher pursed his lips and the other students became subtly relieved. Oh well, thought Annabel, watching Isabella float through the same figure eight she had just forced herself through; at least they knew they didn't have to worry about being bested by her in Deportment—not if she had to wear three books on her head, anyway.

Elementaries of Elegant Ensorcellment was even less palatable. The girls in this class paid far less attention to Annabel than those in her other classes, but since this was because they were all gazing wide-eyed at Melchior, Annabel didn't find it preferable. In fact, it left her feeling distinctly grumpy. It was some balm to her soul to see Isabella, after a brief, incredulous look around the room, sit forward with her chin propped on her palms and a gaze of almost disturbing soulfulness on her face. It must have made Melchior uneasy, because he flicked a look across the room at them more often as the lesson went on, and he seemed disinclined to turn his back on the class. That almost made Annabel grin. Instead, she sat forward like Isabella and added her soulful gaze to the other girl's. With any luck, it would make Melchior uncomfortable enough to pay back all the winking this morning.

Annabel was still grinning about that when she went to meet Melchior. Twilight was stealing over the halls and mingling with the soft hallway lighting by the time she got there, but she didn't mind Melchior having to wait a bit. Serve him right for winking at her so often. She would have knocked when she got to his door, but there were voices from the other end of the hallway, and she preferred not to be seen sneaking into a master's suite. She ducked hastily through the door with a small blue flip of skirts, and shut it behind her just as hastily. There were no startled exclamations or accusatory tones from behind the wood, and Annabel turned around in some relief to find that Melchior was watching her in amusement, one eyebrow up.

"What a pleasant surprise, Nan!" he said. "If you didn't want to be seen, perhaps a darker colour would be a better choice of gown."

"It's not a surprise at all," Annabel said. "You were winking at me so much that some of the girls thought there was something in your eye. Does Mr. Pennicott know how bad you are at intrigue?"

For the first time in several weeks, she heard Melchior's real laugh, sudden and wholly amused.

"Mr. Pennicott has never had any reason to be disappointed in my skills, thank you, Nan! If you had given any sign of acknowledgement, I might have winked a little less."

"You mean you kept going because I didn't react," Annabel said accusingly. "And to think that you told Peter he was infantile!"

"Must we talk about Peter?" asked Melchior. "It's such a nice night!"

Annabel made a face. "I suppose that means you aren't going to tell me if you found out anything at the stops we made along the way here."

"There's no need for me to tell you anything," Melchior said. "For the very simple reason that there's nothing much to tell that would interest you. It's much more useful to know what's going on in the school."

"Oh, is it."

Melchior, without acknowledging the potent sarcasm, asked, "Have any of the girls specifically approached you?"

"They've *all* approached me," Annabel said. She'd found it wearying at the time, and just as wearying to recount it. "I thought Mr. Pennicott was trying to be very careful about how much information got out."

"He was," Melchior said, a little grimly. "Things have changed slightly, however."

Annabel blinked. She had been sure that *something* had changed in the last few months, but Melchior had never said as much before. "What things?"

"Small things," said Melchior. "Nothing we can pin down; just rumours and phantoms and ideas."

"Yes, but *what* ideas and rumours?"

"Have any of the girls who approached you tried to offer you anything in return for certain favours?"

"Yes; Isabella," Annabel said bluntly. "But since you're the one who sent her, I really think you ought to have known that already."

Melchior grinned. "Oh yes, the Firebrand! She's one of a kind. Did you accept her offer?"

Annabel, resentfully, asked, "Did you only want to see me to get information from me?" She had been hoping, at the very least, for a sharing of information. Melchior had always been disinclined to share information with her, but although she had been prepared to put up with that when she was younger, so long as he didn't lie to her, Annabel was now not so willing.

Melchior's hazel eyes rested on her thoughtfully. "What else were you expecting?"

"You should at least share information if you want me to tell you anything!" Annabel protested. "There's no need to be keeping secrets from me; I'm not a child now, Melchior!"

"I see," said Melchior. He was smiling, but his eyes weren't amused. "That's what you meant. I'm very well aware that you are no longer a child, Nan. I believe I've mentioned it several times over the last few months."

"When?" demanded Annabel. "All I remember is you telling me over and over again that you're not a cat any more."

"Exactly," said Melchior. "I really couldn't have made myself much clearer, in fact."

Annabel gazed at him in despair. If there was one thing Peter and Melchior had in common, it was the way they had of dancing circles around her when it came to conversation and cleverness. She was quite well aware that she wasn't clever; that she had to sit, and think, and reason before she came to any sort of conclusion that Melchior or Peter would arrive at in seconds. If only they would say what they meant, instead of hinting and suggesting until it drove her mad!

"Do you know what I like so much about Isabella?" she asked. It had only just occurred to her; it should have occurred much sooner, but until a day or two ago, she hadn't been exactly sure that she *did* like Isabella. Even now she wasn't entirely sure.

Melchior, looking rather startled, said, "No, what?"

"She says exactly what she means," Annabel said crossly. "And she doesn't dance around things and then hint at clever meanings. If she's hiding something from you, she doesn't dangle it in your face."

"I resent the implication that I'm less trustworthy than the Firebrand," Melchior protested. He was still looking more than slightly startled. "She regularly flummoxes people by telling them the exact truth."

"Yes, but that only works with untrustworthy people," said Annabel. "People like you, actually. Melchior, they'll crown me in less than a year—that is if someone doesn't get to me first. If you can't trust me with information concerning my own safety, I don't know what you're expecting of me as queen!"

Exasperated, Melchior began, "As a queen—! When did I say I was expecting anything of you as a queen, Nan?"

"Yes, but I'm *going* to be the queen! So—"

"Then let us say I'm speaking to Nan. Just Nan, not Queen Annabel."

"Yes, but what's the use of speaking to *just Nan*? It's not *just Nan*

that the Old Parrasians are making a fuss about! And it's not *just Nan*
—Well, actually, yes, it is—it *is* just me that wants to know what you
found out about who attacked us. Queen me wants to know as well,
but just me wants to—" Annabel stopped, then complained, "I'm
getting a headache. Why can't we talk like normal people?"

"Exactly what I would like to know, Nan," said Melchior. "Are you
determined to know every fact of which I am master?"

"Yes! Well, at the very least I should know if they're just footpads,
or Old Parrasians, or—"

"Very well. None of the footpads admitted to any sort of political
bias, but we're certain they were hired, so that's no surprise."

"Yes, they said that when they tried to kidnap us."

"Then, Nan, on this point you know as much as I. I sent Raoul
back the way you both came; he visited each of the stops at which you
should have had a meal waiting, including the ones at which you did
have a meal. In each case, none of the hosts could remember someone
sending a message or coming in person to break the promise."

"Then how were the meals cancelled?"

"Raoul seems to think that someone interfered with the record
books at each inn."

"Why?"

"For the very simple reason, Nan, that at each stop where I had
booked a meal for you, the records book has either mysteriously
vanished, been dropped into a bucket of milk, or is missing a page. A
little too much to put down to coincidence, Raoul thought."

"I should think he would!" said Annabel. There was something else
that she wanted to ask—something important that had occurred to
her earlier after Melchior answered one of her questions. Now, if only
she could remember what it was!

"No one caught sight of so much as a face or the sound of a voice
in the commission of those accidents, either," said Melchior, before
she had a chance to do so. He added, "I trust, Nan—I really trust—
that you and the Firebrand won't spend the entirety of the lesson
tomorrow staring at me again! I thought that I was inured to the
open-mouthed wonder of the little girls in First Form, and I even
managed well with the saucy ones in Second and Third Forms, but I

really can't deal with the sort of unnerving stares the Fourth Form is capable of!"

"What have you been doing to make the Second and Third girls saucy?" Annabel demanded. "They're not saucy with the Deportment Master!"

"I like to think, Nan," said Melchior, "that despite all I may be lacking, I am at least better looking than the Deportment Master!"

"That's not much to boast about," said Annabel. She hadn't taken to the Deportment Master. He pursed his lips far too much for her taste, and when he looked at her he gave the distinct impression that he'd smelled something nasty. He gave the same look to Isabella, but at least he didn't purse his lips at her. Annabel had the feeling that while the Deportment Master disliked Isabella, he found her deportment at least to be irreproachable; Annabel, he evidently both disliked and found lacking.

"Be that as it may, I would appreciate it if you both turned your eyes elsewhere during the lesson," Melchior said firmly.

"All the other girls were staring at you," Annabel said. She felt particularly argumentative tonight. "Why shouldn't we?"

Melchior's eyes glinted. "Well, Nan, if you find me to be so irresistible that you can't take your eyes off me, who am I to object?"

Annabel gave a surprised giggle. "What rubbish! You know perfectly well we were only trying to put you off your lesson!"

"If, in fact," continued Melchior, without regarding this in the slightest, "the hardship caused by seeing me only once a day is too great—"

"It's twice, actually, and it's not a hardship—"

"—if the hardship is too great, my door is always open, and my chairs are always available."

"I have my own chairs," Annabel said. "Actually. Isabella picked them out, so they're *very* fashionable."

"Don't tell me the Firebrand has also smuggled in *chairs?*"

"I didn't ask her where they came from," said Annabel. "That's the sort of question better not asked when it comes to Belle. She'll tell me if she wants me to know. But if it comes to that, I'm pretty certain the chairs are different from the ones in the other girls' suites."

"Ah!" sighed Melchior, apparently at random. "I fancy it's not meant as an insult, after all!"

"What insult?"

"Never mind. I don't think I can bring myself to mention it. What I chiefly dislike about you, Nan, is your ability to drag me down to the level of a brangling child with you."

"If you're suggesting that I'm a brangling child—"

"Not a suggestion; an observation."

"Then I think you're being very rude."

"Oh, undoubtedly. Very well, Nan; if you didn't come here to seek information—"

"I did!" objected Annabel. "I just didn't come to give it!"

"If you didn't come here to seek information," continued Melchior firmly, "exactly why did you heed my signals?"

"To tell you to stop winking at me, first of all," Annabel said. "And we need you to check our suite, Melchior. Someone went through it on the first day, poking their nose into our things. We know they didn't take anything, but we want to be sure they didn't leave anything."

"I did that during lunch today," Melchior said. "I found a nice little piece of listening magic above your dressing table, and another over the Firebrand's table. I won't ask how you knew someone had been in your room since I'm quite sure that was the Firebrand, too, but—"

Offended, Annabel said, "*Actually*, I was able to discover that much for myself, thank you."

"Oh, well done, Nan!" said Melchior easily.

The praise might have been more welcome if it hadn't been for the carefully congratulatory manner of it. *Like a grown up talking to a baby*, thought Annabel, very much annoyed.

"There's no need to sound so surprised," she said. "You and Isabella aren't the only ones who can see things, after all."

"Of course not," Melchior said, even more affably. "Don't tell me: they pulled all your things out of your drawers?"

"They were," said Annabel icily, "*very* careful!"

"Of course!" Melchior said, more affably still. "I would never suggest otherwise!"

Annabel eyed him in dislike. "I think I preferred it when you were a cat."

"I believe I've already mentioned that I'm no longer a cat. You should remember that."

"Oh *should* I?" Annabel snapped, and went away to her suite again.

It wasn't until she was sitting at her dressing table later that night, that she remembered. She said in exasperation, "Oh *bother* the man!"

Isabella's grey eyes flicked up from her hat and met Annabel's eyes in the mirror, amused and understanding all at once. "What is it, Nan?"

"I was so annoyed and Melchior talked so much that I didn't get a chance to ask him what had changed! And I just *know* he did it on purpose!"

"Very likely," Isabella said. "What do you mean, *changed?*"

"That's the thing," Annabel complained. "I don't know exactly. Up until a few months ago, very few people knew about me. It was part of the conditions for my leaving Poly and Luck after two years and staying with Melchior for the year before I came to Trenthams."

"And up until a few months ago, nobody did know?"

"Not many did," Annabel said. "There might have been one or two who suspected, and there were a lot of people curious about me anyway, because of Melchior, and because I was staying with him. One or two definitely knew, but they were meant to know."

Isabella nodded. "The Head Guard, I suppose; my little Papa, of course; and possibly the minister for Economics, a few privy council memebers, and the State Secretary. Nobody would have told *him*, of course, but I'm certain he learns things via osmosis."

"Yes; I stayed with each of them for a month or so, getting to know them and learning certain things," Annabel agreed. "And I can understand people beginning to talk about *that*, too. But then, three months ago, I began to get invited to parties, and visited, and bothered until I didn't know what to do. And just now Melchior said that things *had changed a little*. I want to know what he meant by it."

"I see," Isabella said slowly. "Obviously, things have changed, and just as obviously, Melchior knows at least a little bit about it. Is that what he didn't tell you?"

"Yes," said Annabel, in annoyance. "I was so irritated that he wasn't telling me everything he learned about our attack that he talked right past it and I didn't get the chance to ask again. I didn't even *think* to ask again! Oh, it's annoying!"

"I shouldn't worry too much," Isabella said comfortingly. "Melchior is awfully hard to pin down to anything, and I think he knows you very well—though obviously not as well as he thinks he does! We'll plan an informational assault later; something that works with your strengths."

"I haven't got any strengths," said Annabel gloomily. "That's why Peter and Melchior could always talk rings around me."

"I don't know about that," said Isabella, "but I'm certain that if anyone can make Melchior give up information, it's you. We simply have to find the right way of doing it. I'll think something up, don't you worry!"

"It's all right for you to say *don't worry*," Annabel said, "but when you say *don't worry* it makes me think you're up to something, and that's worrying."

"I'm always up to something, Nan; it's best that you know that now."

"I already know it," said Annabel. "Why do you think I'm so worried!"

THERE WAS A WEIGHT ON THE SIDE OF ANNABEL'S BED WHEN SHE woke the next morning. From the direction of that weight, Isabella's voice said thoughtfully, "Do you suppose Melchior is here to chase the informational leak he was very carefully not talking about yesterday?"

Annabel groaned. "I haven't had breakfast yet, Belle! I haven't even gotten up!"

"It's good to discuss problems before breakfast," said Isabella. "It aids the digestion. You should really get up; elegant young ladies may sleep until noon, but Trenthams ladies aren't elegant young ladies until they graduate. Until then, we must force ourselves up at eight o'clock, eat breakfast at nine, and attend classes from ten o'clock."

"Informational leak," mumbled Annabel, gazing up at the ceiling with blurred eyes. She blinked a few times, yawned, and made herself sit up. "Do you mean, he thinks the source of the leak is here? At Trenthams?"

"Not as such," Isabella said. "I had an idea he might be chasing the effects of the leak."

"Now that more people seem to know about me, you mean? That's a good point. But what effects is he looking for, I wonder? Apart from threats and attacks, that is. We already knew about that, and if that's all it was, shouldn't he have made sure he was closer to me? Or put guards in here with us?"

"Yes, and that's what is so interesting," Isabella agreed, brushing her hair. "It makes me think, Nan, that there is a *lot* more we don't know."

"I already know there's a lot more we don't know," grumbled Annabel. "That's why I'm so annoyed with Melchior. All right, if the Royalists found out that I might be the queen heir, what would they do?"

Isabella tied off the end of her plait. "Celebrate, most likely."

"Yes, that's what I thought. Though some of them are a bit—actually, some of them are really scary. I got the impression that they'd prefer me to be living somewhere more...well, Royalist-friendly."

Isabella turned away from the mirror. "Really? Now that is interesting! I've obviously been out of the country for too long. We already know that the Old Parrasians are very annoyed by you, of course; it's very likely they were behind the footpads on the way here. Do you suppose they've sneaked someone into the school?"

"I think that's what Melchior thinks, anyway," Annabel said. It was a cooler morning despite the fact that it was well into summer, and she resented having to get up. Nevertheless, get up she did. Nowadays there were nearly as many things she had to do that she didn't want to do, as there had been when she was younger; she had simply gotten better at doing them anyway. "That's what Melchior was always best at—counter espionage. Do you know, when he first knew Poly he was in four different factions at once? The Royalists thought he was one of them—oh well, and I suppose he was, in a sense—undercover in the Wizard party, and the Wizards were convinced he was one of them but was spying out the Old Parrasians. Actually, he was in Black Velvet the whole time, but a member of each of the others, too."

"I suspected something of that," Isabella nodded. "And if it comes to that, I've always suspected that he had his own reasons for being in Black Velvet, too."

"He was looking for Poly," agreed Annabel. She had guessed quite some time ago that in the past, Melchior had been very fond of Poly. The thought had made a small, niggling annoyance in the back of her mind for the first year she spent with Poly and Luck, until it became obvious that whatever had been in the past, Poly was entirely wrapped up with Luck and Onepiece. More importantly, it was clear that while Melchior was still fond of Poly, he no longer had the kind of feelings that had caused him, several years earlier, to fling himself into magical scrapes of the worst kind in her aid. Melchior, in fact, had told her as much himself.

Isabella, entirely astonished, said blankly, "You *know* about that?"

"Mm," murmured Annabel, brushing her hair. "He told me a little while ago. He was supposed to rescue her instead of Luck, but Luck got in first. I'm pretty sure that's why he joined Black Velvet in the first place."

"Nan," Isabella said curiously, "What did you say when he told you that?"

Annabel thought about that for a few moments. "I think I told him I wasn't surprised. He's the only person I know who could be involved with four political groups who each think he's on their side while he's actually there to do what he wants to do. He's sneaky like that."

Isabella giggled. "Did you really tell him that?"

"Of course I did. Why wouldn't I?"

"No reason at all. I merely wished to corroborate. Did he say anything else about Poly?"

"Just that he wasn't in love with her any more," Annabel said. "But I already knew that, so I don't know why he told me."

"I imagine he had his reasons," Isabella said, her eyes dancing. She was amused at something, but Annabel was too sleepy to fathom it out. "Do let's get dressed and go to breakfast, Nan. I've a feeling today will be a lovely day!"

"What's so lovely about it?" Annabel asked gloomily. Isabella had already laid out a dress for her—or had the maids?—and she was torn between putting it on because it was easiest, or protesting on principle that she was capable of choosing her own dresses.

"Oh, I always enjoy a little Spectator Sport," said Isabella.

"Bother," she said, a little later, in the dining hall.

Annabel might not have taken notice of that small, thoughtful word if it hadn't been for the unexpected undercurrent of anger to Isabella's voice. She had heard a note of annoyance there, upon occasion, but never actual anger.

She looked up. "What's wrong?"

"The table," Isabella said, just a little grimly.

The table looked as it had looked since the start of the week; two chairs, two place settings, and a few sauces and seasonings. There *might* have been less of those today, but not noticeably; the only real difference Annabel could see was that the table linen was now a different colour.

"We shall not sit here today, Nan," said Isabella. "There has evidently been a Mistake Made. Let's sit over here instead."

"That table isn't any different," protested Annabel. "Except for two more seats. What's wrong with our old one?"

"Never you mind," Isabella said darkly. "It must be a mistake, just as I said."

Annabel allowed herself to be herded to another table, but they had only just shaken out their napkins when the Meal Matron appeared at their table.

"Let's have none of that, Miss," she said, possessing herself of Annabel's normal, pink napkin and replacing it with another blue one. She was looking at Annabel, but Annabel had the feeling she was talking to Isabella.

"Are you quite sure you haven't made a mistake?" There it was again, that slight undertone of anger to Isabella's usually light voice. "Blue napkins seem...unnecessary for Nan."

"I've nothing to say, blue or pink," said Matron sharply, "except that I've got my orders, and orders are that it's blue napkins for Miss Ammett."

"Why does it matter whether it's blue or pink?" demanded Annabel, hopelessly confused. "What does a blue napkin mean?"

"It means, Miss," said Matron—entirely, correctly polite and yet entirely, viciously satisfied— "that you're to be put on a reducing diet. And it's no good trying to change your seats again, either, because all the dining staff know about it, now."

"A *reducing* diet?" said Annabel blankly; but Matron had already gone.

"The absolute *cheek* of it!" said Isabella, in amazement. "Who decided this, I should like to know! At any rate, we shan't submit!"

"Oh, we might as well," said Annabel wearily. "It's no use making a fuss about it. It was probably Melchior, if it comes to that; they wouldn't do it without his permission, anyway."

"I wouldn't have thought so poorly of him! Well! There is certainly more than one way to tie one's boot-laces, after all! We shall see!"

Breakfast with blue table linen, Annabel soon discovered, was a vastly different thing to breakfast with pink table linen. Instead of the vast food trollies that trundled deliciously scented trays to the other tables, there was a single, small trolley that carried one full meal and a much smaller one. That full meal was put in front of Isabella, and the smell of it crept over Annabel's much sparser plate of breakfast to jolt her stomach into regretful growling.

Feeling just a little bit raw and annoyed, Annabel asked Isabella, "Do the other girls know what the blue napkins are for?"

"I shouldn't think so," Isabella said, in a lowered voice. "It's one of the things they don't tell us—you either notice or you don't. And the ones who do know are more likely to feel sorry for you than to rejoice at your expense. Or to tell anyone else who can then rejoice at your expense, if it comes to that. Oh, good! Look, there's one of the Awesome Aunts! Let's bother her!"

Gazing down at the single piece of dry toast and the cup of water in lieu of tea—did they suppose she was desperate enough to load tea with sugar if given the opportunity?—Annabel was annoyed into following the suggestion.

It was the Yellow Aunt who was threading her way through the tables, apparently trying to look in any direction but theirs. Today she was in different clothes, but the cameo and main accent was still yellow. She always wore yellow accents, Annabel had discovered; just as the Lavender Aunt always wore lavender accents. Eyeing that yellow ensemble in dislike, Annabel waited until the Yellow Aunt was in closer proximity before she said in a carrying voice, "Good morning, ma'am! Could we speak with you?"

"Oh!" said the Awesome Aunt, forced to look at them. "Well really, my lady, it's quite a busy morning, and—"

"We won't take much of your valuable time," said Isabella, with smiling steel. "Really we won't. Miss Ammett simply wants to know why it is that she's been put on starvation rations."

"Really, Miss Farrah! Starvation rations indeed! You must learn to moderate your language!"

"I don't care what you call it," Annabel said, too annoyed to be less direct. "I just want to know why I've been given it."

The Awesome Aunt cleared her throat delicately. "I understand that there was a directive from your guardian," she said. "I'm afraid there's really nothing we can do, my lady."

She sailed away again while Annabel and Isabella were still looking at each other in differing degrees of surprise and annoyance. Annabel, despite what she had said, hadn't really thought the command came from Melchior. It was evident that Isabella was just as surprised.

"This is another odd thing," Isabella said. "I should ask Melchior about this if I were you, Nan."

"I don't see that it'll do any good," Annabel said, and went back to her dry toast and water.

She said the same thing again at lunch, where the only solace allowed her was an extra half-piece of fruit with her small salad. At the evening meal, Isabella didn't make the suggestion again, but Annabel saw the annoyed pinch to her lips when she put another something on the dining room door.

"What are we putting on the doors?" she asked. Isabella had been discreetly leaving small, metallic pins in each of the doors they passed through that day; always just too deft to be caught, done behind cover of Annabel. "Is it a joke like the smuggling competition?"

"Good heavens, no!" said Isabella. "This is much more important. You said you wanted to begin classes, didn't you?"

"We have begu—oh. Those classes. Yes."

"We've got a place to have them, and I'm certain we've got the interest. I've been leaving invitations all around the school. It's only fair that everyone gets a chance to come if they want to come."

Annabel, who didn't see how a drawing pin could be construed as an invitation of any kind, looked dubiously at it and found herself dragged away by the other girl.

"Don't *stare* at it, Nan!" hissed Isabella. "You'll give it away to the teachers! It's no good as a secret invitation if the teachers find it! We'll have trouble enough with whistleblowers as it is!"

"You mean some of the girls really will tell the teachers?"

"More than likely at least five. The last year I attended Trenthams we had to weed out eleven in the first class and a few sneakier ones after that."

Annabel forgot about her lean breakfast for a brief moment. "If there were still some of them in the second class, how did you avoid being caught by the teachers?"

"That was a somewhat hair-raising year," admitted Isabella. "It was the year that made me realise I would have to be rather more careful in my vetting process. It should be *much* more streamlined now, Nan; never you fear!"

"I understand the first class," Annabel said. "That's easy. You just tell each group of girls that the meeting place is in a different spot, and then have people you actually trust tell you where the teachers show up. But how did you manage not to be caught for the second lesson if there were still some girls there who told the teachers?"

"Honestly," Isabella said confidentially, "that day we all did rather a lot of running and someone did a very good bit of spellcasting that made us all look like the girl who had brought the teachers down on us."

"A very good bit of spellcasting?"

"Certainly," said Isabella. "Don't forget, Nan; I have very little magic of my own."

"Yes," Annabel said suspiciously. "I know. Where did you get the spell?"

Isabella grinned. "That would hurt my feelings if it wasn't so complimentary," she said. "We'd best duck down this hall, Nan; we're going to be late for Deportment if we don't take a short cut. In all truth, it wasn't me. It was Delysia. I was very grateful to her, because if it hadn't been for that, there would have been a lot more trouble about it than there was. I don't like people to know that I'm fallible, but if it comes right down to it, there's always a chance my schemes won't work. It's good for you to know that if we're going to be working together closely."

"That's all right," Annabel said. "If it comes to that, I'm not really very good at planning, but I seem to do all right when things go wrong, so maybe that will work out for the best."

"We'll have to be more careful this year," Isabella said soberly. "If you're joining us, I mean. It won't be merely a matter of the teachers not finding out—it will be a matter of which girls may or may not be reporting back to someone else, and what they'll do if they know we're somewhere the teachers don't know about. It might be as well to make very good use of our library, after all."

"What will happen when the girls see the invitations?"

"The ones who already know what it means will give me notice that they're interested," Isabella said, in a lower voice, as the Deportment Master's head poked out into the hallway, his mouth pursed. "And the others will ask the ones who know. After that, anyone interested will approach me. After that...well, won't it be interesting to see how things fall out, Nan?"

"All right," Annabel said beneath her breath, as they passed the purse-lipped Deportment Master on their way into the room, "but if we get caught, I'm going to tell them that I was led astray by bad company."

✵ 8 ✵

nnabel had not enjoyed her first Deportment Lesson. It was
less enjoyable, she soon discovered, attending a Deportment
Lesson on an almost empty stomach, where the primary
subject matter was Correct Corsetry. The Deportment Master
scowled if her stomach growled, pursed his lips if she wobbled out of
line by the smallest degree, and pursed them still tighter if she swayed
due to a combination of too-tight corsetry and hunger induced giddi-
ness. It wouldn't have been so bad, Annabel thought, if the Deportment Master were not in charge of the lacing of their corsets. He
wasn't *directly* in charge of it—Trenthams was far too careful of its
students to allow any such thing—but his shrieks of *"Tighter!"* and
"Again!" could be heard not only from the imperfect protection of the
changing screens, but probably out into the hall and other classrooms.
Any other girls who were unfortunate enough to be bigger than the
Deportment Master considered ladylike, were watched just as carefully in the changing screens as Annabel herself was. Annabel, being
squeezed tighter and tighter in her corsets by one young girl who was
nearly as red faced as Annabel herself, came to the conclusion that he
must have a gradient for matching the colour of his students' faces
with an appropriate tightness of corsets.

When Annabel at last escaped the classroom, far too hot and

more than a little dizzy, she had to take a moment in the hall to catch her breath.

"Nan?" Isabella's hand was on her arm, but Annabel couldn't quite feel it. "Shall we go to our suite? I think it's about time you were unlaced. Next time, try to be a little closer to me when the Master calls for partners, won't you? I'm really very good at pretending to tighten corsets."

"Don't tell me," said Annabel, unsure whether she was laughing or whimpering, "you did a class on that, too!"

"If a girl is incapable of pretending to tighten her corsets, there's no hope for her in today's society," Isabella said. "Aren't you glad we're going to change the fashions? If all else fails, Nan, you'll be the queen who was known for freeing New Civet's women from the restrictions of corsetry and bringing about a new era of fashion."

"It'll have to be your legacy," groaned Annabel. "Because I'll already be dead by then."

"A few more hallways, Nan; a *very* few more. And perhaps we could bestir ourselves just a little bit more. It wouldn't do to be late to State-craft, after all."

"If I'm dead, I can't go to Statecraft anyway," Annabel said. At this point, she wasn't sure if it was something she actively wanted to prevent.

"Nonsense," said Isabella; "They'd simply drag your non-resisting corpse to the classroom and prop it up nicely."

Still, Annabel was feeling a little less corpse-like by the time she got to Statecraft. Some of that relief was due to Isabella's quick job at relacing her corset; the rest of it was no doubt due to the small cake the other girl gave Annabel to eat while she was doing so. It didn't quite do away with the lightheaded feeling, but it did take away the breathlessness and the sharp pains around Annabel's ribs. Statecraft, on the other hand, produced a sharp pain in the temple that didn't seem likely to be alleviated by anything other than the end of the class. Since there wasn't, thought Annabel gloomily, at least a decent meal to look forward to at the conclusion of the class, there wasn't any other point to the end of the class than the relieving of that headache.

Lunch was the depressing affair Annabel had expected of it; she was given a grapefruit, a cup of water, and a few slivers of the same ham that the other girls were eating heartily. Isabella slipped a few of her own slices of ham over to Annabel's plate when it seemed expedient, but since the Meal Matron was watching them closely, her eyes dark and suspicious, those moments didn't occur as often as either of them would have liked.

"All right, then," said Annabel wearily. "If I can't eat, at least we can plan."

"Very good," Isabella said, and swept a few slices of ham neatly into her napkin as one of the Awesome Aunts sailed between them and the Meal Matron. "We've been rather reactive until now. I don't like being reactive. I like making other people reactive."

That brought a reluctant tilt of amusement to Annabel's lips. She had already discovered that much about Isabella. "I think we should concentrate on finding the spies in the school," she said. "We're already pretty certain they're here, so how do we find them out? I don't mind them being here if we know who they are."

"Very politic," agreed Isabella. "Friends being the Cuffs and Enemies the Collar, as they say. Where would you like to start? It would have to be someone with the ability to get reasonably close to you, don't you think?"

"Yes, that's what I thought. You don't happen to be an Old Parrasian spy, do you?"

Isabella giggled.

"Oh well," Annabel said. "I thought it was worth asking. You'd probably tell me if you were."

"Oh, certainly! There should be no secrets between friends, after all!"

"It doesn't have to be someone too close; I think they'd be satisfied to see me every day. So it needn't be any of the girls who were trying to make friends."

"I agree," said Isabella. "It could even be one of the teachers, at a pinch."

Annabel said rather hopefully, "Is it the Meal Matron, do you think?"

"Oh no!" Isabella said airily. "She merely detests me. There's nothing suspicious in that; just inconvenient."

"I suppose she's a bit too open about it," reluctantly agreed Annabel, poking at her grapefruit half with one disconsolate finger. "What a shame! It would have been nice to throw her in prison. Why does she hate you, by the way?"

"There are some people, Nan," said Isabella solemnly, "who simply take an immediate, instinctive dislike to me. In general, I can point out the ones likely to do so; they share a similar disposition and personality. Odd, I know; but there's no accounting for tastes, after all!"

"I can understand people taking a dislike to you," said Annabel, brutally honest. That brought a distinct sparkle of amusement to Isabella's grey eyes. "But why does she dislike *me* so much? What did I ever do to her?"

"That's instinctive, too, I shouldn't wonder," Isabella said. "You're the queen—well, the queen heir, at any rate. Matron's personality being what it is, I believe she detests you because everyone else is kowtowing to you, and she likes to fancy herself above that sort of thing. What a fortunate thing for her daughter that she considers Trenthams to be all pettifogging and pretension. The poor girl might otherwise have been sent here."

Annabel, whose small village school had been presided over by a teacher who was the mother of one of the children, heartily agreed. "She would have had a worse time than anyone else here."

"Exactly so. Now, if this leak is of any great proportions, I think we can count on more than one spy, don't you think?"

"They've probably all got someone here," Annabel said gloomily. "Melchior for Black Velvet, and one each for the Old Parrasians and the Royalists."

"And then we have to consider that they'll need to get information out of the school grounds," added Isabella. "Which means there's at least two for each party. Melchior has Raoul to do his running around outside the school, and unless the others are much better at magic than I think they are, they'll need someone to run messages out, too.

We'll have to look at all the maids and gardeners' boys; see who is willing to bend the rules and take out messages."

"I'll talk to the maids," Annabel said. "If you're flirting with the gardeners' boys you won't have time to get to them."

"Nan!" said Isabella. One hand was pressed against her chest in a shocked sort of fashion; the other, Annabel was fairly certain, was sneaking that meat-laden napkin into one of her pockets. "I'll have you know that I'm perfectly capable of flirting with the gardeners' boys *and* questioning the maids. It's a matter of timing and prioritisation—the very things, in fact, for which Trenthams best equips a young lady."

"I'll still talk to the maids," said Annabel, grinning. "I'm not very good at flirting, actually. I'd rather you look after that bit."

Isabella sipped her tea. "It needn't be flirting, you know. I simply skew toward that because it seems to work so well. Fancy, Nan! I'm not at all attractive—it constantly surprises me that flirting works for me. And it's so convenient! All it costs is a smile or two, and it's enjoyable for me, too."

Annabel would have asked, in outright astonishment, who had told Isabella that she wasn't attractive, but it seemed to her that Isabella was already dangerous enough. It didn't bear thinking about what she could accomplish if she was equipped with the knowledge that she was attractive, too. Besides, Annabel was hungry, and she was beginning to feel gloomy again.

She was still feeling in equal parts hungry and gloomy when she went in search of a convenient maid or two to talk to during her free period. Annabel was well aware, from bitter experience, that her hunger pains didn't usually fade into gnawing emptiness until the second day; it was likely that she would have trouble sleeping tonight. And if Isabella didn't manage to sneak more into her napkins than she had hitherto managed, by the third day it was likely that Annabel would faint—especially if the Deportment Master had anything to say about her corsets again. Still, Isabella was already out flirting with footmen or gardener's boys, and Annabel didn't like to think about going back to their suite without having something to match what Isabella would no doubt come up with. She wandered casually through

Trenthams, mindful of Isabella's tenet that an unhurried, unworried student was less visible than a secretive one, until she found the back staircases; there, she reasoned, it should be easy enough to encounter a stray maid or two.

In fact, she encountered one before she reached the back staircases; a small girl who was apparently walking the halls for no other reason than to activate a small spell in the glass of each window that faced the pending onslaught of the afternoon sun.

Annabel, who was curious about everyday magic as a result of her complete lack of inherent magic, stopped to watch her and asked, "What's that?"

The maid jumped and gasped, "Miss! Don't *do* that to me!"

"Oh, sorry," said Annabel, very much amused.

"Bother!" the maid said. "Now I've been rude. I remembered to call you miss, though, didn't I?"

Annabel successfully smothered her grin. "That bit was pretty clear. Why? Are you anti-classist?"

The maid looked very shocked. "Goodness, no! It would be pretty hypocritical of me to be anti-classist."

"Would it? Why?" asked Annabel, forgetting both her original mission and original question in her curiosity.

"Well, I'm only a maid because my father lost all his money," the maid said, matter-of-factly. "I wasn't anti-classist when I was rich, so I shouldn't try starting now that I'm poor. It would look a bit too much like trying to light the candle at both ends."

"I suppose so," Annabel said. She thought about it for a moment and added, "Then if I started out poor and got rich, I shouldn't be anti-classist just because I'm rich now?"

"Were you poor, then?" The maid's eyes grew very round. "Goodness, it doesn't show! You've got the chin-tilt just right!"

"I've been practising," said Annabel, very much pleased. "Belle has been working on it with me so the Deportment Master stops glaring at me."

"That won't stop him," the maid said. "Not if you're friends with Miss Farrah. If you're rich now, you should know how to choose your friends."

"I do," Annabel said, in a less friendly voice.

The maid, young as she was, looked up at her with a sharper, more understanding look. "I can see that," she said. "You should call for me if you need anything, Miss. I'm Jess. I know how to keep my mouth closed, too, if that's what you need."

"Actually," said Annabel, "I need someone to be a bit chattery right now."

"You want something to get around?"

"Nothing nasty," Annabel assured her. "I just want the maids to know that I'm looking for someone to run messages quietly."

"Goodness, at your age!" said Jess, showing her a shocked face. "You shouldn't be sending messages to boys, Miss! That's the sort of thing that gets you into trouble around here!"

Annabel giggled. "It's not that. I just want to know which maids are willing to send messages."

"All right," said Jess. "Just make sure you don't ask the little sour-faced thing who looks after the brasses downstairs. She only started a few days before term, but she won't do anything beyond what she's engaged for by the Aunts; won't even look at you when she's out in the village. She's the sort who informs on you to the Head Maid."

"I'll remember that," Annabel said, visited by another, more interesting thought. "Thank you."

"I'll put out the word," said Jess. She curtseyed. "I'll be on my way before the Head Maid wants to know why the second floor windows are all letting in the sunlight to fade the carpets. Good day, miss!"

It was likely, thought Annabel, gravitating more by accident than design toward the library she and Isabella had claimed earlier that week, that the message would get around to the other maids. It would be interesting to see which maids conveniently put themselves in her way over the next few days, hoping for a commission.

She found herself outside the library a moment later and blinked at the bright, peeling door in slight surprise. She hadn't realised she was so close. She gazed at the door for a brief moment longer, considering her options, and entered the library. She had all the information that she could get at the moment, after all; and she was curious to know, now that she could find out without anyone witnessing her potential failure, if she could fit through the library window too.

She had just found a secure footing on the sofa back, her arms comfortably propped up on the window-ledge, when a familiar figure walked past the opening, mere feet away.

Dannick. What was Dannick doing here?

"Oh good!" Annabel said joyfully, startling the Guard considerably. He looked around cautiously, caught sight of the flash of colour low in the wall that was Annabel, and started toward her. Annabel said, "Just the person I wanted!"

Dannick went profoundly red, and bowed at her head and shoulders. "Your Highness. How can I be of assistance?"

"You might not be able to be of assistance at all," said Annabel. "But I thought it couldn't hurt to ask. Have you been at the school all this time, or have you been with Raoul in the village?"

"I've been at the school," Dannick said. "I would have liked to be with the First Guard, but he wanted me here. I've been keeping an eye on the perimeter from the inside; nobody saw me arrive with the carriage, so the First Guard said it would be safest for me to pretend to be a footman."

Annabel, thoughtfully, said, "I suppose you're technically Belle's job, but I don't think she'll mind."

"Job, your highness?" Dannick looked distinctly worried.

"Yes; she's meant to flirt with all the gardener's boys and footmen. I'm supposed to be questioning maids; but I don't think she'll mind if I take you instead."

If Dannick had looked worried before, he now seemed stunned. He asked faintly, "Are you going to flirt with me?"

"Good grief, no!" said Annabel. "Belle hasn't taught me how to flirt yet; she does that part. I'll just ask you questions, that's all."

"Oh," said Dannick. "Oh. Well, I suppose that's all right. What did you want to know, your highness?"

"You're around the other footmen all the time," Annabel began, wedging her elbows into the edges of the window frame and leaning comfortably forward. "Do any of them go to the village oftener than the others? Or just go in and out a lot? And are there any of them that seem a bit too friendly with either the teachers or the students?"

"There's more than a few of 'em that are too friendly with the students," Dannick said forthrightly. "If you'll excuse me saying so, your highness."

"Really? Good grief. This school really is a hotbed of scandal and trouble waiting to happen." Annabel pondered that, and added, "That's what Belle says."

"Miss Farrah is right. But if it comes to that, there are always a few of them hoping for commissions—is that the sort of thing you meant?"

"Perhaps," Annabel conceded. "But what about the ones who don't really mix with the students or the other footmen, but spend a lot of time by themselves or in the village? Are there any of those?"

"One or two," said Dannick. He crouched by the window and asked diffidently, "Is there anything in particular you're looking for, your highness? More than ideas, I mean? Something you want me to keep an eye out for and report to you if I see it?"

"That depends," Annabel said, deciding to be as absolutely, blindingly honest as Isabella. "I mean, I do; but I don't know if I can trust you not to tell Melchior or Raoul."

Dannick spent some time digesting this, and Annabel wondered for a few moments if she had made a mistake. Then he said seriously, "My loyalty is to the First Guard, and he's said to obey Melchior as if it was him, but when we were in school they taught us that our first loyalty was directly to the crown. So if you were tell me what you wanted me to watch out for, and order me to keep it secret from everyone else, I would be bound not to tell anyone else, even Melchior or the First Guard himself."

"Lovely!" said Annabel happily. "Melchior never says things like that. He's too busy being sneaky."

"Is there—is there a particular reason why I shouldn't tell Melchior?"

"There are two particular reasons," Annabel said darkly. "The first one is that Melchior never tells me anything, so I don't see why he should know everything I'm up to. The second one is that if he knows, he'll probably make it hard to do what I've got to do."

"Is it dangerous?"

"Not at all," Annabel assured him. "And even if it is; well, there are things that will be dangerous when I'm queen, too. I should still be able to make the decision to do them without Melchior interfering."

Dannick gave some thought to that as well. At last, he said, "I can't disagree with that, your highness. Only, if you'll allow me to be so bold, I think you shouldn't expect to make decisions without other people being able to tell you they're bad decisions. You don't have to agree with them, but it doesn't hurt to listen."

"You're a lovely, sensible sort of person," Annabel told him, very much pleased. "Are you very fond of being a medical officer in the Guard? With all the moving around, I mean?"

"I like my company," said Dannick cautiously. "But I'm more of a settled person, your highness. And my mother is by herself in the Capital, so—"

Annabel nodded decisively. "I'll remember that. All right, then, do you think you can get some information for me?"

Dannick bowed. "It would be my pleasure, your highness. And of course, you'll be careful to order me to secrecy so that I can't possibly share anything with anyone?"

"Very careful!" Annabel said, laughing. "It's like I said before: I'd like you to look around the footmen and see if there are any of them who are particularly careful not to take commissions from any of the girls—or maybe just take commissions for *one* girl—but who still go to the village quite often. I expect they'd keep themselves away from the rest of the footmen a bit; they might think the footmen childish or frivolous, that sort of thing."

"You're looking for a messenger?"

Annabel nodded. "We're sure there's at least one or two in the school, and I might know of one in the maids."

"Melchior and Raoul are looking as well," Dannick said. "And I wouldn't mention it but for the fact that—"

"Melchior has ordered you to look for the same thing?"

Dannick nodded.

"There's no need to worry about it," Annabel said. "If you find out something, report it to Raoul as well, just as he ordered you. I just don't want them knowing what I'm doing at the moment. Oh, yes; the royal command is that you're not to reveal my orders to anyone, regardless of who they are. Is that clear enough?"

"Very clear," said Dannick. He was grinning, and only faintly red now.

That was an improvement, Annabel thought. She grinned back at him and said, "I'm sorry if I've stopped you from your business by calling you over."

"It's my pleasure, your highness. Besides, the duties of the footmen here always come second to the orders of the young Trenthams' ladies. Actually, it's part of our duties to make sure they know how to properly order a footman. Even if the orders take a long time to give, or perform, a Trenthams footman is always alert, always at the service of his young ladies. Or his queen, if it comes to that."

Annabel laughed. "Is that why the footmen here always look so alert? Still, it's past lunch time; you must be hungry. If I'd been Isabella, I would have flirted with you, taken my information and been merrily on my way. Instead, I've had a very sensible lesson in statecraft that I probably won't forget and made you wait for your lunch. What a shame I didn't put more effort into learning how to flirt!"

"On the contrary, Nan," said a familiar voice. A pair of shiny black shoes appeared in the square of space beside Dannick. "I think you're doing remarkably well. Dannick, isn't there somewhere you ought to be—or at least something you ought to be doing?"

Dannick seemed to struggle with himself for a few moments before he rose, bowed once more to Annabel's torso, once to Melchior, and turned back to the path he had been treading before Annabel hailed him.

"Isn't he nice?" Annabel said, quite pleased with herself. "He notices things *and* he shares them."

"That, I suppose, is a dig at me," remarked Melchior, dropping to his haunches. "A man's amiability is not to be measured by his willingness to answer all your questions, Nan."

"From where I'm standing—"

"Are you standing? I had the impression you were wedged. Are you quite comfortable?"

"Very," Annabel assured him. "Isabella is right; if you take off your bustle, it's really quite easy to get through."

Melchior closed his eyes for a pained moment. "Have you been removing your bustle, Nan?"

"No, I wanted to see if the rest of me could fit through first. Anyway, Isabella says we're going to change the fashion to get rid of bustles, so I only have to wait a bit longer before I don't have to worry about that. What are you doing, anyway? Don't you have a class?"

"If it comes to that, I'm quite certain you're meant to be in class." Melchior's thin lips were particularly sarcastic.

"There's nothing on my schedule right now," Annabel said, perfectly truthfully. Isabella had taken Elegant Carriage on Horseback off the schedule completely. "And you've skidded under the question. What are you doing?"

Melchior sighed, and threw a look around. "Perhaps you should invite me in," he suggested, leaning closer. "For some reason, Nan— for *some* reason—I seem to have the greatest difficulty in either hearing sounds from or getting into a room for which I provided the security spell."

"Are you really?" Annabel asked, pleased with her simulation of surprise. "Isn't that funny? Why do you think that is?"

"I can't imagine. Perhaps a second security spell was added by mistake; such an odd thing to happen, Nan."

"That would be an odd thing," agreed Annabel, wriggling back carefully through the window. "Oh, all right! I invite you in—just this once. No trying to sneak in later. And if you don't answer my questions I'll just kick you out again."

"Will you?" Melchior sounded very affable, but when he slithered elegantly through the window and into the library, his face wasn't particularly affable. It was smiling, however, so Annabel wasn't afraid that he was trying to cause another quarrel. "And how exactly would you propose to do that, Nan?"

"I'd probably use the staff," she said. "Maybe I'd erase a bit of shine off your shoes, too. Why aren't you at your first class, Melchior?"

"The staff is very useful," agreed Melchior, the amusement in his eyes growing. "However, it does presuppose your ability to use it. If you can't move your arms, how do you suppose you'll go about using it?"

Annabel scoffed. "Why wouldn't I be able to use my arms?"

"Any number of reasons," said Melchior, sauntering closer. "But the one that immediately springs to mind, Nan, is this one."

"Hey!" said Annabel in surprise. One swift step forward and a sudden dart from Melchior, and her arms were pinned to her sides, her chin resting roughly where it could touch the top button of Melchior's black, silver-traced vest. "That's not fair! I wasn't expecting a sneak attack!"

"Men don't typically give much warning when they're going to kiss someone."

"Yes, but I'd be on my guard with anyone else," protested Annabel. "And you're not going to kiss me, so why would I be on my guard?"

Very thoughtfully, Melchior said, "I don't know. Perhaps I shall kiss you."

Annabel, remembering the reproofs she had suffered from Melchior over the last few months due to her habit of patting him on the head or sitting too close to him, laughed out loud. "You wouldn't!" she said, still laughing. "I know that!"

Melchior looked both startled and faintly annoyed. "I fail to see why you should know that so well, Nan!"

"Well, it would be like expecting Dannick to want to kiss me!" protested Annabel. She thought about that and said, "Actually, he does go very red when I talk to him, so maybe—"

"I trust, Nan," said Melchior, in a dangerously calm voice, "that you are not planning on asking Dannick if he would like to kiss you?"

"At least he'd tell me he wanted to kiss me if I asked him!" instantly said Annabel. "*He* answers questions. *He* doesn't—"

"Ask me, Nan," Melchior said. His arms loosened a little and slid further down, at the same time freeing Annabel's arms and curving around her waist. There was that smile again, the one that wasn't quite the exasperation of Melchior or the fondness of Blackfoot. "I'll answer you truthfully, I promise. Ask me if I want to kiss you."

Annabel spluttered a small, surprised cough into his top button. "You taught me not to ask questions when I already know the answer!" she said. "You won't even let me pat you on the head! Why would you kiss me?"

To her surprise, that made Melchior drop his arms completely and take a step back. His lips were particularly thin and sarcastic as he said, "I see that I'll be some time yet in reminding you that I'm no longer a cat, Nan."

Annabel was conscious of a desire for Isabella's presence, if only to speculate on Melchior's possible meaning. She pulled in a silent sigh and smothered it before it could become an exasperated one. "But what does that have to do with kissing me?"

Melchior didn't answer at once, and it occurred to Annabel that she recognised the expression on his face. This was Melchior in the lightening quick moment before he made a decision, all the possibilities and outcomes flowing through his mind.

"Don't try to map out the best way to answer," she said. "Just *explain*."

"I could explain," Melchior said, and stepped forward again. "But I'm credibly informed by the Awesome Aunts that Trenthams favours the approach of Demonstration over that of Explanation."

"What demonstration?" asked Annabel, fighting the urge to cough again. Was there something stuck in her throat, or was the library simply dusty?

"A demonstration usually works best when a thing is demonstrated, I find," said Melchior, his hazel eyes bright and narrow. His smile made Annabel's fingers close involuntarily around the pencil staff they had only loosely been clasping, but she didn't try to raise the staff, even when Melchior's long fingers closed over her own and pulled her gently toward himself again.

"Hullo!" said a voice at the door.

Through the freestanding bookcase shelves Annabel could see the blue smock of a junior Trenthams Miss. She turned her startled eyes from the doorway and up at Melchior again, but to her surprise, he didn't let her go. Instead, he gave one more, gentle tug that pulled Annabel right back into his arms, still smiling down at her.

"Oh, hullo," said that voice again. The smock stayed, politely, exactly where it was; trying neither to crane or bend to catch a better look at them. "Sorry to butt in and all that, but is this where the invitation wanted us to go? Only there'll be a few other girls coming soon and unless you want the Awesome Aunts to know that there are people cuddling in the library, you'd probably better tell your beau to sneak out the window."

✺ 9 ✺

Melchior seemed to sigh. That was curious, thought Annabel, because he didn't make a sound. It took her just a little bit too long to realise she had felt the sigh rather than heard it, and that this singular circumstance was because she was still pressed against his chest. She hastily pulled herself away and pointed at the open window. Melchior only looked at her in silence, and for a moment Annabel thought he really would kiss her. Then he brushed past her, as swift as he was silent, and vanished through the window in one liquid movement. Even Melchior as Blackfoot couldn't have done it more elegantly.

Annabel resisted the urge to clear her throat and went to see who was at the door. When she passed around the edge of the bookcase she could see that it was a junior, as she had thought; a young girl with a plain, unremarkable face and a well-kept but unremarkable blue smock. All the junior girls wore them, but they usually tried to give them some distinction—a white lace collar here, a brooch there, or a seam of embroidery in slightly lighter blue along the arms and collar.

"Thought it was you!" said that unremarkable girl. When Annabel opened her mouth to answer, she added, "I don't think it's any use talking to me until you let me in, your highness. I can't hear anything from inside the library; someone's put a nice couple of security spells on it."

"Sorry," said Annabel. "You're invited in."

The girl must have been one of the ones who could read lips, because she tried one tentative step forward and the library allowed her in. "Very nice!" she said. "Good idea to use two spells; sort of a magical kill box that doesn't hurt anyone but still stops the ones you don't want from coming in."

"Yes," Annabel agreed doubtfully. She wasn't sure exactly what a kill box was, but she didn't like to say so in front of an unremarkable junior.

"Been watching you," said that unremarkable junior, in an unemotional voice that made it impossible to tell if she was simply stating a fact, or offering a threat. "Funny thing; three of the footmen look up every time you come into a room. One of the masters as well."

"The Deportment Master is probably just making sure I haven't eaten anything while I'm out of his sight," muttered Annabel. "Are you here for the—"

"That's the thing," the junior agreed. She was very clear and sure of herself—in fact, Annabel was just beginning to wonder if she really was a junior, despite her uniform, when the other girl asked, "Belle not here yet?"

"Certainly I am here," said Isabella's voice calmly, from the window. "Now, Nan, did I or did I not see someone surreptitiously creeping out the window as I just happened to be passing by?"

"Just happened?"

"Naturally. One appreciates useful exits, but one tends to dislike them when other people can make use of them. Of course, that had nothing to do with my presence outside this window."

"Oh, didn't it?" Annabel said. She was unwilling to discuss Melchior—unwilling, she found, even to think about him at the moment—with someone so sharp as Isabella looking on. "Some of the girls are arriving, and that person didn't want to be seen."

"Good day, Alice," Isabella said, wriggling energetically enough to drop through the window, bustle and all. "I trust you've been busy?"

"A bit," said the junior. "Got rid of the invitations for you."

"Very good. Anything else to report?"

"Nothing important yet," said Alice. "I'll make a report at the end of the week. Got a few ideas."

"Ideas about what?" Annabel demanded.

"About what's going to happen tonight," said Alice. "And some other things."

"You thought so, too?" Isabella asked, in astonishment. "Well done, Alice!"

Annabel, her eyes narrowing, said, "So *that's* why Melchior is poking about the halls today! He never said a word to me!"

"Yes, they excused us from his class earlier," Alice said, with some regret. "Shame. I like his class the best."

"Oh, can you do magic?"

"No," said Alice. "Just like to look at him, that's all."

"We do that, too," Annabel said, trying not to giggle. It wasn't proper to giggle in front of juniors, or so the Deportment Master said. "It makes him squirm a lot, doesn't it?"

Alice blinked a little bit and said again, "No, I just like to look at him. A bit gorgeous, isn't he?"

"Oh," said Annabel. "Well, his good-looking nose was definitely poking around the school earlier, so he must know there's something up, too. What *is* going to happen tonight?"

"Don't know," Alice said. "But the whole school has been unsettled all morning, and the Awesome Aunts are more nervous than usual. There've been footmen running here and there on the top floor. If I didn't know better, I'd say they're expecting an important guest. Very odd."

"*Very* odd," agreed Isabella. "Oh well, we'll just have to be attentive tonight, Nan. Goodness, is it the rest of them already? Let's discuss this later."

Much to Annabel's surprise, Isabella didn't attempt any other security than the spells they had already put on the library. Nor did she seem particularly nervous about being interrupted by teachers during the course of her introductions. She outlined very clearly exactly what classes would be offered, and when, and although she didn't give a place for the classes, Annabel was uneasy. She was still listening for the measured tread of the Awesome Aunts, in fact, when Isabella announced the next lesson time and place.

"And there's a reasonable piece of work accomplished!" said Isabella, after the last of the girls had gone.

"Yes, but won't they just tell the teachers?"

"Perhaps they will," Isabella acknowledged, with perfect cheerfulness.

"All right," Annabel said, with reluctant amusement. "I suppose you've got a plan for that, but I wish you wouldn't look so gleeful about it! What's next?"

"Next, we wait for what's going to happen tonight," said Isabella decisively.

SINCE SHE WAS CERTAIN THAT ISABELLA WOULD WAKE HER UP IN time for whatever was happening in Trenthams that night, Annabel went to sleep without thinking twice. If there really was something untoward happening that night, it certainly wouldn't be happening first thing, and Annabel preferred to have as much sleep as possible. Great was her annoyance, therefore, to be woken from a sound, dreamless sleep at the early hour of midnight, by the repeated clattering of people passing in the hallway—carrying, if the sound was anything to go by, the contents of two full suites, escorted by a cohort of guards and a small circus.

Annabel huffed a sigh at the ceiling and pulled her blanket over her head. What a ridiculous amount of noise! No wonder Melchior and Alice were aware that something was going on; everything else about the fact must have been as obnoxiously obvious as the noise outside her door.

She was still trying to go back to sleep for another precious few minutes when Isabella tugged gently at her covers.

Annabel groaned. "What?"

"Something is happening!" Isabella said, helpfully pulling the covers away completely. "Just as Alice said. Come along, Nan!"

"I already know," Annabel said crossly. "They've been making enough noise to wake the dead! I think they want us to know!"

"Well now," said Isabella, stopping still. "There's something in that, after all. There's certainly no way that anyone on this floor won't know that something's afoot. Shall we go peep, anyway?"

Annabel sighed gloomily and climbed out of bed. "Well, I'm awake now, so we might as well."

"That's the spirit!" Isabella said encouragingly. "There's no good in them making a lot of noise to be noticed if no one goes to notice it, is there? I don't like to make people feel unappreciated."

"I don't like to go without sleep," said Annabel, to the soft darkness of the room, "but no one minds that, do they?"

Isabella, at the door, said soothingly, "Never mind, we have a half-holiday tomorrow, at any rate."

Annabel mumbled rebelliously to herself, but slipped her arms into a silky wrapper and stole after Isabella. "If we get caught—"

"We're not going to get caught."

"I know," Annabel muttered, and grinned reluctantly. "It's like you said: it's no use catching us if they do want us to see something. But I'm cross and I'm going to complain anyway."

"Do you suppose," murmured Isabella, as they stepped quietly from the door and stole together down the hallway, "that Melchior is somewhere about tonight?"

"If he is, let's sneak up on him," said Annabel. "I want to make him jump. Actually, if it's the only thing we really accomplish tonight, I'll be happy with that."

Isabella giggled. "I could be satisfied with that, too, I think! Shall we give up our mission? They obviously want us to know; I've counted five noses poking out of doors so far."

"Oh well," Annabel said, "If Melchior is out and about tonight, he'll be where everything is happening anyway, so we might as well keep going."

"This way, I think," said Isabella, beneath her breath, and then, hastily, "Careful! You'll be seen!"

"I don't think so," Annabel disagreed. "She's being awfully careful *not* to see us, don't you think?"

That made Isabella giggle again. "She really is! Shall we have some fun tonight, Nan?"

Annabel gazed at the single Awesome Aunt who was trying very hard not to see any of the hastily opening and closing doors around the next floor. "It's insulting," she said. "Actually. Who told them they could take us so lightly?"

"Never mind, Nan," Isabella said, her voice soft and amused. "No, do move with a modicum of care! It's all very well to make a small miss-step or two, but we should keep it to a believable limit. It is *always* beneficial to be underestimated!"

"That reminds me," Annabel said, keeping to the less noisy edges of the hall behind Isabella. "Melchior is still keeping information from us. It's all very well to say that it's beneficial to be underestimated, but there's too much of a good thing, isn't there?"

"In Melchior's case, I'm not certain it's because he underestimates you. Of course, he does; but I don't think that's why he keeps information from you. I've a feeling that the events in the castle may have shaken him more than you think."

"Yes, but—"

"One gets the feeling, in fact," pursued Isabella, smartly snapping shut a door that popped open too close for comfort, "that Melchior is concerned about you. He's keeping things from you deliberately to prevent you from running into danger."

"Yes, that's what Dannick said," Annabel agreed. "But it's still wrong, just the same. I ought to have a say in what dangerous things I —actually, it's not even about having a say. If I'm going to be the queen, I should be told everything. It's not Melchior's decision to make. I could have him beheaded for treason."

"Probably not just yet," Isabella said, dissolving into laughter at the bottom of the stairwell. "You have to be actually crowned first!"

"Yes, that's probably what Melchior thinks," said Annabel darkly. "But I can *kick* him for treason, anyway. He won't be able to do this sort of thing when I'm crowned."

"I've the fancy he's trying to make sure you make it to the point of *being* crowned," Isabella remarked. "Of course, I could have read him wrongly, but I really don't think so. One of Melchior's specialties is allowing the people he loves to face the things they need to face, while throwing his all at the things trying to stop them from doing so."

"A most astute observation, Firebrand," said the curtains of the stairwell window, and pulled Annabel within their clutches.

"Oh, really!" said Isabella's voice, as Annabel made a small noise that was muffled against the softness of someone's waistcoat.

She pulled back crossly, and said, "Why are you always so perfectly dressed when you sneak out of your room at night?"

"I'm shocked, Nan," said Melchior, his eyes glinting down at her in the moonlight. "Are you suggesting you'd prefer me to be wearing less? I'm sure that's not what a fine school like Trenthams is teaching you."

Annabel snorted softly. "What rubbish! Most of the girls sneak out to kiss the footmen."

"Is that so?" Melchior sounded thoughtful. "Well, if it comes to that, why are you always in your night-things when you sneak out?"

There was a small *tsk* from outside, and Isabella said, "I shall leave you to discuss the matter in privacy. Good heavens!"

Her shadow flitted lightly away up the stairs before the startled Annabel could protest that she had no intention of discussing anything with Melchior, in privacy or otherwise.

Annabel snapped, "If I'm in my night things it's more likely the Aunts will believe I'm sleepwalking."

"A very good bit of thinking," Melchior said politely. He adjusted his hold on Annabel and said, "No, don't wriggle, Nan; the curtains will move. There isn't much room in here and I'd rather not be discovered at this point."

"They already know we're here," Annabel said exasperatedly. "They've been making so much noise that the whole school is probably awake by now."

Melchior ducked his head to murmur in her ear. "More quietly, if you please, Nan. I'm not talking about the circus that you followed here. I'm talking about the little byplay going on under cover of the circus."

Annabel leaned forward, pinching Melchior's waistcoat between her fingers to keep her balance, and peered around the curtain edge closest to him. There, in the crack beneath Lady Caro's door, was a softness of light creeping over the carpet. Not enough to make anyone think the lights were on, but certainly enough to make a curious passerby think that someone had a lamp or a small light spell. And as Annabel watched, leaning into the warmth of Melchior's hands, that same door cracked open just enough for someone's head to peek out and look carefully up and down the hall.

He waited until she saw what he had seen, his hands warm beneath her elbows, before he said softly in her ear, "Now isn't that more interesting, Nan?"

Annabel looked up at him and found that he was smiling down at her. She drew a breath. "*Much* more interesting! When did you discover this?"

"Just now," Melchior murmured. "Why do you think I pulled you in here so swiftly?"

"What about Isabella?"

"There's no room for the Firebrand."

"But what if she gets caught?"

"The Firebrand can look after herself," Melchior said firmly. "And I've no intention of spending the next half hour with my arms around her, if it comes to that."

"Half hour? Will the Lavender Aunt be in there that long?"

"I've no idea," Melchior said. "But they've been in there since before the noise began, so I think we can count on them being in there at least another half hour before they think it safe to come out."

"Wait, *them*? I only saw the Lavender Aunt."

"The Lavender Aunt seems to be the lookout," Melchior said. "She's not particularly good at it, so you'll undoubtedly see her a few times more yet. More interestingly, Nan, there's another girl in there —about your age, I should think, and dressed to the ears."

"The cheek of it," Annabel said mildly. Now that she knew why she needed to keep still, she was quite content. It had been such a long time since Melchior had let her close enough—or for long enough—to feel the warm comfort of him. "Thinking we're stupid enough to fall for something like that."

"You and the Firebrand were happily following the circus," pointed out Melchior, with a softness of amusement to his voice. "Aren't you grateful I chose to share with you what I found?"

"You only did that because you were afraid the Lavender Aunt would poke out her head again while we were there and give you away," said Annabel, but she said that mildly, too. She didn't particularly feel like arguing with Melchior at that moment. "Oh, wait!"

She had heard the soft click of the door opening again, she was sure. Annabel leaned forward to look through the curtain again, but Melchior was there first. She made a small *pft* of annoyance into his waistcoat and made space for herself by pushing him gently against the wall.

Melchior's startled face looked down at her and then, slowly, turned until he was looking back out at the hall. The Lavender Aunt was peeking from the door again, her eyes blinking too often; but this time, instead of closing the door after she had looked up and down the hall, she opened it wider.

There was someone behind the Aunt; someone, Annabel could see even in the faint light, who was dressed in bright, expensive colours. She had elegant cheekbones, but that was all Annabel could make out in the dim light; the girl was painted very skilfully to make the best of that low light, but it gave Annabel very little idea of what her face really looked like. Trenthams didn't encourage the kind of cosmetic usage that obscured the wearer's face from recognition, so it was most likely that this girl had arrived today. She could have been around Annabel's age, but Annabel didn't recognise her from any of her classes—or any of those Isabella had seen fit to excuse them both from. She had the feeling she would have remembered those cheekbones.

Annabel, watching the Aunt and her guest swiftly vanish into the darkness, whispered, "She must have arrived today. But if those were all her things, why did the Aunt want to hide *her*? If the things are here, someone must be with them."

Melchior didn't reply, and when Annabel glanced enquiringly up at him, he was no longer looking through the curtain. Instead, he was gazing down at her, the faintest of frowns between his brows as if he, too, was trying to solve a perplexing puzzle.

"Oh, sorry," said Annabel, straightening. "But you were taking up all the space, and I wanted to see."

She would have disentangled herself from him, but Melchior's arms tightened around her waist instead. He spun her in a flurry of wrapper and curtains, and nudged her back against the wall with rather more firmness than Annabel had shown to him.

"I would like to know, Nan," he said, ducking his head until he was almost nose to nose with her, "exactly who has been teaching you to do things like this?"

"Who do you think?" demanded Annabel. "I learn everything from you, so if you don't like what I do, you only have yourself to blame."

"I don't believe I was complaining," remarked Melchior. "Actually."

Annabel spluttered a laugh. "You can't say that!" she said. "That's mine!"

"Perhaps we're learning from each other," Melchior said thoughtfully. "Nan, what are you doing?"

"I'm going back to bed," said Annabel, pressing both of her palms against his chest to push him away. "Trenthams doesn't approve of young ladies being out of their beds at this time of night."

"Unless they're the ones causing it," Melchior agreed, stepping back. His hands covered Annabel's where they touched his chest, but Annabel didn't think it was consciously done; Melchior was gazing down the hall after the Lavender Aunt and her midnight guest, his cheek brushed by the curtain edge. "Very well, Nan; you'd best go to bed before I accidently teach you anything else disreputable."

As Annabel had expected, it was significantly harder to get up on a morning that was not only a half-holiday, but had been preceded by a night out of bed far too late. She got up anyway, because Isabella was very carefully making just enough noise in her morning ablutions to keep Annabel awake in spite of her desire to sleep longer.

"All right, what is it now?" she demanded, dipping her feet into her slippers. "You've been trying to get me up this past half hour and more. What do you want?"

Isabella didn't even try to dissemble. She grinned, bright and unabashed. "Do you know, Nan, what is the most enjoyable part of any half-holiday at Trenthams?"

"Sleeping in," Annabel said, and padded over to the tea kettle to make herself a cup of tea. "And it's no use trying to tell me it's anything else, because I won't believe you."

"Well, then; the *second* best," allowed Isabella. "No, don't guess; you'll only be grumpy again. Have your tea first. Well, Nan, the second best thing about any half-holiday at Trenthams is permission to visit the village and purchase anything we so desire—or at least, anything for which we have the money."

"And anything that's allowed into Trenthams, I suppose."

"Oh no!" Isabella assured her. "You can *buy* anything. You simply can't get anything into the school. Unless you're me, of course."

"Of course," echoed Annabel, watching spirals of steam rise from the kettle spout in the early morning sun. "That reminds me. When are we going to start making bustles unfashionable? It's too hot to be walking to the village in a bustle and corset."

"Nan!" Isabella said reproachfully. "Have you lost all that vim and vigour you showed to Melchior? How can we investigate these interesting occurrences at Trenthams when you're moping about bustles and corsets?"

"I'd like to know how I can investigate anything in a bustle and corset," Annabel remarked. "I don't think anyone can—unless they're you, of course."

"Of course!" Isabella agreed, laughing. "Never mind, Nan; we began phasing out bustles earlier this week, in fact. Did you really not notice?"

"What was there to notice?" demanded Annabel, reverting to her previous glower. "I've been squeezed within an inch of my life by the Deportment Master whenever I so much as *breath* in his direction, and I'll have you know that every dress I've worn this week has been bolstered by a bustle."

"Well, I suppose that's true," agreed Isabella. She still sounded far too cheerful for someone who had just admitted to failing in a most important mission, but at least she looked sympathetic. "But have you not noticed, Nan? I've been putting out a smaller bustle for you each day. In fact, your gown for today doesn't need one at all; it's already worked into the design. The merest suggestion of a bustle made from ruched cloth and the tiniest bit of padding! And I've raised the waist-line, besides."

"Oh," said Annabel, who *hadn't* noticed. She poured two cups of tea and asked, "Do you think the Deportment Master will stop making my corsets so tight if I look smaller without a bustle?"

"Anything is possible, I suppose," Isabella said. "But one is inclined to doubt it. One is inclined, in fact, to come to the conclusion that the Deportment Master merely hates you and is trying to do all he can to make your life miserable."

"He hates you too, but he doesn't squeeze you within an inch of your life," pointed out Annabel. "Oh! Those evening wrappers—"

Isabella nodded. "All part of the plan, Nan! After all, there's no reason for a wrapper to accommodate or provide a bustle, is there? And we certainly had the chance to show our fashion last night, did we not?"

"Don't remind me," Annabel muttered. She sipped her tea and said hastily as Isabella approached with an armful of clothing and a determined expression, "All right, all right, I'm getting dressed; there's no need to bring my clothes over! You'd make an awful maid!"

"I'd make a wonderful maid," contradicted Isabella, dropping the clothes on one of the sofas in favour of the tea Annabel had poured. "I'd dress you to perfection every day and be awfully rude to your face but full of fiery brimstone to anyone who dared to say a thing against you behind your back. Only, one suspects one ought to be angular and pinched to be that kind of maid, and I'm not sure I could forgo the chocolate cake."

Annabel gave a smothered giggle. "Never mind," she said. "All you have to do is have someone appoint blue napkins to your place settings and you won't have to worry about it!"

The village was much bigger than Annabel remembered. It could have been the fact that they hadn't had a chance to walk its full length on the day after they arrived, but Annabel was more inclined to think it was because they had already walked from Trenthams, and the length of the village itself was an unpleasant addition to that exercise when she was already too hot, too breathless, and dizzy from a sad lack of any kind of sustenance for breakfast that didn't involve a peel or a glass of water.

There was a flock of younger girls, intent upon spending their money on whatever sweet things—or alive things, Annabel realised, sighting one girl who was bouncing by the cages of birds for sale on the village street—they could conceivably manage to sneak back into the school. The older, more sober girls were led away swiftly by Lady Caroline, who didn't look as though she had been up the previous night, either in haggardness or general guiltiness.

Annabel frowned at that. She didn't particularly want Lady Caro's company—or the company of those other girls she had so confidently led away—but it gave her the uncomfortable feeling that there was something in the wind.

"In most cases," Isabella said confidingly to her, as Lady Caro and her flock sailed away, "I would advise this as a very good chance to steal a few of Lady Caro's supporters. I'm certain there are several of them who are ready to leave her and see if the waters are any warmer with you. However, since we're going to be purchasing things of a decidedly more suspect nature—"

"Yes," agreed Annabel thankfully. "Since we don't know we can trust them not to talk, it's safer to be on our own."

"For now," Isabella said. "For now. It does seem to me that Lady Caro is just a *little* bit too determined to lead everyone away from you, and there's more of a coherency to them this morning than I'm comfortable with. One has the feeling, Nan, that something has drawn them together and made them uneasy to be seen with you in public."

"Yes," Annabel said. She'd seen the sort of thing that happened when cliques that had been loose began to draw together; and the timing was just a bit *too* coincidental with the visitors to Lady Caro's room last night. "I thought so too. Do you suppose someone has been spreading rumours about me?"

"Of course they've been spreading rumours," said Isabella. "Lady Caro has probably been spreading most of them, if it comes to that."

"Do you think it's got to do with whoever arrived last night?"

Isabella considered that meditatively, steering them both rather bizarrely in the direction of a blacksmith. "Now there's an idea, Nan! I doubt Melchior will tell us even if he knows—and I strongly suspect this has been a surprise to him as well. Well! There's no need for him to be creeping about the halls and being silly with curtains if he knew about it, is there?"

"Oh," said Annabel. "Well, actually, there was a reason for that."

"I'm quite certain there was," Isabella said. She was grinning, though Annabel wasn't sure why. "You were a little late coming back last night, Nan, if it comes to that."

"That's what I was saying," Annabel said. "I forgot to tell you last night—"

"I'm not surprised," murmured Isabella irrepressibly. "You were too busy cuddling with Melchior."

Annabel, taken by surprise, coughed. "I wasn't cuddling!"

"Really? What a waste, Nan! I was under the impression that that was why you'd forgotten to tell me what else happened last night."

"It wasn't!" Annabel said crossly. She had certainly felt off balance and odd last night, but she had also been very tired. "I forgot because I was tired. The Lavender Aunt who didn't follow last night's circus came to Lady Caro's room last night with another girl."

"*Really?*" Isabella's eyes brightened. "Oh, how interesting! I can't imagine it was one of the regular girls, can you?"

"I didn't recognise her," Annabel agreed. "I don't know all the girls, though."

"I wonder," said Isabella meditatively, "I really wonder if Melchior knew about this in advance."

"He said he was just in the right place at the right time."

"Very suspicious!" nodded Isabella. "And that brings something to mind, Nan! Do remind me when we get back to the school that I've got a few ideas about how we can get a little information out of Melchior."

"All right," agreed Annabel. Melchior had far too much knowledge that he wasn't sharing. He might not have known exactly what was going to happen at Trenthams last night, but he had certainly been aware that *something* was going to happen. "Belle, what on earth do we need from a blacksmith?"

Isabella grinned. "Certain things that can't be purchased anywhere else. Come along Nan—and let this be a lesson to you not to judge from appearances!"

This pronouncement, Annabel soon learned, meant that the blacksmith was not merely a blacksmith; or at least, that his son wasn't inclined to follow his trade. At the back of the forge was a small room that opened onto the forest behind the house, small and tidy and herby-smelling. It was so tidy and herby-scented, in fact, that if Annabel hadn't been able to read some of the small, neatly labelled drawers around the room, she might have thought it was merely a chemist. She had no ability to see magic the way Poly and Melchior did.

In surprise, she asked Isabella, "We're buying spells?" She was sure that Isabella had said that the attempted smuggling of spells was bound to be caught by Trenthams' magic sensors.

"Not exactly," Isabella said. "That's the sort of thing that Trenthams catches up with sooner or later if one keeps doing it. Besides, I like to be able to manage without magic where I can, given the distinct lack of magic inborn in me. No, the Blacksmith's son is a far more useful person—he does sell spells, but he also has a range of useful things not dissimilar to my smuggling garters. I always like to browse here whenever I come into the village. The poor boy needs encouragement, and I'm ever in need of useful things."

Annabel couldn't see that Isabella was in need of anything more than her usual quick wits, but she was content to be browsing in a shop for a little while. It had struck her almost immediately after the other girls separated from herself and Isabella, that two slowly strolling men always seemed to be in view when she glanced over her shoulder. She wasn't sure if Isabella had ducked into the shop to ascertain for herself whether or not the men were following them, but certainly the men were still there when they entered the street again.

There was nothing to stop two men strolling down the street, of course, but had that one been reading the paper he was holding so assiduously to his nose? Annabel didn't think so. He put it down casually and moved after the girls, his reflection fluctuating in the shop windows, and the other man, who had at first seemed not to be there any longer, now stepped out from the shadow of the bakery door.

"Bother!" said Isabella beneath her breath, startling the entirely absorbed Annabel. "Nan, do you suppose you could move a little more quickly? I fancy we're about to have some excitement."

❧ 10 ❧

"They won't attack us in the street, will they?" protested Annabel.

"Ah." Isabella looked pleased. "I thought you'd seen them, too! Well, perhaps they won't, but from here I can see at least three different ways in which they can corral us before we reach the end of the street, and I'd really rather they didn't."

Annabel looked over at her in some respect. "Actually three? Good grief. All right, I'll move more quickly. What shall we do?"

"Keep walking at this speed until *that* cart draws even," said Isabella rapidly. "And when it does, we'll pass around *those* boxes ahead. There's a street there: duck down it as quickly as you can. I'll dart across the road and meet you by the bakery in a couple of minutes if I can. If I can't, I'll meet you just outside the village and we'll try to make it back to Trenthams when the other girls come out."

"Yes, but what about you?" protested Annabel, quite well aware that Isabella was taking the more perilous route. She might not be able to see three ways in which they were in danger, but she could certainly see one—it was across the street, where Isabella was planning on running. Besides the two men who had been dilatorily following them, a third had been watching them from across the street as they drew closer.

"No time, Nan!" Isabella said cheerfully. "Off you go! Keep in the shadows, won't you!"

Annabel, shoved down the side street summarily, threw a brief look over her shoulder as she ducked into the cover of protruding brickwork. Isabella dashed across the road, accompanied by something that billowed along with her and could have been either another person or a cloak she had snatched up and taken with her.

"Rude," Annabel muttered to herself. Isabella was by far too bossy —worse, she was completely reckless of her own safety in her behaviour. Annabel hesitated, and as she did she knew she wasn't going to keep walking down this street. Instead, she hurried back to the turning, hanging back just enough to shelter behind the crates there.

If she had been Isabella, she would have waited until she saw all three threats disappear. Since she wasn't, and since she wasn't entirely sure what threats Isabella had seen apart from the obvious three men, Annabel simply waited until she could bring herself to wait no longer, and ran across the road. Where exactly had she seen Isabella's tidy bustle disappearing? There—that small gap between shop and shop that wasn't even wide enough to be an alley—she had seen Isabella last near that. None of the three men could possibly have fit down there, so there was a good chance that Isabella had gotten away clean.

Too worried about her own, more generous size combined with her bustle, Annabel didn't attempt to follow Isabella's probable path exactly. Instead, she skirted around the gap and found it again after circling a shop completely. There were a few small threads of blue caught on the rough blockwork there, suggesting that Isabella had not found it as easy to exit as she had to enter, but of Isabella herself there was no sign. Nor was there any sign of the three men Annabel had recently seen in hot pursuit of Isabella.

Annabel looked around herself dubiously. Behind the shops in the main street was a rather dingy place to be; cottages backed on the exits of the shops, and if Annabel had been wondering where all the garbage from either of those two lines was stored, she was no longer left in doubt. It was piled up against the rear of both shops and cottages, with little attempt at neatness or general cleanliness other than a few haphazard piles. Annabel stole quietly past those piles, her eyes darting from one side of the alley to the other. It was out of the question for Isabella to be hiding in the garbage, she was quite certain; she must have darted down one of the other cracks of light that led to a normal, sanitary village road.

Annabel followed the alley toward the darkness of forest at the end, cheered by the fresh scent of the trees sweeping through the fetid air, and saw a gate that was just slightly ajar. It was a very small gate, set crookedly in the wall, and it didn't look particularly promising. Still, it was something a little different from the rest of the alley, and Annabel wasn't keen to try her bustle through any of the gaps between stores. She carefully pushed open the gate, afraid that it would squeak and give her away, and stepped into a small courtyard that was just as grimy as the alley she had come from and made no less confusing by the sheer amount of archways it contained. Once, it must have been a common courtyard leading to the back doors of several of the buildings around it. Now it was slick and grimy with disuse, and a third of the archways were haphazardly blocked up.

As Annabel opened her mouth to call quietly to Isabella, there was the sound of a muted gasp from one of the archways.

Someone said in disbelief, "She *bit* me!"

"I warn you, sir," said Isabella's voice icily, "that I have a hatpin poised where you do not wish to have it poised. If you do not release your hold on my waist immediately—thank you. I can assure you that Miss Ammett is well back on her way to Trenthams by now, and any attempt to take me prisoner will be resisted to the utmost."

Pencil staff in hand, Annabel stepped lightly through the archway. Perhaps those few deportment lessons had been useful for something after all—she had always been able to step lightly, but she didn't think she had ever done it so easily. None of them heard her approach; there were three of them surrounding Isabella, kerchiefs wrapped around the lower halves of their faces. Isabella still had her long, deadly hatpin in one hand, but two of the men facing her had pistols, their barrels even longer and deadlier than the hatpin.

"What are you going to do?" asked one of the men grimly. "Stab all of us? Don't move, Miss Farrah; Lord—"

"No names, you fool!" hissed the one with a bite mark on his hand.

"Oh, how ridiculous!" snapped Isabella. "You're wearing the same perfume you wear to every summer ball, Lord Arrian! And if I couldn't recognise Mr. Collette from that really very distinctive nose, I'm certain I couldn't avoid noticing the family crest he's still wearing on his signet finger!"

"Oh," said Mr. Collette. "Does that mean we can kill her now? She ruined my best waistcoat a year ago in Broma, and I really think that bite mark is going to scar."

"I *told* you to take off your signet!" said Lord Arrian, in very nearly as much disgust as Isabella. "You can shoot her when we've got the queen heir. You'd best begin calling for her, Miss Farrah."

Isabella sighed deeply, and said earnestly, "If you were in such bad need of coaching for negotiations, you should have come to me! What could possibly be a motive for me to call for the queen heir now? I already know you're going to kill me, and of course I shall refuse, in pure spite."

"You—but—"

"You're both idiots," said the third man, bitterly.

Annabel considered them silently, and reached with her other hand into the pocket that held her sketchbook. She didn't really need it to use the staff, but it was familiar and safe; and while Isabella was facing pistol barrels, Annabel preferred to be extraordinarily careful. Neither of the men with pistols seemed particularly clever, but it didn't take cleverness to pull a trigger.

"I agree," said Isabella, as Annabel drew two pistols into her notebook, tracing the chamber of each carefully. "You're both idiots. It really makes me regret allowing myself to be caught by you. I don't like to think of people knowing I was captured by such people."

"Let—! We caught you fair and square!" protested Mr. Collette.

"And you might just as well take off your kerchiefs, since I know who you are, anyway," Isabella continued. That made the third man laugh. To him, Isabella said kindly, "There's no need for you to take yours off, of course, unless you don't feel perfectly comfortable in it. I've really no idea who you are, but since you've not brandished a pistol in my face, I feel inclined to approve of you."

"Very kind of you," said the third man politely, and bowed.

Annabel, sketching rapidly in her little book, finished the last lines and ran her eye carefully over the completed drawing. She had made a study of each new type of pistol that came out; partially because it was important, Melchior said, to keep up with the latest in the new craze of firepower, but mostly because pistols were new and fascinating and a little bit loud. Besides, it had seemed useful, since the staff took the form of a pencil with her, to know how to draw one if needed.

Finished with her drawing of the two pistols belonging to Isabella's captors, Annabel turned the page and drew another, more compact version with two fat little barrels. She made sure to draw this one with full chambers, just as she had been very careful to draw the others with empty chambers.

She felt the weight in her pocket before she quite finished the drawing, and took a step toward the others as she finished the final shading on the double-trigger. Perhaps she wasn't careful enough; the third man looked over sharply, prompting the first two men to turn around.

Lord Arrin's eyes grew very wide above his kerchief, and then narrowed in what Annabel was quite certain was a satisfied smile. "Very good timing, your Majesty!"

"Wait!" commanded the third man, sharply.

"Actually," said Annabel, drawing her pistol and levelling it as she came, "I'm not *your Majesty* until I'm crowned later this year. Until then, you're supposed to call me *your Highness*. Don't move, please."

"We've got pistols too!" snapped Mr. Collette. "You can't tell us what to do!"

"Try and fire them," Annabel invited. "Go on; I'll wait."

Lord Arrin and Mr. Collette looked at each other, then back at Annabel's levelled double-barrels. The third man gave a short, sharp hiss of annoyance, seized Lord Arrin's pistol, and put the dainty barrel against Isabella's temple. The heavy click of the hammer falling sounded loudly in the silence.

Isabella said, "I call that rude, I really do!"

The third man hissed once more through his teeth. He dropped the pistol contemptuously to the cobbles, and said to Isabella, "We'll meet again, Miss Farrah."

"Will we really?" Isabella asked. "How lovely. I'll make sure to be ready for you this time."

He laughed again, and ducked through one of the archways before Annabel could threaten to shoot him, much to her annoyance. She probably wouldn't have shot him, but it would have been nice to have him still there when Melchior and Raoul came to see what the fuss was about. They should be along shortly, if Annabel knew anything about Isabella; she was almost certain that the other girl had a distress spell somewhere about her that linked to Raoul.

Annabel corrected the tilt of her pistol to take in the two figures of Lord Arrin and Mr. Collette, who now, with a single, useless pistol between them, stared at each other.

"Since you were so full of suggestions earlier," she said, "I've got one for you. It involves you sitting down on one of those very comfortable piles of rubbish until a friend of mine comes to ask you some questions."

"It's no good running, after all," Isabella reminded them. "I know who you are, so even if you do run, all you'll get out of it is sweat, and someone waiting for you when you get home."

"Is Raoul coming?"

"Goodness, how did you know about that?" Isabella sounded almost startled.

Annabel grinned, very pleased with herself. "Why else would you let yourself get captured after conveniently losing me in another street? I suppose you had an alarm spell somewhere outside the grounds—actually, the Blacksmith's son probably had it for you."

"Perhaps I'm losing my edge," complained Isabella. "That man earlier nearly swept me away earlier than I intended to be caught, and now this!"

"I might have been surprised if I hadn't been living with you for a couple of weeks," Annabel told her comfortingly.

"*Might have* is no comfort to me!" said Isabella. "Oh well; these gentlemen of dubious intelligence——"

"I say!"

"Watch what you say, Miss Farrah!"

"——these gentlemen of dubious intelligence," continued Isabella, in a very clear voice, "don't seem to have suspected anything, so that's a comfort, anyway. Raoul and Melchior should be here in a few more minutes. Less, if they take the right path through this nasty little muddle of archways and unwashed cobblestones."

"Firebrand!" said Melchior wrathfully, striding into the courtyard a moment later, "If you continue to lead my Nan into the kind of danger that you routinely court and enjoy, I warn you that you won't have to wait for the Old Parrasians to end your life! I shall take the greatest pleasure in wringing your neck myself!"

"Told you," said Mr. Collette to his co-conspirator, in a low, gloomy voice. "Everybody finds her an annoyance."

Raoul, following swiftly behind Melchior, cuffed Mr. Collette so hard behind his ear that both of the conspirators were sent sideways into the garbage. "That doesn't give you leave to point pistols at her!"

"Raoul!" said Isabella, considerably startled. "I've never appreciated you enough! Thank you! I've been wanting to do that for the last fifteen minutes at least!"

"D'ruther that than your sharp tongue, anyway," muttered Mr. Collette, who didn't seem to know when to stop.

"Are you hurt, Nan?" Melchior demanded, bypassing Isabella completely and scanning Annabel from head to toe.

"Of course not," said Annabel, tucking the pencil staff back into her pocket. "I had the staff. Oh. And now this."

She wriggled the small pistol in Melchior's face.

"And Isabella did try to keep me out of it," she added. "She pushed me down a side street and led them this way. I came because I didn't want her to get hurt."

"That's very good of you, Nan," Isabella said, in a pleased sort of voice. "In fact, I tried *very hard* to keep you out of danger. I've never appreciated how very annoying it is to have someone dance willy-nilly after one when one has been careful to leave them safe in another place. I feel as though I ought to apologise to you, Raoul."

"Well, it's about time," said Raoul. He was unsuccessful in preventing the pleased grin from spreading over his face, though his voice was gruff.

"Oh, and I *do* think an apology is warranted from you, Melchior," Isabella mentioned politely.

"From him! You haven't even apologised to me yet! You just said you ought to!"

"I tried my utmost to leave your Nan safe and lead away the—"

Annabel coughed. "*Whose* Nan?"

"I apologise unreservedly, Firebrand," Melchior said, after scanning Annabel one last time. "Where did you get that firearm, Nan?"

"The staff, of course," Annabel said. "I've been practising."

"Designing, too; or is this a new model I've not seen?"

"It's a prototype," said Annabel, "but Hendersons has been very accurate, so I didn't wait for them to approve it. I like this size."

"It's all very well to stand here and discuss firearms," Isabella said, "but it strikes me that those two are trying to wriggle away, and I really think we'd do best to get information from them before it occurs to that other man to have them killed."

Mr. Collette, who had indeed been trying to wriggle unnoticeably away, followed by Lord Arrin, froze and said in a shocked voice, "Yes, but he won't try to have us killed!"

"Of *course* not!" Isabella assured them, in a voice too innocent, too kindly. "But do tell me! Which of you considered that he would put a pistol to my head and pull the trigger?"

There was a very uncomfortable silence before Lord Arrin said sulkily, "Collette wanted to kill you, too!"

"Naturally," agreed Isabella. "I find it's a pretty common desire when people interact with me. On the other hand, very few people actually put a pistol to my head and pull the trigger when they know the pistol is loaded."

"It's not much use putting it to your head if it's not loaded," Annabel remarked.

"Exactly so. Your friend is really a lot more ruthless than either of you are—or than either of you thought he was, I imagine. Are you really so sure he won't try to have you done away with?"

Mr. Collette and Lord Arrin exchanged another glance as Raoul chivvied them to their feet, and Lord Arrin said, "Don't take us by the main road, then, for pity's sake! There were a few of us stationed along there, waiting."

"I'll take these two as far as the posting house," Raoul said to Melchior. "The other guardsmen are waiting in the alley, so they won't have a chance to run. You can accompany her Highness and Miss Farrah back to the school if you'd like."

"Would you like to borrow my pistol?" enquired Annabel, in a helpful spirit. "It's no use using theirs—they won't work at the moment."

Raoul looked in disfavour from Annabel's tiny, useful pistol to the two more manly ones that were utterly useless, and sighed. "Thank you, your Highness. I'll send it back by Dannick."

"I'll come back for it later," Melchior said briefly. "I'll need to be present for the questioning in any case."

"Rude!" said Annabel. "We do all the work to capture two dangerous agents for the Old Parrasians and we're sent back to school!"

"Just as things were getting interesting!" instantly agreed Isabella. "It really is too bad!"

Annabel nodded, but caught Melchior's eyes, which were glinting with decided warning. She added hastily, "On the other hand, a cup of tea would be nice, and I've no idea what interrogation techniques are effective today."

"You're more familiar with the traditional ones!" agreed Melchior, his lips narrowed sarcastically. "Imagine how much use you could make of the more modern, magic-based methods!"

That surprised a giggle out of Annabel. She took the arm Melchior offered by way of indicating that she wasn't really averse to going back to Trenthams, and on Melchior's other side, Isabella took his right arm.

"Now don't you agree," Isabella said persuasively, "that you've entirely misjudged me, and that my intentions are merely to be of as much use as possible to the queen heir?"

Melchior grinned a little. "Very well, Firebrand. I admit I was in the wrong. Are you content?"

"Not at all!" Isabella assured him. "Now I must bring to your attention the matter of your constant snide remarks, not to mention your sad habit of assuming the worst whenever Nan and I are out of your sight..."

CLASSES SEEMED TO DRAG MORE THAN USUAL THAT AFTERNOON. Annabel wasn't sure if it was the discomfort of her corsets, so strictly enforced by the Deportment Master, or the lack of food combined with their strenuous morning—or even the fact that she was impatient to know what Melchior had discovered from his questioning of the two men she and Isabella had captured.

Melchior hadn't returned to Trenthams by the time the dinner gong sounded brassily through the halls. Neither was he in his room when Annabel, after a weary and entirely unsatisfying hour in the lunch hall, visited it in hopes of finding him there. Isabella wasn't in their suite when she got back there, either, which made Annabel wonder if she had excused herself from Isabella in order to find Melchior, or if Isabella had excused herself from Annabel for her own reasons. In any case, it was likely that it wasn't just Melchior who was busy at his own business; Annabel shrewdly suspected that Isabella had another, more secret class to lead at Trenthams.

Not entirely to her surprise, there were no evening visitors to the suite she shared with Isabella. Annabel hadn't encouraged it after the first day, but even if she had been the most enthusiastic of hosts, she had the feeling that the supply of visitors would have failed that night anyway. Girls had been less inclined to speak to either Isabella or Annabel that morning, and although Annabel was content to have Isabella's friendship and the occasional exchange with Delysia or Alice, she wasn't quite prepared for the level of unfriendliness that was on display that afternoon. During class, the girls who had originally crowded into her suite to stare over their teacups with bright, considering eyes and compliment her carefully as *Miss Ammett*, now tittered behind their fans when the Deportment Master icily instructed her for the fourth time to *mind her carriage!* More, they were actively spiteful at dinner, their voices high and carrying, and Annabel was glad to get away from the childishness of it all.

Failing to find Melchior in his room or Isabella in their suite, Annabel made herself a cup of tea and decided that bed was the only place to be. She was more tired than she'd thought, and the removal of her corset with the help of one of the gadgets Isabella had procured from the blacksmith's son only assuaged some of the discomfort.

When Annabel woke the next morning, her teacup was back on the sideboard where it belonged instead of on her night stand, and Isabella was pacing the floor in a manner as energetic as it was silent.

"Ah, you're awake!" she said, without pausing that exercise. "That's good. I've a feeling, Nan, that this will be a trying day."

"Well, that's good, then," said Annabel, a little grumpily. She was already feeling far too hot, and there was a damp patch where her shoulders rested through the night, suggesting that she had been far too hot for quite a while before she woke. "If I was looking for a frame of reference, do you consider yesterday to have been a trying day as well?"

"Yesterday was an interesting day," Isabella said. "Not trying, as such. I'm very much afraid that today will be more unpleasant."

Annabel groaned and sat up, throwing off the covers. It was too late to try going back to sleep; she might as well have a cup of tea, despite the heat. "What, do you think the Royalists will try to kidnap us today?"

"I shouldn't imagine so—oh, and that reminds me. One of the maids asked me to give you a message. You've been having more luck with the maids than I've been having with the footmen, I take it?"

"What message?"

"I've no idea; she wrote it and twisted it up for you. I didn't think it polite to try and read it so I made you a cup of tea instead."

Annabel was surprised into a hiss of laughter, and accepted the cup of tea. "Really? That must have been a bit of a strain."

"You have no idea!" Isabella said devoutly. "Do read it, Nan—

perhaps it will shed some light on our situation. Failing that, we'll have to bother Melchior again."

"We'll have to bother him again anyway," Annabel remarked, untwisting the screw of paper. "We want to know what those two said during their interrogation."

"Do you suppose he'll tell us?"

"I don't know," said Annabel honestly. "I thought you had some ideas about how to get the information out of him if he didn't want to tell."

"I do," Isabella agreed. "I'm really not sure you'll like them."

"I don't like a lot of things you make me do," Annabel said. "But I don't suppose that's going to stop you, so I might as well make the effort."

Isabella leaned over her shoulder. "Don't be like that, Nan. It'll be fun. What does your little maid have to say?"

"Oh, that's odd," Annabel said, perusing her note. "Jess says it'd be a good idea if we were to wander up to the fourth floor after dinner tonight. She says there's something I should see."

"Some*one*, belike," remarked Isabella. "Yes, but we already know about her, don't we?"

"Perhaps we'll know more if we go to the fourth floor," Annabel suggested. She looked at the cup of tea Isabella had given her and wondered if it was really wise, after all, to drink it when she was already so warm. "Ooof! Isn't it *hot* today? Why is it so hot?"

Isabella, quite cool and unbothered despite being significantly more dressed than Annabel, told her, "Croquet season began this week. It's always hotter after croquet season starts. Nan, since I'm forwarder than you in dressing, I'll start off now, shall I?"

"Up to something, are you?" asked Annabel, unsurprised. This time, she didn't think it had anything to do with whatever side project Isabella was working on apart from Annabel, but she was quite certain that Isabella *was* still up to something. "There's something going on in the school and you don't know what it is, so you want to find out from pure spite."

Isabella grinned. "Well, perhaps so. Besides, I told you; it's going to be a trying day for us both, and I'd rather find out how best to miti-gate the annoyance if at all possible."

"All right," agreed Annabel. She had to try and sneak into Melchior's room before it occurred to him to run away, anyway. She would like to know more about the two Old Parrasians they had caught yesterday. "Shall we meet at breakfast?"

"I believe so. If I've not found what I need before then, I doubt I will."

There were very few girls in the hall when Annabel finished dressing. She was glad for it; she was still feeling too hot, and she had the dreadful suspicion that her face was already pink and slightly glossy from the exertion of dressing. She preferred not to face people when she was pink and glossy if she could avoid it. The maid who came in to help her with her corset must have been in league with the Deportment Master, because her corset was laced far too tightly, and by the time she slipped into Melchior's room, Annabel was feeling pinched, cross, and hard done by.

Fortunately—or perhaps unfortunately—Melchior was still in his room when she got there, so Annabel was left with no reason to remain cross, although she felt that she would have liked to do so. He was in the process of tying a tidy black cravat when she slipped through the door, and if he hadn't seen her in the mirror, Annabel thought she might have taken him by surprise. Melchior as a cat had been very hard to startle, but it had always been amusing to catch him by surprise; human Melchior was just as enjoyable to startle.

"Disappointed, Nan?" he asked, raising one brow at her in the mirror.

"Yes," Annabel said, deciding on absolute honesty. "I haven't made you really leap in at least a year."

"If I recall correctly—"

"That time doesn't count," she objected. "That time it was a runaway bull, not me."

"I remember doing a lot of leaping," murmured Melchior, going back to his cravat. "And spending a lot of time in an apple tree, if it comes to that. Are you here to bid me good morning, Nan, or are there other forces at work?"

Annabel watched him tie the ends of his cravat and tuck them neatly away with an air of gloomy interest. "Other forces, actually. You don't usually tie it like that, do you? It looks different."

"It is different," Melchior agreed. He turned his head to look directly at her, and his lips were curled curiously. "It's a variation upon my usual theme; and I have to say, Nan, I'm surprised that you noticed."

"Of course I noticed. You've been wearing it the same way for the last three years, and today it's different." Annabel sat down on one of the fat red couches. Melchior would put on his cufflinks now, two plain silver squares that glittered just a little too much to be *just* silver, and then he would make himself a cup of tea that he would drink in his vest and shirt sleeves before he put on his coat to go out. She had exactly that long to find out what the two men from yesterday had said. She said, "My prisoners from yesterday—"

A gleam of amusement came to Melchior's eyes, though to his credit, he didn't smile. He pinched his left cuff together and slid the cufflink through, and said, "Yes, Nan; your two prisoners?"

"What did they say?"

"You'll have to be more specific. They said a great deal, but not much of it was useful, and less of it was polite."

"What did they say about their employers, then?"

"They insist that they were single movers, and were trying to kidnap you for ransom."

Annabel was surprised into hissing a laugh. "They expected you to believe that?"

"In these cases, it's not so much a matter of whether or not we believe, but whether or not we can *prove* our suspicions," Melchior said mildly. "New Civet might be currently queenless, but she is not lawless. If we want to find out who is behind this attack, and what else they plan, we'll have to question them further. They know they're in a bad spot, but they're finding it hard to betray their cause. And then, there's the fact that kidnap for ransom carries a lesser sentence than treason, of course."

"I'll change that when I'm queen," Annabel said darkly. "You said they didn't say *much* about their employers."

Melchior smiled faintly as he turned a teacup upright on its saucer. "Still unsatisfied, Nan? Very well; they're Old Parrasians. They didn't necessarily come outright and say so, but they were full of all the usual sentiments and complaints."

Annabel looked at him disapprovingly. "We already *know* that, Melchior! Belle recognised both of them! I meant did they say *exactly* who their employers were? And what about the girl who arrived last night? What do they know about her?"

"The girl from last night?" Melchior poured a dark stream of tea into his teacup, and then the milk. "Why would you assume them to be connected, Nan?"

"That's not an answer," Annabel said. "Oh, don't start dodging again, Melchior!"

"It merely seems unlikely that a kidnapping attempt is related to a new student, no matter how secretly she arrived," said Melchior. "I find it insulting that you immediately assume I'm not telling you everything."

Annabel eyed him shrewdly. "I'd bet my breakfast you're not telling me everything," she said. "It's not much, but still!"

"It is not always the case, Nan, that I'm keeping things from you in order to spite you—"

Annabel couldn't help grinning. "Not *always*! Just every now and then!"

"Exactly so," agreed Melchior. "Has it ever entered your mind to trust me a little?"

"That's—" Annabel stopped, bewildered. "Oh, that's not fair! I've always trusted you!"

"I'm one who can admit my failings," pursued Melchior, without giving her a chance to catch her breath, "so I'll acknowledge that it was perhaps my fault that you first came not to trust me."

"*Perhaps*—!"

"I lied to you and didn't tell you everything in the castle. You were justifiably annoyed with me over that. But have I ever lied to you since then, Nan?"

"Not until just recently," Annabel said bluntly. "And I *do* trust you!"

Melchior looked directly back at her, and she found that it was difficult to hold his eyes. "Is that so, Nan? Then perhaps you would be good enough to trust me to tell you exactly everything you need to know? And perhaps it would occur to you that I don't tell you everything because not everything is important?"

Annabel blinked a little. "Yes, but then why would you be so secretive about so many things all this time!" she protested. "If they're nothing important, why are you acting like it is important and dodging questions!"

"I would also like to remind you," Melchior said, after the briefest pause, "that I have not, in fact, lied to you since the castle. I have simply not told you quite everything. It's an important distinction which I would like to have preserved."

"Yes, but—"

"Shall I tell you exactly what I had for breakfast this morning? Perhaps you'd like to know what the Awesome Aunts were about yesterday while playing badminton? Ah! I have it! Were you aware that one of the maids is following Dannick around the school like a particularly lovesick puppy?"

Annabel had been inclined to become resentful, but at this she stifled a giggle and demanded, "What maid? There's a maid following Dannick around?" If that was true, Dannick's face was currently likely to be a permanent shade of red.

"Ah," sighed Melchior. "Thus the reward for sharing all that I know!"

He refused to tell her anything else, either significant or insignificant, and Annabel left his room rather more hot and annoyed than she had entered it. She would have gone right back to her suite in the hopes of finding Isabella there, but she had already seen Isabella flitting down a far corridor as she entered Melchior's room. Isabella too, was still up to something. That particular fact left her far less inclined to resentment than the same conclusion had in Melchior's case, and that made Annabel stop and think. Isabella, like Melchior, was almost entirely certain to be up to something. Why, then, didn't it matter as much to Annabel? Isabella hadn't so much as mentioned to her that she had something going on; nor was she likely to explain to Annabel unless Annabel directly asked her about it.

A little earlier, it wouldn't have occurred to Annabel to mark the difference. Now, fresh from Melchior's accusation that she didn't trust him, it struck her that she had been looking at both Melchior and Isabella very differently.

"Then whose fault is it that I do?" she muttered. Melchior had adopted a mysterious attitude with his lack of communication that was annoying enough to leave her in a permanent state of irritation. Someone as clever as Melchior should be aware that he was only making her angry.

Unless, of course, he was *trying* to make her angry.

Annabel stopped dead in the hall and thought about that. It was possible. But if Melchior really had been trying deliberately to make her angry, why? Each time she had lost her temper, she had also lost her chance to ask more about the things she was interested in knowing, and that was telling. But if, as Melchior suggested, not all of those things were important, was that really why he had been trying to make her lose her temper?

She was still thinking about it when she found Isabella in the dining hall. She was too caught up in her musings, in fact, to entertain any more thoughts of her sparse breakfast than the feeling that her head felt just a little bit too light.

Isabella passed her a few slices of egg under cover of a passing horde of giggling juniors, and when those juniors had gone, said darkly, "There was nothing, Nan!"

"Nothing?" Annabel asked vaguely, hiding the egg slices in her very small breakfast roll.

"Nothing for me to find, anyway," sighed Isabella. "It's dreadfully frustrating, Nan! I know something is happening in the school, and I know Lady Caro knows something I don't, and that it has something to do with the visitor from last night, but it's beginning to feel as though everyone at Trenthams is aware of something I'm not! Absolutely unacceptable!"

"It must be very hard for you," Annabel agreed, listlessly. It could have been the effect of just a little egg, or not enough egg, but she was feeling decidedly lacking in energy.

"Never mind," said Isabella, turning her mood in a moment. "I'm sure we'll find out very soon; the whole school is poised to blow at any minute. Ah! And speaking of which—!"

"Speaking of what?"

"Explosives, of course! Well, explosives and lock picking. Now is the time."

"We weren't talking about explosives and lock picking," objected Annabel. "And what time is it?"

"Now is the time, Nan," continued Isabella, with far more glee than Annabel considered to be reasonable, "Now is the time where we find out if I've been successful in weeding out all of the pretenders!"

"I thought you'd already had more classes!" protested Annabel, catching up to the other girl at last. "There was the one at the start of the week—"

"Explosives," Isabella agreed, nodding.

"And the one in the middle of the week—"

"Secondary Explosives, for those girls who have experience."

"Oh, so that was why one of the second story windows shattered."

"Exactly so. The point at hand, Nan, being that I have now successfully cleared the beginners Explosives classes of any spies—I do assure you that none of those girls who weren't seriously there will dare to come again. The Secondary class was already clear because it consists entirely of girls who were in the first class three years ago. Delysia was overjoyed, if you can believe it. I rather fancy that's why we had a little excitement."

Annabel blinked, for a moment distracted from her original protest. "Delysia? Really?"

"Isn't it surprising? She looks so ladylike and delicate."

"Ladylike, anyway," Annabel said, remembering the slight gleam of steel she'd seen in Delysia's eyes the first time she'd met her. "She has a bit more backbone to her than people think. It props up all the giggling and silliness."

"I really shouldn't be surprised at the things you see, by now," Isabella said musingly. "And yet, I always am. You remind me of another monarch I know; although I have to say you're nothing like as terrifyingly ruthless as he is."

"Perhaps I will be when I've reigned for a few years," remarked Annabel. "Perhaps the power will go to my head. Belle—"

"I know exactly what you want to ask. You want to know how I can know for certain that we've cleared the pretenders from the Explosives Class."

"Actually," said Annabel, "I want to know when the Lockpicking class is going to start. You've all been having fun with explosive, and what I want to do is learn how to pick a lock."

"In that case, you're in luck," Isabella remarked, "because that's the class we're going to start today. Immediately, as it happens."

"Have you managed to get rid of all the pretenders from this class?"

"That's the delightful bit," said Isabella, with sparkling eyes. "I'm not sure! Come along, Nan! No time to waste!"

The class, thought Annabel some little time later, was awfully quiet. They were in one of the smaller sitting rooms with the curtains drawn against the stifling heat of the sun, and the muffled feeling could have come from that, but Annabel didn't think so. The silence may also have been because each of the girls was busy looking over an open half lock in varying degrees of dismay, or because any noise was drowned out by the faint buzzing that seemed to cling around her ears. Annabel was more inclined to think, suspiciously, that each of the girls was waiting for Something To Drop. They had a distinctly flighty look to them, as if each girl was calculating her odds of being able to leap out the window, swarm up the chimney, or dodge through the door under an unwary teacher's arm. If they'd been taught anything very much from Isabella, they probably were. Even Isabella was watchful, her eyes bright and light grey, enjoying the suspense—or perhaps a joke that only she knew. That comforted Annabel a little. If

Isabella was laughing at her own private joke, it was unlikely that a visit from the Awesome Aunts would achieve anything but expulsion for the student who had informed them of the meeting.

And if the class looked flighty, they also looked a little...uncomfortable. Annabel hadn't heard any of the same carefully loud rudeness from any of these girls that she had heard from the general Trenthams population, but it struck her some time after Isabella encouraged them to observe the workings of the locks and see if they couldn't figure out how they worked, that none of the girls were particularly friendly, either. They were merely confused.

It wasn't until one of the girls, a bold-eyed thing with a bright red ribbon through her curls, wandered casually through the other sitting girls and said in a low voice to Isabella, "Are you sure *she* should be here?" that Annabel knew it really was about her. More than that, she knew she was meant to hear the question, because she could see the questioner watching her from the corner of her eye. More amused than annoyed, Annabel didn't rise to the bait and look up properly.

She studied her lock, and heard Isabella say, "Miss Ammett? Why ever not?"

Anyone who knew Isabella well would have caught the distinct chill to her voice. Annabel, her head bent over the lock, grinned into its exposed mechanics.

"Well..." the girl hesitated, then said, "I'd heard something about her not being exactly who she—well, who she claims to be, if you get my meaning."

"Miss Ammett is not Miss Ammett?" asked Isabella, all innocent confusion.

"Well, that is—"

"Miss Ammett has only ever claimed to *be* Miss Ammett," Isabella said, very sweetly. "I'm certain that no one has heard her claiming to be anything else."

"Ah," said the bold-eyed girl. "Well, that's true enough, if it comes to that."

Isabella's voice was distinctly warning this time. "That is not to say she won't ever claim to be something else, if you perfectly understand me."

"Are you really standing behind her?"

"Nan, am I standing behind you?"

"I hope so!" Annabel said frankly, wiping sweat from her brow. It was disgustingly hot in the sitting room. "We can't forget about your little Papa, after all. Belle, is this really the only way to learn how to pick locks? I thought there might be more teaching involved."

"There will certainly be more teaching involved," agreed Isabella. "There, Fern; does that answer your question?"

Fern's dark eyes flitted from Isabella to Annabel. "Yes," she said slowly. "I think it really does. You might want to have a few words with Lady Caro, in that case."

"I'll do so," said Isabella. "But at this time I really think it would be a good idea for you to return to your seat."

"Really?" The girl's eyes flicked from Isabella to Annabel again—then passed Annabel entirely and widened. "Crumbs! Thanks!"

"It will make this occasion so much neater!" Isabella said, as one of the doors opened swiftly across the room.

At least half of the girls stood up to flee, but the other door was already opening, too. Through the first came the Lavender Aunt, sailing majestically; through the second came the Yellow Aunt stalking magnificently. Behind each Aunt were two broad-shouldered footmen, who looked as though they couldn't decide whether to be amused or sheepish, but who were equally impassable either way. As one, the girls sat again.

"Ma'am, Ma'am!" said Isabella cordially, nodding to each Aunt. "What brings you into our sitting room this morning?"

"Miss Farrah, I must ask you to sit down," said the Lavender Aunt crushingly.

"Of course, Ma'am," meekly said Isabella.

Annabel, who had not attempted to rise from her seat due to the combined effects of a sudden dizziness and the conviction that it would do no good, tried not to grin. If the Aunts had any sense of self-preservation at all, they would have left the minute they saw Isabella was unbothered; and doubly quick at Isabella being meek.

"I am surprised, Miss Ammett," said the Yellow Aunt, surprising Annabel considerably, "to see you in such company."

"Oh," Annabel said blankly. "Really? But I like these girls."

Across the room, she saw Fern grin.

The Yellow Aunt looked disapprovingly at her. "In your position, Miss Ammett, you really ought to be more careful about who you associate with. It may very well lead to some doubt as to your...ahem... that is, it may lead people to disassociate themselves with you."

"If that's all it takes, I don't think I'll mind," Annabel said.

"Do not speak back to me, Miss Ammett!"

"Oh, sorry," said Annabel. Now that was odd. The Aunts had been calling her *my lady* until yesterday; and today she was *Miss Ammett*?

"I trust you understand the full extent of your misconduct, then, Miss Ammett."

"Actually, I'm a bit confused," said Annabel. She was still dizzy, and now she was also rather tired of being *Miss Ammett*ed so accusingly. "None of us are due in class yet; aren't we allowed to um, associate with each other? Our Conversation won't become more Advanced if we don't study."

"This is not a matter of associating outside of class!" the Lavender Aunt said impressively. "It is a matter of Scandal! Of Clandestine Classes and Nefarious Doings! If it was not for the very good sense of Lady Margaret, who informed us of this travesty via a note, the good name of Trenthams might well have been soiled!"

There was a polite but very distinct shuffling of girls away from the named Lady Margaret, who put her nose in the air with very red cheeks and glared angrily at her retreating classmates.

Isabella said in bewilderment, "Soiled by learning how to adjust *carriage clocks?*"

"There is no use in prevaricating, Miss Farrah," said the Lavender Aunt. "Lady Margaret has already informed us that this disgraceful class is for the purposes of learning how to pick locks. The locks are clearly evident."

"Locks?" Isabella's face was the picture of astonishment. "Dear ma'am, what locks? Each of the girls has before her an open carriage clock of the most popular—oh! Dear heavens! I quite see where the mistake has been made!"

There was the scrabble of wooden chair legs across the floor, as the newly solitary Lady Margaret leaped to her feet. "Mistake? There's no mistake! You've been teaching everyone how to pick locks since we got here!"

"I really do think," said Isabella, "that if you look just a *little* closer, you'll discover that each girl has before her a carriage clock of the most popular sort—the lock shape has gained popularity in Broma and Glause already due to its functional and really very pretty design. It can be locked around the utility strap, you see! Such a useful design, don't you think?"

The Yellow Aunt, her face suddenly aghast, snatched up the closest lock—which, now that Annabel looked at it with new eyes, didn't have a great many of the characteristics that might have been expected in a lock, and had quite a few of those she would have expected from a very small clock.

Lady Margaret said shrilly, "They've been changed! She's changed them by magic into clocks!"

"Miss Farrah," said the Lavender Aunt, with the coldness of absolute annoyance, "does not perform magic."

Despite that, she passed the carriage clock to her sister, who, Annabel had learned, was the more competent magic user of the two. The Yellow Aunt looked at it closely, though she did so with a certain grimness that suggested she didn't expect anything from the examination.

At last, she gave it back to the Lavender Aunt and said, "It is merely a carriage clock. Nothing more and nothing less. Lady Margaret, I believe we have some matters to discuss, if you would be good enough to accompany us."

She turned and sailed majestically back the way she had come, followed by her two footmen, who were now grinning. Lady Margaret, her face patchily white and red, followed her in a stiff kind of way through a channel of entirely silent, watching faces.

The Yellow Aunt paused only long enough to say, "It would behove you, Miss Farrah, to be very careful," before she emulated her sister and stalked magnificently away through the same door she had entered. Fern wandered innocently behind her, winking at the footmen who closed the door; and at the other door, another girl was doing the same.

Isabella gave them the slightest of nods. In tandem, they opened their doors a crack and settled themselves comfortably with an eye to that crack with all the comfortable familiarity of long practise. Isabella, rising, stood again before the cleanly swept fireplace and smiled at them all.

"Thus ends the first lesson," she said. "How to tell the difference between a lock style carriage clock and an actual lock. Very well done, all of you. Top marks to all the class."

"What?" said someone blankly.

Someone else giggled.

Annabel laughed and shook her head, more to clear the buzzing than from disbelief, and the buzzing faded. With it faded feeling and sight, and Annabel fell into dark coolness that was more welcome than hot reality.

"Nan? Nan?"

"Ow," said Annabel, aware first and foremost of a pain in her forehead, and then more slowly of far too much warmth around her. "Who hit me?"

"You hit your own head," Isabella told her. "Face-first into the floor—it was very graceful. Do you think you could open your eyes, Nan?"

"Good grief," Annabel said, opening her eyes. The buzzing in her ears was gone, and the reason she was far too hot was because she was being carried by Dannick, whose chest and arms seemed to fairly radiate heat. "Did I faint? Why?"

Isabella's face was decidedly stormy. "One can only presume a lack of sustenance. Through here, Dannick."

"Miss Farrah, I *really* don't think—"

"You can stay with us if you fancy we're liable to dig through Melchior's things," offered Isabella. "We're not, but you might as well make yourself useful and make us some tea. Oh! And some biscuits!"

"I thought you said you weren't going to dig through his things," Dannick said, and went even pinker when Isabella laughed in delight.

"That's no way to treat your future monarch!" she said. "Nan just fainted from lack of sustenance, and you want to keep such paltry things from her as a few of Melchior's biscuits?"

"Why are we in Melchior's room?" protested Annabel. Dannick put her down in one of the red chairs and wandered away—presumably in search of biscuits and tea—and she tried to recapture the sense that her head actually belonged to her.

"Because I want a few words with him!" Isabella said, in a martial sort of a way.

"So do I, but mostly I want food."

Firmly, Isabella said, "Both are to be had here. I won't see the Meal Matron starving you so that you faint, and I would like to know what Melchior's about to let it happen."

"It's probably more the Deportment Master's fault," Annabel muttered. "He's the one who keeps making sure I can't breathe."

"A change of maids is in order, one feels," Isabella said. "How do you think that girl Jess would feel about doing your corsets?"

"Does she *know* how to lace corsets?"

"Very likely not, but she can sit down to a nice cup of tea while I lace them. So long as we have the appearance of respectability, there's no need to have the real thing, I think."

"That should be your motto," Annabel said.

Across the room, there was a muffled sound from Dannick. His back was to them, but Annabel was quite certain she had seen those broad shoulders shaking for the briefest moment.

"Are you quite well, Dannick?" enquired Isabella. "Shall I help you with the tea things?"

"It's nothing, miss," said Dannick.

"Was it not? Are you sure?"

"Perhaps he feels, as I do, that two young ladies shouldn't be discussing their corsets in front of him," said Melchior's voice.

"Oh," said Isabella, with a distinct lack of cordiality. "There you are."

One of Melchior's brows went up. "I trust you're glad to see me, Nan?"

"Yes," said Annabel, who still felt as though it was a little too hard to raise enthusiasm for anything but a cup of tea.

Melchior's other brow went up. "Perhaps I'm unnaturally quick," he remarked, "but I'm catching the sense that neither of you is particularly happy to see me. May I remind you both that this is, in fact, my own room? What is it this time?"

"Miss Ammett fainted," said Dannick. Annabel didn't think she imagined the less-than-cordial tones with which he said it.

"Miss Ammett," continued Isabella, with even greater coldness than Dannick, "has been refused a full serving at every meal. *Naturally* she fainted, with the heat!"

"Nan?" Melchior said sharply. "What is this about?"

"Why are you asking me?" Annabel said tiredly.

"Really, Melchior!" remonstrated Isabella. "I thought better of you!"

"Pardon?" Melchior said blankly. "What do you think I've got to do with it?"

Annabel stared at him. "It's no good pretending you don't know about it."

Melchior, who looked as annoyed as Annabel had seen him for a very long time, drew in a deep breath through his nose and said, "Nan, I'd like to know exactly why I'm to be suspected of depriving you of food to the extent that you fainted!"

"The Awesome Aunts said the orders came from you."

"The Awesome Aunts are misinformed!" snapped Melchior, "And I still take great exception to being accused of causing you to faint! Dannick, you may go!"

"How was I supposed to know that?" Annabel asked indignantly, finding the strength to sit up in the midst of that indignation. "And you can't just tell Dannick to go!"

As Dannick left, his shoulders hunched as if to avoid the disagreement, Melchior said coldly, "I believe I can; it is my suite, after all, Nan! And as to how you were supposed to know—well, one imagines that one's oldest friend knows one a little better than that!"

Annabel, automatically accepting a cup of tea and two biscuits from Isabella, felt that her appearance of righteous indignation had been disturbed. She said vigorously, "The Awesome Aunts *said*—"

"Nan, if you tell me just *once* more what the Awesome Aunts said—!" Melchior stopped, and pinched the bridge of his nose between his fingers. "No one at the school knows I'm your guardian, and I assure you that there have been no letters to the manor. They couldn't have got my permission!"

"Oh," said Annabel. She ate one of her biscuits, pondering this, and then pointed out, "Yes, but you said I could stand to miss a few meals, too, so I really think—"

"*When* did I?" demanded Melchior; and then, goaded, "Are you throwing up something I said to you when we were in the castle?"

"It wasn't *that* long ago," Annabel protested. "And I haven't got much thinner!"

"Let me make two things perfectly clear, Nan," said Melchior. "When I said you could do with a few less meals, it wasn't a comment on your weight: it was an objection to the way you were using eating as an excuse."

"Oh," said Annabel, in a small voice. That, as far as it went, wasn't so far from the truth. She *had* used it as a defence of sorts. *I'm too fat to do this. I'm too big to do that.*

Melchior's eyes narrowed on her. "That," he said, as if he perfectly understood exactly what she was thinking, "and that thing you do where you make a wall out of it. *No one can hurt me if I've got a nice bit of padding.* That sort of thing. Don't think I didn't see it."

"What's the second thing?"

"Pardon?"

"You said there were two things," Annabel said. She'd prefer more time to think over the first. "What's the other one?"

"Yes, what *is* the other thing?" demanded Isabella, her eyes sparkling. She had been watching them avidly, and now she blinked demurely at Melchior. "*Do* tell, Melchior!"

"Nan, did you have to bring the Firebrand with you?"

"I believe I did the bringing," Isabella pointed out.

"With Dannick's help, anyway."

"Besides, it would be shocking for a female student to be alone in the sitting room of one of the male masters," Isabella said, even more demurely. "What is the other thing, Melchior?"

"Never you mind," Melchior retorted. "Out, Firebrand; out! I've another lesson to prepare, and Nan needs quiet."

Annabel hadn't meant to grin, but it happened anyway. "It won't matter if you don't prepare," she said. "They'll hang on your every word anyway."

"I'll have a word with Miss Cornett," Melchior said, refusing to acknowledge the jibe. "I won't have them starving you. And you—Firebrand! Make sure they don't lace Nan's corsets too tight. It's unhealthy."

"We ought to cover our ears," Isabella said confidentially to Annabel. "Shall you begin screaming first, or shall I?"

"Miss Cornett says we ought to cover our ears and scream if a male begins to talk about undergarments in our presence," Annabel said to a very startled Melchior.

"I conclude that it's entirely acceptable for young ladies to talk about undergarments in the presence of footmen, however!" Melchior said sourly, when he had recovered a little. "I'll thank you not to put ideas into Nan's head, Firebrand!"

"Well! Of all the ingratitude!" gasped Isabella. "I'll have you know, Melchior, that I am *entirely* responsible for the blue ensemble in which Annabel is currently attired!"

Melchior's brows went up again for the briefest moment. "In that case, Firebrand, I unreservedly apologise."

"There was nothing wrong with my clothes before this!" protested Annabel.

This time, it was Isabella who was firm. "Yes, there was. It's no use arguing with me. At any rate, it disguises exactly how tight—or otherwise—your corsets are done, which is advantageous to us. Very well, Nan; you remain where you are. I've other matters to attend to in any case—I'm sure Melchior will make sure you're taken care of."

Annabel meant to protest, but found that she didn't have the desire to do so. "All right," she said. At Melchior, she added, "But if you expect me to do anything, I'm going to faint again."

❧ 12 ❧

Annabel wasn't sure exactly what else Melchior did than talk to Miss Cornett, but she was certain he did something else. Certainly Miss Cornett, with her nervous flutterings, couldn't have produced the distinct appearance of deflation with which the Deportment Master conducted his lesson the next day. She mentioned as much to Isabella at lunch time, which was served with the normal pink napkins again, and was surprised to see Isabella consider the idea seriously.

"I wouldn't be quite so sure, Nan," Isabella said thoughtfully. "Miss Cornett is a surprising thing. She always seems as though she's on the brink of a nervous collapse, but she can be occasionally savage when one least expects it."

"Really?" asked Annabel doubtfully. "All right, I suppose you know better. At any rate, wasn't it nice not to have the Master shrieking *Tighter! Pull it tighter!* all through the beginning of the lesson?"

"Not to mention real breakfast and real lunch," agreed Isabella. "Which reminds me, Nan; what do you think about establishing a food bank for Blue Napkin students? We meant to establish a stash in the library, after all, but I quite forgot!"

"Absolutely not!" said Melchior's voice.

Annabel jumped, but Isabella only gazed up at him innocently.

"Are you serving some punishment, Melchior? Presiding at breakfast *and* lunch! Dear me!"

"Be a little less free with my name, if you please, Firebrand," Melchior said warningly. "And it's nothing of the sort. I'll be presiding over the dining hall tonight as well."

"You're making sure my napkins really are pink," said Annabel, feeling pleased and content in spite of the fact that the heat was even worse today than it had been yesterday.

"Believe it or not, Nan, there are reasons for the things I do that don't have directly to do with you."

"Really?" asked Isabella. "What would they be? We're *very* curious, Melchior!"

"Very curious," Annabel agreed, refusing to feel slighted. The girls around the dining hall were watching in mingled curiosity and jealousy as Melchior lingered by their table, and that struck her as dangerous attention to have. "Belle, do you think we should go now?"

"Very wise," nodded Isabella. "Come along, Nan; we've work to do."

"Work?" Melchior was suddenly very alert. "What work?"

"Study, of course," Annabel said.

At the same time, Isabella said, "Dressmaking."

They exchanged a glance. Melchior looked between the two of them and opened his mouth.

"Off we go," said Annabel firmly, pulling Isabella away by the elbow. "Oh! And don't talk to us at the dinner table, Melchior. The other girls notice and it's annoying."

"Annoying—!" began Melchior in outrage, but the girls were already half way down the dining hall.

"Oh, well done, Nan," Isabella said in a congratulatory, albeit hushed, manner. "Wasn't he annoyed! You're doing awfully well, I think."

"I thought so," agreed Annabel, very pleased with herself. "All right, we'd best be off to lessons, I suppose. Or is there somewhere else we actually need to be right now?"

"I'm sure I gave you a schedule, Nan."

"I shouldn't have to read my own schedule," Annabel said, putting her nose in the air. "That's what I've got you for."

Isabella giggled. "You've had one victory over Melchior and run mad with the heady success! We haven't a class until Elegant Elementaries of Ensorcellment; until then, we're free to enjoy Interim Activities."

"You want to poke around, then," said Annabel, unsurprised.

"Certainly I do. Alice has been busy—I told her we'd look at whatever was happening inside the school, and she was quite pleased with that because she's focusing on something outside the school. I've got a few other girls looking around the school in general, but the fourth floor is all ours."

"Do you suppose it's Lady Caro who's set it around the school that I'm not really the queen heir?"

"More than likely," Isabella said. "But a rumour like that doesn't spread well without a bit of encouragement. I believe I would like to know who helped it spread. The Deportment Master, obviously—"

"Obviously."

"But I'm quite curious to know if it was Miss Cornett or the Aunts who really gave it wings. Lady Caro wouldn't spread a rumour like that without reason—she may dislike me, but she's clever enough to know who to support, and in this case, that person is you."

"So there's still something important we don't know," Annabel concluded gloomily.

"Exactly so," said Isabella. "However, the more we know, the closer we come to discovering exactly what that thing is. All the known things start to cast the not known thing into relief, after which it becomes much easier to tell what the not known thing is. And I've a feeling that the relief-work bit is about to become a lot clearer. Let us make a nuisance of ourselves today, Nan."

Annabel was perfectly agreeable to making a nuisance of herself now that she was properly fed, but it did strike her that it would be more enjoyable to make a nuisance of herself in the nominally cooler halls of Trenthams than wandering the gardens in the sun. She said as much to Isabella, in a less than cordial tone of voice, but although Isabella said, "Yes, perfectly horrid, isn't it?" she said it in a cheerful tone of voice and showed no sign of either slowing her brisk walk or moving to one of the shaded walks. Annabel was inclined to resent this until she saw that Isabella's eyes were directed up toward the school windows more often than the walk she was engaged upon, though she was careful not to tilt her head and give away as much.

"Who are we trying to see through the windows?" she asked. "That girl who arrived?"

"Naturally," said Isabella, nodding. "Why else would we be outdoors on such a horrid day when there's nothing to be gained from exercise but a headache?"

"I suppose your pet first year girls told you they'd seen something," Annabel said, with one eye on Isabella.

Isabella looked slightly guilty, but grinned. "Well, but Nan! There are three or four of them who simply *love* climbing trees! You have no idea! So why not put such skills to good use?"

"When did they tell you?"

"Just before lunch," Isabella said. "I would have told you sooner, but you pick things up so quickly that it's fun getting you to guess. Besides, Melchior was prowling and trying to listen. We'll have to be careful at dinner if he's going to be presiding again."

"Ye-es," said Annabel, rather slowly. "Belle, those windows are the ones that belong to the suite you wanted to have, aren't they?"

Isabella narrowed her eyes at them. "Well, I never!" she said. "The absolute cheek of it! They've put that secretive guest in our suite, Nan!"

"Rude, isn't it?" asked Annabel, enjoying herself just a little again, despite the heat. Her face was far too hot and her corseted waist felt as though it was slowly cooking, but Isabella's outraged face was too amusing to allow her to dwell on the discomfort. "The Awesome Aunts are taking their revenge on you, Belle!"

"What nonsense is this?" Isabella murmured to herself. "I was sure it would make things clearer, but this only makes things more confusing. What are they playing at?"

"Not croquet, anyway," Annabel said, skipping nimbly out of the way of a croquet ball that bounced through the hedges and would have clipped her ankle. "How rude. Where did that come from?"

"Gangway!" shouted a voice from the other side of the hedge, as an approaching hat bobbed up and down above the hedge.

"Much good that does!" said Isabella in amusement. "It would have already taken out an ankle by the time we heard any warning."

"Oh! Is there someone there?" called the bobbing hat. There was a shaking of foliage and the muttered complaints of the voice as its owner was scratched in her attempts to push through the hedge, then a young lady of about their own age tumbled through onto the path, hat first, and brushed herself down.

Her name was Gwyn, if Annabel remembered correctly; she had been in one of the first groups of girls who came to see Annabel on that first day of receiving visitors. Then, she had looked from Annabel to Isabella in narrow-eyed appraisal.

Now, she looked at them in undisguised surprise. "Miss Farrah! Miss Ammett! I expected you both to be in the school!"

"We occasionally take the air," murmured Isabella. "If it comes to that, Gwyn, I'm surprised to see you on the croquet field. I thought you didn't care for it."

"Oh well," said Gwyn, shrugging elegantly to remove a clinging leaf from the hedge, "we're just trying to get a look in the windows on the fourth floor. That's why the croquet ball keeps going astray."

"Are you?" Annabel asked, in undisguised surprise.

"Goodness me!" said Isabella, much more languidly. "That seems like an odd thing to be doing!"

"I thought that's what you were doing, too," Gwyn protested. "How else are we to get a look at her before breakfast tomorrow if they won't let us visit her?"

"Her?" Isabella's tone was, if possible, even more languid.

"Haven't you heard?" Gwyn's face was the picture of astonishment. "But you hear *everything* first!"

Annabel tried very hard not to giggle, because Isabella had gone almost imperceptibly stiff. "Who is it that you're trying to see?" she asked, since Isabella seemed to have been deprived of words in one fell swoop.

"It's the Queen!" Gwyn confided, leaning closer but speaking more loudly. Annabel had the feeling she enjoyed telling Isabella something the other girl didn't know. "The queen heir, I mean! She's just now arrived!"

For a moment, Annabel nearly laughed at the absurdity of it. Was Gwyn attempting, in this singularly ridiculous way, to try and trick her into an admission of being the queen heir? Not even one of the less clever girls in the younger classes would do that.

"I didn't see anyone arrive today," she said, but now all she could think about was the girl she had seen exiting Lady Caro's room two nights ago, the stickiness that had clung to Lady Caro's clique for the past two days. According to Gwyn, the supposed queen heir was in the very room she had just seen the mysterious girl. Coolly, she added, "I haven't heard anyone arrive since we've been out in the garden, either."

"Not *exactly* just now," Gwyn corrected herself. "But two nights ago. Just think! The queen heir at Trenthams for real!"

"I beg your pardon?" Isabella said, at last. "You are saying that the *queen heir* arrived two nights ago?"

"You must have heard the fuss!"

"Goodness me!" said Isabella, losing that tiny edge of stiffness completely. "Fancy that, Nan!"

"Fancy!" said Annabel for the first time in her life, and with something of a hollowness to her voice. She didn't want to be queen—she had never wanted to be queen—but there was something very odd about her stomach suddenly. Something that said although she hadn't wanted it, it was her responsibility. And something that said it was very odd for another potential queen to turn up at Trenthams exactly when Melchior and Annabel were both there.

"And we were certain it was you!" Gwyn turned her look of sugary surprise on Annabel. "Who can have set such a rumour around, I wonder! We're *so* very sorry!"

"Now this," said Isabella, her grey eyes sparkling, "is more like it! Come along, Nan! We're going to go see the queen."

"You'll find it hard to get in to see her!" Gwyn called after them. Her voice was a mix of spite and disappointed surprise; she had obviously hoped for a bigger reaction from both of the girls. "She's not accepting all callers, you know!"

Annabel found herself being dragged along the path by the force of Isabella's arm, skinny and determined, crooked through her own. "Why are we—shouldn't we tell Melchior that the girl is pretending to be the queen heir?"

"Why should Melchior have all the fun?" demanded Isabella.

That struck Annabel as a perfectly just sentiment. She said, "Yes! Why should he! He's been awful for weeks. Let him find out for himself."

"Exactly so!" said Isabella nodding. "And he probably already knows—if he didn't know from the very start."

"Oh bother!" Annabel said in disgust. "He probably does."

"I'm more astonished at myself, quite honestly. It seems perfectly obvious now; the Aunts and their *Miss Ammett*ing lately, not to mention the suite, and a hundred other things!"

"Yes," said Annabel, feeling disgruntled. She felt that she should have put the clues together much better. "How annoying! And Melchior—"

"Never mind about Melchior. At least you can be casually knowledgeable if he brings it up."

"*If* he brings it up," remarked Annabel darkly. "All right, who is this person pretending to be me? Let's go find her."

"That's the spirit! Goodness! You look perfectly warlike!"

"I feel perfectly warlike," said Annabel. It was very surprising. "I didn't spend weeks running around a castle having my life threatened and being tested as the next queen just to have someone else pop up without taking the trouble of a test."

"They must have something," Isabella said thoughtfully. "Something that makes them think it safe to bring out a pretender right now."

"Yes," said Annabel. "Because it would be stupid to turn up without something that looks like the staff."

"More importantly, they wouldn't turn up without the support of at least four influential families. I do wonder how long Lady Caro knew about this."

"Why is that more important?"

"Because a staff can be faked—"

"I don't think it can, you know."

"And even if it can't—well, get the support of enough families, and everyone will politely overlook the lack of a staff. No one, in fact, will even mention it. I hope you're prepared to use the staff if necessary."

Annabel, who hadn't in fact thought about it, found herself saying, and with some decidedness, "Yes."

"Very good. Now, Nan, who do you suppose is behind this latest outrage?"

"Do you know," said Annabel thoughtfully, "the first thing I thought was that it was probably the Old Parrasians?"

Isabella nodded. "That's as a good a guess as any, given the fact that we've mostly dealt with Old Parrasians; but it would be a bit odd for Old Parrasians to want a queen on the throne, don't you think?"

"That's the bit I'm not sure about," Annabel said. "But so far as we can tell, all the fingers in this pie have been Old Parrasian ones. And isn't it awfully handy for the real queen heir to disappear just as another one comes along? The only other real option is that some of the powerful families have gotten a bit too used to being powerful and don't like the idea of giving up power when a queen comes along. Perhaps they've been using the Old Parrasians to do their dirty work."

"That's more likely," Isabella said, nodding. "And they're so awfully clique-y in the old families! If enough of them agreed to something like this, they'd probably think it worth trying."

"Some of the clique-y families have hidden Old Parrasian roots, too," said Annabel, unwilling to give up on her own idea. "At any rate, it's rude to be putting pretend queen heirs in the school while I'm here."

"*So* impolite."

"Yes," said Annabel, grinning suddenly. "Accepting sham queens isn't the sort of behaviour you expect from a school like Trenthams. And giving her *our* suite, too!"

"I knew you'd see it my way," Isabella said, with a very small, sparkling smile. "Goodness, no wonder the girls have become so unbearable over these last couple of days! They won't just be trying to put you down, either; they'll be trying to put me down now that there's a chance to prove I've picked the wrong side."

Annabel looked at her curiously. "Aren't you used to that sort of thing?"

"Goodness, yes! In this place factions form over which breakfast settings are allowed to be used by which families. That's not what I meant. I meant that you might find the pushback to be stronger than if you'd been by yourself; it might have been easier for you if I'd not shown my outright support. I honestly didn't consider such an eventuality. This will do me such a lot of good in terms of personal growth, don't you think?"

"I don't mind hissing and spitting," said Annabel, ignoring Isabella's last, cheerful pronouncement. Nasty words and disgusted looks didn't much disturb her—no one who had been friends with Peter since childhood could be affected by something as insubstantial as words. She had once thought that was because of the comfortable layer of flesh she had worn for so long, but she was beginning to understand that it was a strength built somewhere much deeper within her than that. It made her wonder, suddenly, how it was that Melchior managed to get under her skin so easily these days.

"All right, then; what should we do about this? We need a real plan —not just going to see the Pretender and seeing what we can find out, I mean."

Annabel stopped short. "Ah. I didn't think of that."

"Of course not. You're merely annoyed—perfectly understandable. Did you know, by the way, that you haven't been walking toward the school building?"

"My subconscious must be smarter than I am," Annabel said, beginning to laugh. "Oh well, since we're out here now, we might as well sit down and work out a plan. I suppose you've already got a few ideas?"

"Of course!" said Isabella cheerfully. "I wouldn't be much of an advisor if I wasn't prepared for most situations, would I? Let's hatch a little bit of reverse-treason, shall we?"

"I suppose," said Annabel thoughtfully, a little later, as they sat beneath a conveniently shady tree, "at least we know why everything was just a *little* bit late when we first got here."

"Indeed," Isabella agreed. Her grey eyes were reflective and thoughtful, and Annabel was quite certain that whatever she herself was thinking, Isabella was thinking of that and something else as well. "Which is somewhat worrisome, given the sheer amount of instances in which Trenthams staff have been just a little bit late about doing things. They wanted to be sure they had a foot in the door if things went your way, but they weren't very certain things *would* go your way, and—good heavens! Miss Cornett!"

"Pardon?" Annabel asked blankly.

"How awful! I've maligned her!"

Annabel frowned. Isabella might be irreverent, facetious, and entirely concerned with how the world affected her own affairs—or at least, the affairs of her little papa—but she was usually careful to make sure she didn't actually mock any of the teachers.

"When?"

"Well, not aloud, but I did think she came to see you to be a hanger-on—she probably knew I thought so, too. It must have been very hard for her."

"You mean she didn't?"

"She's an odd, fluttery thing, and she can be ridiculous, but she does have a very strong sense of right and wrong. I suppose she knew about this and she was showing her solidarity in the only way she could."

"Oh!" said Annabel. "That's rather nice."

"Yes." Isabella looked vexed. "Goodness me, it really is a salutary year for me! Wrong more than once in the first term!"

Since Annabel was quite well aware by now that this was merely Isabella's way of mocking herself when she was particularly annoyed at her own hubris, she didn't point out that Isabella was, in fact, often wrong. Isabella was very well aware of that.

"Are we really going to see the other one?" she asked.

"Do you not want to go?"

"No," said Annabel. "I want to go. But I keep thinking that we've been scrambling behind everything since we started out to get here—Melchior, Raoul, the new girl. I want to do a bit of research first."

"When you say research—"

"Yes. I want to break into the Records Office."

"That should give us a good idea of things." Isabella looked very satisfied. "Although, I feel I should warn you that it's likely to get us both caught and expelled. Even I have never made it into the Records Office—and not, I should like to point out, from lack of trying!"

"That's all right," Annabel said, grinning her own satisfaction. "I've never actually *shown* you what the staff can do, have I?"

"How exciting!" Isabella said. "I've been wanting to ask you for a demonstration ever since we were in the alley with the Old Parrasians, but I thought that was too frivolous, even for me. Do go ahead."

"Not here," said Annabel. "There. At the Records Office. Actually, probably in the room next door. No one will see us if we're in there, will they?"

"There are two rooms by the Records Office, one on either side. There's the teachers' tea room, and the Awesome Aunts' main office. The Awesome Aunts' office is probably the safest—they only use it when they meet with parents and Important People."

"All right," Annabel said. "We'll use that one, then."

"Shall we? I daresay you're right, but I find myself wondering exactly how you're planning on spiriting us through a good foot of solid masonry and into the next room."

"You'll see," said Annabel. "All right, take me to the Awesome Aunts' office."

Annabel could see the questions fairly bubbling on Isabella's lips by the time they got to the Awesome Aunts' office. She would have liked to have drawn out the moment a little longer, enjoying the rare sensation of displaying an ability utterly beyond Isabella's skill set, but Isabella was so honestly interested that she didn't have the heart to show off.

Instead, as she had always done in the Castle, Annabel sat cross-legged on the floor, digging for the pencil staff and her small note-book. This one was a new notebook, a present from Melchior at the start of the year, but it had already begun to feel fat and comfortable in her hand when she picked it up. Peter had given her other note-books, too, but somehow she had always liked the feel of the ones she got from Melchior better, and they'd filled more quickly than the ones from Peter.

Now, in contrast to the last few sketches, which had been sketched with a normal pencil, and would only ever remain drawings, Annabel took up her pencil staff and started on a sketch that began to exist as she drew it. She drew a door; a simple, elegant, *useful* door in the wall opposite her, dwelling thoughtfully on the mason-work that Isabella said was between the two rooms. If they had to get through masonry, there would need to be a door-frame in heavy, sculpted stone-work, fitted together beautifully and casting deep shadows on the slender door it contained.

"Good heavens!" said Isabella, her eyes turning in wonder from the drawing, to the wall, and back to the drawing.

Annabel didn't look up, because she already knew what she would see if she did. "You can open it, in a minute," she said, circling a door-knob with shadow and light. "I don't know what will be on the other side, though, so be careful. If there's a bookcase, you could knock down a few books. If there are any breakable things, well..."

"Certainly," said Isabella, in fascination. "Oh! Are you finished?"

"Yes," Annabel said, and shut her notebook around the pencil staff. She would have to erase the door later—in a hurry, if anything went wrong—and she didn't want to have to flip for it. The door was there ahead of her, just as it had been on the page. Once, she had felt a potent mix of excitement and fear whenever she saw something she had drawn come to life. These days, Annabel merely felt a sense of satisfaction. "You might as well open it."

"Shall I?" Isabella sounded dubious, but her hand was already reaching out.

Annabel grinned. Isabella could never have resisted that urge, even if Annabel hadn't said anything.

The other girl turned the doorknob with one careful, precise movement of her wrist, and pushed gently at the boards. The door moved, but heavily, and Isabella said, "Ooof! It's heavy! Perhaps it's a bookcase after all, Nan! How odd!"

"Actually, that happens fairly often when I don't know what's in a room," Annabel said, matter-of-factly. "And it is a Records Office, after all. There are bound to be account books somewhere."

"What a fortunate thing the staff wasn't entrusted to me!" Isabella said frankly. She slipped through the door and gazed around her. "Good heavens, what I couldn't do with something like that!"

"The staff is all right," Annabel said, stepping through carefully into the Records Office after Isabella. As a matter of fact, she was very fond of the staff; sometimes it felt more like a pet than an inanimate object. "It wasn't much fun running around in the castle to get away from Mordion, though."

She turned a brief circle in the Records Office, taking in the two full walls of filing cabinets, and the shelving that framed the real door with tiny wooden hutches, each hutch containing something small and knicknacky that was different for each hutch. The wall they had entered by was indeed a wall of bookcases, but nothing there looked very interesting unless accounting was a subject of particular passion.

Isabella followed suit, and turned a complete circle. "Look on the bright side, Nan," she said, with a lingering look at the pigeon-holed and slightly chalky wall. "At least it meant you were able to turn Melchior back into a human."

"Not to mention giving the country a queen heir again," added Annabel, irresistibly amused by the order of importance Isabella assigned to the business. "Though I suppose Melchior is happier as a man than a cat, so it's not all bad."

Isabella carefully closed the door after them both and asked curiously, "Do you really miss Blackfoot that much?"

"Oh, well..." Annabel trailed away. Isabella so rarely said what she expected her to say. "Not as much as I used to, but more lately. Melchior is being difficult all the time, and even when he was sharp as Blackfoot, at least he was always *there*. He doesn't lie to me anymore—actually, I don't think he's lied to me since then, even a little bit—but he's still tricky about what he does and doesn't say."

"I can't help feeling that Melchior is being a bit too clever for himself," murmured Isabella. "What do you think, Nan; where shall we start?"

"The filing cabinets, I suppose."

"What exactly are you hoping to find?"

"I don't know," Annabel said, "but I keep wondering—if *she's* here, how have they got her filed? I mean, what did they say about her as a student—where did she come from? What are their instructions regarding her? Or is she not in the filing system at all?"

"If it comes to that, I'm curious to know how they've filed you," Isabella said. "I should think they had the same problem with you."

"Oh," said Annabel again. "Belle, I've just thought—what's her name? The Pretender, I mean?"

"Good heavens," said Isabella, and giggled. "Now that *is* something of a problem, isn't it? Fortunately for us, the filing cabinets seem to be organised by year, and then alphabetically—it will take us a little longer, but I'm sure we'll find it. Why don't you look for hers?"

"Why, what are you doing?"

"Looking for ours, of course!" Isabella said irrepressibly.

She was as good as her word; Annabel was still searching through the second filing cabinet for any sign of an unfamiliar name when Isabella found the second of two files and sat down in a corner with every appearance of impish amusement. Annabel might have complained if she hadn't come across an interesting name herself the next moment.

"Belle?"

"Mm?"

"Do we have a Lady Selma Morton at Trenthams?"

"Dear me!" said Isabella thoughtfully. "We don't! More interestingly, neither New Civet nor Parras has a Morton title attached to any of its nobles."

"Isn't that a bit dangerous?" asked Annabel, pulling the file out. It was very slim—slimmer even than the one Isabella was currently reading, which had Annabel's own name on it. "Wouldn't it be very easy for people to discover that?"

"Not at all," promptly replied Isabella. "There's nothing easier than creating Old Parrasian nobles, Nan! It's not particularly successful with me, since I've a rather more detailed source of information than most people, but it should be enough for anyone else."

"A detailed—what, Luck? Does he care about nobles?"

"Not particularly," said Isabella, "but he does have a library with a few one of a kind books in it that have been tampered with. He used to give me access to his library in exchange for looking after Onepiece once in a while when he and Poly first got married."

"When you say *one of a kind*—"

"Oh, nothing magical," Isabella told her, beckoning her forward so that they could both look at the Lady Selma file. "They've just been, well, *tampered* with."

"I would have thought that would make them less useful rather than more useful," said Annabel, settling herself down next to Isabella. "But that's just me. Look, her file is even thinner than mine."

"Very suspicious," agreed Isabella. "The books are useful, Nan, because of *who* it is that tampered with them."

"All right, who tampered with them?"

"Nobody knows for sure," said Isabella. She added, frankly, "Well, nobody who is willing to share it with me, at any rate. I have an idea that Poly and Luck know who it is, and from a few things Melchior has said, I gather there's somebody altering tiny pieces of the past to help shape *now* in the way it's meant to be shaped."

"I didn't think it was possible to travel in time," Annabel said. "At first, anyway. Peter said it was impossible and he's usually right about things like that. But then we got caught in the castle and when it spat us back out, there we were, three years in the past. If someone has been meddling in the past, Peter will want to know about it. Oh! Perhaps that's what he's doing at the moment. Melchior wouldn't tell me."

"That's probably why Poly and Luck don't talk about it much. At any rate, in Luck's library are the only books in the Two Monarchies that someone has altered, at the time they were written, to include correct information—and clues about mysterious happenings that should certainly happen."

Annabel giggled. "Are you sure it wasn't Luck himself? It sounds like the sort of thing he'd do—he's always dropping hints. Oh! Well, if it comes to that, it's right up Rorkin's alley, too!"

Isabella sighed enviously. "I do envy you, Nan! You've even met Rorkin!"

"You shouldn't," Annabel said bluntly. "He's even worse than Luck to understand. I only like him because he seems to like me, otherwise I wouldn't like him at all."

"That's an odd reason to like someone," remarked Isabella. "However, since I'm never sure whether Raoul likes or loathes me, I shouldn't speak too loudly. I don't think this file will be terribly useful, Nan; it's bare bones and not very interesting bones at that."

"At least we know her name is Lady Selma Morton," Annabel said. "For what that's worth!"

"It's information worth having, if only for the fact that we know she's a Pretender noble as well as a pretender queen heir. I'm very much afraid, Nan, that the investigating of Lady Selma Morton's real antecedents will fall to Melchior's lot—I have a few connections, but none that will be useful for this sort of questioning. It's the sort of questioning I usually do on my own behalf, but I fancy we won't have the chance to ask around New Civet about a newly minted Lady Selma."

"Bother," said Annabel gloomily. "Oh well, I suppose that's all right. I want to talk to Melchior anyway."

"Should you talk to him just yet, do you think, Nan? Shouldn't you like to have some more information first?"

"I don't think so," said Annabel decidedly, climbing to her feet once again. "I'm certain he's not going to tell me anything; but I want to give him the chance to tell me before I find out what I can from elsewhere."

"In that case, I approve," Isabella said. She rose and dusted herself delicately, and replaced the files she had purloined just as delicately. "Shall we meet once again when class begins? I believe you're right; we can achieve more each alone."

Annabel wasn't entirely sure how much she could achieve alone, but she had the feeling that for this interview with Melchior at least, she would prefer Isabella not to be present. She was quite sure she wouldn't be successful in getting information out of Melchior, and she was even more certain that she preferred to be without witness to her failure.

❧ 13 ❧

Melchior wasn't in his room when she got there, so Annabel sat down near enough to the window to be able to see what was happening outside without being seen herself through the window. It was the stable side of the school, so it wasn't likely that any of the girls who were trying to peep through the Pretender's windows would see her, but she would rather not take that chance while she was visiting Melchior. On the other hand, it also meant there was little for Annabel to see in the way of alleviating boredom; the occasional footman wandered briefly between the cover of the stable roof and the covered carriageway, and Annabel once caught sight of Alice flitting around the stables—delivering a message to Dannick?—but there was otherwise very little to see.

Annabel left the window and was making herself a cup of tea by the time Melchior got back. He didn't seem surprised to see her in his room, though Annabel thought his face might have brightened.

"Making yourself at home, Nan?" he asked.

"What's yours is mine," Annabel said. "Didn't you know?"

"That includes the biscuits, does it?"

"Especially the biscuits," Annabel averred. "They don't give us these lovely gingery ones at tea; I don't think they're high class enough for the richer girls, and they're far too big to be dainty finger food."

"I wasn't aware that ginger was such a plebeian root," said Melchior. "Oh, are you making a cup for me as well? How kind of you."

Annabel, pouring another cup, shrugged. "I might as well. If we're going to be talking back and forth, we might as well have something to drink."

"I suppose you're here about the Pretender," said Melchior, surprising her a great deal by cutting directly to the chase.

Annabel's eyes opened very wide. She didn't resist when Melchior, smiling faintly, took his teacup out of her hands. At last, she said, "You already knew about this, didn't you?"

"If I remember correctly," Melchior said, with a curl of his thin lips that Annabel found far too sarcastic—or perhaps mocking—for her taste, "we were together when we saw her."

"Yes, but I want to know exactly how you *knew* to see her," Annabel retorted, sitting down again. "It's all very well to say that we were together, but it's very unlike you to be sneaking around the halls without a very good reason for being exactly where you were."

"Are we always to be arguing now, Nan? I suppose you won't believe me if I reiterate once again that it was entirely by accident that I saw the Pretender, and that I didn't know her for the Pretender then?"

Annabel, remembering one of their recent, more thought-provoking conversations, tried to consider this fairly. Was there any reason why she shouldn't trust Melchior? She had trusted him since she was a child; and, except for a brief period after discovering he had been lying to her for some time, she had trusted him since escaping the castle.

"Well," she said, "if you say that you knew nothing at all about a Pretender—"

There was a thoughtful silence that Melchior didn't fill with either a confirmation or a denial. Annabel thought back to the way he had worded his statement, and her eyes narrowed.

"Well, that's rich! Telling me I don't trust you and asking me why we're always arguing, when you're very carefully *not* telling lies in a deceptive way."

"Ah, Nan!" sighed Melchior. Annabel was almost certain there was laughter in his voice, but there was a kind of solemnity to it as well. "Once you learn to be suspicious, you seem to have the dreadful knack for separating right between the bones. Very well, perhaps I knew something of a Pretender. How I knew it, however, I can't share."

"Why not?"

"I can't share that, either."

"Rude," said Annabel again, gloomily unsurprised. Isabella was right; they would have to use other means of questioning Melchior. There was certainly a lot that he wasn't telling her, and Annabel wasn't content not to know it. It wasn't that she didn't trust Melchior to tell her exactly what she needed to know; it was that she wanted to be the one to decide what she needed to know, and Melchior didn't seem to share that desire.

"All right," Annabel said, drawing a small, determined breath through her nose and setting down her teacup. "Then you'd better watch out, Melchior."

"Had I?" murmured Melchior. There was a smile lingering around his mouth, and a brightness to his eyes that Annabel hadn't seen for some time. "What will you do, Nan?"

"You'll see," she retorted. "And it will be too late to complain then, so don't regret it!"

And Melchior, with what Annabel suspected, in surprise, to be a completely sincere anticipation, said, "I look forward to it, Nan. Oh, are you going at once? You might as well finish your tea—and where else will you get a ginger biscuit the size of a saucer?"

"All right," Annabel said, careful to convey the air of one conferring a favour. "But only on account of the biscuits."

Annabel found Isabella in their library a little later. There must have been an explosives class going on, because when she slipped through the door, at least half a dozen voices yelped, "*Don't step there!*"

Annabel froze. "Delysia, is that you?"

Delysia looked up, her cheeks rosy and her curly hair free about her face. "Oh! Nan! You're just in time! Please don't step on any of the little brown buttons, though."

"What brown—good grief, I can hardly see them! What are they?"

"Button explosive!" disclosed Delysia, her eyes bright. "Such fun! I'm testing them to see how destructive they are. They don't make as big of an impact as I wanted them to make, so I was trying to strengthen them a bit and now they might be just a bit *too* strong."

"What she means by that is that we've got one less bookcase now," mentioned Isabella. She was reclining on one of the sofas, watching the class with avid interest. "Nan, I don't believe you've met our teacher, have you?"

Annabel nodded politely to the small, mousy teacher, who blushed and curtseyed.

"It's all right, Miss Farrah," said the teacher. "You can go now if you need to. I think I can stop them from blowing up anything else today. Delysia's mix is more stable than at the first, and I've prepared a few containment spells just in case."

"Very well," agreed Isabella, with surprising alacrity. "One shouldn't be late to class, after all, should one?"

"What class?" Annabel, when they were strolling down the hall together. "We don't have class for another hour."

"It's not one of those," Isabella said, with meaning.

"Don't tell me you've set up another class! Don't you have enough to do with lockpicking and explosives?"

"It's not one of those, either."

"Oh. Well, what is it, then? Who's it for?"

"You, of course," said Isabella. "I take it you have nothing from Melchior?"

"Exactly," Annabel agreed. "But I didn't expect to get much out of him—all I really wanted to know was if he was expecting something like this to happen, and he was."

Isabella nodded. "Very well. Then I think it's high time he was made to share his information. The class will commence!"

"Will it?" asked Annabel, in a fascinated voice. "When?"

"As soon as we get back to the suite," said Isabella. "Come along, Nan."

A little later, in the suite, Isabella said again, "Come along, Nan! Out of that frumpy thing and into *this*! Isn't it pretty? Isn't it light?"

Annabel looked suspiciously at the pretty froth of light blue material, and then suspiciously at Isabella. "Yes. It's very pretty. But why should I change?"

"Think of this as one of the lessons," said Isabella, shaking the froth at her persuasively. "And merely follow instructions. It will make things so much more simple, believe me!"

"Simple for whom, exactly?" Annabel asked, pointedly.

Surprising her, Isabella said, "Me, of course! If it helps, it will also make things much easier for you; but I haven't noticed that you let the easier option weigh much with you. It's one of the things I like about you. Mind you, it's also rather irritating."

"Oh, good," said Annabel. She liked to think that it was actually possible to annoy someone so unbelievably affable as Isabella. "All right, all right, I'll put it on."

"And after that, we're going to do your hair."

"Are we? Why?"

"We can't have Melchior seeing you with your hair like that."

"He's seen it a lot worse," Annabel remarked. "If it comes to that, he's just seen it. He's seen me wearing a lot worse than this dress, too."

"That doesn't at all surprise me, but it makes not one iota of difference," Isabella said firmly. "Now, isn't that more comfortable than that other awful thing?"

"Yes," Annabel agreed, pleased and surprised in equal measure. "Actually, I think I've changed my mind. It's a waste to have you as part of my ambassadorial team. You should be the head tailor."

"I suppose I could smuggle information in the clothing I made," said Isabella, as though she had given it previous thought, "but it's really more of a hobby. Enjoyable, but not enough to live by. Even dressmaking can pall, no matter how many beautiful things one makes. Do sit down, Nan. I'm quite tall, but I believe I'm not tall enough to do your hair while you're standing."

"Wait," protested Annabel, pushed down summarily at the dressing table. "I don't think I understand. Isn't this—I thought we were trying to pump Melchior for information! Are we doing something else?"

"Certainly we are pumping Melchior for information," Isabella agreed, rearranging a small, loose curl beside Annabel's ear. "However, first we will soften him for a few days. You will learn, Nan, that there are some forms of intelligence gathering that require careful attention to one's appearance."

"Yes, but that's the sort of intelligence gathering you usually do."

"And if it was anyone other than Melchior we're trying to gather it from, I would be happy to do the job," said Isabella promptly. "However, since I'm a great believer in using the tools most suited to the job...well, here you are!"

"Melchior won't tell us anything," Annabel complained. "That's exactly the reason I've been trying to think of other ways to get the information! If he didn't even tell us he was coming here, or small things like what he found out about the attack in the village, I don't see that he'll tell us anything about the Pretender, even if he does know anything."

"Don't you worry," Isabella said, turning Annabel around and closely observing her from the front. "I've a very effective method that should work wonders. Part of that method involves *not* losing your temper when you eventually begin to question him, by the way."

"Why?" Annabel asked gloomily. "Melchior only smiles when I lose my temper, anyway. It's annoying, but there's nothing else to it."

"Exactly so," Isabella said. "When you lose your temper, you stop thinking clearly. Melchior is not the kind of man around whom one can stop thinking, especially if one is trying to get something out of him that he doesn't want to give. Fortunately for us, we have a secret weapon."

Unimpressed, Annabel asked, "What secret weapon?"

"You, of course. So long as you don't lose your temper."

"Do you mean the staff?" It was there in her pocket as always, where her hand could easily fall on it for either use or reassurance. "I don't know how you expect me to use the staff on Melchior."

"Certainly not. I mean that you yourself are the secret weapon."

"That doesn't make sense. I'm not secret and I'm nothing like a weapon."

"Didn't I say that I'm a great believer in using the right tools for the right job?"

"I'm not a tool, either," muttered Annabel. "How am I the right tool for the job? All I have is the staff, and I can't go using that on Melchior."

"Good heavens, when you get an idea in your head you do follow it!" said Isabella. She sounded as though she was caught between irritation and admiration. "Nan, do forget this idea of yours that you can't accomplish anything without the staff—do! It's not at all true and it's decidedly restrictive!"

Annabel would have reminded Isabella that she had no magic and that everything she had done to date was because of the staff, but it occurred to her just in time that it wasn't quite true. More, perhaps it was even like her attitude toward her weight when she was younger— *I'm too fat for this, or too fat for that.* Just another excuse to stop her from doing what needed to be done. *I don't have magic so I can't do this. I don't have magic, so I can't do that.*

After all, Rorkin, along with a lot of things that weren't true—or perhaps they were true, Annabel had never been quite sure when it came to Rorkin—had also told her that there could have been more than one potential queen heir. The idea of the staff had been to pick between the potential heirs, and it had picked Annabel as much as she had picked it.

"All right, all right," she said. "We're not using the staff on Melchior, and I'll need to not lose my temper."

"Exactly so. I've the suspicion that Melchior will continue trying to make you lose your temper, too, so it's especially important to remember."

Annabel sighed. "All right. What else?"

"I think it would help," Isabella said, very slowly and thoughtfully, "if you were to be just as comfortable and affectionate as when Melchior was Blackfoot."

"I *was* comfortable," said Annabel gloomily. "And then Melchior started being prickly about me sitting too close or patting his head."

"I said that *you* should be comfortable," Isabella said. "I've no intention of Melchior being comfortable—in fact, I would like him to be as uncomfortable as possible."

"Wait," Annabel protested. "That is—do you mean you want me to *flirt* with him?"

"Certainly I do. What else would you do with him?"

"But—"

"It's no good saying *but* this and *but* that," Isabella said firmly. "I'm certainly not going to do it; I might joke about you having me beheaded, but I certainly don't want it to actually happen!"

"But I *can't!* It's Melchior! He'll see straight through it."

"Believe it or not, Melchior is just as prone to self delusion as the next man," said Isabella. "Or the next cat, if it comes to that."

"Yes, but I don't know how to flirt!" Annabel said, in despair. "It's not something they taught me at the village school, and it's not as if Rorkin taught me how, either!"

"Not to fear, Nan; we will begin very simply. At first, we will simply dress you a little more carefully each day, by way of leading up to it. I'm not inclined to think that it will take a great deal of acting in the actual event, and it's always best to finesse Melchior in any case. Less is more where he's concerned."

"He'll only snap at me and tell me that ladies don't lean on the backs of couches or whisper in gentlemen's ears," Annabel warned her. "I don't think he's very fond of flirting."

Isabella's grey eyes sparkled. "Well, we'll see, won't we? Remember, Nan; I said I wanted Melchior to be uncomfortable."

"Yes, but Melchior never is uncomfortable! Even when I lose my temper—"

"We are *not* going to lose our temper," Isabella said firmly. "And if it comes to that, you may very well find that you're enjoying yourself, Nan. Let me tell you that there is *nothing* more satisfying than keeping your calm while the person opposite you is becoming unsettled."

Annabel looked askance at her. "That explains so much about why you have so many enemies."

"I have so many enemies because other girls are envious of my delightful manners and fashionable clothing."

"I don't think that's it."

"Don't let's argue about unimportant things," Isabella said. "Dear me, you are a quick learner, aren't you? I won't be sidetracked—you're to flirt with Melchior, and if I have anything to say in the matter, you will flirt *very well*."

Annabel huffed out a disgusted breath, but grinned despite herself. "Getting better, aren't I?"

"I'm very proud."

"All right, but if he laughs at me, I'll want to know the reason why," Annabel warned her.

"There are very few things in life that I feel I can promise," said Isabella, with a sparkling smile. "But I believe that may be one of them. Now, listen, Nan! I want all of your attention!"

By the time the girls arrived at the dining table for breakfast the next morning, Annabel was heartily thankful that Isabella had chivvied her into spending a ridiculous amount of time in doing her hair and dressing. Not only was it another sweltering morning that the lighter frock and high hair style made easier to bear, but the halls were full of loitering girls. Some of them even muttered as Annabel and Isabella walked between them, a dark undercurrent of distrust and spite that sometimes resolved into words that surprised Annabel with their nastiness.

"Not to worry, Nan," murmured Isabella, her chin tilted easily at an unconcerned angle. "It's merely a gauntlet of words. They'll probably do it every morning for a while until they get sick of it. Aren't you glad you let me dress you properly this morning!"

Since it was exactly what she'd just been thinking, Annabel giggled.

That small token of amusement must have taken some of the girls by surprise, because someone said, very clearly, "Laughter's good if you don't have to eat it. Trenthams doesn't like liars."

"What nonsense!" said Isabella, without pausing her step. "Trenthams is the first to teach habitual lying as a way of conversing. Now,

Nan; I've never tried to eat laughter, but I suppose anything is possible if you're hungry enough."

"It's a *saying*," the voice said, in bewildered annoyance. As it fell behind them, it was still protesting, "No, it's a *saying*—"

"Do you think they're waiting for the other one?" Annabel asked in a low voice, as they approached the dining hall. The double doors were open, and through those open doors, she could see that it was almost entirely empty. There were a few girls here and there, mostly clumped together at tables, and Annabel could recognise each of the girls as ones she had seen in either the lock-picking or explosives classes.

"Almost certainly," Isabella said decidedly. "What do you think, Nan?"

Annabel looked over at the other girl and saw that her eyes were dancing. "About what?" She hadn't meant to feel so, but somehow she felt both insulted and irritated by the appearance of this other contender to the throne.

"Will she be a Beauty, a Brain, or perhaps a Pawn?"

Before Annabel could respond, Lady Caro's voice said from behind them, "She'll be the Queen, and that's all that really matters, isn't it?"

"There's still some dispute about that," murmured Isabella.

Lady Caro displayed elegant unconcern. "Is there so? I hadn't heard it; I *had* heard that there was a Pretender *you* were supporting, Miss Farrah, but I'm sure that isn't true."

"Are you? But then, people often are sure of things that aren't accurate, I find."

This time when Annabel looked across at Isabella, she found that Isabella was watching her curiously, her lips apart as if she would say something, but was waiting for Annabel's...permission?

Was Isabella waiting for permission to directly champion Annabel's heirship?

Annabel hesitated for one moment, and said, "If it's me you're talking about, you're only half right. Come along, Belle; we don't want someone else to take our table."

"If I were you, I'd be less concerned about someone taking your table," said Lady Caro, "and more concerned about someone taking something much more important."

"Thanks," said Annabel. "I'll remember that. Hadn't you better go meet Lady Selma? I don't think she'll be pleased if you're not there when she leaves her suite."

Lady Caro's eyes rested on her thoughtfully, but Annabel merely towed Isabella away toward their table, ignoring Isabella's delighted smile.

"Oh, well done, Nan!" Isabella said quietly, when they reached their table. "I should have dressed you with your hair up much earlier than this! You made even Lady Caro think twice! She's wondering if she's picked the right side now. She's wondering if she'll regret going to Lady Selma's side with the Aunts."

"What I'd like to know is whether they actually believe she's the real queen heir," Annabel said, seating herself and replying to a wink from one of the girls by winking back solemnly. Was that the bold-eyed girl from the lock-picking class, the one who had asked if Annabel should be there? Obviously she had made up her own mind in the matter. "It's the first thing I want to know, actually."

"Is it?" Isabella considered that. "I suppose you're right, though I'm inclined to think that if they don't know, it's more by an exercise of deliberate rather than accidental ignorance. It's convenient for them to have Lady Selma as the queen heir—she can represent their interests, and can't get too powerful if they're the reason she's in power at all. I'm inclined, Nan, to consign them all to prison directly without too much concern about the finer details of their treason."

"If I'm going to jail people for treason, I'd like to make sure they actually knew that's what they were doing," said Annabel. "I don't want the Awesome Aunts running Trenthams again, in either case. It's privately funded, but I met the old lady who does most of the funding, and I'm pretty sure she'll have something to say to all of this."

"That's just as well," agreed Isabella. "My younger sister Susan will be here later on, and I really don't think the Awesome Aunts are capable of keeping her in order."

"I don't suppose you want to run a finishing school, do you?"

"Certainly not. How dreadfully boring!"

"I wouldn't have called this term boring," Annabel said. "Actually. But that's just me."

"Generally speaking, we usually have a lot less in the way of treason, treachery, and intrigue," said Isabella. "In a word; boring! You're not trying to back out of our agreement, are you?"

"I wouldn't dare!" said Annabel frankly, which made Isabella giggle. "Oh! Here she comes! Should I drink my tea in an unconcerned manner?"

"If you like," Isabella said. "But I'm going to stare, so you might as well stare, too."

As they watched, Annabel in growing interest and Isabella in what seemed to be rising amusement, Lady Selma sailed across the dining room, nodding to all the girls in a regal manner and ignoring Annabel and Isabella's table as if it had ceased to exist.

She was a tall, impressive girl with a classically Old Parrasian exterior, all long face and long nose, and a kind of elegance about her. They couldn't have found a girl more different to Annabel, thought Annabel, becoming amused in her turn. Even the golden hair that sprang from a smooth, oval brow was braided low and elegant at her neck, in contrast to Annabel's high, sweeping brown bun.

By the time Lady Selma sat down at the table obviously reserved for her, Lady Caro motioning to the young girls who had bagsed it to pull out Lady Selma's chair, there was a veritable swell of goggling girls surrounding the table. All of them obviously wished to sit by Lady Selma; and, just as obviously, not all of them could fit.

"Goodness, what a fuss!" said Isabella. "She certainly knows how to lead a room! They'll be making one long trestle table out of all those separate ones in a moment—yes, there they go! Everyone wants to sit next to her."

"I'm glad you didn't make me do that," Annabel said, with another sudden tickle of amusement in her belly. "I don't think it would have worked."

"Oh, well, perhaps not!" allowed Isabella. "However, one of my favourite kings is the sort of person you'd much rather not be sitting next to, thank you very much, even if asked, and—"

"You have an order of favourite *kings*?"

"Certainly, I do! The King of Glause is a lovely, sleepy, clever man, and he's absolutely terrifying. I would have tried to marry him if I wasn't so frightened of him."

"I'll remember that," Annabel said, more than slightly worried. Someone who frightened Isabella was someone she didn't really want to meet.

"Oh no! He'll adore you. Just make sure you don't agree to do anything without thinking it over in fifty different ways first. He'll still probably manage to get something you didn't expect, but he might not get the other forty-nine things he wanted, and that's the most important thing, after all."

"I'll make sure you handle all the negotiations," said Annabel hastily. "Or your little Papa. What do you think of Lady Selma, Belle? Will she be someone to negotiate with?"

"Perhaps," Isabella allowed. "If she's being paid, that is. If not, it's unlikely; and given the way she dresses, I find myself doubting that she was promised money. She seems as if she has dressed well all her life. We'll have to work awfully hard to keep up with her, you know. She won't be easy to oust when it comes to fashion."

"I don't care," said Annabel, who didn't.

Isabella looked at her with fascinated eyes. "I believe you really don't," she said. "Well, we can't have that."

"Why can't we?" protested Annabel. "Why can't I be comfortable and not care about fashion?"

"There is absolutely no reason to sacrifice comfort for fashion—or fashion for comfort, if it comes to that," said Isabella. "I'm sure I mentioned this when we first met, Nan. When it comes to fashion in New Civet, you're in a unique position as the future queen. It's a great shame, because it means that full-figured girls are going to come back into fashion, and that's not at all good news for me."

Annabel sniffed. "What rubbish. At least you have a lovely figure."

"Nonsense," Isabella said. "I'm *tall*. That's the best that can be said of me. Tall, and I've made sure I know how to stand. You though— you have a *figure*. And because you're queen, you're bound to lead the fashions so long as you listen very carefully to me."

"But I want to be—"

"Comfortable, yes," nodded Isabella. "Don't worry about that. We've already done some very solid work toward removing the bustle from fashion—we'll work further on that as the weeks go by. Even more, if the Pretender decides to make a fashion of her own for exaggerated bustles. It's a distinct possibility; no doubt Lady Caro will think of it if Lady Selma doesn't. When she comes a cropper we'll have won that battle by default—two birds with one stone, so to speak. But battle we must, on the field of fashion as well as the field of succession, and there's no reason why we can't do so comfortably. Well, Nan—why do you think I made my smuggling garters?"

"Because you wanted to sneak in contraband," Annabel said, without hesitation.

"Yes, but they're beautiful, aren't they?"

"And comfortable," said Annabel slowly.

"Exactly so!" Isabella said, in a pleased voice. "Clothes should be beautiful, useful, and comfortable. You wouldn't think it, but all of my clothes are fitted just so—enough for me to be able to run really very fast at a pinch. That's what's important to me. A nice gusset under the arms for freer movement, too, and a gathered pinch at the waist; all made from a nice fabric that allows airflow."

It was Annabel's turn to eye Isabella in fascination. "Did you have to run very fast when you were helping your father at ambassadorial functions?"

"Of course! And with my complexion I'm bound to look awfully red if I have to scurry about too much without gussets and other allowances. The current fashion for bustles is something of a mixed blessing; I can add some extra material there to make it easier to run, and it's delightfully easy to smuggle things, but the corresponding weight is something else to think about."

"That's why you wear light materials."

"Exactly so. In your case, since you're bound to be sitting so often and moving about court and drawing rooms so often, I've been starting with a higher waistline and a nice bit of gathering at the back. Isn't it a good thing you've got such a slender waist!"

"A what?" blankly said Annabel, who was quite aware that her waist was at least three inches larger than most of the girls at Trenthams and a good six inches wider around than Isabella's.

"Goodness, don't compare it with mine!" scoffed Isabella. "You have to compare it with the rest of you. Look at me: straight up and down. My hips are barely wider than my waist, and it doesn't get any better further up. I'm a straight line up and down; it's why I appreciated bustles so much. Now you—you've got actual hips, an actual waist, and what Miss Cornett refers to as '*your—ahem—décolletage*' is in proportion to your hips. There's no need to emphasise anything with you. Just a *little* pinch at the back and a firm-to-loose gathered front, and you'll be perfectly comfortable. It will be the death-knell for bustles, you mark my words!"

Annabel tilted her chin toward the swiftly growing table at which Lady Selma and Lady Caro sat together, conversing coolly. Some of the girls now joining it were ones she knew from the classes Isabella ran. "It's all very well to talk about battling on the field of fashion, but what are we going to do about that?"

"Continue classes, of course," said Isabella promptly.

"I meant what are we going to do about the—"

"I know," Isabella assured her. "We continue classes, of course! I may not have mentioned this earlier—"

Annabel regarded the teapot in despair. "Oh, what *now?*"

"Don't be like that, Nan. The smallest thing!"

"Don't tell me—you've been running an illicit class in espionage."

"If it comes to that, all the classes are illicit," Isabella began, and added hastily, "All right, all right, perhaps this one is a little more illicit than the others. It's not exactly espionage, however; it's a class on Undetected Information Gathering."

"Espionage!" Annabel said firmly. "How did that little group not get caught in the raids?"

"It isn't a class that can be signed up to," said Isabella. "Invite only, and dreadfully exclusive. The only way to get in without a personal invitation from me is to find your own way in. I knew which girls were going to be in it before I got here this year. Although, we did have one girl find her own way in this year—"

"So *that's* what that was about!" Annabel declared triumphantly. "I knew I'd figure it out if I kept paying attention!"

Isabella looked at her in awe. "I know I've said it before, Nan, but your resting face is really very deceptive! I never know if you're paying attention or not! It makes it very difficult for me to know when I've really passed something under your nose and when I haven't."

"Good!" Annabel said. She much preferred things that way, and it was probably very good for Isabella to have someone she couldn't read with perfect ease. Isabella, thought Annabel, got things her own way just a little bit too easily at times. "And I know you were *just* about to tell me, but how exactly does keeping up classes in Undetected Informatio—Wait. Were you thinking of using the girls as scouts?"

"Not all of them," said Isabella thoughtfully. "Just one or two of the much better ones, like Alice. If it comes to that, Alice has already been nosing around the school, and a bit of field work will be very good for some of the others, too."

"Yes, but is that safe?" Annabel asked doubtfully. "Even if they're our age—"

"They're all first and third year girls," Isabella said. "It's no good getting the older girls; they're already worked into perfectly groomed little Trenthams girls who know better than to be sneaking information where it isn't offered—unless, of course, it's in the service of gossip."

"Should we really use them like that?"

"Oh, why not?" Isabella said blithely. "They've got to start somewhere, after all."

"Yes, but what if it's more dangerous here than we thought? Lady Selma is here, after all, so why not a couple of footmen and a few maids as well?"

"That's the good thing about being in a girl's school," Isabella said. "It's awfully difficult to bring in really dangerous elements. They don't like dangerous elements in any shape or form, unless they happen to be undergarments. And unless the Old Parrasians or Royalists have found a way into the school that doesn't involved battering the front gate down or a mountain of paperwork sufficient to frighten the hardiest of revolutionaries, I really don't think we need worry too much."

"Still..." Annabel said reluctantly.

"Oh, don't be stick-in-the-mudish about it!" begged Isabella. "The girls want their chance, I do assure you! They've been waiting for something like this to happen; in fact, they approached me. Alice has some idea of something happening that she's been chasing for a little while now, and I really don't think we could stop her just by forbidding her."

"I suppose not," said Annabel, though she had the suspicion that Alice would stop on the orders of Isabella, even if she didn't on the orders of Annabel herself. She ate another spoonful of her fruit-covered porridge, wishing that now she could technically eat properly again, she could really enjoy it. If it wasn't pretenders to the throne, it was worrying about young school girls being hurt in her service.

"I still think," she said, remembering the lurch and pistol-crack of the attempt when she and Isabella were travelling to Trenthams, "that it could have been planned this way from the start. The Old Parrasians try to kidnap me so they can put their own queen on the throne, starting now."

"It's possible," agreed Isabella. "In my experience, the Old Parrasians go straight to the most convenient solutions rather than the elegant. But supposing it occurred to them to get rid of an inconvenient queen, and replace her with one of their own, all before the official introductions. Even if Black Velvet did object—and honestly, Nan, I feel that they would merely slip back into the shadows and bide their time—who would believe them? I'm beginning to think it's not a bad conclusion of yours."

"That's what I thought," Annabel said. She was oddly satisfied with that answer. It left her in no doubt at all as to whether she really would fight back. Before she had been annoyed; now she was merely determined. "Belle, if I were to skip a class—"

"No, no," objected Isabella. "Impersonal hypotheticals, please, Nan!"

"All right, all right—if someone were to skip the next class, do you think that someone else would be able to make enough of a distraction that it wouldn't be noticed?"

"If the two someones are the ones I'm thinking of, naturally! Are you off to have fun without me, Nan?"

"Just a bit," Annabel said. "I need to ask Dannick a few questions, and the sooner the better."

Isabella sighed, then grinned. "Never mind. It's good practise for me to have to be patient. And one can never have too many opportunities for making distractions—it keeps one upon one's toes."

"It keeps everyone else on their toes, too," said Annabel; and in spite of everything, she grinned too.

❧ 14 ❧

nnabel might have worried briefly about being able to locate
Dannick within the space of one class, but he was easily
found, after all. He was easily enough found, in fact, that
Annabel wondered if he had been watching out for her. She had no
sooner wandered into the main, lower hall of the school that led to
the grand stairway when he appeared; and, bowing hastily, dragged her
away from the hall and into a small antechamber.

"Are you well, your highness?"

"Why?" asked Annabel, much amused. Dannick really was a sweet
little thing. "Just because of the Pretender? Don't worry, we'll deal
with her soon. Have you been waiting to speak with me?"

"I'm glad," said Dannick, his face lighting up in a smile. "That is,
yes—I've been waiting for you all morning."

"You could have come by our suite," Annabel told him. "Isabella
knows everything, anyway."

Dannick, looking uncomfortable, coughed.

Annabel narrowed her eyes at him, and asked, "Did Melchior ask
you not to tell me?"

Dannick coughed again, this time in surprise. "Well—he didn't
exactly *ask* me anything."

"He ordered you not to tell me anything?"

"Not exactly," Dannick said. He looked as though he would have liked to cough again, but found it impolite to cough in her face three times. "He said—that is, he told me that if he found me anywhere near you or your suite, he'd tunnel me into the walls and shut me up there to give me a chance to cool down."

"Good grief!" said Annabel, very much startled. "Is there something he doesn't want me to know as badly as that?"

"He doesn't know what I know," Dannick said. His pleasant face had darkened, and that firm chin of his had become very mulish. "And it's not that important; it's just that you asked me particularly, and I wanted to let you know."

"This is getting ridiculous!" said Annabel, exasperated. "I really think he's keeping unimportant things from me and pretending they're important just to annoy me! Well, I won't have him threatening you! I'll tell him so."

"If you don't mind, your highness," Dannick said diffidently, "I'd like to look after that by myself."

Annabel gazed at him for a moment or two. He grew pink under her gaze, but the mulishness of his chin didn't change, and at last she said, "All right, then. I'll leave it to you. Tell me if you change your mind."

"I won't change my mind, your highness."

"All right. What did you have to tell me? I have to go to my next class in half an hour, so you'll need to be quick."

"You asked me to look out for footmen who might be up to something. Ones who were too good to be true, or looked after just one person?"

"You found one?"

"Not a footman," Dannick said, his eyes sparkling, "a maid!"

"Oh, is that the one Melchior said has been following you around?"

Dannick went very red. "No! That's—that's something else! It's an awful little girl who—never mind that! Anyway, it was because of that awful little girl that I noticed the other one. She doesn't take commissions from anyone and keeps her nose in the air, but as soon as that Lady Selma arrived, she was sneaking out of the building and lurking behind bushes to pass notes to the bicycle girls."

"The bicycle girls?"

Dannick nodded. "There are two girls who cycle past the school wall every day. They've been doing it since the start of term, and Jess said—"

Annabel, still very much amused, couldn't help asking, "Is Jess the awful little girl?"

"Yes," admitted Dannick. "But I didn't encourage her, your highness!"

"I don't think she would have needed encouragement," Annabel said. She could understand exactly why Jess found Dannick attractive —he had the same air of impoverished nobility that Jess herself had. Annabel wouldn't be surprised to find out that Dannick was the third son of a rich family, or even the first son of recently impoverished nobility. Jess would have hailed him as like called to like. "Did she tell you to tell me, as well?"

"Yes. She found out that I'm helping you and said since she's helping too, we ought to team up. Now I can't get rid of her, no matter what I do."

"I wouldn't try, if I were you," Annabel advised him. "She's a clever girl, and not very stand-offish."

"Yes, your highness," Dannick said. "I did get that impression. At any rate, Jess said that the bicycle girls have been riding past every day, but *this* time, they stopped to pick up something white from the road. I'd just seen Lady Selma's pet maid lurking behind the bushes before that, but I wasn't high enough to see who she was passing the note to. Jess was coming back from the village, so she saw the bicycle girls while I saw the maid."

Annabel nodded in satisfaction. "So Lady Selma is passing notes outside the school. I wonder who they're going to."

Dannick, looking bashful again, said, "I made a few inquiries, your highness."

"Oh, well done you!" Annabel said cordially. "However did you manage that without letting Melchior and Raoul know?"

Dannick appeared to struggle with himself. "Well, actually, your highness—that was Jess, too. She said she didn't want to be left out of it, and really I didn't have the heart not to let her help. I think that's the most awful thing about her; I just haven't the heart to say no to her about anything."

Annabel made a brief, successful attempt not to laugh. "Did she follow the bicycle girls?"

"This morning. They're boarding at the Red Hen, and according to the landlady, they bike all day, every day. The cycle out from the Red Hen every morning at nine o'clock, pass the school, and take the road out of the village with a packed lunch. They don't come back until it's well into the afternoon, either."

"They must be very sturdy girls," Annabel said doubtfully. "What else is there when you leave the village in that direction? Another village?"

"Jess says there's not much, just a few local places of interest and a manor that's are only used in the hunting season."

"*Is* it hunting season?"

"I suppose it depends on what you're hunting," Dannick said. "There's always pheasants now, but if it's gnau you're after, it's the wrong time of year. Gnau hunting season is when the manors will all be full as they can hold."

"So the bicycle girls could be taking the messages to the Red Hen, to that manor, or to somewhere else out in the country."

"Yes," Dannick said. "Sorry, your highness. I'm hoping to have more information soon."

"That's enough to be going on with, anyway," Annabel said. She was quite well pleased—the more so because in this at least, she fancied she had the information before Melchior had it. Now if only she could manage to convince him to tell her what he was keeping from her, she would be very well satisfied.

It was this determination that made her seek out Isabella again as soon as class broke up. The girls were still milling around in the classroom, laughing and talking without being too concerned about going on to their next lesson in any prompt manner, but it wasn't until Annabel looked around and saw the absence of any teacher, that she understood why.

Of Isabella, she asked quietly, "What did you do to the teacher?"

"Nothing at all!" Isabella said, with wide eyes. "I do assure you, Nan! Only I fancy she won't be coming out of her room at any stage soon, because I *did* hear there was a snake in her room. Imagine, Nan! The poor creature must be confused—it keeps circling the bed as if it can't see which way to go!"

"I suppose the teacher's on the bed," Annabel said, trying not to grin too much. "Wait, wasn't this a Place Setting class?"

"I wonder why I gave you a schedule, Nan; really I do."

"But isn't it the Meal Matron who takes this one?"

"Astonishing, isn't it?" Isabella said. "The Meal Matron is such a strong, fearless woman. Who would have imagined that she would crumble so completely in the face of a harmless little grass snake?"

"You, probably," said Annabel, without mincing words. "Belle, how in the world can you handle snakes when you're afraid of horses!"

"Snakes," said Isabella firmly, "are lovely, soft, sensitive creatures who are greatly misunderstood. Horses—now *horses*, Nan, are a wicked combination of muscle and sheer, errant determination not to do what is expected of them."

"All right," Annabel said, still grinning. "But I'd prefer to deal with horses rather than snakes."

"So, it appears, would the Meal Matron. Perhaps our dinner will be late."

"Perhaps," agreed Annabel, "but perhaps they'll just get Melchior to do it again. And speaking of Melchior—"

"Naturally! I should think you're just about ready, Nan. Shall we try tonight? I take it that Dannick had some useful information for you?"

"It's *nearly* useful. I don't think Melchior knows about it, but I think he might know some other things that will help me understand that thing a little more."

"In that case, we'd best repair to our suite before dinner," Isabella said. "There's a new ensemble I'm determined to have you wear to the dining hall. It will have the dual effect of taking the shine out of Lady Selma considerably, and utterly astonishing Melchior, if I have anything to say about it."

"All right," Annabel said. "But if Melchior kicks me out straight away, it's your fault, ensemble or no ensemble. I'll put all the blame on you without a second thought."

"Naturally!" said Isabella again. "Oh, won't we startle Melchior today! I wish I could be there to see it, Nan; really I do!"

Melchior was certainly very startled when he saw her before dinner that night, though Annabel wasn't sure if that was because of Isabella's ensemble, or because he caught her winking solemnly at Dannick as he passed in the hallway.

"Miss Ammett," he said, with a particularly sarcastic curl to his lips, that did nothing to help Dannick's already red face, "Trenthams encourages a good relationship between staff and students, but it does insist on some distance."

"Does it really?" asked Isabella, as Dannick hastily removed himself from the scene. Her voice was just the right mix of curiosity and innocence. "Are you sure, sir? Really sure? I can't say I've observed it, but I suppose a master would know more than a mere student, after all."

"What does Trenthams suggest when a student has something in her eye?" Annabel demanded, going on the attack immediately after Isabella. Melchior's eyes narrowed, and there was a pleasing moment where she felt an entirely mischievous satisfaction.

He looked swiftly up and down the otherwise empty hallway, and Annabel had only a moment to feel in somewhat vague alarm that she'd made a mistake, before he cupped her face between his hands, spreading his fingers carefully around that eye, and blew gently in it.

"This, Nan," he said. "This is what Trenthams suggests for a student who has something caught in her eye."

"Well, really!" said Isabella. "It appears that Trenthams also makes a difference between staff and masters."

"Belle is hurt because you're behaving as if she's not here," Annabel informed Melchior.

"Naturally! It's a most unfamiliar and uncomfortable sensation."

"I find, Firebrand, that I don't particularly care."

Annabel, still captured by the face, blinked up at him. "You should probably let go of me before any more of the girls come along."

"Should I?" Melchior sounded unconvinced, but he did release her.

"You're late to dinner, too, actually," Annabel said. "If you're the monitor tonight, that is."

Melchior said something impolite below his breath and strode away toward the dining hall doors. Watching him, Isabella said, "I really do applaud my own timing, Nan! Tonight will certainly be the best time for you to get information out of Melchior."

"If you really think so," Annabel said, unconvincedly. "But if he kicks me out straight away—"

"Yes, yes; you'll blame me utterly. I will take that responsibility. Now, Nan; while you're busy with Melchior tonight—no, let's not go in right away. The girls will seize on anything to cause gossip at the moment, and if we go right in after Melchior with your face as pink as it is—"

"Is my face pink?" Annabel asked, in astonishment.

Isabella looked at her narrowly. "Did you really not know, Nan? Dear me! You do constantly astonish me! No, never mind that—while you're busy with Melchior tonight, I'll see if I can't arrange for someone to intercept the note between Lady Selma and the bicycle girls next time they try. We might find something interesting there."

"All right," agreed Annabel. "And we'll meet again after in the suite to discuss our strategy. Don't fall asleep!"

"I wouldn't dream of it!" Isabella said happily.

LATER, WITH HER HAIR DRESSED HIGH AGAIN IN A WAY THAT MADE her feel very elegant and poised, Annabel stole quietly down the hallway. She had purposely chosen the lull between dinner time and the rush back to suites that happened just before lights out, and the halls were as empty as she had hoped. There wasn't a girl to be seen when she let herself into Melchior's room, shutting the door after herself with a pleasing sensation of accomplishment.

"Nan!" said Melchior in surprise as she entered, jerking upright. He had evidently not been expecting her; his black and silver waistcoat was unbuttoned and loose, and his shiny black shoes were nowhere in evidence. Much to Annabel's delight, his hair was also slightly ruffled—he looked, in fact, very much like the Blackfoot whose head she had used to pat.

"There's no need to get up," she said, since he seemed to be about to do so. She felt that it would have ruined the friendly feeling to the picture—or perhaps he looked defenceless for a change. Annabel was very well aware that she would need whatever advantage she could get in her campaign this evening. "It's not as if I haven't seen you with your waistcoat unbuttoned or your shoes off before."

Melchior smiled faintly and sat back again. He gazed at her with his head leaning against the back of the sofa, and it struck Annabel that he had relaxed utterly, as if he had somehow been waiting to see her and now that he was looking at her, could finally rest. She crossed the room, aware of the gaze that followed her but not uncomfortable under it, and fetched two teacups out. There was a faint *clink* as the fireless hob started the kettle on its boiling cycle, though Melchior hadn't moved again.

Annabel said, "Thanks," in a friendly sort of way.

She made two cups of tea as Melchior turned his eyes back to his book, but Annabel had a feeling that he wasn't reading the book so much as gazing at its pages. That was all right, she thought hopefully. She didn't need him to be completely ignoring her—so long as his eyes were engaged for long enough, that was all she needed. It would have been rather off-putting, in fact, if he had been ignoring her completely.

Annabel carried both cups by their saucers and brought them around the back of the couch. There was a small table there, she remembered. Enough space for a teacup and saucer, and a small plate of something—or, in this case, two teacups with their saucers. She put them both down together; and, mindful of Isabella's instructions during her two official lessons on Informational Flirting, began with the familiar. The familiar, in this case, meant leaning on the back of Melchior's sofa and wrapping her arms around his neck to prop her chin on the top of his head.

There was a brief moment where Melchior didn't seem to notice—or perhaps where he relaxed again by the most infinitesimal amount—

before he straightened in surprise, dislodging Annabel's chin but not her arms.

"Nan, what did I tell you about hanging over the back of gentlemen's chairs? Let go of me at once."

"I don't want to," said Annabel. "And if you keep wriggling like that, things will get undignified. Your hair will probably get messier, too." It was the thing human Melchior most had in common with cat Melchior—that dislike for having his hair rumpled the wrong way.

"I see," Melchior said. She couldn't see his face, but she heard the undercurrent of amusement in his voice. "May I ask why you've come to my rooms merely to hang around my neck?"

"I missed you," Annabel said. "And also I was feeling lonely but I didn't think Dannick or Raoul would appreciate me hanging on their necks, so—"

"Absolutely not!" said Melchior, jerking forward.

Annabel clung to his neck even more firmly. "Anyway, you said I could come and sit with you sometimes if I wanted to see you."

"I did," agreed Melchior. He sank against the sofa back again. His book was still open, but it had dropped to the sofa beside him. "I had no idea that you would miss the sight of me so soon!"

"Don't be irritating tonight," Annabel said into the slightly curling hairs at Melchior's temple. There were one or two silver ones there, despite the fact that Melchior was only, as far as anyone knew, twenty five or six years of age. "I'm comfortable and I don't feel like losing my temper."

"*Are* you comfortable?" enquired Melchior, and Annabel saw the curve of his cheek as he smiled.

"Very!" she averred. "What are you reading, anyway?"

"Matheson's Treatise on Preferred Methods of Spell Protection."

"Oh," said Annabel. "Is it interesting?"

"Not in the slightest," Melchior said. "If we're to judge it on the merits of its teaching alone. Fortunately, it isn't necessary for me to pay attention to the teaching of the book—most of the methods are completely incorrect, and the others are methods by which I am unable to work."

Annabel threw a curious look down at the book on the seat of the sofa. "Then it seems like a waste of time to read the treatise, but I suppose you know what you're doing."

"Thank you so much, Nan.

"Someone has scribbled in the margins."

"I'll have you know, Nan, that it is *not* scribbling—these are my notes from when I was a child, studying this book."

"Why were you studying this book? I would have thought it wasn't much use to you if half of the methods don't work and the other half don't work for your magic."

"Perhaps not," Melchior said, and she could see that he was smiling faintly by the curve of his cheek. "But someone told me I might find it useful, and so I did."

"Why would someone—is that something to do with Black Velvet?"

"Not directly," said Melchior, surprising her by answering. "Before Black Velvet there was Rorkin and a couple of other, er, young meddlers. They like to leave me messages in odd places."

"Messages about what?" Annabel asked, looking at the scribbled-over book more carefully.

"The Sleeping Princess, the Castle—Mordion. Someone hid messages in the text."

Annabel, in some astonishment, said, "That's what Belle said!"

"Oh, the Firebrand knows about that?" Melchior's voice sounded uneasy. "Sometimes I get the distinct feeling that the Firebrand knows more than Black Velvet."

"Probably," agreed Annabel. "But Poly has already been rescued, and Mordion is gone, and the Castle will be coming back soon. Why still study the book? Who else do you have to learn about?"

Melchior turned his head just enough to turn a mocking look on her. "That, Nan, is a secret."

"I'll ask you about that later, then," Annabel said. There were other things to ask first, after all. "Did you manage to get anything more out of the Old Parrasians that we captured, Melchior? You said they didn't have much to say, but I suppose you kept trying?"

"Naturally," said Melchior. He was looking down at the lace of her sleeve where it draped over his arm, and Annabel thought he was smiling. "Well, Nan; Raoul tells me that those men have been somewhat more cooperative given the possible charges of treason that could be levelled against them. They admitted that they were part of the attempt to kidnap you earlier, and gave up a meeting place for our information."

"Did they say anything about the Pretender?" asked Annabel. "And did you find out anything at their meeting place?"

She knew she'd been too eager as soon as she asked the second question, and clutched more tightly around Melchior's neck in expectation of another struggle. Instead, Melchior only turned a little until he could see her more clearly.

"I was convinced, Nan," he said, smiling up at her, "that you were here merely because you missed me. I begin to feel that it's not the case."

"No," said Annabel, going by another of Isabella's maxims—*Attack with Truth!* "I'm here to get information out of you. You were nice and told me a little about the Old Parrasian thugs, so now I'm going to pat you on the head."

"Ah, I see," Melchior said. The light of laughter was back in his eyes. "This is to be an exchange, then? For each item of information I give you, I'm to be patted on the head?"

"Not exactly," said Annabel, happily scruffing his hair. "But I think you're inclined to be lovely tonight, and it's nice to pat you on the head again."

"*I* see. You still have more questions."

"And it's no good trying to wriggle away," Annabel warned him again.

"I've no intention of wriggling away," Melchior told her. "I feel that I should be encouraging you in your attempted informational gathering."

Immediately suspicious, Annabel said, "Oh, do you?"

"Certainly, Nan. Come, what else do you have to ask about? Perhaps I'll tell you."

Since that made her even more suspicious, Annabel thought a little before she answered. Then she said, "The day that Lady Selma arrived."

"I remember. What of it?"

"You were sneaking around that day," Annabel said. "I remember because you threatened to kiss me."

"Threatened?" There was the suggestion of Blackfoot's purr to Melchior's voice.

"Yes," Annabel said, digging her chin into his shoulder. "I think you knew what was about to happen—or maybe you just knew something was going to happen."

"I knew the Aunts were up to something," Melchior agreed. "There was nothing concrete, of course, but it was rather obvious."

"There must have been something suspicious about the Tea Crafting Class, too," Annabel added. "You made sure that Isabella and I were in your class so we couldn't be in that one, didn't you?"

"Dear me, Nan!" said Melchior, turning his head so that his nose almost touched hers. "You have been paying attention. Very well, then; it was obvious that the classes were carefully arranged this term, and it was all arranged around that particular class. I fancied things might be more dangerous for you both if you attended. Now I know that it was for Lady Selma's benefit—to give her a chance to meet friends and influence people, as it were, but at the time it seemed reasonable to suppose that it was merely to allow for an attack."

Annabel, who might have pulled back with pink cheeks if she hadn't been in Melchior's room for the express purpose of flirting, said, "Blackfoot's nose was softer, but I like yours better," and tapped that nose gently with one finger.

Much to her astonishment, this simple sentiment seemed to deprive Melchior of both words and breath. He gazed at her in silence, his lips barely parted and his eyes at the same time curious and unsure, and didn't seem inclined to move.

"That's how, anyway," she said to him. "The Tea Crafting Class, that is. That's how I knew you knew a lot more about Lady Selma than you were saying."

"I knew that the Awesome Aunts were bringing an important guest in," said Melchior slowly, thoughtfully, "and that there was the possibility of a pretender. That's the sum of my knowledge, Nan."

"I think," said Annabel, remembering a previous conversation with

Melchior, "that you've been pretending to know a lot more than you do know."

"Oh, do you so?"

"Yes. It makes it very difficult to know exactly how much you do know and aren't sharing, and don't know but want me to think you do. And I want to know why you're pretending."

Melchior's hazel eyes danced with amusement. "Oh, do you so, Nan?" he said again, his lips curved in a smile she hadn't seen for some time. "Then I suggest you think about it a little more. Heaven knows, you might arrive at an answer, at this rate!"

"I will," Annabel said darkly. But since he had given her more information than she had had just a little while ago, she patted his head again. Instead of pulling away from it, Melchior leaned into it, and she thought he smiled a little more.

"You said, Nan, that I'm pretending to know more than I know. Shouldn't you ask me why?"

"Yes, but that's not an important question, right now," said Annabel. "First, I want to know more about Lady Selma and who's behind her."

"Lady Selma, as far as I can tell, is being heavily sponsored by more than one group in particular," Melchior said. "Some of the families in her favour are Old Parrasian, and some of them are Royalists who seem to think she's the real heir. There have even been a few murmurs from Black Velvet about taking her aboard."

"Rude!" said Annabel. "When they know I'm the real heir, I think that's a bit much!"

"Not myself, of course," Melchior told her. "And not Mr. Pennicott either, so there's nothing to worry about there."

"Is Mr. Pennicott that powerful?"

Melchior's mouth tipped up ruefully. "I would very much like to claim that distinction for myself; however, if I didn't have Mr. Pennicott's support, there would be nothing I could do to stop Black Velvet supporting Lady Selma."

"Rude!" Annabel said again. "Why would they—oh. I see. She's someone who can be leveraged and moved in the right direction at the right time. They have no direct control over me."

"Exactly so, Nan."

"Oh. Then in that case, I think it's lovely of Mr. Pennicott to support me when he hasn't even met me."

"Why is it that I feel so disappointed to be passed over?" murmured Melchior. "I feel that my support should be acknowledged, Nan."

Annabel leaned a little further over the sofa back and kissed his nose. "I think you're lovely, too," she said.

There was a brief silence, and it seemed as though Melchior had followed her as she drew back, because his nose was still where it had been when she was leaning over. It occurred to Annabel that she was about to be scolded, and she had to bite back a small sigh.

Instead, Melchior cleared his throat. "Nan."

"What?"

"As pleasant as this game might be, I believe it's time for you to leave."

Annabel was conscious of disappointment and a little bit of indignation. Isabella had said that Melchior would be significantly more malleable—she had had to work very hard for every piece of information he had given her, and now she was being kicked out anyway. More than that, she had been really enjoying herself for the first time in quite a while when it came to Melchior. She hadn't realised how much she'd missed the closeness they had shared when he was a cat and she was a girl.

Only, if it came to that, it wasn't exactly the same kind of closeness.

To hide the disappointment she felt, Annabel said, "Rude. You're always kicking me out, these days."

"Believe me, Nan, it gives me absolutely no pleasure at all to kick you out," said Melchior, and there was a shade to his hazel eyes that almost made Annabel believe him despite his previous, constant rebuffs. "However, I think that this has gone on for quite long enough. How could I face Mr. Pennicott if I gave away all of Black Velvet's secrets, after all?"

"You'll have to give them to me anyway, when I'm queen," Annabel reminded him.

Melchior didn't reply to that; he simply took the arms that were around his neck and lifted them away without effort. Annabel found herself led to the door by the hands, and gently but firmly pushed out of Melchior's room.

"Won't I have a few words to say to Isabella!" Annabel said wrathfully. She wasn't sure if she ought to be feeling embarrassed or annoyed—the feeling of which she was most conscious was still disappointment. "She said you'd tell me everything!"

"Isabella was entirely correct," Melchior told her. "Why else would I eject you from my room but if I wasn't afraid I would tell you everything? Off with you, Nan! I won't be tempted!"

ISABELLA WAS STILL AWAKE WHEN ANNABEL GOT BACK TO THEIR suite, but since she was entirely unapologetic about Annabel being kicked out of Melchior's suite at such an hour—was, in fact, entirely *gleeful* about it—Annabel didn't waste time complaining about it. Instead, she gave Isabella a swift rendering of what little she had learned while she changed into her nightgown.

"I suppose Alice was very useful as usual," she added, as she climbed into her bed. She thought her voice sounded a little bit sour, but Isabella didn't take exception to it.

"Naturally!" she agreed. "She says she'll liaise with Jess and Dannick with regards to the bicycle girls. If even Melchior doesn't know who Lady Selma is really affiliated with, it's necessary for us to do a little investigation on our own. We may have our suspicions, but we can't be sure, after all. And if Melchior isn't aware of the bicycle girls, well! So much the better. It's no good frightening them away by *too* much investigation, after all!"

"Yes," said Annabel darkly. "I think Melchior is trying to be very clever, and I don't know why, so I don't see why we should share with him."

"That's the spirit!" cheerfully said Isabella. "Take that spirit with you to the Deportment Lesson tomorrow, and you'll surprise the Master by being the most majestic, untouchable young lady in the lesson!"

❦ 15 ❦

U nfortunately, the next day's lesson in deportment was out in the gardens. The gardens might have been pleasant if it wasn't for the sun, which waxed warmer and warmer as the morning went on. This made the Deportment Master beam more brightly, as if to match, while his students steadily grew pinker and more shiny. This lesson, as Annabel quickly found out, was to learn how to best avoid the appearance of strain in the sun, how to graciously suffer discomfort, and how to properly deport one's parasol. Since the disposal of the parasol wasn't taught until the latter quarter of the lesson, by the time it finished, Annabel was hot, sweaty, and possibly sunburned.

Isabella didn't seem to be suffering from any such ailments; she walked in an offensively sprightly manner beside Annabel as they re-entered the school, and once they had gained their own suite, she said cheerfully, "What a good thing that Trenthams has followed the trend and introduced Interim Activities to the school day!"

"What now?" demanded Annabel. She was tired, hungry, and far too hot to be doing anything that involved walking, bending—or, in fact, movement of any kind. Instead, she flopped down on her bed, trying to ignore the way her dress stuck to her back. "The only

Interim Activity I'm interested in is sipping iced beverages in the dining hall! Don't try to make me do anything else!"

"You can sip an iced beverage on the way," Isabella said persuasively. "There's no time to be hot and bothered, Nan. And if you slip into the outdoors frock I made you, I really think you'll find yourself a lot cooler. Look! Isn't it nice?"

"I don't want to slip into anything," Annabel complained, but she sat up anyway. The back of her dress was still sticking to her lower back, and the frock Isabella held up for her inspection was a light, free thing with only the barest suggestion of a waist.

"You're such a wonderful, grumpy little thing," said Isabella cheerfully. Annabel tried not to feel gratified, and didn't quite manage. "It's like having a small pet cactus."

Annabel, who had been unbuttoning those buttons she could reach, had to stop because she was laughing too much. "Oh, don't make me laugh when it's so hot!" she begged. "I'd just managed to stop sweating! Why don't they let us use personal hygiene spells here, I'd like to know!"

"Real ladies," said Isabella, making her mouth prim, "do not sweat, Nan. Real ladies *glow*. Did you not hear the Deportment Master?"

"If I have to put up with heat like this for much longer, the Awesome Aunts will be able to light the dining hall with me. Why aren't you glowing, if it comes to that?"

"That's because I've graduated beyond being a real lady," Isabella said; but she came over to help Annabel unbutton. "And also because I smuggled a few things in before term started. I should have mentioned it this morning, obviously."

"You smuggled them in *before* term?"

"Of course! They have their magic sensors when term begins. I couldn't very well smuggle them in then; the Awesome Aunts would have caught me, smuggling garters or no smuggling garters."

"Don't they have the sensors working before term starts?"

"They can't have, or they would have caught me," said Isabella. "It was in the way of an experiment, really; and what a convenient thing for us, Nan!"

"What did you smuggle in?"

"Some anti-perspiration spells, a few chairs, and some things I'll need for my hat making."

Annabel said blankly, "You really did smuggle in the chairs! I told Melchior I thought you had, but I didn't really believe it!"

"Naturally, I did! You have no conception, Nan, of how dreadfully uncomfortable the chairs at Trenthams are! And don't you think these are stylish?"

"Yes, but how?"

"I bribed some of the footmen," said Isabella. "There are always a few of them hanging around the halls, hoping to be bribed."

"I don't think that's why they're hanging around in the halls," Annabel said, gazing around at the chairs. Chairs were not the first thing she would have thought of smuggling in if she had been trying to smuggle something into Trenthams. "It's a pity you didn't think to smuggle in a communication spell."

"Oh, I did think of it," Isabella assured her. "It would be a waste of effort. Only think, Nan! No one replies when I try to contact them! I'm sure it must be because I'm sold defective communication spells. As it is, I vastly prefer to work face to face. I'm sorry, did you say something?"

"No," said Annabel, taking her face out of the pillow. "I was just laughing. Carry on."

"At any rate, I have enough anti-perspiration spells to last us through the term, so you can't use that as an excuse to avoid the badminton court."

"I'm not," Annabel said, flopping back on the pillow again. "I'm avoiding the badminton court because everyone is so wafty and lady-like, and it's no fun playing badminton like that."

"They *appear* wafty and ladylike," said Isabella, "but if you send them a few tricky shots you'll see how very competitive Trenthams badminton girls can get. They're very nearly as ruthless as the croquet girls, as a matter of fact. They begin in a ladylike manner, but by the time they've been cut to the soul a time or two about missing a shot, they become positively warlike. That aside, the badminton court is one of the best places to find really good allies."

"Are we looking for allies?"

"Certainly we are! Now that another queen heir has appeared with Lady Caro, we'll need all the allies we can reasonably get."

"I'd rather just have Alice and Jess," Annabel said, but she got up and began to unbutton herself in spite of that. "They're worth more than all the others combined. Except maybe Delysia."

"Yes, Delysia is a darling!" said Isabella promptly. "Here, Nan; try this."

Annabel accepted the spell, and it spread coolly over her from the top of her head to the toes of her overheated feet. She sighed in relief. "I know the coolness won't last, but it feels lovely while it does!" she said. "And at least I won't have to worry about sweating in front of Lady Selma, if she's trying to make allies on the badminton field, too."

"Yes, that's rather an annoying thing," Isabella agreed. "She doesn't seem to be flustered, or hot, or even worried by anything. I'm curious to know if she's unflappable or merely stupid."

Annabel, who was inclined to be more concerned about the singular unflappability of Lady Caro, asked, "What about Lady Caro? Have you known her for a long time?"

"We began at Trenthams in the same year," Isabella said. "She was determined to be a leader in the school, and I was determined not to be nose-led by anyone other than my little Papa. Naturally, this caused something of a split in the class, and things have see-sawed very interestingly ever since. While I've been gone for the last couple of years to look after Papa, it seems that Lady Caro has been very busy."

"Not busy enough," opined Annabel. She was no lover of intrigue or court politics, but she was sharp-eyed enough to be able to see them at work. Lady Caro might have worked very hard, but Isabella's arrival back at Trenthams had precipitated a sweeping change in the atmosphere of the school that was as widespread as it was sudden. Annabel was quite well aware that although all of the girls who lined up at her door had done so firstly in order to see herself, fully three quarters of them were just as curious to confirm that Isabella—*the* Miss Farrah—had actually returned and was in residence. More, she was certain that there had been a great deal of discussion about whether the secret lessons would begin again.

"Oh, yes," she said now. "Your classes—do you think there will be less girls attending?"

"Perhaps technically," Isabella answered carelessly. "Essentially, no! The numbers will perhaps fluctuate for a little while as some of the girls try to decide whether to stay or leave."

"That's all right," Annabel said, slightly cheered. She couldn't blame some of the girls for wanting to see which way things would settle before they became settled themselves, but it did make her appreciate Isabella, Delysia, and the bold-eyed Fern just that much more. "Belle, do I have to actually *play* badminton, or am I a haughty spectator?"

"Haughty spectator," said Isabella promptly. "Lady Caro will no doubt challenge me to a match as soon as we arrive, so there's no need for you to be involved physically just yet. You'll possibly trade verbal blows with Lady Selma instead—unless, of course, she's refusing to acknowledge you again."

"Sort of like a bug on her plate," agreed Annabel. "All right, but that might annoy me."

"Might it? Well, so long as you're not shrill or stupid, there's no reason for you to remain silent, after all. Do as you think best, Nan; I've no advice to offer."

Annabel gave the tiniest of sniffs. "That's unusual."

"Isn't it? It hurts a great deal to say so, but you've surprised me often enough. I feel all the confidence in the world that you'll say exactly the right thing at exactly the right time. I shall therefore put all my energies into the game."

"All right," said Annabel. "But you'd better win, or I'll get myself another advisor."

Isabella giggled. "That's exactly what I mean! I shall certainly win; see if I don't!"

There was already a game of badminton ongoing when Annabel and Isabella arrived at the court, cool and comfortable in their fresh frocks. Annabel felt the touch of the sun on her face again, despite her hat, and was glad of the anti-perspiration spell she could feel still coolly lingering.

"Ugh!" said someone as they arrived, over the *swish* and *pop* of the delicately plied badminton rackets against the shuttlecock. "Really! Some people fancy they'll be welcome *anywhere*! It really is too bad!"

"Isn't it?" agreed Isabella at once, ostentatiously clearing a space for Annabel within easy sight and hearing of Lady Caro and Lady Selma. "I'm constantly astonished at the brass face of people in general. Even in Trenthams! Goodness me, the boldness of the social mushroom would be really admirable if it wasn't for the fact that it's so laughable."

Annabel saw, out of the corner of her eye, Lady Selma stiffening. Score one point to Isabella, then.

Lady Caroline, looking bored and effortlessly bronzed in the sun, said lazily, "You've a lot of energy today, Miss Farrah. You ought to try a match against me, if you've that much energy."

"Certainly," Isabella agreed. "However, do you think you should leave Lady Selma alone like that?"

"Lady Selma is perfectly safe," Lady Caroline said. "She has quite a few friends here at Trenthams, unlike some—what did you call them? Mushrooms?—I could mention."

"Do mushrooms grow on the badminton field?" Annabel asked of no one in particular. "I thought it was rolled out every week."

"Some mushrooms," said Lady Selma, turning her large, blue eyes on Annabel, "are very persistent!"

"It's not much use being persistent against a stone roller," said Annabel, "if we're going to be dragging this metaphor out as long as humanly possible."

Someone giggled. On the badminton field, the two current players looked at each other, then abandoned the field. They obviously thought there was more sport to be had off the field than on it. Nothing loath, Isabella and Lady Caro took the field, Lady Caro spinning the handle of her racquet between her fingers with every appearance of aptitude, and Isabella swinging hers lightly by her skirts.

As they did so, Annabel caught a flutter of blue between the bunches of greenery surrounding the badminton field. The badminton field was set at the base of a natural basin, and the surrounding trees were thick and well grown—enough to block an inconvenient breeze, and certainly enough to block approaching people from view. Enough, too, thought Annabel now, to hide the entire badminton field from view of the school windows.

She narrowed her eyes at the trees that edged the badminton field closest to the school wall, and saw someone slip through the trees. No, not one—two, then three, then four, then enough to make her hand slip into her pocket by sheer habit and close around the pencil staff.

On the badminton field, Lady Caro looked sharply to the trees, her racquet swinging easily up as if it was a sword instead of a racquet, and Isabella said, "How odd. Nan, did you—"

"I saw," Annabel said, with some grimness. "Girls, you'd better all start going back to the school building, I think."

"Why should we do as you say?" demanded one of the smocked girls around Lady Selma. "Who are you to be telling us what to do?"

"I don't think it particularly matters who *I* am," remarked Annabel; "but there are at least half a dozen men sneaking through the decorative shrubs at the moment, and you might want to know who they are. Actually, I'd rather we all just went back to the school building, but I suppose you can stay and ask them who they are if you'd like."

Lady Caro, her eyes narrowed on the foliage, didn't respond.

On the other hand, Lady Selma blinked her pale blue eyes and said, "How ridiculous."

There was a sudden murmur of uneasy girls that was cut short by a very sharp, very distinctive *click*.

"Bother!" said Annabel. She knew that sound very well by now. "They brought pistols."

Through the trees came three men, their pistols ready cocked and levelled; another two came silently from either side, backing the girls into the tree-shaded net that formed the other side of the badminton court.

It was at that moment Annabel truly realised the accuracy of Isabella's statement that the badminton court was the best place to make allies. Not one of the girls around her attempted to scream. Each from a rich and influential family, these girls had been well taught in the arts of being held hostage and kidnapped for ransom.

Annabel had been taught the same things—albeit in a more practical fashion than most of the other girls—and she was very familiar
with the concept of quiet acquiescence while watching for opportunity, as well as the well-drilled idea of keeping alive to stay alive.
Training or not, however, it wasn't so easy not to scream when a
pistol was thrust into your face ready loaded and cocked, and
Annabel felt the first stirrings of real respect for the girls of
Trenthams.

"I call that rude," opined Isabella. Annabel wasn't sure when she'd
moved—perhaps that had been Isabella backing across the field, as
though frightened—but now the other girl was very close. In a much
quieter voice, Isabella added, "I suppose the chances of your being
able to do the same thing you did last time...?"

"Pretty good," Annabel murmured. "*If* they're not the same ones
from the other day and know what I could be up to, and *if* I can have
a bit of time to myself without them seeing what I'm up to."

"Not to worry, Nan," Isabella said, her voice quiet and satisfied. "If
there's anything I know how to do, it's make a distraction."

"You two," said the one who seemed to be the leader. He was
pointing at Lady Selma and Annabel; as they watched, that pointing
finger beckoned. "Over here. You too."

You too was aimed at Isabella, who shrugged elegantly and came to
join Annabel and Lady Selma at the forefront of the group of girls.
Lady Caro, who had edged forward too, hung back just slightly, and
Annabel wondered if she had imagined the other girl's hand slipping
into a hidden pocket. Did Lady Caro, too, have a small pistol
holstered about her thigh? Annabel, feeling the tightness of her own
pistol strapped around her leg, was thankful that she'd made herself
continue to wear it despite the heat.

"Over to the side," said the leader, to the three girls. "And don't
move too quickly, if you please, ladies."

"Stay away from the little plump one and the skinny red-head,"
called one of the other men, sharply. "Gregor says he doesn't know
how they did it, but one of them managed to slip the firing pins right
out of the pistols."

A small murmur spread through the huddled girls. Annabel had wondered if there would be rumours from that day—it seemed as though there had been.

"Oh, was that what it was?" Isabella asked agreeably. "The firing pins? *So* fortuitous!"

"It won't be so fortuitous for you, Miss Farrah," said the leader of the Old Parrasians—for Old Parrasians they must be. "And it's no good trying to figure out who we are this time, either."

"Is it not? I'll remember that."

The leader nodded toward the girls. "Check their pockets. That one had a pistol last time."

"What nonsense!" said Isabella. "A girl of Trenthams, with pockets? Simply not to be thought of—ask the Awesome Aunts, and they'll tell you at great length the risks associated with Allowing Young Ladies to Obtain Pockets."

Despite that, however, both Isabella's and Annabel's seams were examined with great attention; and when at last their captors declared them to be without weapon, it wasn't without Annabel feeling a chill of fear that they would somehow manage to find the leg holster Isabella had purchased from the Blacksmith's son, and the slit in her right hand pocket that gave access to it.

"Now," said the leader, "we can start having a bit of fun. We're here for the queen heir."

"Which one?" asked one of the girls. It wasn't until Annabel caught sight of a dark head of hair being tossed, and a distinctly sarcastic smile that she realised it was Fern. "We've got two queen heirs here, and you've already separated them. Which one did you want?"

"Perhaps they're looking for quantity over quality," suggested Isabella. "A sound strategy in the general run of things, but I can't help feeling that's a little short-sighted in this case."

The Old Parrasians looked between themselves and then to their leader for guidance. He opened his mouth, closed it, and finally said, "Both of them," but not before Fern's sarcastic smile had a chance to become even more sarcastic.

"All right, you've got us," Annabel said, nodding at Lady Selma. "Two queen heirs. You don't need the rest of the girls, do you?"

"Can't let 'em go; they'll tell the teachers," said one of the men.

Annabel glared at him. "Well, can't you take us elsewhere, then? You don't need to take all the other girls, just me and Lady Selma."

"And me," Isabella said. She smiled sweetly at the grouped Old Parrasians. "You've no idea how much trouble I can cause when left behind. *Far* safer to have me with you, don't you think?"

"Don't try to trick them," said Lady Selma, turning her cold blue eyes on Annabel. "The queen heir can't die a stupid death because you wanted to save a few lives."

"It's common sense, not a trick," Annabel said, feeling her first twinge of real, personal dislike for Lady Selma that wasn't prompted by the fact that she was pretending to be what Annabel really was.

"We're not taking any of you anywhere," the leader said shortly, "so you might as well stop squabbling. The sooner you cooperate with us, the sooner you'll be let go. There's no need for anyone to try and be clever, or get hurt."

"We might have a better chance of cooperating with you if you told us what you wanted," Annabel said, with some asperity. "Why do all of you Old Parrasians *talk* so much? You never get to the point."

"We didn't say we were Old Parrasians!"

"You talked about the firing pins," Annabel said. "Who else would you be? Are you stupid?"

"Exactly my feeling," agreed Isabella. "A failure to get right to the point presupposes a muddled mind—amply proved already, I fancy—and one should always be careful when dealing with those possessed of muddled minds."

"Who are you calling muddled, you—"

The leader turned a glare on the rest of the Old Parrasians. "That's enough. It was when they got the others to squabble that they took the firing pins. Pay attention."

"All right, then," said Annabel, who felt like this debacle had gone on for quite long enough. Even girls who had been trained for the eventuality would become sick of having pistols waved in their faces at some stage, and she was quite sure that Lady Caro was prepared to do something by herself if no one else did anything. She was also quite sure that Fern, who was suddenly very close to Lady Caro, had formed the same idea; she was significantly less sure of how many girls might be shot if things went badly. "All right then. You've got pistols, and you want our attention. We're paying attention. What is it you actually want?"

"The staff," said the leader of the Old Parrasians. "We want the staff."

"It won't do you any good," Annabel told him. "It won't work for you."

"It wouldn't work for you, either," Lady Selma said, cutting in on the distinctly interested babble of noise that had woken in the girls from the other group. "Since you're not the queen heir."

Annabel said, with a distinct steel to her voice, "We'll have a conversation about that later. In the meantime, do you have anything for these...gentlemen?"

Lady Selma tilted her chin just enough to make a clean-cut line of her jaw. "Of course not. Why should I?"

"You," the Old Parrasian leader said, turning his pistol on Annabel, "where's the staff?"

"Do you think I've got it in my pockets?"

"Exactly so!" agreed Isabella. "Did I not just tell you about Trenthams girls and pockets?"

"Actually, I have got pockets," Annabel said, since the Old Parrasians showed no signs of taking notice of Isabella's aside. "Would you like to see what I've got in them? My sketchbook and pencil. One handkerchief. You can wipe your noses with that, but it's about the only thing that'll be useful to you."

One of the girls in the other group giggled, and several Old Parrasians glared at Annabel through their masks. Impervious to giggles and glares alike, Annabel merely held out the few things from her pockets, and with a heart as cold as ice said, "See for yourself. Just give them back when you're done—I haven't finished a few of the drawings."

The Old Parrasian leader looked at her with suspicion but instead of snatching the things out of her hands, as she had been very much afraid he would do, only snapped at the others, "What are you doing? Check her pockets properly!"

"One wonders," said Isabella to no one in particular, and gazing at no one in particular, "exactly how it is that one is supposed to fit something as large as a staff in one's pockets. Presuming one *has* pockets, of course, which as I have already told you, is unlikely in the extreme."

"You!" said the Old Parrasian leader suddenly to Lady Selma, as if he had only just remembered her. "What have you got in your pockets?"

"I have no pockets," Lady Selma said coldly.

"Oh," said the leader. "Well, check her for pockets, too, I suppose. It won't do any good, but you might as well."

Isabella gave a sudden gurgle of laughter that made more than one girl from the other group look at her in distinct worry. To Annabel, quietly, she said, "Oh, how amusing!"

"Actually," said Annabel, in a likewise lowered voice, as the Old Parrasians tugged at the outraged Lady Selma's skirts for any sign of pockets, "I don't know about you, but I'm pretty tired of being held at pistol point."

"Yes, but isn't it amusing!"

"I suppose," Annabel said quietly, refusing to feel in the slightest bit amused, "that you're talking about the fact that they can't seem to decide who to treat like the queen heir."

"Exactly so! Which besides being a *little* bit clever, is more than a little bit stupid in quite another way; not to mention counter-productive."

Gloomily, Annabel muttered, "I told you it was probably the Old Parrasians behind Lady Selma."

"I acknowledge that you were entirely correct!" Isabella admitted, at once. "It was very forethoughtful of you, Nan! They're certainly being very careful not to give the idea that they know she isn't queen heir, at any rate, while at the same time focusing all the more invasive attention on you. Not to mention they've already tried to kidnap you twice; but that's by the by, I suppose."

"I would like to know—actually, no, I'll try to figure it out later. I'd better do something about the Old Parrasians, first."

"Do you think you can?" Isabella's voice was speculative. "I hate to seem to doubt you, Nan, but there are at least six of them, and they all have pistols. I'm not particularly fond of many of these girls, but I wouldn't like to see them injured."

"If I don't, Lady Caro is going to," pointed out Annabel.

Isabella asked, in surprise, "Lady Caro?" but by then the Old Parrasians were finished with Lady Selma, and she didn't have the chance to speak again.

As Annabel put away her sketchbook and handkerchief, and wrapped her hand a little more tightly around the pencil staff, she saw Isabella gazing at first thoughtfully, and then more speculatively at Lady Caro. So Belle had seen the pistol too, had she? Isabella didn't seem surprised about it, merely more watchful. That put to rest any hopes Annabel might have had about Lady Caro holding her peace to let others fix the problem. Obviously, Lady Selma was as averse to sharing information with her co-conspirators as was Melchior.

The Old Parrasian leader drew back a little, eyeing the other group of girls with narrowed eyes, and Annabel had the faintest thread of an idea—both of what he would do next, and of what she could do to stop it.

He was going to grab one of the girls—the closest one, probably Fern or Lady Caro, who had somehow managed to be right at the front—and he would offer, in the friendliest way possible to begin shooting one after the other until she told him where the staff was. And so Annabel, as the Old Parrasian leader took a step forward again and started to say, "If that's how you're going to play things—" lifted her pencil staff to the ready and drew without leaving a line in the air before her.

She had never drawn an invisible thing before, and it was difficult to tell if there was a slight shimmer to the air between the Old Parrasian leader and Fern, for whom he was reaching, or if Annabel was only imagining it.

Lady Caroline already had her pistol out, pointed directly in front of her with her body turned to the side, and the Old Parrasian leader, his own pistol still only half raised, froze with his other hand part way toward Fern.

Was that an oddness to the air? Had it worked? Annabel, cold to her stomach, wasn't sure. She and Isabella were exposed, Lady Selma with them, but that wouldn't matter if only she had managed to keep the other girls safe for now behind an invisibly-drawn barrier of magic.

Every other Old Parrasian pistol pointed at Lady Caroline; who, with her pistol directly against the Old Parrasian leader's head—and there was, wasn't there? the vaguest suggestion of shimmer between the two?—pulled the trigger.

There was a muffled pistol-shot that didn't crack as loudly as it should have done, and a blackened patch of gunpowder burst against the shimmering air between Lady Caro and the Old Parrasian leader. It stayed there, too; a visible indicator that there was indeed an almost invisible wall of magic between the girls and their assailants.

"Good grief!" said Annabel, her ears ringing a little. "Did she know the protection was there, do you think?"

"With Lady Caro, it could be either," Isabella said. Lifting her voice a little, she called, "Is everyone uninjured?"

There was a general chorus of agreement, between which Annabel heard Lady Caro say distinctly, "Unfortunately." Her eyes were locked with the eyes of the man she had very nearly shot, and he was actually sweating.

It was in that little piece of shocked time that Annabel drew out her own pistol and levelled it at the leader as well. "You should really drop your pistols, now," she said. "Actually, I'd like to shoot you right now and save the trouble of executing you later, but I don't think I've got the authority until I'm officially crowned. Also, my friend doesn't like her clothes to get dirty, and I'm pretty fond of her."

"Put *his* down?" said one of the other men, incredulously. "We've all got our pistols on you! What do you think will happen if you pull the trigger?"

"If it comes to that, what do *you* think will happen?" Annabel asked, hoping they couldn't see the sweat on her brow. "Last time, your pistols lost their firing pins. What do you think will happen this time?"

"She's bluffing," said another of the men. "She can't have taken care of all of the pistols. All she did was hold up that—she held up the pencil! That's the staff!"

In the brief silence that followed, Annabel saw Lady Caro kick the invisible magic wall in disgust. She wasn't sure if Lady Caro was merely disappointed not to be a part of the fight any longer, or if she was irritated at Annabel's handling of the situation.

Ruefully—because, really, she hadn't handled it very well—Annabel lifted her pencil once again, and reversed it. No time for subtleties this time.

"You'd better both duck," she said to Isabella and Lady Selma, and erased the first pistol without too much care for the fingers that were holding it.

A shot whistled past Annabel, far too close for comfort, and Lady Selma bolted away toward the trees. Isabella hissed and ducked, though to Annabel's considerable approval, she didn't try to drag Annabel down with her. That gave Annabel the chance to keep erasing pistols without losing concentration. She was erasing the third as a second shot went wildly astray, and half of the Old Parrasians turned to face the opposite direction.

"Good heavens!" said Isabella. "It's Melchior! Nan, you'd better keep erasing pistols, or he's going to be shot."

"What a show-off," said Annabel. She furiously erased the fourth pistol as Melchior leaped down the hill toward them, his necktie askew and his hair utterly disarranged. "He's making his coat billow like that on purpose. I bet he's even using magic to do it. Why couldn't he stay out of the way until the pistols were gone!"

"I don't think he cares about the pistols," observed Isabella.

Regardless of their pistols, the rest of the Old Parrasians turned to face the new threat. Annabel grimly moved on to the fifth pistol, but Isabella dragged her to the ground as a burst of something strong and possibly magical threw most of the Old Parrasians into the bushes.

"Won't I have words with Melchior!" Annabel heard her say. "If these stains don't come out, I shall take it personally!"

Annabel wriggled until she was on her stomach without considering her frock, and continued to erase pistols. She could see Melchior properly now—he might well have been flinging magic, for all she could see, but he was certainly swinging punches. Very much impressed, she asked Isabella, "Did you know he could fight? Oh, what a nice hit! I hope your nose is broken, you awful man!"

Isabella giggled. "I believe Melchior is a little annoyed. Good heavens! Is that one dead, do you think?"

"No," said Annabel, who knew that clenched, open-mouthed, non-breathing posture. "He's just winded."

"Is that all the pistols?" asked Isabella, her grey eyes narrowly observing the scene.

One of the Old Parrasians helped up another, and Annabel, who had been about to shout a warning to Melchior, instead watched in astonishment as they turned away and ran for the bushes.

"Yes—bother! They're running!"

"I should think so!" Isabella said. "Melchior may not have a great deal of magic, but he has a great deal of motivation, and he seems to be quite conversant with using his fists."

Now that Melchior was in little danger of anything worse than a punch in the nose, Annabel had the time to take in the various open-mouthed and outright adoring looks from the girls behind the wall of magic. She frowned.

"Oh no," she said. She made a small adjustment to it with the pencil end of the staff, shading in the invisibility of the wall until the girls disappeared into a slight haze. "I'm not having that. He's *my* cat."

Isabella looked startled. "Nan, he's not *really*—"

"No, but he's *mine*," Annabel said, climbing to her feet and dusting herself off. "I won't have other girls patting him on the head."

"Perhaps you should tell him that."

"Yes, but he *knows* that! Who else does he belong to if not to me?"

"Who knows the minds of men, Nan? Is that the last one?"

"Yes," said Annabel, watching in unqualified approval as Melchior saw to the last Old Parrasian remaining. The others were running or limping through the trees the way they had come, in various states of bloody disarray, and Melchior didn't seem inclined to pursue them.

Instead, he strode across the now-scuffed badminton court and demanded, "Are you hurt, Nan?"

"Just dirty," Annabel told him cheerfully, brushing herself off and carefully replacing her pistol through the slit in her pocket. "Why didn't you tell me you knew how to punch people, Melchior? That was *awfully* satisfying!"

"I wouldn't like you to think it was selfless," said Melchior, after the briefest of pauses. "It merely never occurred to me as a method of self-aggrandisement when it comes to you, Nan. Judging from the bloodthirsty gleam to your eyes, I'll need to rethink that position."

"Perhaps you could rethink it later," suggested Isabella. "And perhaps we could remember that although the girls can't see anything, they can certainly hear if we speak loudly enough."

Melchior, more quietly but scarcely less sarcastically, said, "If you're suggesting a dumb show of my emotions at this moment, Firebrand—"

"Absolutely not!" Isabella said at once. "I won't stand for it! Merely that we move away from the blockade. Should we let them out, do you think?"

"Not yet," Annabel said, remembering those adoring gazes and certain she didn't feel energetic enough to deal with that at the moment.

To her surprise, Melchior agreed. "Let the Awesome Aunts deal with it," he said. "They should be coming along at any moment—as soon, in fact, as they hear about it."

Annabel opened her mouth to remark that that would happen just as soon as the Old Parrasians told the Awesome Aunts, but it occurred to her in time that the definite connection between the Awesome Aunts and the Old Parrasians was something that Melchior didn't know. She was still not inclined to share information with him.

Instead, she said, "Lady Selma will probably tell them when she comes out of hiding. And speaking of coming out of hiding, how did you know what was happening?"

"I've got little spells all around Trenthams," Melchior said. "If any kind of threatening magic breaks out, I get a warning. If the staff does something—"

"You come right away to see what I've done," said Annabel, nodding. She accepted Melchior's help over the last of the hill, but instead of leading her back toward the school, he drew her toward the covered gardens.

"Exactly so," he said. "I can't say that I was expecting to see you holding off seven Old Parrasians with a pistol, however."

"Oh, are we going into the gardens?" asked Isabella. "How unusual. I suppose it's best to stay away from the school until they sort everything out themselves, but I would have thought we were all a bit tired of the heat."

"This part of the garden is covered," Melchior said, without releasing Nan's hand. Instead, he tucked it through the crook of his arm. "Nan, I hate to ask, but did the Old Parrasians happen to see—"

"Yes," said Annabel baldly. "Sorry. They know it looks like a pencil."

"It's a bit of a bother, isn't it?" Isabella said reflectively.

"Yes," Annabel said glumly. "But what could I do when they were about to threaten the other girls? I couldn't let them shoot anyone just to get their hands on the staff, could I?"

"I think not," agreed Isabella. "Besides, Nan, one could always say that although they now know what the staff looks like, they don't *have* it; and I'm certain they would have had it if they'd started offering to shoot the girls. You did well."

Annabel sighed. "I suppose I could ask it to change, or draw it to change, but then I'd have to learn to use it again. I know how to use it when it's like this."

."There's no need to change how it looks," Melchior said. He was frowning down at his black and silver waistcoat, where a tear in the fabric left spiky silver threads sticking out. He sighed, too. "Nan, this was a new made waistcoat."

"Sorry," said Annabel, removing her hand from Melchior's arm and patting his head by reflex. He twitched his head away, narrowing his eyes at her, and Annabel made a face back at him.

"A pat on the head," he said coldly, "is hardly enough to compensate for damage to a new waistcoat."

"Oh," said Annabel. She tiptoed and kissed him on the cheek instead. "Sorry."

"You shouldn't give him ideas, Nan," warned Isabella. "As my Aunt Oddu says—"

"I'll thank you to stay out of this, Firebrand!"

"Yes, but Aunt Oddu is very concerned about the Ascendancy of the Male in Polite Society, and—"

"I'll thank your Aunt Oddu to stay out of it, too."

"Oh, but Aunt Oddu never stays out of things," Isabella said. "Particularly not when it comes to the Ascendancy of the Male in Polite Society."

"I suppose you spent a lot of time with her when you were growing up," Annabel said. She poked the loose threads back into Melchior's waistcoat, which both made him jump and surprised him into silence. She drew the threads back in with the pencil staff as she pinched the material firmly together. "There," she said. "The staff has probably never been used for such a purpose before. I hope you're satisfied."

"Very," said Melchior, and Annabel could have supposed him to be Blackfoot again for the briefest moment, because he had certainly *almost* purred.

Isabella made a small, disapproving *tsk* sound. "Well, Aunt Oddu wouldn't approve at all."

"Firebrand—"

"Very well!" hastily said Isabella. Her grey eyes were dancing despite the disapproving nature of her remarks, and now she grinned. "Shall I leave you both alone?"

"Yes," said Melchior.

At the same time, Annabel said in surprise, "Why?"

"Dear me! Perhaps Aunt Oddu would approve after all!"

"Firebrand," said Melchior between his teeth. "I will give you until precisely the count of *five*—"

"I'm off, I'm off!" Isabella waved at them airily and floated away down another avenue that led toward the school building.

Left alone with Melchior, Annabel would have asked what it was they had to discuss, but Melchior didn't give her a chance. He took her hand again without asking and pulled her away from the other avenue with enough firmness to make it clear to Annabel that it wouldn't be much use making a fuss unless she really didn't want to go with him. Since she didn't mind, Annabel didn't make a fuss.

She did say, however, "Isn't it more proper for me to be walking along with my hand in the crook of your arm?"

Melchior threw a look down at her. "If you're minded to make remarks about the Firebrand's Aunt Oddu as well, Nan—"

"I don't know her," Annabel said peaceably. "So I can't make remarks about her. I wasn't complaining, I was just asking."

"Considering the dreadful behaviour you exhibited toward me just last night," began Melchior, "I should think that my holding your hand for a few moments is hardly the depths of depravity."

"Oh, yes," Annabel said. "Sorry about that."

"Are you?" Melchior gazed down at her again, his eyes curious. "I'm really not sure whether I should be insulted or not."

"I don't know why you should be insulted," Annabel said, putting her nose in the air. "You're not the one always being scolded and pushed out the door for being too affectionate. *I* should feel insulted."

"I should like very much to know whether you actually *do* feel insulted," Melchior retorted. "I've seen no evidence of it!"

"I suppose I should just cling around your neck when you tell me not to do it, or when you tell me to go away," remarked Annabel. "Well, I won't."

That made Melchior's eyes deepen in colour with amusement. "Until you want more information, I suppose."

"Until then," agreed Annabel, this time more cheerfully. It didn't *sound* as though he was angry, even if he had sent her away in disgrace last night. In fact, it almost sounded as though he hadn't minded at all —or that he had enjoyed the closeness as much as she had done.

Well, she thought, mulling that over, no matter how prickly he was being now, there was no one she preferred to be around than Melchior, and the same was probably true of him. They had spent too many years together to be wanting to be apart for long. No matter how much Melchior pushed her away, he probably missed her just as much as she had missed him.

She said accusingly, "I don't think you minded me hugging you last night."

"When, Nan," said Melchior, with a smile dancing not only on his lips but in his eyes, "*when* did I say that I minded?"

"You pushed me out the door," she pointed out. "Actually, I think it's a bit much for you to be walking me around by the hand when you pushed me out of your room last night."

"At some stage in the near future, I'll explain it to you. For now, resign yourself to being walked around by the hand while we have some discussion, if you please, Nan."

"So we *do* have something to discuss!" Annabel said, in mild triumph. "I thought you were just trying to annoy me. What are we discussing?"

Melchior closed his eyes briefly, and said plaintively, "I'm certainly insulted. Very well, since you're so inclined to humour me, shall we begin with the new safety measures that are so obviously wanting, or the fact that you seem to have incorporated half of the school's servant staff into your own personal spy network?"

❧ 16 ❧

It hadn't occurred to Annabel that any of the girls might have been concerned about her, so it was something of a surprise to her at breakfast the next morning when most of the girls who had attended the badminton court approached her table during the meal.

More, none of them directly said they had been concerned—or that they were glad she was uninjured. Most of them simply approached, curtseyed, and continued on to their tables. One or two of them brought small presents of candied fruit or chocolates, and said some variation of *It's nice to see you this morning, Miss Ammett*, as if she had been confined to her room for a week. Since Annabel had been aware, if not interested, in her classes on Advanced Polite Conversation, she understood by this that each of the girls was, in their own way, happy to see her alive and uninjured.

"I call that a good day's work," said Isabella happily, after the latest of these. "And I don't think Lady Selma can say the same! She was in very little danger, but at the first sign of it, she abandoned her supporters. Trenthams girls, even the most devious of them, are the sort to remember that kind of thing."

"Oh," said Annabel. She had noticed Lady Selma and Lady Caro sitting at their usual table together, and if she had been asked to say what was different about it, she might have said it was a little less busy than usual. "Do you think the other girls will be more inclined to support me now, then?"

"Certainly. They've seen that you're ready to defend them at the cost of your own life. Most of them appreciate that. It's not the killing blow I would like it to be, but it has certainly made our job somewhat easier. We'll still need to fight, but we're certainly not at a disadvantage. Yes, Nan; I call that a very good day's work!"

"Do you think the Awesome Aunts will acknowledge the fuss yesterday, or will they ignore it completely?"

"They're more likely to pass over it gracefully—make a reference to an *Unfortunate Disagreeableness* or a *Slight Fuss*—and try to pretend it was the smallest of disturbances. The girls will tell their parents, of course, but the Aunts will be ready for it by then."

"And nobody will think of taking their daughters out of school while the queen heir is attending, anyway," Annabel said, with the feeling that she had become hopelessly jaded. "Even if no one is sure who the real queen heir actually is."

"Naturally. Which reminds me—we really need to prepare for half-term when there's a moment free from lessons and Old Parrasian attacks."

"Oh yes," said Annabel gloomily. "The parents. Do you know, I thought the castle would be the standard for awful and life-threatening experiences, but I think Trenthams might actually be worse."

"Speaking of the castle," said Isabella, sipping her morning juice tranquilly, "when exactly is it supposed to come back?"

"I don't know exactly," said Annabel. It hadn't been possible to keep track of the days, even for Melchior, since neither of them had any idea when the castle had appeared again in the first place. "But I think it should come back at about half-term, too."

And that, she thought, a little sourly, was exactly like life at Trenthams—no chance to catch a breath.

"They'll be wanting to crown you straight away, I should think."

"Melchior says he'll introduce me to the parliament first. Officially, that is. At least half of them already know."

Isabella made a face. "What a bore! Necessary, of course, but still a bore. You should ask Poly to tell you what happened on the day *she* was introduced! Now there's a nice, stirring tale for you!"

"That?" Annabel grinned suddenly. "She told me. Actually, I was pretty curious about how she avoided being made queen, with everything that happened."

"It wasn't for lack of trying on the part of Wizard Council, I can tell you! As for the Old Parrasians—well, they tried to convince her, brainwash her, and kidnap her. I think one or two of them even tried to kill her. A bit foolish when Luck was looking after her, but still."

"A bit foolish of them considering what she can do, too!" said Annabel. "Anyway, it's pretty rude of them to be trying to threaten me as well, in that case! At least I'm queen heir by Right of Choice; Poly was just mistaken for the Civetan Princess!"

"I don't think the Old Parrasians care about Right of Choice, Rorkin or no Rorkin," said Isabella. "Not if the Chosen Royal in question isn't an old Parras-line Royal. They're not very reasonable people. You would think, Nan, that three hundred years would be enough time to do away with the bad feelings that invasion invariably excites, but when it comes to Royalists and Old Parrasians, it seems like it was yesterday."

"I suppose it's just a matter of surviving Trenthams until half term, then," Annabel said. "Poly and Luck said they'd come along to support me in parliament, so I'm not afraid of being killed there, at any rate."

Isabella sniffed. "Not unless you die a slow death of boredom, annoyance, and nit-picking."

"At least it's a different parliament now," said Annabel peaceably. "Not so many wizards all together, for one thing."

"A parliament is still largely a parliament," Isabella said dryly. "A little more diverse these days, at least, but it's still a vast, slow-moving machine that can't be brought to see what's under its own nose until you've shown it several times. They might not be obstructive by design now, but they certainly are by sheer incompetence."

"Yes," said Annabel. She still felt vaguely resentful about the amount of work she was going to be responsible for as soon as the crown was on her brow. "Melchior has been showing me how to do paperwork and make speeches for the last three years."

"Aren't you glad you'll have such a good ambassador!" said Isabella. "Just think how nice it will be not to have to worry about that appointment, at least!"

"I'm very grateful," said Annabel, and tried very hard not to roll her eyes. "By the way, did you see the bicycle girls this morning?"

"Of course. They're rather good at what they do, Nan; they didn't stop at all while they were in sight from our windows. One presumes they must have stopped where the wall dips in a little, since that's nearby where Dannick saw the maid retrieving a note. A very nice little drop, I think. One of them needs only to stop and tie a shoe or adjust her hat, and the thing is done!"

"And since they come back after riding out, there's no need to wait for an answer," agreed Annabel. "All they have to do is check when they come back. Well, if that's the line of communication between the Old Parrasians and Lady Selma, we'll have to get a look at a message or two somehow."

"Without giving away that someone has seen them," Isabella said, nodding. "I'm certainly not averse to sneaking a peek at their conversation, but I would like to remain undetected if possible."

"All right. I'll ask Jess exactly what time they come by," said Annabel. "But you'll have to distract the maid who collects the note. If we put it back right away, she shouldn't notice anyone has looked at it."

"Very well. In the meantime, I shall liaise with Alice; she's been absent to a few classes during the week and she hasn't reported to me since last night. I feel that I shouldn't contribute to the delinquency of the girls any more than necessary, so perhaps a small word or two is in order. I shall see you in time for Elegant Elementaries of Ensorcellment, Nan."

In fact, Annabel saw her rather sooner. Shortly before Advanced Conversation began, Isabella accosted her as she exited the library to join the class.

Her usually curved brows quite furrowed, Isabella said, "Nan, have you seen Alice today?"

"I thought the point was that you couldn't see her," remarked Annabel, closing the door behind her. She didn't like to leave it open;

no one could enter it without direct permission from either Annabel or Isabella, but if people *couldn't* enter it they tended to report the matter to the Awesome Aunts. With the door closed, the security spells made the library significantly harder to see to all but those invited in.

"I don't mind other people not seeing her," Isabella said, and it occurred to Annabel that her freckles were just a little bit more prominent than usual—was Isabella actually pale? "But she should have spoken with me last night, and again this morning. That wouldn't worry me, but the other girls say she hasn't attended lessons since yesterday morning. There are five demerit marks next to her name in the dormitories."

Annabel asked sharply, "What was she looking for?"

"That's the thing," Isabella said, biting her lip, "she didn't tell me. I could have pushed, but I should have hated to share anything if I weren't sure of it, either, so I let her have her head. She's a bright little thing, and she has only been poking about the school, so she couldn't have run into too much trouble. Surely not, Nan?"

"Do you think she's been watching Lady Selma?"

"I think not," said Isabella. "Whenever I did catch sight of her, she was out at the stables. There's nothing unusual in that; she loves horses and I'm almost entirely certain there are a couple of hidden passages I haven't found that start there and come into the school, but even hidden passages pall after a while if there's no excitement or adventure forthcoming. If she was investigating something she thought big enough to curate, it was out there."

"We'd better go out to the stables, then," Annabel said. "Shall we send another one of the girls with a regret slip and a request to see the nurse, or should we try to disrupt the whole lesson before it starts?"

"Certainly I was born to this life," said Isabella, a brief flash of amusement in her grey eyes, "but then there are the unexpected people like you, who come to this life and make it their own. You will certainly be a very good queen. I've an idea you'll be a good general, too, if it should come to that. By all means, let us disrupt the entire lesson; the more distraction, the better."

"I'll send one of the girls to ask Delysia to smuggle something explosive into Advanced Conversation," said Annabel. "Shall we meet at the stables at eleven?"

"At eleven," said Isabella, nodding.

At eleven exactly, there was a small, dull pop from the direction of the Advanced Polite Conversation classroom, and an accompanying puff of chalk dust through the three open windows. Annabel, who was passing below the classroom, smiled briefly and went on her way. Isabella was already at the stables, her expression roughly that of an engaged terrier, and was poking methodically into corners, nooks, and crannies with a whip.

"You'll have to check the stalls with horses," she said, when Annabel appeared. "I can't go in those ones."

Annabel blinked at her. "Are you allergic?"

"Certainly not," Isabella said. "I am allergic to nothing—in fact, I am entirely, disgustingly healthy and I only sneeze by design or request. I believe I mentioned at the beginning of term that I happen to dislike horses."

"Dislike?" Annabel found herself grinning. "You mean you're scared of them!"

"A queen should not jump to conclusions."

"A subject shouldn't tell her queen to search stalls that are full of horses," Annabel countered. "The royal person could be trampled."

"Oh, well, I suppose that's true, after all," said Isabella. "But I'm afraid it doesn't alter the fact that I can't enter any of those stalls actually containing horses!"

"Never mind," Annabel said, still grinning. "I'm mostly ambivalent about horses."

Fortunately enough, the horses were mostly ambivalent about Annabel as well, and it was a simple though smelly job to search each of the stalls. She had already gone through two stalls that were empty but for straw, a horse, and a few piles of manure, when she found herself in one that was empty even of a horse, but evidently hadn't been cleaned in a day or two. Annabel stepped through the door, frowning. Although it contained no horse, the door had been shut as though it did, and there was a horse blanket thrown carelessly in one corner.

Annabel looked down at that horse blanket with the vague feeling that a horse blanket ought not to have hands and feet, and said quietly, "Oh."

It wasn't a horse blanket. It was a small, crumpled figure with a horse blanket thrown haphazardly over it, as if the person who had thrown both into the stall hadn't been too concerned one way or the other about how well the body was wrapped, or how well disguised it was.

It hadn't occurred to Annabel until that moment that she had expected Alice to be in no worse trouble than being locked in a stall as a joke by one of the stable boys. She said, her voice cracking a little, "Belle!"

"Did you—oh!" Isabella stopped in the doorway for the briefest of moments, then hurried forward and dropped to her knees, regardless of straw and dust-coated manure alike. "Alice! Alice, can you hear me?"

"Do you think it's magic?" Annabel asked anxiously.

"No, I fancy that's blood beneath her head," said Isabella. She was even paler than before, although her voice was quite steady. "I believe someone has hit her quite hard—not, thankfully, enough to kill her, for she seems still to be breathing. Nan, do you suppose you can carry Alice's feet if I support her head and shoulders?"

Annabel didn't waste time with a reply; she lifted Alice's feet as Isabella raised the girl's head and shoulders from the horse blanket. The blue uniform revealed when they lifted Alice away from the horse blanket was torn and grubby, as if Alice had run for quite a way, then crawled, and finally wriggled through something both sharp and dirty.

"The Sanatorium!" panted Isabella. "Quickly!"

They bore Alice to the Sanatorium, stopping for neither wide-eyed classmates nor the hall monitors who began to call out a warning for tardy students and stopped abruptly at the sight of Isabella's pale face. Annabel, sick to her stomach with the thought that she had not only allowed but encouraged Alice to poke about as best she saw fit, thought she might be about the same shade as Isabella. One of the lockpicking class girls saw them as they came and ran ahead toward the Sanatorium, her feet loud against the hallway floor, to bring the nurse out to meet them.

"Put her on one of the beds," said the nurse, falling back to hold the door. "I'll see to her at once."

They did as they were told, gently lowering Alice onto the clean white bed, and although Annabel couldn't see it, she was certain the nurse was already working her own particular brand of magic. There was a line between her brows; and her eyes, scanning Alice from head to toe, seemed to see things that Annabel couldn't see. The nurse stared at Alice's head for some time with that same expression, and there was an anxiousness to the air that built up not only from Annabel but from Isabella as well.

"Take her shoes off, Miss Ammett, if you please," said the nurse. "Miss Farrah, hold her right hand and my left. I shall use you as an energy source."

Isabella did as she was told without question. Her face might have grown whiter, but Annabel, gently removing Alice's shoes, didn't think Isabella grudged the giving of that energy. Although she swayed, she continued to hold both hands until the nurse said, "That's enough."

"She's still too pale," Annabel said, biting her lips.

Isabella said, "I can keep going. You needn't stop on my account."

"That should do it for now," said the nurse, releasing both of the hands she had been holding. "I've stabilised the wound on the back of her head and started the healing process. We'll need to clean it, but it won't get any worse. I've also started a sustenance magic to build her up enough to wake."

"Will she be all right?" asked Isabella anxiously.

"She'll wake, if that's what you mean," the nurse said. "Who did this? Someone chased her to exhaustion and then tried to kill her!"

"We don't know," Isabella said, her eyes blazing in that too-white face. "But we will certainly make it our business to find out!"

"See that you do," said the nurse, surprising Annabel a great deal. "I've no idea what Alice was playing at, but I'm quite sure it had to do with you, Miss Farrah. That girl adores you."

"It was my fault, actually," Annabel said, still sick to her stomach. "She was looking into something for me."

"Don't be silly, Nan. You asked me if it was safe, and I said yes. It's entirely my fault. Will she really be all right, Nurse?"

"She'll be unconscious for another few days," the nurse said. She seemed to relent at their aghast faces, because she added, more encouragingly, "I won't wake her on purpose if she can wake naturally; I can't see that anything's been damaged badly, and my Sight is pretty good. If she'd been hit any harder—or any lower—it would have been another story. Whatever you're doing, Miss Farrah—fix it."

"We will," promised Annabel.

A little later, safely in the library, Isabella said, "I really don't understand." She wasn't so pale as she had been, now that the nurse had said there was no danger to Alice beyond another few days of unconsciousness, but her mouth was still very tight. "There should be no one in the school capable of this sort of thing. If it were the village I could understand it, but even Lady Caro would think twice about hitting another girl over the head."

"Are you sure?" Annabel was doubtful. Everything she had seen about Lady Caro indicated an entirely ruthless personality when it came to her machinations. "She *did* shoot at that Old Parrasian."

"Exactly," said Isabella. "At the Old Parrasian. She wouldn't hurt a Trenthams girl. Insofar as Lady Caro has loyalty, it's to Trenthams. I've no idea why, but I fancy her life at home isn't the kindest one. No, it must be one of the footmen or perhaps a master—but I don't fancy the Deportment Master doing it, and Melchior is the only other master here."

"Could someone have got inside the grounds?"

Isabella's brow furrowed, but she said, "There are too many wards. Too many rich girls, too many influential parents—the Awesome Aunts wouldn't leave that to chance."

"But if no one from the outside got in," Annabel said, finishing Isabella's unspoken conclusion, "then how did Alice nearly get murdered?"

"Exactly so."

"We can add that to the list of *Things We Want To Know*," said Annabel. "In the meantime, shall we have a guard on the door? If someone in the school *is* responsible for hurting Alice, they might think they killed her. When they find out—"

"Indeed," Isabella said. Her eyes were still very bright. "In this case, I fully advocate for telling Melchior. He'll put Dannick on the door—or Raoul, if it comes to that. What next should you like to do, Nan?"

"I want to find out what Lady Selma and the bicycle girls are sending notes about," said Annabel. "Because if one of the Old Parrasians did that to Alice, I want them out of the village and out of the school. I want to poke them all out of their dirty corners until this place is clean and safe again."

THE NEXT MORNING DAWNED BRIGHT AND HOT, BUT ANNABEL HAD no difficulty in rising. There was a sharpness of worry to her stomach that she couldn't quite place until Isabella said from across the room, "It's all right, she hasn't died."

Isabella was already up—had been up for quite some time, if her well-dressed appearance was anything to go by—her face bright and her eyes dangerously sparkling. "Nurse says she's perfectly fine, but she still wants her to wake naturally. Since Alice has already been through enough, I thought that best, too."

The sharp gnawing of worry eased a little, but Annabel asked, "Did you stop the other girls already?"

Isabella nodded. "Every one. They're not happy about it, but they'll obey. Dannick was pretty unhappy, too—he says he'll only take the order to stop directly from you."

"I'll have a word with him later," Annabel said. "All right, how are you going to distract Lady Selma's maid this morning?"

"Already done, Nan; already done!" airily said Isabella. "Lady Selma's maid is discovering a distinct lack of left shoes in her room, and a distressing want of stockings. If you should like to nip down to the drop point, I shall go back to loitering around the maid's room just in case anyone is kind enough to help her find the things she needs."

Annabel dressed hastily. Surprisingly, Isabella had already left out a frock for her, even though the attempt to gain information from Melchior was over, and she was hurrying down the stairs fifteen minutes later.

Down by the crook in the wall, Jess had said, when Annabel asked her exactly where the bicycle girls stopped, *and just past the two pencil pines. They'll wrap it around a rock and throw it over.*

It was a good place to drop notes, thought Annabel, strolling across the school grounds with careful casualness. A swell in the ground soon hid her from the view of anyone at ground level, and the pencil pines completed the job by hiding her from the view of anyone looking from the windows. There were more than a few pebbles and rocks there, too; if Annabel hadn't been looking specifically, she didn't think she would have seen the one that was wrapped with stone-coloured paper and tied with brown string.

"Got you!" she said happily, and pounced on it. She pulled one of the tag ends of sting just as a twig snapped behind her.

Annabel jumped guiltily, but it was only Isabella.

"Well, Nan?"

"I nearly jumped over the wall myself!" grumbled Annabel. She unravelled the string and separated the stone-coloured paper from the stone. "Oh. It's just an invitation card. Goodness knows how they got it wrapped around the rock—it's pretty stiff."

She smoothed it out against her leg, but when it was finally uncrumpled enough to read, there were only six words to take in.

Wednesday, Blackwood Manor, Midnight, Supper Provided.

Annabel blinked. "Is that all?"

"Every bit," nodded Isabella, gazing closely at it. "Not a drop of magical or invisible ink there."

"How would you know?" demanded Annabel.

"I'm very good when it comes to secret inks," Isabella told her. "Luck says it has something to do with my personality. Trust me, Nan; if there was anything else there, I would know it. Dear me! It appears that we have an appointment two nights from now."

"Yes, but—Well, is that all? Really?"

"Old Parrasians like to be ornate," Isabella said, "but despite the fact that it looks like an ordinary engagement, it will almost certainly be for the purposes of welcoming Lady Selma to the ranks. Not to mention deciding what next to attempt. One can only hope they don't intend on a complete overthrow of the government while they're about it!"

"Then we should go, too," Annabel said. "If they're going to be plotting over what to do to overthrow me before I'm even crowned—"

"Naturally we should go! I have an interest in finding out exactly who has been damaging my poor Alice's head, not to mention keeping you on your trajectory to official crowning."

Annabel wrapped the card back around the stone and retied the string. Now that she knew Alice was well on the way to recovery, she was feeling distinctly more cheerful. "I'll make sure to arrange a particularly nasty cell for whichever one of them did that," she said. "All right, we'd better get going before Lady Selma's maid comes along."

Isabella giggled. "If she can find another boot! Lady Selma is a trifle enraged, Nan—I heard her shrieking from her suite as I came down."

Annabel *tsk tsk*ed solemnly, but asked, "Will it be all right to go to the meeting? Both of us without any real magic, I mean? I can't use the staff to make us invisible, you know."

"Yes, there's the real difficulty," sighed Isabella, sober at once. "I believe I'll have to visit the Blacksmith's son during Interim Activities today, Nan. If I'm *very* tricky, perhaps I can manage to smuggle us in a decent invisibility spell."

"But the magic sensors—"

Isabella sighed again. "I know. But we'll need something of the kind. We could try to go early and sneak into a cupboard, but I couldn't guarantee we'd end up in a useful cupboard, and I don't approve of useless effort when it comes to informational gathering. Leave it to me, Nan. We'll discuss it further at breakfast."

"All right," agreed Annabel. It struck her that Isabella was perhaps a little sanguine for the difficult nature of her task, but Isabella was generally sanguine. It wasn't until breakfast arrived without Isabella also arriving that Annabel wondered if she had already run into difficulties.

Annabel was pouring her juice when she saw Isabella approaching through the press of students arriving at the same time. There was something of an annoyed bob to Isabella's walk.

"Nan," she said, plopping herself down in her usual seat, "there are *spies* in this school!"

Blinking at her breakfast ham, Annabel said, "I thought that was the idea."

"These ones," Isabella said, stiff with outrage, "are not mine! The absolute *cheek* of it, Nan!"

Annabel tried not to giggle. "What happened?"

"The Awesome Aunts sailed all the way down the hall to our suite just before breakfast to remind me that magic of any kind is not permitted at Trenthams, and that all pupils will be examined upon return to the school from the village after Interim Activities. They also suggested that a visit to the Blacksmith's son was tantamount to smuggling spells into the school and very pointedly told me they would see me today in the village, as they're going for an Outing."

Still trying hard not to giggle, Annabel said, "Someone must have seen us there when we were in the village last time. I daresay that's how the girls knew about us being attacked by the Old Parrasians, too. I don't suppose the Awesome Aunts will mention that, though."

"I find it unlikely," agreed Isabella. "Nan, it's at times like this that I realise what a trial a bad personality is! Merely because the Aunts have warned me that they will be watching, I have the greatest desire to smuggle some form of magic into the school, and it wouldn't at all do! After all, there's no sense in doing reckless things just because one has been warned not to do them!"

"Do you think someone knows we know about the meeting?"

"I certainly hope not!" Isabella said frankly. "No, Nan; I'm more inclined to think that they merely know we've been obtaining certain things that aren't strictly allowed at Trenthams, and are trying to make our lives more difficult. Mere spite. However, if the Aunts really are watching me—"

"You'll have to be careful you don't get caught," Annabel agreed.

"There's the difficulty," said Isabella darkly. "The kind of spell we need is a very strong one—premade, you see. As much as I'd like to spite the Awesome Aunts, I won't be able to sneak it in if they're carefully watching me. Oh, how vexing! If either of us had a decent amount of magic, this wouldn't be such an effort."

"What a shame you didn't think to cultivate a friendship with a strong magic user," Annabel said affably.

"Exactly so!" Isabella said, her eyes dancing. "What a cross little thing you are, Nan! As it is, we may very well have to shift for ourselves and do without invisibility. We couldn't leave something that strong hiding outside the school to get later without the chance of losing it. And now that the Awesome Aunts are watching, I don't see much chance of us being able to visit the Blacksmith's son or sneak anything through the Trenthams magic sensors either. I might have had a chance before that, but not now."

Annabel grew brighter with a sparkling, mischievous idea. "What if we didn't try to sneak one in? What if we snuck one out?"

"I take it all back," said Isabella instantly. "You're not a cross little thing, you're a delightfully devious little thing! I take it Melchior has something that could be useful to us?"

Annabel nodded. "A top hat. It's a really strong one because Peter made it for him—only I don't know when he made it for Melchior, because he and Peter have been quarrelling ever since they met each other."

"Not the sort of selfless thing I expected from Peter," agreed Isabella. "Are you entirely sure that the hat works, Nan?"

"Oh yes," Annabel said. "I've seen him disappear in front of my own eyes, and Luck says it's very hard for a spell to make someone disappear in front of your eyes."

"Very well," said Isabella. "In that case, the Blacksmith's son may very well already have helped us, after all."

"If you think Melchior will actually loan it to us—"

"Of course not. But the hat we must have, so we must needs try. I shall prepare accordingly. I will meet you outside Melchior's suite after lunch today, Nan."

❧ 17 ❧

I t was interesting to see Isabella work—actually work. Annabel, meeting her outside Melchior's suite, was quite certain that Isabella had spent at least some of the morning in the Sanatorium with Alice, but no trace of the softness she had seen the day before now remained on Isabella's face. Instead, there was only a certain, bright joyfulness. That look, Annabel was beginning to learn, was Isabella's battle face. Battle was joined for Isabella, whether it was in the matter of finding a spell to get them into the Old Parrasian meeting, or in finding the person who was responsible for putting Alice into the Sanatorium, and until it was done, she would sail through the world in a laughing, devious way, determined to do what needed to be done.

Herself more inclined to glower at the world than laugh at it, Annabel felt that it was something she would never quite understand about Isabella.

As for Melchior, he might not have understood it, but he was certainly wary when he opened his door to Isabella's sparkling face and Annabel's expressionless one.

"Absolutely not!" he said at once.

"Rude," said Annabel, blinking at him. "We haven't even asked you anything."

Melchior's hazel eyes rested mockingly on her. "Is that so? It's a social call, then, Nan?"

Annabel grinned, breaking the flatness of her expression. "No. We want something. But you could at least wait until we ask before you say no!"

"Very well," said Melchior. "But you had better ask quickly. What is it you want?"

"It's nothing at all," Isabella said sweetly. "Merely that we wish to borrow a small spell or two from your really very impressive collection!"

Melchior's gaze glanced from Isabella's innocent face to Annabel's once again expressionless one. He said crushingly, "Absolutely not. I seem to remember being kept out of a certain library last time one of you plagued me for a spell. I refuse to be on the receiving end of anything for which you plan to use a borrowed spell."

"Actually, it was Raoul's spell we used to keep you out," Annabel said. "Your spell keeps out everyone but you, and Raoul's spell keeps out everyone but him. He can't get in without an invitation, either."

"I'm sure you intended to soothe my feelings by telling me so," said Melchior, "but let me tell you, Nan, I am not soothed!"

"Oh," said Annabel. "Well, there's no need to be sniffy-nosed about it."

"I am not," said Melchior stiffly, "sniffy-nosed! And if you're planning on trying to winkle information out of me again—"

"Hopeful, or fearful?" Isabella asked, irrepressibly.

"That's quite enough from you, Firebrand!" said Melchior, after the briefest of pauses. "Exactly what spell were you hoping to borrow from me, Nan?"

"Don't tell him, Nan!" said Isabella, her eyes dancing. "He's not going to give it to us anyway."

At the same time, Annabel said, "Well, that's just insulting."

Melchior grinned. "Is it so, Nan? *Now* who's sniffy-nosed?"

"I'm not going to be baited into telling you, either," Annabel told him. "So don't even think about trying to make me lose my temper."

"What a shame!" mocked Melchior. "In any case, I've no intention of lending you any spells, no matter how pleadingly you look at me. If there is anything you require, you can simply ask for my help."

"We are," said Annabel, uncrushed. "We're just not telling you why we want it. You should trust us, Melchior. Actually, I seem to remember somebody saying something about trust, and not always telling things that aren't impo—"

"I daresay," Melchior interrupted. "However, I'm quite sure that anything you're up to is something you shouldn't be up to, and I refuse to help willy-nilly, without knowing what you're attempting."

"That's rich," Annabel said. "Never mind, Belle. We'll manage without magic."

"Manage what, exactly?"

"We want to break a school rule," said Annabel, once again borrowing Isabella's mantra of direct truthfulness. "And we can do it without magic, but it's easier with magic."

Melchior looked amused. "I see! Be that as it may, you'll have to do so without my help. Off with you both!"

"Rude," said Annabel again, but she said it cheerfully enough, and she thought that Melchior looked far less suspicious than he had done when they first asked the question.

"Oh, well done, Nan!" Isabella said, when they door had closed safely behind them. "You took down his suspicions completely! We will have to be very innocent and girlish over the next day and a half."

"Will we?" asked Annabel. "What will we do then?"

"We'll steal it off him, of course," said Isabella.

ANNABEL AND ISABELLA WERE THEREFORE GIRLISH AND INNOCENT when they went to breakfast the next day. Annabel fancied that Melchior was watching them a little more closely through breakfast than usual, but by the time they had been innocent and girlish through Melchior's lesson—with a brief respite to gaze avidly at him every time he looked in their direction—and girlish and innocent during the lunch break and their Interim Activities, his suspicions seemed to be absolutely allayed.

Since Annabel was by then very tired of being girlish and innocent, this was something of a relief. Isabella, who didn't seem to find the exercise a struggle, merely passed from girlish innocence to a bright-eyed anticipation as their evening appointment grew closer.

"Such a lovely night to sneak out!" she said, when Annabel commented a little sourly upon her evident enjoyment. "And such a lovely feeling of satisfaction, too, Nan, since it seems as though Melchior really doesn't know about this meeting! And the Black-smith's son was very useful after all, since I'd already smuggled in something that I got from him on our first day in the village. Very pleasing altogether!"

"That's all right," Annabel said, refusing to be cheerful, "but how are we going to get into Melchior's room without him knowing it?"

"We're not," said Isabella happily. "We're going to let him know we're there. He'll invite us in, in fact. I trust you know what the hat looks like?"

"He's only got three top hats," Annabel said. "It's the stateliest one. You know, the old fashioned kind. Belle, if Melchior invites us in, how are we going to steal the hat?"

"Sheer trickery, and my smuggling garters," said Isabella. "And perhaps a suggestion or two to misguide Melchior. Come along, Nan. Let us pay a call upon Melchior."

The door to Melchior's suite was opened by a wary and entirely sarcastic Melchior, who leaned against the door jamb and said warn-ingly, "I trust you're not here to badger me into loaning you a spell again?"

"Not at all," said Isabella. Her voice was perfectly agreeable, her face neither too innocent nor too conniving. "We're here for quite another reason."

Melchior was probably as well aware as Annabel that Isabella refused to lie except in the most exigent of circumstances. He consid-ered this and nodded. "Very well. In that case, come in."

Isabella sailed in, followed closely by Annabel, who was more concerned with sitting down on one of Melchior's comfortable chairs than sailing gracefully across the room like Isabella.

Melchior watched them both with something of a twisted mouth, and asked of Annabel, "Why are you really here?"

"We're hiding," said Annabel, with some truth. "The Deportment Master is looking for me, and the Awful Aunts are looking for Belle. They think she's up to something."

"It's all perfectly innocent," Isabella added. "Of course, *naturally* we came to eat your food, take up your time, and pilfer your things, but you can't really expect us to admit to those, so—"

Grinning, Melchior said, "Oh, is that all? It's very kind of you to tell me so! Very well, I'll grant you sanctuary."

"We thought so," nodded Annabel. "Aren't you going to offer us a cup of tea, Melchior?"

"I do beg your pardon. Bromian or Civetan?"

"I'm sure we're not difficult guests," Isabella said sweetly. "Whichever is easiest for you, of course!"

Melchior looked mistrustfully at her. "I find myself wondering exactly why it is that I feel worse than before."

"He doesn't trust us, Nan," said Isabella. "I think that's rude, don't you?"

"Very," agreed Annabel.

"Especially since I haven't done anything the *least* bit fire-brandy since we got to Trenthams! You can't—you *can't*, Melchior—possibly count the affair of the spell we procured from you, since that was entirely Nan's idea."

"There's more than a little truth in that," Melchior said, turning his hazel gaze on Annabel instead. "Nan, are you being a bad influence on the Firebrand? I wouldn't have thought it!"

"It was my idea," Annabel said. She felt rather pleased with herself about that. "So you can't really blame Belle for it."

On the other hand, quite a lot of what Isabella had done thus far in the term could have been considered distinctly fire-bearing, even if Isabella herself evidently didn't consider so.

"Belle is innocent," she added. "Ask the Awesome Aunts. Actually, ask the Meal Matron. Belle hasn't made a step out of line all this term."

"I'm misunderstood," said Isabella. "Never mind, it's evidently my cross to bear."

"All right, all right, there's no need to overegg it," Melchior said hastily. "I confess my fault and acknowledge that I've slandered you. I have evidently now only to call you in a less incendiary fashion: how do you feel about Carrots?"

Isabella inclined her head graciously. "An estimable vegetable."

"Now that I've apologised thoroughly, could we establish whether you care for Bromian or Civetan tea?"

"Civetan," Isabella said, with a small, prim smile. She apparently accepted Melchior's apology as her rightful due, without the slightest difficulty. Annabel would have found it hard to swallow in her place.

"We want biscuits, too," Annabel interrupted. She would have like-wise found Isabella's docile manner just a bit too much to swallow if she were Melchior, but as far as Melchior knew, Isabella really hadn't done anything wrong that term. "Since you don't mind us being difficult."

"Entirely my pleasure, Nan," said Melchior. He clicked his fingers with a snap of magic to set the kettle boiling and sauntered across the room to the door. "I'm sure you won't mind waiting?"

Annabel, equally as polite, said, "Not at all."

"I should mention," said Melchior, lingering at the door, "that I will undoubtedly be checking my suite for any foreign magic when you both leave."

"Rude," Annabel said.

A slight warmth of amusement lit Melchior's eyes. "Very well," he said, and closed the door behind him.

Across the empty tea table, Isabella's eyes met Annabel's. Annabel shook her head very slightly and said, "You know, I really think the Deportment Master has eyes in the back of his head! He wasn't even watching us this morning, and he still—yes? What do you need, Melchior?"

"Reassurance," said Melchior, from the open door. He vanished, closing the door behind him again, and this time Annabel was sure he wouldn't come back.

"Oh, well done, Nan!" said Isabella in a congratulatory manner. "Shall I take the hat, or shall you?"

"You might as well," Annabel said. "You're the one with the smuggling garters, after all—you did wear them, didn't you?"

"Of course! Why else should the Trenthams motto be *Don't put on your boots unless you expect to stand in the manure?*"

"I'm pretty sure the motto is *Always be prepared, ladies,*" said Annabel. "Actually."

"Exactly the same thing," Isabella said firmly. "Just a little more polite. Now, where does Melchior keep that spelled hat?"

"With the others," said Annabel. She found that rather amusing. "Is the other one still attached?"

"Certainly." Isabella adjusted her skirts and disengaged the top hat there from her smuggling garter. "Here, you take this one. I'll affix the other. I don't trust Melchior to be gone for long."

"I'm more worried about him realising we've swapped the hats," Annabel said. The hats looked almost exactly alike, but she couldn't see the magic to know for sure. She'd drawn the hat herself, and although she was able to draw items made from magic, she hadn't yet been able to draw a spell into one of them. Isabella had added the smallest touch of Don't See magic to the hat herself, with the fatalistic pronunciation that it would Have To Do.

"Nan," said Isabella, turning the real top hat over and peering at the hatband, "are you really certain Peter made this hat for Melchior?"

"He said so," Annabel said in surprise. "Actually, Peter said so, too." She remembered that day quite well—it was after a particularly acrimonious spat between Melchior and Peter, while Peter was trying to sweep out of the room with dignity. He had knocked over the hat stand in the hallway instead; and, being Peter, had picked up every hat and coat with the same attempted air of dignity, until he came across the top hat. Eyes narrow, he wheeled on Melchior, who had come out to watch him with a sarcastic curl to his lips, and demanded, "What's this?"

"You made that for me," Melchior had said, with what seemed to Annabel to be an entirely malicious amusement.

"I did?" Peter looked down at it again, frowned, and turned it over. He glanced back up at Melchior; then, to Annabel's surprise, he gave a laugh and tossed the hat to Melchior. "So I did," he said. "You'd better look after it, then. It's a good job."

And Melchior, his smile certainly more genuine than it had been, had said, "I shall certainly do so."

"It was one of those times when they were being mysterious," Annabel said now. "I never know if Peter knows what Melchior's talking about, or if he just refuses to admit he doesn't know. At any rate, they both said he'd made it."

"Yes," said Isabella, doubtfully, "but Nan, this hat is at least one hundred years old! And it's no good telling me that the spell wasn't put in at the time it was made, because it couldn't be this strong if it wasn't!"

This time it was Annabel who said, thoughtfully, "Yes. That's something I've been meaning to ask Melchior about, too. I would have asked Peter, but he's disappeared. Put it away quickly, Belle! If he comes back while your skirts are up like that—!"

"It's unwise to rush the attaching of things to the smuggling garters," said Isabella impressively, but she rearranged her skirts again just the same. "Now, Nan! We are presenting dulcet harmlessness for the remainder of our visit. In other words, don't stick out your tongue at Melchior."

"Isn't the blacksmith's son a useful person?" said Isabella happily, that night. True to her prognostications, it had been a very simple thing to sneak out of the school building itself, and if Annabel had had to climb a little more than she cared for these days in getting over the wall, at least the magical protections hadn't tried to stop them from sneaking out. Annabel was inclined to think that was a flaw in the Awesome Aunts' understanding of Trenthams girls in general and Isabella in particular.

"Who would have thought, Nan, that we would live in a day and age where such things as spell splitters exist! And completely non magical in nature!"

"My hat is too big," Annabel complained. "Who did you borrow it from?"

Isabella stifled a giggle. "Raoul."

"Does he know you borrowed it?"

"Certainly not!" Isabella said, shocked. "He would have been suspicious, and then he would have said something to Melchior. I'm certain Melchior would have been able to put two and two together. Do you want to wear Melchior's hat? It's a bit smaller."

"No, I just wanted to complain," said Annabel, more cheerfully. "My ears stop it from covering my eyes, so at least I can see. Actually, I'm surprised you don't have something like this of your own."

"I owned something very similar, once," agreed Isabella. "However, a sad series of events befell the poor object, and that was the end of that! They're not at all cheap to buy, and I fancied that it was better for me to be capable of managing without magic if I needed to do so. It is also why I bring very little magic into Trenthams."

"I thought you brought very little in because of the magic detectors," Annabel said.

Isabella grinned. "Oh, well! Perhaps that weighs with me as well! However, when it comes to anything other than personal hygiene, Nan, I really do think it's best to learn how to manage without magic. Well! This term, we've only had to beg or borrow—"

"—or steal—"

"I prefer to think of it as borrowing," Isabella said firmly. "After all, we are going to give it back, are we not? We've only had to beg or borrow two spells. I call that a good use of our own resources, really I do!"

"And we haven't been caught with either of them," agreed Annabel, who only considered it a good use of resources if the outcome was also useful. "Belle, you do know where this Blackwood Manor is, don't you?"

"Certainly I do! Why do you ask?"

"Jess said that it's quite far away, and we're on foot."

"I believe I've mentioned, Nan—"

"We're walking because you're afraid of *horses*?"

"There was no alternative," Isabella said. "Don't be like that, Nan! There's nothing better than a nice, brisk walk at twilight, after all!"

"And breaking our ankles or necks by tumbling down the bank," pointed out Annabel.

Still, by the time there were promising lights against the bruised pink and purple of the summer night sky, neither of the girls had suffered anything worse than the scratching of a blackberry cane or two. Even Annabel had begun to feel more cheerful. It was a delightful night, with a light, cool breeze that was very pleasant after the heat of the day at Trenthams, and as they approached Blackwood Manor, they encountered a single traveller on foot, who amused Annabel a great deal when, lacking the ability to see or hear the girls with their purloined hats, he concluded that the skirt he brushed against was likely to be a ghost and hurried on again with as much haste as he could manage with the singular tightness of his trousers and coat. Since this caused him to trot on ahead of them with roughly the gait of a sentient coat peg, Annabel found it difficult not to giggle. She found it easier when they actually approached the gate to the manor and turned down a short, stately driveway that was very full of Old Parrasian carriages and Old Parrasians on foot.

"Not very well managed," Isabella said, in a disapproving murmur. "Anyone could tell that it's a secret meeting! Even if they've given it about that it's a comet-gazing party, well! Just look at the carriages and the guests! They're in their everyday outerwear."

"Clumsy," Annabel agreed. "Perhaps they're expecting spies and they don't want to go to too much bother."

Isabella appeared to ponder that. "Well, perhaps so, Nan, but is that any reason not to do the thing properly? I call that an insult, I really do! But in any case, I recognise nearly every carriage here tonight, and there are none that I would have said don't belong here. I've never thought much of the intelligence of the Old Parrasian party as a whole—they make up what they lack in brains with ferocity and sheer determination—but I did expect a little more from them."

"They *are* out in the country, after all!" protested Annabel. "I mean, I don't think they're awfully clever either, but you can't expect them to take the same precautions in the country where no one is likely to see them, can you?"

"Perhaps not," Isabella said. "But I would certainly do so."

"Yes, but you're a suspicious sort of person."

"How impolite!" said Isabella cheerfully. "Do hang back a trifle, Nan."

Annabel, who had been looking ahead, was already slowing. There was nothing obviously different about the doorway through which each guest was passing, but it was slightly unusual for each of the guests, even those who had arrived together, to pass through separately. She wasn't sure if it was the footmen enforcing the separation, or if the guests themselves were familiar with the process and were going on just as usual, but it was quite obvious that there was some kind of check in place on the door.

"They've got a magic detector," she said. "I really don't like Old Parrasians, Belle! They're rude, they have pistols, and just when you don't expect them to be clever, they do something a little bit clever."

"A *little*," allowed Isabella. "However, the Old Parrasians have a tendency to fail when it comes to follow-through."

"You think they haven't got detectors on any of the other doors?"

"Exactly so! And I'm almost entirely certain they won't have any on the windows, either. What do you think, Nan? Should you like to try a window or the servants entrance?"

"I'm not climbing through another window," Annabel warned her. "You had me trying to climb through that window in the library, and Melchior nearly caught me at it. Dannick *did* catch me at it!"

Isabella grinned. "Don't be like that, Nan! Every girl should climb through a window or two in her youth so that she never forgets how to do the thing. You might need to revisit the skill when you're older."

"I'll thank you then," Annabel said. "Let's try the servants' entrance."

The servants' entrance was certainly busier than the front entrance, with maids popping in and out, and footmen calling to one another through the windows, but at least it seemed to have no magical protections attached. At any rate, there was no alarm that Annabel could hear when they entered, and nobody came running to see who had sneaked in. She and Isabella crept through the bustling kitchen, and once they had passed into the comparative safety of the dining room, where a vast array of food was laid out, Isabella said beneath her breath, "Goodness, aren't they luxurious! If I didn't know this is a disreputable meeting for the purposes of treason, I'd be inclined to think that the Old Parrasians are just pretending outrage for the purposes of eating a good dinner together every so often. It would explain why most of them are either very old and grey-haired, or young and bored."

Annabel tried very hard not to giggle. "You mean treason and espionage to stave off the loneliness of life?"

"Well, perhaps I wouldn't go right to treason," Isabella allowed, "but I do think an espionage club in one's old age is a perfectly lovely idea. Think of the interesting friends one could make! Outings included, and nothing boring allowed!"

"Do you think they'll have the meeting over dinner?"

"Certainly not! Not even Old Parrasians are so completely lacking in decorum. They'll have their meeting in the library—which, Nan, if I remember rightly, is just down the hall—and when the scent of dinner becomes too strong to resist, they will all abandon the library in a rush."

"If you remember rightly," said Annabel, passing over the facetious manner of Isabella's delivery, "is there anywhere we can hide if this hat spell goes wrong?"

"The spell won't go wrong," Isabella said in surprise. "It is perhaps the best one I've ever seen—not many invisibility spells, Nan, give the wearer the added measure of complete silence. But if you are asking where a convenient exit is should we be compelled to run for some reason, well, there's an antechamber that bridges the library with a sitting room. So convenient! That sitting room has large windows that are all quite easy to open."

"I see," Annabel said. She found she was smiling faintly as she followed Isabella down the entrance hall. A few of the meeting-goers were in the hall as well, but they were sparse enough to avoid easily thanks to the magic detector at the front door. "And exactly how often have you had the opportunity to be at Blackwood Manor?"

"Exactly once," said Isabella, her grey eyes flicking between the Old Parrasian ahead of them and the library door. "But I find it's useful to know where one's exits are, Nan!"

"That doesn't surprise me at all," Annabel said.

By the time they slipped through the door and into the library, there was already a small crowd of Old Parrasians gathered there—some women but mostly men, old and young alike. Instinctively tiptoeing even though they couldn't be heard, Annabel stole around behind the sofa closest to the second door, a dark, unobtrusive thing that was half hidden by bookcases and a drape of cloth. Judging from Isabella's approving nod, this was the door to the antechamber—and escape—should things go badly.

Across the room, Annabel could see the man who had led the attack on the badminton field. If he had been the leader of that particular group, he didn't seem to be the leading light tonight; that honour went to the gentleman with very large sidewhiskers and an even larger voice.

"Lord Tremare," Isabella said softly.

"Oh," said Annabel. She remembered Lord Tremare—or rather, she remembered him being particularly absent at any party she had attended. He had been so conspicuously absent, in fact, that it had been impossible to ignore.

Lord Tremare said, in his booming voice, "We've had a temporary setback, but it isn't without consolations. We're now familiar with the form the staff has taken, even if we've been unable to get our hands on the staff itself. When Lady Selma gets here, we can discuss further steps for discrediting the other heir—"

"Rude!" said Annabel. "*She's* the Other Heir!"

"—and solidifying Lady Selma's influence at Trenthams. Mistakes were made, but I'm sure that with the correct tools, Lady Selma will regain any ground she has lost. The other heir has no magic abilities of her own and should it come to a contest between the two of them, we have no doubt that we will prevail."

Isabella snorted quietly. One of the assembled men must have been similarly unconvinced, because he asked, "You said that, my Lord. You also said that we would have no difficulty in obtaining the staff with our last attempt—which failed miserably, if I remember aright. Indeed, the previous *two* attempts—"

"Mistakes were made," Lord Tremare said again, loudly. "However, should even this latest expedient fail, there is another plan in place. Do you think that one magic-less girl will be able to stand against every magic user in the Old Parrasian ranks?"

The man who had objected looked startled. "Is that why—"

Lord Tremare nodded. "Blackwood Manor is currently housing some of the strongest magic users in the Two Monarchies, and should all else fail we are prepared to move."

"When you say *move*," said the man who had objected, even more startled, "do you mean a direct attack? Were you able to find a way through the defences after all?"

"There was a small amount of trouble that was dealt with," Lord Tremare said, radiating smugness from his very sidewhiskers. "How else could we have joined Lady Selma on the badminton field at Trenthams. Should it be needed, we have the ability to attack directly."

"Goodness!" said Isabella. "I thought they had been let in by someone!"

"Do you think the trouble he's talking about—"

"Alice," Isabella said gravely, nodding. "Nan, when I find out who did that to Alice—! Oh! Here's Lady Selma now! Things should get quite interesting now."

Annabel looked over to see Lady Selma at the door, her mouth tight.

"You'd best stop speaking so loudly," she said to Lord Tremare, worrying Annabel by looking around the room with her pale blue eyes narrowed. "Somehow one of those awful girls got hold of my invitation, and you can be certain they told that new master at Trenthams. He's probably figuring out how to sneak in here if he isn't here already."

"Did I not say," hissed Isabella, in Annabel's ear, "that there were a sad amount of spies at Trenthams? Absolutely riddled!"

Lord Tremare leaped to his feet. "They know we're here, tonight? Why didn't you send word, you stupid girl?"

"I just learned about it," Lady Selma said. Coldly, she added, "If you're so concerned, you'd best run an unmasking spell. I'm going back to the school before it's noticed that I'm missed."

"Going back—You can't leave!"

"I became a part of this because you told me it was safe!" snapped Lady Selma. "During the course of my stay at Trenthams, I have been shot at by *your* men, not to mention being partnered with a girl who told me that if I injured any of the other girls in the course of my activities, she would shoot me herself! I have seen the things of which Miss Ammett is capable, and I refuse utterly to put myself into danger from her!"

"The other heir," said Lord Tremare, with the air of one barely holding onto the frayed threads of his patience, "has no magic! If it comes to a contest of magic, you will certainly prevail! Gregor has prepared—"

"He gave it to me," interrupted Lady Selma. "And now I'm going back. If you fancy remaining here to talk while that Trenthams Master could be sniffing about, I have nothing more to say. Good night."

She swept back through the door and it snapped shut behind her with ominous loudness in the quiet room. As Annabel watched, the Old Parrasians exchanged uneasy glances, and someone said, "We'd best run an unmasking spell."

Annabel said, "Belle—"

"Not to worry," Isabella said softly. "An unmasking spell won't work against something this strong. I really must congratulate Peter if I see him again."

"Run the spell," said Lord Tremare shortly to the man who was sitting behind him with crossed legs. That man hadn't even moved when Lady Selma came through the door, his face still in shadows, but Annabel thought he looked familiar. His hands rose in a graceful symbol that was foreign to the non-magical Annabel but seemed to her uneasy mind to be distinctly malignant.

A flutter of movement rippled across the corner of the room behind Lord Tremare—a shadow, or a shape that was lounging, top hatted, and distinctly familiar...

"Belle!" Annabel said, in a panicked whisper. "Belle! It's Melchior! He really is here! He's here and he's *wearing the wrong hat!*"

"Dear heavens!" said Isabella blankly. "What an awful man! How in the world did he find out about this?"

Annabel repressed a frustrated squeal with some difficulty. "You said they weren't very careful about it—he probably found out from Raoul. This is what happens when he doesn't share things with me!"

"Now, Nan," Isabella said calmly, as Melchior's shape grew solid in the corner of the room, his hazel eyes watchful, "I'm very much afraid that Melchior is going to be captured."

Annabel observed the scene gloomily. "Yes, I think so. All right, there's no need to look at me so worriedly! I'm not going to rush in and try to save him in the open unless things go badly. I can do better here where they can't see me. The staff is lovely, but it's better used when I don't have to worry about magical attacks as well as physical ones."

"And you can remonstrate with Melchior later," agreed Isabella.

"He'll probably remonstrate with me, too. We did steal his hat, after all."

"I ask you, Nan; how could we possibly know he'd do something so foolhardy as sneak into an Old Parrasian meeting with nothing but a Don't See hat?"

"He would have been all right if he'd come with the real hat," said Annabel, feeling rather badly about everything in general. "But he's not going to be all right in that little Don't See thing."

As she said it, the spell completely flickered and died. Just a little bit too far away from the door stood Melchior, a rather startled look on his usually composed face and very clearly aware of all the eyes that were now on him.

"Got you!" said the magic user, sitting forward with a satisfied curl of the lips.

Melchior said something very rude and opened one of his tunnels in the wall. Annabel, with a sick, jumping heart, watched it close again and felt the first trembling signs of relief.

"Stop him!" screamed Lord Tremare. "Gregor! Stop him at once! He carries a spell of recording for trial use!"

Annabel stiffened, recognising the magic user far too late. "That's the one who pulled the trigger—"

"Exactly so," Isabella whispered. "I remember with remarkable clarity. Nan, do you remember me saying that you ought not to rush out and attempt a rescue?"

"Of course I—what do you mean?"

"I mean that it may well become necessary. That man doesn't care enough and that's dreadfully dangerous in this sort of work."

Annabel watched the scene anxiously, wishing, not for the first time, that she could see magic as other people did. "Do you think he's got very strong magic?"

"I am very much afraid," said Isabella quietly, as Gregor raised his arms and made a large, sweeping circle with them, "that his magic is *excessively* strong."

At first, it seemed as though the grand circle had achieved nothing. Annabel, who had slipped the pencil staff out of her pocket at the very first sign of Melchior's danger, felt the barrel of the pencil digging into the pads of her fingers and was almost tempted to loosen them. Then the section of the wall that was still spinning slightly with a suspicion of darkness where Melchior's spell had affected it, stopped absolutely and seemed to reverse its spiral.

"Oh *bother*!" said Annabel, and flipped open her notebook as well.

Across the room, the darker section of wall hadn't reversed, exactly; instead, it had begun to revolve from top to bottom, a glass-like slickness growing where it spun until it began to look less like a spiral and more like a sphere. A sphere, Annabel realised, that was beginning to separate itself from the wall as it revolved, glassy and round. Nor was there any doubt as to the purpose of that sphere or its contents; as it separated from the wall, the revolving blackness within cleared to a vague suggestion of filminess and there was Melchior, sitting down calmly, cross-legged. Annabel might have thought he was resting comfortably if it wasn't for the fact that she could see the lines of strain beside his eyes, and the way his arms were extended on each side, open palms pushing against the empty space between himself and the walls of the bubble.

If she was right, he wasn't breathing very deeply, either. Annabel asked, in a voice that was suddenly far too thin, "How much air do you suppose he's got in there?"

"What I think," said Isabella, "is that you ought to get him out of there as quickly as you possibly can without getting us all caught. He seems to be holding off the spell on his own, but I believe he's having difficulties breathing."

"All right," said Annabel, who had been busily drawing. "But what I'm going to do will make it even harder for him to breathe for a little while. I don't want to kill him if it takes too long."

"In normal circumstances I would be the most avid supporter of caution," said Isabella. "However, in this case, Nan, Gregor is clearly unconcerned as to whether Melchior lives or dies. I really think Any Means Possible should be our watchword at this point."

"Amongst your classes," said Annabel, with a throat that seemed to close up on the words, "I don't suppose you did one on Revivification?"

"Now, funnily enough, Nan—"

"I'm glad to hear it," said Annabel, smudging a last shadow on her drawing. There was a distinct swelling in her throat, with a corresponding hotness to the back of her eyes, and she wasn't sure if she was angry, crying, or both. Melchior's cheeks were very pale now, his lashes fluttering dark against them as he struggled to keep his eyes open, and the backs of his hands dropped against his knees as the bubble drew in around him.

On one page of her notebook there was another Melchior, drooping and waxy but resistant still, his eyes nearly shut and his palms just barely keeping the curve of the bubble at bay. On the other side was a third Melchior, this one lying on his back in the parlour that lay on the other side of the antechamber, his eyes still open a slit.

"Go to the parlour," Annabel said. "Quickly! Revivify Melchior."

"What will you do? Nan, if the hats are too far separated—"

"Revivify Melchior. I'll be along shortly. I can't leave this one just yet; I need to make it complete and Melchior doesn't have that much time!"

"Nan—"

"If you don't Revivify Melchior," said Annabel, her voice as sharp as the point of the pencil staff, "I won't ever speak to you again, Belle."

"I won't fail," Isabella said, and she was gone in a light flutter of skirts.

❧ 18 ❧

nnabel drew. With the library shouting and flying with magic all around her, she shaded furiously until the Thing she had drawn was real and present enough to keep the Old Parrasians engaged. Then she stood, her knees far weaker than she would have liked, and stole through the melee toward the antechamber door. Nobody saw as she slipped through the door and shut it behind her, and there was nothing in the antechamber but for the dust that clouded as she passed through.

On the other side, Annabel paused for a moment, her heart beating too fast. What if she hadn't drawn it correctly? She had never seen the parlour on the other side of the door; she had merely drawn a plain section of wall with the edge of the antechamber door peeking in to give the staff a direction. But if the door here was different to the one on the other side—if she hadn't given enough details—would Melchior really be there? The painted wood of the door felt cold beneath her fingers.

Annabel swallowed and opened the door all at once, in a rush.

"Nan!" said Isabella's voice thankfully. She was crouched directly beside the door. "I thought you were one of the Old Parrasians!"

That was certainly Melchior sprawled on the floor, Isabella's hand resting lightly on his stomach. Annabel felt a flush of relief, and then a second wave of coldness when she couldn't tell if his chest rose and fell.

"Is he—I mean, can you wake him up? It'll be hard to get him back to Trenthams like this."

"It's no good," said Isabella. "He's alive, but could be some time before he wakes up. I've seen this kind of magical exhaustion before. I'm afraid we're on our own, Nan."

Annabel drew in a deep breath that wobbled in the middle. "All right," she said, "but if this doesn't work, I'm going to tell Melchior it was his fault."

"If what doesn't—oh. Oh, I really admire your way of thinking, Nan!"

"Good," said Annabel, with one eye on the door that was forming in the parlour wall under the influence of the pencil staff.

Isabella watched it with her mouth open. "I could really fancy it to be the door to Melchior's suite!"

"Good," said Annabel again. "Because it is. Sort of. Could you open the door, Belle?"

"That's the question, isn't it?" said Isabella, but she reached out anyway. The knob Annabel had drawn without paper turned beneath Isabella's fingers and opened into a softly lit room that was almost as familiar as their own suite. Through the antechamber door, faintly, Annabel heard shouts of *The parlour! In the parlour!* and her hands went cold. They must have called down the other magic users to help disintegrate her drawing.

"Oh well done, Nan!" said Isabella encouragingly, as if there was no one else but the three of them within earshot. "I've got his feet—goodness, isn't he heavy!"

They wrestled him through the door as quick footsteps sounded in the antechamber, and Annabel, panting put Melchior's torso down on the carpet with rather less gentleness than haste. She slammed the door again, her back pressed against it and her heart beating very fast.

"Ah," said Isabella. "I didn't think about this part—oh, Nan, do you really think it's wise to erase the door completely?"

"I'm not," Annabel said, furiously erasing. "That's why it took me a bit longer—this door isn't in quite the same place as the one from the parlour."

"I thought I was seeing double from the stress. Goodness! Do you think they'll be able to beat on the door for much longer?"

Annabel, who had jumped violently at the thumping assault on the other side of the door, continued to erase the doubled line around Melchior's door. Much to her relief, the noises faded as the second doorway did, and by the time it was gone the thumping had vanished just as entirely. She opened the door anyway, her fingers icy, and the familiar hall at Trenthams wafted cool, school-flavoured air into Melchior's room.

"Well," said Isabella. "That was a little more fraught than I had counted upon, but really, I think we can blame Melchior for that as well. Our own plans were very nearly perfect."

Annabel stared at her through the doorway, then dissolved into ridiculous giggles. "I'll be sure to tell him that when he regains consciousness!" she said.

"Melchior would be the first to admit it," Isabella said firmly. "Come back in before you wake the hall, Nan. *That*'s better. Perhaps we can carry Melchior to the sofa before we give in to our laughter."

"It's too late now," said Annabel, hiccoughing. "Oh, Belle, shouldn't we take him to his bed?"

"Absolutely not! He's a great deal heavier than I anticipated, and if he was so foolish as to wander into an Old Parrasian meeting with nothing but a Don't See on his top hat, I really think—"

"All right, all right," Annabel said, giggling again. She wasn't sure if she was overtired or overwrought, but it was far too easy to giggle ridiculously with Isabella around. "No, no, leave him to me, Belle. Go to bed before we both get caught in a master's room past lights out. I'll stay with him until he wakes up and make sure he's all right."

"Very well," agreed Isabella, and added piously, "But if you get caught in your bad character I'll not stand by you, and so I warn you!"

Since she waved goodbye at the door with an airy, "Give him something to drink if he wakes up, Nan!" Annabel was left to the comforting conclusion that there was nothing wrong with Melchior that a night of rest wouldn't fix. She covered him with the soft lap quilt that always made a bright patch of colour against the brown armchair and sank to her knees beside the sofa where she could see Melchior's chest rise and fall in a reassuring manner.

A<small>NNABEL HAD BEEN QUITE SURE THAT SHE WOULDN'T FALL ASLEEP.</small> There was still an unpleasant feeling in her stomach that said Melchior could have—and very nearly *had*—died, and she knelt where she was with the confident assurance of watching over Melchior until the morning came, if need be. Certainly she didn't lose the feeling of unpleasantness that moved uneasily in her stomach, but in spite of it, Annabel slept. She woke once during the night when Melchior stirred enough to murmur, "Nan?", and tucked the hand that was rather aimlessly trying to reach out and touch her face back beneath the lap quilt. Melchior allowed it with a lack of protest that made her think he was still quite weak, and went back to sleep.

This time, when Annabel fell asleep, she did so with the comforting warmth of Melchior's open eyes in her mind. She woke to the bright dawn with her head resting on Melchior's chest, and the brighter gleam of Melchior's eyes as they gazed at her.

"Good morning, Nan," he said, his eyes entirely awake and sensible.

Annabel, with a gleeful laugh that he was alive, and whole, and bright, seized his face with both hands and kissed him full on the mouth.

Melchior last night might have been fainting and lacking strength, but Melchior this morning was entirely recovered. Two arms folded themselves around her at once, and Melchior kissed her back with as much enthusiasm and considerably more skill.

Very much startled, Annabel pushed herself away and stared at him.

"Dear me," said Melchior, gazing up at her. "I seem to be making a remarkable amount of mistakes lately. Nan—"

But Annabel, at first frozen and confused and then merely confused, was already darting from the room. She didn't remember closing the door behind her, or the hall passing beneath her feet. She didn't remember anything, in fact, beyond Melchior's voice calling out her name, until she found herself sitting on the floor in the library, out of breath and with a heart that beat too fast.

Disbelieving and entirely bewildered, Annabel clutched her arms around her knees. Why had she done that? Why in the world had she kissed Melchior? Worse, why had she run away? If she hadn't run away, she could have blamed it on her relief at seeing him awake and alive. But she had kissed him, and she *had* run away, and now she couldn't even pretend to herself that she had kissed him merely because she was glad he was alive. How could she face him again? How could she even face herself in the mirror?

Annabel groaned and buried her face in her arms. There was no reason to be suddenly kissing Melchior. Wouldn't he scold her! After he had been twitting at her for weeks not to hang around his neck and pat his head; not to whisper in his ear or be too familiar like she had been used to be with Blackfoot! Between that and her Isabella-instigated flirting, she would never hear the end of it.

Annabel groaned again. She thought it might not be so bad if she could only explain to *herself* what had happened, but she couldn't even do that. She had simply been so glad to see Melchior's face—so glad to see his eyes open and bright, so glad to know he was alive, and here, and hers—that she had kissed him before she knew what she was doing. And yet, that wasn't all it had been. There had also been a thought that—a thought that—and had Melchior kissed her *back*?

"Oh, this is no good!" she muttered, and climbed grimly to her feet. She was going to go for a walk in the garden. A *long* walk. A walk where it would be extremely unlikely for her to run into Melchior—or Isabella and Isabella's sharp eyes, if it came to that. Annabel didn't think she could bear to be under Isabella's knowing gaze. That gaze left her with the feeling that Isabella knew a great deal more than Annabel did, and that if she asked, Isabella might just tell her those things. Annabel wasn't sure she was ready to hear anything from Isabella right now.

Unfortunately for that particular plan, she met Isabella just outside the library door.

"Oh good!" said Isabella affably. "I was hoping I would run into you here!"

"I don't want to talk about it!" Annabel said at once. She could already see the keenness to Isabella's grey eyes. "I'm going for a walk!"

"Very good," approved Isabella, clinging to her arm, "only *not* that way, Nan! If you go that way you'll meet Melchior. He seems to have a pressing desire to find you. Shall we go through the servants' exit?"

"Yes," said Annabel hastily, "let's!"

They exited the building with something of the air of prisoners escaping into the freedom of the outside world, glancing around hastily at the open stretch between themselves and the dubious cover of the garden.

"The gardens it will have to be," Isabella said. "We can be seen from the windows, but we have the added advantage of being able to see anyone approaching, so if Melchior sees us, we'll have ample opportunity to escape before he gets to us. Now Nan—"

Annabel, marching away toward the garden hedges, said firmly, "I told you I don't want to talk about it!"

"Oh, this is no fun!" protested Isabella. "Not those hedges, I think, Nan; we want to be able to see anyone approaching, after all!"

"All right," Annabel agreed reluctantly. She had walked almost instinctively toward the cover of the larger hedges, but Isabella was right—the higher hedges were no cover from the windows, and it would only make it harder to see Melchior if he did come out to find her.

"One would think, Nan," Isabella pursued, with a flagrant disregard for Annabel's stated preferences, "that you had done something unseemly. One would think—"

"I kissed Melchior," Annabel interrupted. "And if you keep talking about it, I'm going to use the staff to—"

Isabella clapped her hands. "Oh, lovely! No, no; don't threaten me with the staff. I know you won't do it, you see! I'll be still now."

Annabel eyed her suspiciously. "Oh, *will* you?" It was more than she expected.

"Certainly," Isabella said, inclining her head. She sat down on a stone bench that was on the edges of a courtyard just within the first few hedges, and smiled sunnily. "My curiosity is now partially sated and I can withstand some little areas of uncertainty until I know the whole."

"You're not going to know the whole," Annabel told her, sitting down beside her.

Isabella only continued to smile in a way that made Annabel think she believed that even less than she had believed Annabel's threat to use the staff. That smile, however, faded a moment later.

"Bother," said Isabella, gazing across the courtyard. "We seem to have escaped one annoyance only to find another. Shall we get up and take another path?"

Annabel looked up to where Lady Selma was purposefully approaching them, and came to a surprising and unwelcome conclusion. "No, I wouldn't bother. I think she'll just follow us."

"Yes, she does appear to be sailing with intent," agreed Isabella. "Judging by what we heard last night, I'd think she's under orders, wouldn't you?"

"Probably," Annabel said gloomily. From a flutter of movement in her periphery, she was aware that a great many Trenthams girls were also approaching through the gardens. Either they'd seen the pending meeting from the windows and flowed down to see it in person, or, more likely, Lady Caro had spread it about that there was about to be a confrontation. "Oh well, we might as well get it over with. I don't want to go back into the school right now, and the girls are all coming out anyway, so I suppose no one's having breakfast this morning."

"Good day, Miss Ammett!" called Lady Selma. "No, don't run away."

Annabel looked pointedly down at the bench upon which she and Isabella were presently seated, and then back up again in time to see the impatience that flashed across Lady Caro's face. So Lady Caro really was finding it difficult to deal with the heir she'd chosen!

"We two," said Lady Selma, drawing off her gloves in a business-like manner, "should have some discussion."

"This probably seems like a good time to you," Annabel said to Lady Selma, in what she was aware was one of her grumpier voices, "but I'm having a really bad day today, and it's actually not."

"Since when should the Queen of New Civet care about whether or not something is at good time for one of her subjects—particularly a treasonous one?"

"I'm glad you brought that up," said Annabel. Her tone degenerated from mere grumpiness and into sheer annoyance. "Belle, is it your opinion that the queen heir of New Civet should consider the feelings of a treasonous subject?"

"It is not."

"Oh good," said Annabel. "That's what I thought. Lady Selma, I've had a very bad night and a trying morning, so I'm going to give you one chance to pack your bags and leave Trenthams before I have you confined to jail pending trial."

Lady Selma laughed, a light, brittle thing that seemed aware her followers only barely matched those that were beginning to gather around Annabel. "What nonsense is this? I'm the real queen heir!"

"If you're the real queen heir," Annabel said, in a voice very clear and carrying, "you ought to know about the staff."

There were a few murmurs of agreement from Annabel's side, and a mutter of "Honestly, who cares about Rorkin's Staff nowadays?" from Lady Selma's side of the courtyard.

"People who care about New Civet lasting a bit longer than Parras did," said Delysia, daintily shouldering her way to the front of the crowd. "So there, Elvira!"

"You can't talk to me like that!" instantly retorted Elvira. "You're only a third daughter of a Mister!"

"I might only be the third daughter of a Mister, but I'm as much a New Civetan as you are," Delysia said promptly. "In New Civet, one can say exactly what one likes, so long as one is prepared for the consequences." She looked Elvira up and down, and added, "You might want to think about whether or not you're prepared for the consequences of what you say, El! Did you know I can make pottery that explodes?"

Elvira squeaked. "I'm not saying Miss Ammett isn't the heir!" she protested. "I'm just saying that the staff is outdated and our government is more stable now than when the idea of the staff was first brought up. If we're going to bring back the monarchy we ought to be able to choose who we want on the throne without consulting a *staff*!"

"*I*," said Lady Selma, ignoring the larger part of that speech, "am saying that Miss Ammett isn't the heir!"

"That's all very well," Annabel said, "but there's still the matter of the staff, isn't there? I thought that was made pretty clear on the badminton field a few days ago, actually."

"What about it?" Selma asked. Her pale blue eyes were even harder to read this morning; Annabel couldn't tell if she really didn't have anything prepared and was going to bluff it out, or if she was so confident in her preparations.

"Rorkin left it so that there wouldn't be any insecurity about who's the rightful Heir," Annabel said. "And you agreed with that on the badminton field, too. So let's see it. Your version of the staff. We might as well get it over with while it's a bad day already."

"My version?" Selma said. "It's not a version, it's the real staff! Well, show me yours, if you're so certain of yourself!"

"You've already seen it," said Annabel, drawing the pencil staff out of her pocket.

"That thing?" asked Lady Selma scornfully. "Oh well, if you call colluding with the Old Parrasians to make it look like you've got the real staff proof—!"

Isabella stifled a laugh. "Good heavens, really? Oh, Nan, this is no fun! It's far too easy!"

"You won't find it so easy to dissemble this time," Lady Selma said, and there was enough coldness in her voice to make Annabel gaze at her, frowning. The other girl smiled and displayed an elegant wand, gold-toned and beautiful. "Shall we see what the real staff is capable of, Miss Ammett?"

"Go ahead," Annabel said, sighing. Lady Selma was going to do exactly what she wanted to do anyway; Annabel might as well wait and see what there was to undo once Lady Selma finished. Perhaps she could put an end to this uncertainty once and for all.

Lady Selma, smiling, gestured daintily with her pretend staff, and at least half of the girls present gasped.

Oh dear, thought Annabel. Lady Selma was obviously a very good magic user. There was a brief rustling behind Annabel, and before she knew what was happening, every girl on her side of the courtyard was snatched up into the air. There was a volley of screams from both the suspended girls and some of those on Lady Selma's side, and a wild rustling of white petticoats and flailing feet.

"What are you doing?" demanded Lady Caroline, wheeling on the other girl. "They'll be hurt if they fall from that height! Let them down at once!"

"Shall I?" Lady Selma smiled coldly at her, and the girls above them dropped three feet, shrieking.

Isabella's voice said doubtfully, "I really hate to be a bother, Nan, but I don't find myself enjoying this turn of events."

Annabel, with her eyes on the suspended girls, felt for her sketchbook; and, drawing it out, began to sketch.

Lady Selma laughed. "Is that all you're going to do? I think you'll find your drawings are no match for the staff, Miss Ammett. It's really very powerful, and if you're not inclined or able to save the girls, may I suggest that you leave?"

"I'm not going to leave," said Annabel, busily sketching a strong, invisible floor below the girls. Perhaps it was because she had already been scared out of her wits last night by Melchior's brush with death, or perhaps she had simply worn out her store of emotions earlier this morning, but now she only felt faintly annoyed.

"Really? You might think better of it, Miss Ammett, when I tell you that if you don't return to the school and pack your things to leave right now, I shall allow your supporters to fall from where they are. Miss Farrah is a bouncy kind of girl, but do you really think she'll survive a drop from that height?"

Lady Caroline turned on her with dark, wrathful eyes. "Lady Selma—!"

"This is just ridiculous!" Annabel snapped, dropping the sketchbook as she stood. She wasn't prepared for a battle of magic—she wasn't equipped for it, and if it came right down to it, she wasn't inclined to go through any such farce when she could avoid it altogether. She reversed the staff and erased Lady Selma's pretend staff in a businesslike manner.

"Don't!" cried Lady Caro, but the pretend staff was already gone.

The girls above them, their petticoats ruffling in the breeze, dropped an inch and stopped abruptly.

Lady Selma's eyes narrowed. "What did you do? How dare you erase my staff!"

"I really think the question under your consideration ought to be whether your own side will scrag you, or if you're content to wait until the rest of us get back down there," said Isabella, from above. "Those are the questions that spring immediately to *my* mind. Of course, one of life's beauties is that each of us has a differing point of view, but I fancy the point of view on this is pretty similar all around."

Delysia, tapping one foot gingerly against the invisible platform on which they all stood, called out, "Miss Ammett, Miss Marriot says please could you possibly get us down now because she didn't wear her long drawers today and it's a bit breezy."

There were stifled giggles from above, and Miss Marriot could still be heard protesting when Annabel retrieved her sketchbook and drew in some slightly more visible stairs by which the stranded girls could descend. She left it to Isabella to encourage the more frightened girls down from their platform, and turned her eyes on the girls behind Lady Selma.

"You," she said to them. "Are all of you really going to keep standing behind a person like that?"

There was a shifting and a murmuring. Lady Selma, her face pink and stiff with outrage, said, "You'll regret this, Miss Ammett."

"I really don't think so," said Annabel, her voice hard. "Go back to your room and start packing your things. Don't bother me again. And if I see you put another girl's life in danger while you're still here, I'll erase your legs until someone can come to lock you up properly."

Lady Selma's face went perfectly white. She picked up her skirts and fairly ran across the lawn toward the school, bringing to Annabel's attention the fact that most of the teachers were spilling from the school, Melchior with them.

"Don't thank me!" she said to the rescued girls who were crowding around her, safe and excited and chattering, "just make sure the teachers don't catch up with us!"

"Oh, are we fleeing?" asked Isabella in high amusement, as the girls flocked toward the teachers as one. "It's all very undignified, but all right!"

They ran for it while the other girls surrounded the teachers, circling back around by the taller hedges until it was clear to slip through the library window to safety.

Once there, Isabella, retying her bustle and rearranging her skirts, said cheerfully, "Well, Nan what shall we do now that we've thoroughly routed the Pretender Heir? Shall we go and find Melchior?"

"No," said Annabel, repressing a shudder. She found that she would still prefer to face the problems brought about by the Old Parrasians. "Why do you think we ran away?"

"I thought you believed in facing your problems immediately," said Isabella innocently. "How dreadfully disappointing!"

"There are still problems from the Old Parrasians!" protested Annabel. "Alice is still unconscious, and you heard Lord Tremare—!"

"Oh yes," said Isabella, immediately serious again. "If he wasn't simply trying to make Lady Selma and the others feel better, they've really found a way into Trenthams. No doubt that's why Alice was hit on the head—she must have caught them at it."

"Yes. And if Lady Selma is inclined to make trouble, she might try to get a message back to them."

"Ah."

Annabel watched the flickering of thoughts as they passed over Isabella's face, and said, just as Isabella's face lit up, "Belle, do you suppose that Delysia has finished with—"

"Her explosive?" Isabella's face sharpened in a combination of enjoyment and consideration. "A very good question! A more important one, I believe, would be if she has finished making it explosive from a safe distance."

"Exactly," said Annabel, nodding. "And I think we're going to need as much as we can get."

IT WAS WELL PAST MIDNIGHT WHEN ANNABEL RETURNED TO HER suite. She had very carefully tried not to think about Melchior while she was helping Delysia to package explosive in small, palm-sized amounts with a pretty ribbon around the top of each package. She tried not to think about him while she planted explosive all over the Trenthams lawn in the chirping darkness, and she tried even harder not to think about him while she helped Isabella scour the stables for any sign of hidden passages through which any Old Parrasians could clandestinely enter the schoolgrounds.

"That's no good," said Isabella at last, when they were both wearied of horses and manure. "There's not a sight of an outside passageway! I'm beginning to doubt that even Alice could have found one. Never mind, Nan; we'll keep making preparations, just in case. I've no objection to becoming smelly and stained in a good cause, but this does seem like a useless endeavour."

"Yes," Annabel said listlessly, following her back to the school building. "Completely useless."

Completely useless to think about Melchior, or that kiss, or anything really. Certainly he had kissed her back, but what use was there thinking about that? He had probably been surprised—he had spent the last few months rebuffing any attempts at closeness from Annabel. Or, dreadful thought, he hadn't been surprised, but had taken pity on her.

And that was the worst of it, thought Annabel gloomily, as she bathed quietly in the darkness of the suite, conscious of Isabella's upright figure at her own dressing table. The worst of it was that she had kissed him, and that she had probably wanted to do it for quite some time now. No, the worst of it was that she had probably been in love with him for as long as she could remember—that Melchior, apparently realising that, had begun to push away her affections.

"Useless," muttered Annabel again, to the shifting water in her wash basin. "Completely useless."

19

"Well, Nan," said Isabella, when Annabel opened her eyes the next morning, "I think we can say your engagement with Lady Selma was a complete rout!"

"Good grief," said Annabel, rubbing her eyes. "Why are you awake? Why are you sitting on my bed?"

"To give you the good news, naturally!"

Annabel sat up and yawned. "She actually left?"

"No one has seen her since your meeting yesterday morning," said Isabella, nodding. "I really congratulate you, Nan! You should allow yourself to be perturbed more often; it leaves you ruthless to the more mundane things in life—though I believe *I* would consider kissing a certain someone to be more mundane than a magical battle. That's all a matter of perspective, however, I dare say."

"Yes, it is," Annabel told her balefully. "Never mind being funny about that now, Belle—what do you think the Old Parrasians will do once they find out Lady Selma's gone?"

"Chase her, I shouldn't wonder," Isabella said. "Bring her back and give her more money."

"No," said Annabel slowly, "I don't mean that. I mean—well, she and the bicycle girls were just like Melchior and Raoul. She was on the inside, and the bicycle girls are on the outside. I saw the bicycle girls out there last night, waiting at their spot. I don't think she told them she was going."

"Ah," said Isabella. "That is unfortunate."

"That's what I thought." Annabel, who by now had some reason to know the general unreasonableness and quickly lit nature of Old Parassians, pinched her lips together. "If the bicycle girls don't get a message to take, and they come back and see that she's not here—what will they do then?"

"Yes, I see your point," murmured Isabella. "If she didn't send a message, they're bound to think she's had an accident."

"Yes, I thought that, too. And they're the sort of people to attack first and ask questions later. Especially if they think we're holding her prisoner in here somewhere."

"Then I suppose it's a good thing we'd already begun our preparations for incursion," said Isabella. "Do you think, Nan, that Delysia will have finished with the second lot of explosive by now?"

"I hope so," said Annabel devoutly. "I've got an awful feeling that we're going to need it. If only Alice could tell us what she knows!"

"That being the case, I really do think we ought to let Melchior know what's happening. It's best to make sure we're all prepared, after all."

"Ye-es," Annabel said uncertainly. "Yes, but can't it wait a bit longer, Belle?"

"I shouldn't like to leave it much longer," Isabella said. "And it's no good asking me if I'll tell him, either, for I shan't."

"You're an awful adjunct," said Annabel, scowling at her. "All right, I'll do it, I'll do it! But not until after breakfast! And I won't go to classes today!"

"Neither will I, if it comes to that," Isabella said reflectively. "Nan, do you think there's enough explosive spread around the grounds?"

Annabel groaned. "If I never have to dig another hole—!"

"Very good. I've been stockpiling a few useful things, and I've passed the word that if anything...unexpected...happens in the next week or so, that everyone should gather in the first floor dining hall. It's good to be prepared, I find."

"Are we sending in excuse notes today?"

"Funnily enough, Nan, none of the classrooms are usable."

"Aren't they?"

"The doors don't seem to be able to open," mused Isabella. "I'm not entirely sure how that happened—"

"Oh, *aren't* you."

"I very carefully outsourced the job to three or four very creative and gleeful juniors with access to glue, screwdrivers, and a motley assortment of other goods," said Isabella. "As it happens, I'm not aware of the measures they've used, simply that none of the classroom doors will open, and that it doesn't seem to be magical in nature. The Awesome Aunts would usually have announced a cessation of all classes for the day by now, but Miss Cornett doesn't seem to have seen them this morning, so all the girls are still in their rooms or in the dining hall."

In surprise, Annabel asked, "Do you think the Awesome Aunts have run for it, too?"

"Goodness knows, but I shouldn't be surprised! I haven't seen Lady Caro at all today, either."

Annabel eyed her in some awe. "How long have you been up this morning?"

"Oh, an hour or two. When I'm motivated I find it difficult to sleep, and I am quite well motivated at the moment, Nan! Isn't this fun!"

Annabel could have disagreed, but she didn't have the energy. "All right, what do we need to do today, then?"

What they needed to do was a great deal, much to Annabel's secret relief. The business of making sure there was enough explosive, easily accessible weapons, and food supplies kept her out of the Melchior's way. He always seemed to be just around the corner when she least expected him to be, today. Aware that she would have to speak to him sooner or later, Annabel preferred to put off that meeting until later, and continued relentlessly with the preparations. Nobody seemed to be concerned about opening the classroom doors, so most of the girls crowded in the parlours to play old maid and jack-straws, presided over by the watchful teachers, and it was an easy matter to dart about the school without being seen by anyone but the servants, who had developed a watchful sort of look to them. They knew Trenthams, and they knew mischief when they saw it, and they wanted nothing to do with it. Annabel didn't blame them. She would have preferred to be out of it, too; but since she couldn't be, she was determined at least not to think about Melchior.

By the time early evening came, she had almost been successful. Much to her relief, Melchior had vanished entirely from the school halls, and she didn't have to peer about so anxiously every time she walked through a doorway.

"Oh good!" said Isabella, when they met in the dining hall. "You're looking much less hunted now, Nan! By the by, there's no need to tell Melchior about our little problem, I think. Raoul has already started to get an inkling, and no doubt he'll already have reported it to Melchior."

Annabel let out a breath. "Did you do everything you needed to do? Shall we go back to our suite now?"

"No, I think not," said Isabella decidedly. "I rather think I have another engagement. You go ahead, if you're finished."

Annabel was suspicious, but not, she very soon learned, in the way that she ought to have been suspicious. When she returned to the suite, fancying herself safe, the first thing she saw was Melchior, lounging comfortably in one of the windows.

Annabel jumped convulsively. "What are you doing in here? You're not allowed to be in our suite!"

"What distinction," began Melchior, strolling toward her, "No, don't run away, Nan; I'd only chase you—what distinction do you make between you sneaking into my suite and me sneaking into yours?"

"Oh," said Annabel, trying not to clear her throat, "well, I only come to your suite when I need something."

"I see," Melchior said, a smile playing around his lips. "And exactly what was it you needed from me yesterday morning?"

"Oh," said Annabel again. It really was very hard not to clear her throat. "Well, you'd been injured—"

"Indeed. We will have to discuss the circumstances of my being injured a little later, I believe. I was injured...?"

"Yes, and I had to make sure you were all right."

"I feel very healthy," Melchior said. His eyes were glittering—with laughter, Annabel was sure. Was he actually teasing her? "Invigorated, in fact. What else, Nan?"

"All right, I kissed you!" Annabel said grumpily. "I didn't mean to, and I'm sorry, and I won't do it again!"

Blankly, Melchior asked, "I beg your pardon?"

"I said I won't do it again!"

"I don't accept that."

Annabel blinked. "No, but I promise, Melchior! I won't do it again."

"That seems problematic," responded Melchior, with the air of a man belabouring his point, "given the amount of time we'll be spending together in the very near future."

"Yes, but I *promised*, and I really do think—"

"Nan!" exasperatedly said Melchior, "I'm trying to tell you that I love you and want to marry you!"

Annabel was conscious of a delightful relief. Melchior *had* really kissed her back, and it wasn't because he felt sorry for her, or because he had been startled. "Well, that's all right," she said, bright with relief. "I don't think I'd want to marry anyone else, actually."

"You—I beg your pardon?"

"Who else would I marry?"

"I thought—Peter, or—"

"No," Annabel said decidedly. "Why would I marry Peter while you're here? Why do you think I told him I wasn't going to marry him?"

Melchior opened his mouth, closed it, and said plaintively, "I really don't understand, Nan! Do you mean to say that I could have declared myself at any point this last year and you would have said yes?"

"I've been in love with you since you turned out not to be a cat," said Annabel simply. "I don't think I quite realised it until I thought you might have died. But I've been patting you on the head and clinging around your neck for long enough that I think *you* might have realised it, Melchior."

"Do you know how *hard* I've been working to get your attention?"

"Is that what you call it?" Annabel said, unimpressed. Quite a few things were now becoming very clear to her. "Ignoring me, being rude, and deliberately baiting me? I don't think Belle would call that a proper courtship, and—"

"Understand, if you please, Nan!" Melchior said. "For the last year you have treated me no differently from when I was a cat—in fact, the only time you treated me like a human male these last three years was when you were so furious at me for not being Blackfoot any more. It occurred to me that it would be worth the trouble of bringing you to that state of mind again."

"Oh, well," said Annabel. "Well, if it comes to that, I suppose it wasn't a bad plan. Actually, I'd got so used to having you there all the time that it just didn't occur to me that things could be any different, so maybe I did need a nudge. I do think you could have been nicer about it, Melchior! I thought last night that you must have realised I'd fallen in love with you, and that you were trying to make some distance between us because you didn't like me."

There was that tired, fond look that Annabel was coming to quite like. "Is that why you ran away?"

"I don't think you should be wondering why a young lady ran away after being kissed," Annabel said. "Actually. Miss Cornett says that a gentleman never kisses a lady without warning."

"Is that so?" Melchior's eyes glittered. "And what does Miss Cornett say about young ladies who kiss gentlemen without warning?"

"She doesn't say anything about that," Annabel said, refusing to acknowledge the pinkness of her cheeks by so much as a small throat-clearing. "Isabella is of the opinion that means she approves."

"Certainly *I* do," Melchior said frankly. "And if one may ask, Nan, what sort of warning does Miss Cornett consider to be suitable before a gentleman kisses a lady?"

Annabel, who thought that Melchior had had things his own way for quite long enough, said, "I'll ask her and let you know."

"In the meantime," said Melchior, advancing with the swiftness and silence of Blackfoot, "consider yourself warned, Nan!"

It could have been Melchior who backed her into the window, or it could have been Annabel, with her hands clutching his collar, who pulled him there. Whichever way it happened, the coolness of the window touched Annabel's shoulders, making a delightful dichotomy of cool and heat between the touch of the glass and the soft pressure of Melchior's lips against her own; the two warm hands cupping her face.

"Nan," said Melchior, when at last he pulled away, "I do apologise. I should have allowed you to cling around my neck as much as you chose. Perhaps we can remedy that by—"

"By what?" demanded Annabel, both suspicious and amused. Melchior didn't reply, and it was slowly borne in on her that he was looking at something through the window over her shoulder.

He sighed regretfully into her temple and said, "I very much fear that the Old Parrasians have decided to make good their threat to commence an all-out attack should Lady Selma prove to be unsuccessful. We will have to postpone our discussion until a more opportune time."

"No!" said Annabel, into his collar. "Tell them to come back later!"

"Nan," Melchior said, "you know I'd do anything humanly possible for you, but I really don't think my powers extend to telling an army of Old Parrasians to come back after we've finished our discussion."

"What, a whole army? Really?" Annabel asked, considerably startled. She turned her head and saw with a burgeoning dismay that there were decidedly more Old Parrasians around the school stables and building than she had supposed there to exist. Worse, some of them were certain to be the magic users that Lord Tremare had mentioned. With an annoyance she hoped would hide the breathlessness of her voice, she said, "Well it's rude, anyway! I suppose they came from the stables; we were afraid they might do that, but we couldn't find the passageway."

Melchior grinned in spite of the paleness of his face. "Perhaps if you tell them off, they'll go away in disgrace."

"I suppose I'd better let Isabella know," Annabel said glumly. "She probably already knows, but we'll have to start up our defences."

"Our—we have defences?"

"Oh yes," said Annabel, turning decisively to the door. "We thought it wouldn't be long before they did something like this, and we couldn't be sure exactly where they'd come from because Alice hasn't woken up yet. I don't think Belle expected something so large scale. I wonder if we've got enough resources to deal with it?"

"How long has the Firebrand had to prepare?"

"About a day and a half," Annabel said. "But if comes to that, I think she already had a plan for just this circumstance, in case we needed it."

"A day and a half is more than enough when the Firebrand has the bit between her teeth," said Melchior, with certainty. He followed her out into the hall. "I've my own resources, of course; and if I can manage to get a message through to Mr. Pennicott, we may just be able to hold out for long enough. As it turns out, I was too busy chasing a certain queen heir around the halls to send out a message as soon as I was on my feet. How long do you think we can hold out?"

"At least a day or two," Annabel said. "More, if we can retreat floor by floor without anyone getting in at the windows."

"Don't worry about the windows," said Melchior, with a particularly grim smile. "I may not have suspected the extent of the threat that was coming, but I didn't like the idea of people being able to climb in and out of the school building at will, so that's taken care of. It's a shame I didn't have time to lay a few traps around the doors, but we'll have to shift as best we can without that."

"Well, we were making explosive in the library last night, so—"

"Then I suppose we can only be thankful that you didn't blow the place up!"

"Actually, the rule with explosives is Safety First," Annabel told him. "Because Nice Young Ladies need all of their limbs to pour tea."

"Not to mention their usefulness in lock picking," said Isabella's voice. She appeared around the corner a moment later, as beautifully dressed and coiffed as ever, despite the army outside. Perhaps, even, *because* of the army outside. "What beautiful timing you have, Nan! I trust you and Delysia had an enjoyable evening planting our lovely bundles strategically about the place?"

"I thought," said Melchior, in failing tones, with his eyes shut, "that you were gardening last night."

"Isn't it lucky," said Annabel to Melchior, without regarding his plaint, "that Delysia is so very good at explosives? I didn't know a talent for snuff-mixing could be so versatile!"

Melchior opened his eyes again, but he still looked ill. "Are there really parcels of explosive hidden around the grounds?"

"It's all *perfectly* safe," Isabella said airily. "That's thanks to Delysia, too. She's made something she calls magical immediacy fuses; they're connected to the explosive and set them off with a single touch of a button. Nothing will blow up unless we really want it to blow up."

"Ye-es," said Annabel slowly. "Only do let's blow up some of them, Belle! It was such a lot of work, and what a waste not to use them!"

"We're going to need all we can use to keep that lot off," Isabella said, nodding at the windows. "I shouldn't worry about that, if I were you."

"I'm worried," said Melchior. "*I'm* worried! I'll have you know, Nan, that before I met you, I wasn't possessed of so much as a single grey hair. This morning, I discovered three. *Three!*"

"Two of those are probably because your hat spell didn't work," Annabel remarked. "And you can't really blame us for that."

Melchior closed his eyes briefly and opened them again. "I would like to remind, you, Nan, that the reason the hat spell didn't work was because you had switched my hat spell with a normal top hat. And if it comes to that, the spell did work! It worked for you and the Firebrand, and I was unfortunate enough to be taken captive."

"How on earth could we know that you would be taken captive?" protested Annabel. "At least you have magic! Belle and I don't have a bit between us—"

"—not strictly true—"

"Not much between us, anyway; and if you can't tell the difference between a top hat with a Don't See on it and a properly spelled top hat, I think there's something wrong with your magic."

"That might have been my fault," Isabella said, a little guiltily. "I may have threaded just the *tiniest* dab of magic into the hatband—just enough to make it look like the spell we put on it was a lot stronger than it actually was."

"Oh, you might, might you?" Melchior looked at her balefully. "I was prepared to give you the benefit of the doubt, Firebrand, but no more! And if the Old Parrasian army isn't inclined to go away without an hostage, I warn you that I will hand you over without a second thought!"

By the time they got to the dining hall, almost all of the girls and teachers had assembled already, pale, frantic, and each speaking over the other in their panic. The Awesome Aunts were still entirely, conspicuously absent, but Miss Cornett was vainly trying to keep the situation from descending into a rabble, and when she saw Melchior with Annabel and Isabella, she looked almost sick with relief.

"Girls! I thought you were outside!"

"We're safe," Annabel said, smiling at her. Miss Cornett might be fluttery and sometimes annoying, but she was also rather lovely. "Do you think you can get everyone's attention? We have an announcement."

"An announcement? Surely, girls—er, your hi—Miss Ammett—surely there are more important things at the moment?"

"That's what it's about," Annabel said. "We were a bit worried that something like this might happen, so we've been preparing. We need to let everyone know where to go to keep them safe."

"Not to worry, your highness," said Raoul, startling her by appearing by her side. "I've got a few of the Guards and some footmen who want to help as well. We'll get their attention for you."

Without further warning, he put two fingers in his mouth and gave vent to the most piercing whistle Annabel had ever heard. A shocked, wincing silence fell over the assembled girls, and someone said, "Ouch." One by one, their gazes fell naturally on Annabel.

She looked around at the sea of faces and felt a momentary panic. If she wasn't able to keep off the Old Parrasians and their wizards, there was a good chance that most of the girls would be hurt. She swallowed the panic and said in a louder voice than she'd meant to use, "You've all got to go upstairs to the Sanatorium. There's an army of Old Parrasians out there, and they'll try to use you as hostages if they can. Don't let them. Go upstairs and stay safe—Miss Cornett will go with you. Don't come downstairs no matter what you hear happening."

"Make an orderly line!" said Miss Cornett, as if they were simply lining up for carriages at an outing. "And *march*, ladies!"

As the girls marched into the next room and toward the stairs, Raoul drew closer with Dannick and Melchior, the footmen crowding behind him. He said, "I really don't think we ought to try to defend this room. It's too big and we can't protect the stairway from here."

"No, no," said Isabella, in a businesslike manner, "all of the blunderbusses are in the main hall, behind the sofa where the windows face out. I put them there last night while Nan and Delysia were planting explosive. There are a few pikes, too; but I really don't think we'll need those."

"We can defend the stairs from there, too," Annabel said.

They followed Miss Cornett and the girls into the hall, where Melchior and Raoul swiftly paced the length of the outer facing windows and the guards helped the footmen to bring out the blunderbusses.

"They're still trying to get in at the front doors," said Melchior, glancing carefully around the curtains. "We'll need a blunderbuss at every window, behind the curtains where they won't be able to see you."

"We haven't got enough people for every window," Dannick said. "Unless Miss Farrah or Miss Ammett can handle a blunderbuss?"

"Alas!" said Isabella. "It's a skill I never learned! I shall fetch shot and powder instead."

"I'll take one of the windows," Annabel said, "but I'll use the staff. It's no use using a blunderbuss when I've got that."

"I'll take one," said a voice from the now-empty stairway behind them. A single figure came back down in wake of the general exodus, her steps light and unconcerned. Annabel turned to tell the new arrival that she would have to join the others upstairs, when she recognised who it was.

It was Lady Caroline. So she *hadn't* disappeared with Lady Selma.

"What are you doing?" Annabel said, in astonishment. Was Lady Caro here to spy on them and wait for a chance to let the Old Parrasians in, or merely to sabotage their efforts?

"What do you mean, what am I doing here? An army of Old Parrasians is trying to take over Trenthams."

"She means," Isabella said, "why are you *here* with us instead of wherever *there* Lady Selma has gone?"

"That?" said Lady Caro coolly. "A fair fight is one thing, but I can't stomach a queen who won't look after her subjects. If it comes right down to it, *I* didn't pick you as queen, and what do I care about Rorkin and his staff? If it was going to be a fair fight between the two of you, then I wouldn't interfere. But they're trying to take over Trenthams, and I won't let that happen. Girls get hurt when things like that happen, and I don't like our girls being hurt."

"You'd better go up with the others, then," Annabel said. "It's not safe down here. We'll probably have to retreat as soon as they make it through the doors and up the stairs to us—they've got an awful lot of magic users."

Lady Caroline grabbed one of the blunderbusses as an explosion outside threw a plume of dirt and grass into the air beside the window. "I'm not going upstairs with the others."

"Good heavens, Delysia's started already!" said Isabella. She tossed a look both amused and slightly respectful at Lady Caroline. "Do you think you can manage that, Lady Caro?"

"I'd like to see you keep off that lot without me," Lady Caro said, tilting her chin at the window. "And if it comes to that, I've been using Nurse's old blunderbuss since I was about three."

"That seems like a dangerous pastime for a three year old," remarked Isabella. "But I dare say your nurse knew best, after all."

"I think some of them are screaming," said Annabel, peering out her window to look at the Old Parrasians below. A double explosion rocked the ground below, followed by a volley of blunderbuss roaring beside her, and the scene below erupted into chaos.

Lady Caroline gave something that was very similar to a grin, as grim as it was, but Annabel wasn't sure if it was at Isabella or the distress of the Old Parrasians. "My brothers didn't like me a lot," she threw at Isabella. "And they were all quite a lot older than me. They had a very lively appreciation for how soft a child's head is at the age of three, and of how easily their bones break. Fortunately for me, my nurse was a *very* angry old woman who wasn't very fond of boys."

"Yes, I suppose that would have come in very handy," Annabel said, not sure whether to be amused or horrified. "You can take this window, Lady Caroline. We want to keep them from the door as long as we can."

"Don't be mistaken," said Lady Caro. She sighted along the blunderbuss and half closed one eye. "I still dislike you both. I simply refuse to have this school torn apart by a rabble of underbred Old Parrasians who have yet to move into this century. It's the one place I've had a few moments of happiness."

"That's all right," Annabel said cheerfully. She tapped the staff lightly against one of the drawings she had made last night, and a series of small, potent explosions drove the Old Parrassians briefly away from the front doors. "We don't like you much either."

"There's no need for liking each other," said Isabella, passing another blunderbuss to Raoul with business-like dispatch. "Look at Raoul and I—we neither of us like the other, but we're the best of friends!"

"Is that what you are?" Lady Caro raised a brow. "I keep meaning to ask you about that."

"Oh *do* you?" Isabella's eyes danced. "I think we had this conversation once before, Lady Caro."

"Oh, well!" Lady Caroline shrugged. "I'm sure I'm not the one who claimed that men and women can't be friends!"

"May I suggest," said Melchior, from the next window, "that you direct your shots at the Old Parrasians, Lady Caro?"

Lady Caroline fired. Annabel, who was busily erasing the ground from beneath a few Old Parrasians, at first thought she'd missed. Then she saw the wall behind the Old Parrasians flash with something opaque and rainbow for an instant, and four Old Parrasians were bowled over into the hole she'd just made in the front lawn.

"*Very* nice!" murmured Isabella. "Did you know it would do that?"

"Some of the girls are throwing spells from the roof to help out, and magic reacts with magic," said Lady Caro. "What *do* you do during Basic Magic?"

"I design hats during Basic Magic," said Isabella, without embarrassment. "In fact, the one I'm wearing today was designed during a particularly—"

"I wasn't really interested," said Lady Caro. She settled herself back in the window. "Your highness, do you think you could make another hole right there next to the bike shed?"

"All right," Annabel agreed, finishing the shading on the solid wooden cover she'd drawn over the first hole. Unless the men were *very* strong magic users, they wouldn't be getting out of the hole any time soon. It wasn't until Isabella caught her eye that Annabel realised it was the first time Lady Caroline had ever called her *your highness*.

"It is a day of Interesting Things, isn't it?" said Isabella. "Oh, bother! There go the front doors!"

Annabel heard the *boom* a moment later, and the building seemed to tremble.

"Cover the stairway!" yelled Raoul, and the Guards turned as one, blunderbusses toward the hallway door. With them, Lady Caro turned on her toes without the slightest hesitation, her own blunderbuss trained on the hallway.

The hallway seemed to bulge, or perhaps that was just Annabel's imagination. Melchior said something through his teeth and made a savage thrust with one palm at that bulging reality. Despite that, too many Old Parrasian wizards pushed into the hall—far, far too many for them to have fit through non-magical means. The blunderbusses roared in almost complete synchronicity, and the Old Parrasians sank back like jelly sucked back into a mould, completely uninjured. The end of the hallway bulged once again—the jelly coming back out, Annabel thought—and there was the businesslike rattle of each Guard's second shot being cocked.

"Retreat!" yelled Melchior. "Back! Get back to the stairs!"

Lady Caroline said something very unladylike and fired her second shot into the heart of the Old Parrasians that were still bulging into the hall. They stumbled but this time they didn't retreat more than half a step. The invisible something at the end of the hall quivered.

"Get back to the stairs," Annabel said to the others. She tossed another blunderbuss to Lady Caro, who had thrown down the first in disgust, and said again, sharply, "Upstairs! Now!"

"They're waiting for you," said Isabella quietly.

"I know," Annabel said. Her sketchbook dropped to the ground, leaves folding and flattening, and she raised the staff pencil. "I'm coming. But you all need to be out of the way first. Keep firing, Lady Caro!"

"I wasn't planning on stopping," Lady Caro said grimly, as the others reluctantly began to file toward the stairs, shepherded by Melchior. She fired one shot, this time higher than the first, and something went *ping* far too quickly for Annabel to follow. Someone in the centre of the Old Parrasians gasped and dropped, but there was no sign of faltering from the others this time. Lady Caro fired her second shot, and at the same time, Annabel reversed her pencil and slashed with the eraser end.

Lady Caro said something else unladylike, and dropped the second blunderbuss, teetering on the murky edge of what had once been floor but was now nothingness. The Old Parrasians on the other side yelled and stumbled backwards, but the hallway chandelier above them fell with a great, grand weight to it, and the floor shuddered beneath them. Annabel saw five or six of them disappear into the void, but she had no time to feel either victorious or sick about it; Lady Caro was still teetering on the edge of that chasm from which not even the strongest of magic users could escape. Annabel grabbed her by the braid and pulled her back from the edge before she could topple after her blunderbuss, and Lady Caro stumbled back, gasping.

"What did you do to the floor!"

"Never mind," Annabel said. "It's not there anymore—nothing is. It's a big bit of nothing that will swallow you if you get too close. We'd better go up now."

One of the men across the room said, "This won't stop us for long. We've got our own magic users, you know."

"Of course we know, you stupid little man!" said Lady Caro. "How else would you have got this far!"

"That's the problem with rabble," agreed Isabella, her head

appearing above Melchior's shoulder. "There's no thought process to mention, and it tries to prove that might makes right."

"I hate to interrupt you both," Melchior said, "but do you think we could complete our retreat instead of trading verbal blows?"

"We might as well," Lady Caro said. "It's boring down here now, anyway."

She followed Annabel, a cold-eyed rear guard against the glares from the Old Parrasian wizards, and when Annabel stopped short at the next floor, she was the first to say, "What?"

Melchior looked sharply at her. "Nan? We really can't stop here; not without making a few more preparations."

"Go upstairs," Annabel said to Lady Caro. "Make sure all the girls are on the top floor. Not on the roof, mind you—and make the girls who have been throwing magic come down to the fourth floor as well. Come back when you're finished."

"Nan?" Melchior said again, and this time there was a question to his voice. "What are you about?"

"I trust you're not thinking of sending me to the top floor," Isabella said. She was bright-eyed and a little bit pale. "I won't go, you know."

"We're not going to the top floor," Annabel told them. To the line of mixed guards and footmen, she said, "And you might as well leave the blunderbusses here, too; they're obviously not working anymore. How many of you are magic users apart from Melchior?"

"Healing magic only," said Dannick. "Sorry. And not much of it."

"You'll stay with us," Annabel said. "We'll probably need you. Anyone else?"

"All of us," said Raoul. "Not enough to hold off that lot for long, but enough to make it difficult for them to get to you. We could possibly hold them off until Mr. Pennicott gets here."

"*If* he gets here quickly enough," nodded Annabel. "No, we're not going to do that. The staff is the strongest thing here; there's no use hiding it away just to keep me safe. Rorkin told me that I was one queen heir out of a few possible heirs."

"No," said Raoul. "We're happy with you, your highness. We'll make sure you don't die for long enough to take care of that lot—or at least until Mr. Pennicott gets here if you can't do it."

Melchior said, "Nan—"

"Don't worry," said Annabel, straightening her shoulders, "I'm not going to die. You'd better stick close to me, though."

Melchior sighed faintly. "I seem to have the misfortune of watching my loved ones facing threats from which I can't protect them," he said. "I won't be protected, Nan! We'll fight side by side, but I won't hide behind you, and so I warn you!"

There was the light tread of Lady Caro on the stairs. Annabel asked swiftly, "Are the other girls safe?"

Lady Caro nodded shortly. "For now. I made them come off the roof, at least. But I hope you know what you're doing, your highness; because if you can't save all of us down here, all of those up there aren't safe, either."

"Don't worry," said Annabel, reversing her pencil staff again, "we're all going to survive. Please stand away from the wall—no, not just the stairs, the whole wall."

Lady Caro, her eyes widening, hurried away from the wall. The guards and footmen followed her with alacrity, and Annabel began to erase once again. As she began on the lowest step, there was a shriek, and Delysia tumbled into the room, leaping over the quickly disappearing stair in a flutter of petticoats.

"Delysia!" Annabel said in astonishment, as Isabella, laughing, caught the other girl. "What are you doing? I could have erased you!"

Panting, Delysia said, "I thought you might need the immediacy fuses for the bits of explosive around the yard, and Lady Caro wouldn't let us stay on the roof. You're—you're going back outside, aren't you?"

"As soon as I separate the top of the school from the bottom of it," Annabel said, nodding. "I'd rather not have the wizards inside with the girls, even if they can't get to them right now. They're tricky and nasty, and I don't trust that Gregor."

"Dear me!" said Isabella. "I'm proud, I really am! I have the most delightful friends!"

"I thought you were convinced you were the most delightful of them," remarked Lady Caro, causing Raoul to cough.

"Well, perhaps I am, in general," agreed Isabella. "But not today, I think. Now, I hesitate to be unhelpful, Nan, but once you've separated the top of Trenthams from the bottom, how do you propose we get outside again?"

"That," said Melchior, as the last vestige of the upper half of Trenthams separated from the lower beneath Annabel's pencil staff, "will not be a difficulty."

Delysia squeaked and darted away from the dark circle that had begun to revolve in the outer wall. Annabel, to whom the phenomenon was as familiar as Melchior himself, was already moving toward it when it ceased to revolve and became a low, dark tunnel in the wall. With Melchior at her side and Isabella flanking her, Annabel stepped from the broken, out of place level in Trenthams school building, and into the sunlit turning circle outside the front of the school, gravel shifting beneath her feet.

"They're coming out again," Melchior said. "They've been watching. School entrance."

The front doors hung drunkenly on their hinges, splintered wood digging into the stonework landing, and through that wreckage of wood strode the remaining Old Parrasian wizards, bringing with them a storm of magic that Annabel couldn't see but felt the weight of despite that. The pencil staff felt very damp in her fingers. She watched the Old Parrasians approach, struck in a small, hazy part of her brain that wasn't trying to calculate odds and possibilities, that Gregor was flanking the leader—not close enough to the front to be a leader, but not far enough behind to be picked off if anyone approached from the rear. He was in a place, in fact, that meant it would be the easiest for him to run away if things went badly.

Annabel put that aside to think about later, and asked Melchior, "Can you make a protective barrier around us?"

"I can, Nan," he said, and Annabel wasn't sure when his arm had gone around her shoulders, but it was there now, warm and protective. "But it won't last long against that lot."

"That's all right," she said. "Just make it as strong as you can. I only need a few minutes with the staff. I shan't bother with paper."

She couldn't see the barrier as it went up, but she saw Raoul and the grouped guards and footmen exchanging a look, and when the foremost Old Parrasian wizard extended one hand with a triumphant smile, Annabel felt nothing.

At her side, Melchior hissed. The sound woke Annabel from her stupor; she raised the pencil staff, sharpened tip pointing at the Old Parrasians, and began to draw without paper, without recourse if things went wrong, and entirely without mercy. The Old Parrasian wizards that thinned at the edges of the crowd twitched and began to change, their limbs shrinking and hardening. There was a dismayed shout from the wizard ranks, and some of the ossifying wizards began to look a little more lively.

"*No,*" said Annabel mulishly, shading the texture with greater precision. "You're *stone!*"

And they were stone, shrinking or falling or sinking in on themselves until a small, ugly gargoyle rocked on a stone base in each place where once there had stood a wizard. Annabel, with the sweat sitting on her brow, knew that there were still too many wizards—she could hear the groaning of Dannick and Raoul, and one of the footmen passed out on the verge, his eyes rolling white and unresponsive. But she couldn't do anything else, so she continued to draw wizards into gargoyles while the air grew hot and stifling around her.

The barrier must have trembled around them, because Melchior shivered. Pressed against him, Annabel shivered too, and to the side Dannick dropped to his knees in the gravel driveway.

"Perhaps," said Melchior, with a great deal of effort, "perhaps you could draw a little more swiftly, Nan."

"I will," Annabel said, but the staff was heavy between her fingers and no matter how many gargoyles littered the lawn there were always more wizards crowding forward.

Still the staff grew heavier. Heavier and heavier, until it felt as though she couldn't hold it up any longer, and until her strokes grew wide and wild. Raoul slumped, bracing himself against Dannick on one side, and the verge on the other, and this time when Melchior shivered, it seemed as though the entire world shivered, too.

"Oh bother," said Annabel.

20

M elchior shivered, and the world shivered. The Old Parrasian wizards swayed closer, while the staff grew so heavy that it seemed to weigh Annabel through the ground.

"Oh bother," she said again.

And then, something *shifted*.

"Oh!" gasped Annabel, as her legs gave way beneath her. She saw the cold flash of triumph in Gregor's eyes; felt sharp gravel beneath her knees and the coolness of damp grass beneath one of her hands as she vainly reached for the sloped verge to steady herself.

"Bother!" Isabella said. "Nan, I really don't think you can stop now. If I try to—"

"No," said Annabel.

"I really think, Nan—"

"No."

Melchior laughed, soft and low, and crouched beside her.

"Nan—"

"You said to tell you if you're being bossy," Annabel said to Isabella, pinching a blade of grass between her fingers and wondering how it could feel so much plumper and alive than it had felt just yesterday. "Stop being bossy, Belle. I'm going to tell you what to do, and you'd better do it, because I won't let you push me down an alley again."

Pale as she was, Isabella grinned. "What do I need to do?"

"Get behind me," said Annabel. "Actually, all of you need to get behind me."

"Nan, what did I tell you about hiding?"

"Not you, then," Annabel said, smiling faintly. "But everybody else."

Lady Caroline's voice was sharp. "Are we retreating?"

"No," said Annabel, using Melchior's shoulder to climb to her feet. "The Castle has come back. Now, we are going to advance."

Melchior didn't tell her, as she had half expected, that it was nonsense. Nor did he mention the fact that she didn't have any kind of magic—nor the fact that she couldn't sense any kind of magic with that handicap.

Instead, he asked, "How do you know?"

"I don't," Annabel said. "The staff does. Oh, that felt odd!"

"Ah," said Melchior, closing his eyes briefly. She saw his lips curving, and when he opened his eyes, there was a distinct glitter to them. "If I'm not mistaken, Nan, the Castle knows you're in danger. It's offering its own strength to shore up the staff."

"I suppose that explains why it took so long for the castle to come back when we were in it three years ago," Annabel said, laughing a little. "Or are in it, if it comes to that! I suppose Peter and I and you are all still in there right now. How ridiculous!"

Gregor heard her laugh, and a laugh passed across his own lips, ghostlike and puzzled.

"I knew I should have killed you," he said. He was backing away as he spoke, and Annabel saw in astonishment that he would abandon the Old Parrasian wizards just as he had abandoned his fellow-attackers in the village. He would abandon them and return again later to cause what trouble he could. "The little one in the stables was too easy to be much fun—tell her I'll be back to look after her when this ends. Then you and I can have a bit of fun, too."

He raised one hand in farewell, half turning from both sides and toward the stables.

"Delysia," said Isabella, her eyes glittering in a way that Annabel had never seen before, "where did you put that explosive garden gargoyle?"

"It's right next to him," Delysia said. "Only, Belle, it's a bit unstable because—ow!"

The gargoyle, as if too impatient to wait for her words, quivered for half a breath. And as Delysia said *ow!*, her plump finger pressed against the trigger of an immediacy fuse by Isabella's long, white one, it exploded.

To Annabel's dazed eyes, a man and a gargoyle stood side by side for the space of another half breath. Then there was a roaring and a cloud of red gravel, red grass and red dirt, and a shock of air that rocked the remaining Old Parrasian wizards off their feet. Even the barrier erected by Melchior and Raoul trembled.

Annabel felt the earth move and be still once again, held in place by Melchior's arm around her shoulders. He asked, smiling faintly, "Are you well, Nan?"

"Yes," she said. "But don't let go of the protection; I'm going to be busy for a little while."

As the wizards scrambled to their feet again, Isabella, so pale that Annabel could have counted every freckle on her face, asked, "Is he dead?"

"Very, very dead," said Lady Caro's blunt voice. "Delysia, what *did* you put in that gargoyle?"

"I didn't put anything *in* it," Delysia said, her face plump and trembly with tears. "The whole thing was pure explosive."

Lady Caro eyed the crater in the lawn with a fascinated eye, then turned that eye on Isabella. "Now, that's effective! Did you mean to kill him?"

"No," said Isabella, in a hollow voice. "I didn't know it would be so powerful. I was just furious and I thought he'd lose a leg or an arm— something to stop him coming after Alice again."

"He won't come after Alice again," agreed Lady Caro, with a last, lingering look at that crater.

"Good," said Annabel. Isabella's eyes came up to meet hers, and dropped to the pencil staff that was in between Annabel's fingers, eraser foremost. Annabel didn't remember flipping it, but she was aware of the thought that was still uppermost in her mind: If not for that explosion, she would have erased Gregor into oblivion where he stood, one foot poised to escape and make more deadly mischief while Annabel was kept busy with the other Old Parrasians.

Isabella swallowed, and said, "We'll still need to look after the others, Nan."

"Yes," said Annabel, and she reversed the pencil staff one last time. This time, with the power of the castle behind her, she didn't even need to draw. She simply pointed the pencil at each wizard in turn and said, "You're stone."

The Old Parrasian wizards vacillated before the staff, white-faced and uncertain whether to fight or run, and Annabel turned them into gargoyles without remorse and without hesitation, one by one. They would run any second now; their ranks were already diminishing with terrifying speed, and the sound of the rabble that had been rummaging around the first floor of the school building was already gone. Even the girls had stopped throwing things from the windows.

From an almost overwhelming force of magic and numbers, the old Parrasian wizards had shrunk until they were a small, outnumbered group surrounded by their newly ossified members.

Lady Caro, watching with a professional sort of interest, said, "I suppose we should replenish the gargoyles, since we blew one up. That one's bit ugly, though, isn't it? What will people think, if they come to Trenthams and see that sort of gargoyle sitting around the grounds?"

"They're not going to stay here," Annabel said. The lead wizard caught her eye; wavered.

He turned and ran for the stables, and Annabel stabbed the staff at him. The rest of the wizards scattered, leaving Annabel to hastily capture them as they began to flee, littering the carriageway with an uneven line of gargoyles.

Lady Caro sighed. "That's boring. Your highness, I don't suppose you know how we're going to get the other girls back from the upper floors safely?"

"Don't bother her while she's capturing Old Parrasians," Isabella said. "It's impolite, not to mention foolhardy."

Lady Caro shrugged and went to help the footman who had fainted. Annabel, turning the last Old Parrasian wizard into an immoveable gargoyle, said, "That ought to hold them in place until Mr. Pennicott gets here, oughtn't it?"

"I should think so!" Isabella said, her voice awestruck and a little closer to its usual exuberant tones.

"I really do feel as though I spend great deal of my life seeing wizards turned into different forms," sighed Melchior. His hazel eyes were glinting with a great deal of sarcastic humour. "I suppose at least this time I can be thankful I'm not among them."

"And at least this time they can't run away," pointed out Annabel. "Onepiece is lovely, and very clever, but I can't help feeling that he was thinking like a dog instead of a boy when he turned those Council Wizards into cats."

"A little gratitude, if you please, Nan!" said Melchior. "If Onepiece hadn't done what he did, you and I would never have met!"

"Good grief, yes!" said Annabel, appalled. "I might have ended up marrying Peter!"

"Remind me to bring a present to Onepiece next time we see Poly and Luck," Melchior said. "I have certainly not been thankful enough. Nan, I hope you're satisfied with your bloodless and stony victory—"

"—not quite bloodless—" remarked Lady Caro's voice from somewhere behind them.

"—because I very much fear that our protective shell is about to collapse."

"Oh, sorry," said Annabel. "You can let it go now. They're all stone. All the ones I could catch, anyway. I think some of them might have gotten away into the tunnels."

"Don't worry about that," Melchior said, and there was a note of decidedly dark amusement to his voice. "I know where the tunnels are now; and if there's anything I know, it's how to stop a tunnel going where it's meant to go. They'll be safe there until Mr. Pennicott arrives."

"Safe?" echoed Annabel, remembering the dark and perilous feeling of walking through one of Melchior's tunnels without any human companionship.

Melchior, even more grimly, said, "Perhaps I shouldn't have said safe. At any rate, they won't be able to leave without ridding themselves of a great many clinging roots and quite a lot of affectionate dirt. I imagine they'll be quite happy to see Mr. Pennicott when he arrives."

"I suppose it's no use trying to finish out the year, now," Annabel said glumly to Melchior and Isabella somewhat later, when they were surveying the school grounds below from the rooftop. She felt that it would have been nice to see what Trenthams could be like under normal circumstances—or at least, as normal as a queen heir attending finishing school could find it.

"I don't think anybody is going to finish out the year, if it comes to that," said Melchior. He was almost offensively cheerful—had been so since they had rescued all of the girls from the Sanatorium and sent most of them home. Annabel wasn't sure if he was cheerful because Mr. Pennicott was taking charge of the gargoyle-shaped wizards below in his usual fussy, precise way, or if he was glad that Raoul had taken Dannick back to the village. Since she now knew exactly what it was about Dannick that Melchior found so offensive, Annabel hadn't been able to bring herself to do more than wave the guards off without being too friendly about it.

Melchior, looking more relaxed than she had seen him in some time, stretched in a very Blackfoot sort of way and added, "Half the school is missing because you erased bits of it, and the other half is peppered with explosive that no one has found yet."

"Not to mention that the Awesome Aunts and a good half of the school staff and servants have gone missing," agreed Isabella. "They'll have to shut the place down just to see to repairs, and someone will have to be found to take over as principal."

"That's easy," Annabel said. "Miss Cornett can do it. Until Lady Caro graduates, anyway. Then they can look after it together."

Isabella giggled. "I'm really not sure if Lady Caro will be pleased or appalled! The explosive, now, that will be found in time—"

"I'm certain it will!" Melchior said, somewhat grimly.

"And I'll draw back the bits I erased, too," Annabel said, a little more hopefully. "I remember what bits I erased, and even if I didn't, the staff would. And Jess locked Lady Selma's maid in her room before all of this began, so—"

Melchior raised a brow at her. "It's no use trying to stay, Nan. Not now that everyone has seen Rorkin's staff—not to mention seeing you use it—and now that the castle is back. There are already messages shooting across the country in the message tubes."

"It is a rather large castle," agreed Isabella. "Nan, I really think you need to reconsider your marriage with Melchior. If you leave it until after you're crowned, or after you finish the year at Trenthams, you'll never manage the time—and if it comes to that, there will probably be quite a few objections—"

"I beg your pardon?" Melchior turned a cold eye on her.

"It's no use looking at me like that," Isabella said firmly. "You might be old family Parrasian and rich to boot, but you really can't expect no one to object when you announce you'll marry the queen heir! It's expecting too much."

"Good grief, yes," agreed Annabel. "They'll send letters to the newspapers and make postings in the news stands. *Should the queen heir of New Civet be contemplating marriage with a former cat?*"

Isabella giggled, a small splutter of noise.

"We've established," said Melchior, tugging Annabel closer by the slightly grubby skirt of her dress, "that I am no longer a cat. Shall we discuss it further?"

"What I mean to say by that," continued Isabella, as if neither of them had interrupted, "is that you should probably consider getting married before the fuss starts. Before, if it comes to that, your younger selves disappear from the castle and it becomes open to the general populace once again."

"Firebrand, I've misjudged you!" said Melchior. He tugged once more at Annabel's skirt seam, and Annabel sat down beside him on the view seat. "Certainly we should be married first!"

"Besides, Melchior is a useful kind of a person," Isabella continued. "And since I'm sure that people will still be trying to kill you up until and after you're crowned, it's good to have a useful person with you all the time."

"Firebrand, have you ever heard the phrase *To leave the Happening while there's still punch in the bowl?* I suggest that you adhere to the spirit of it."

Isabella beamed at him. "I've never adhered to any such spirit in the course of my life. What an odd suggestion!"

"Very well," said Melchior, "then here's another for you, Firebrand —make yourself scarce! There is only one seat on this rooftop, and there is certainly no room for you on it."

"How very rude!" Isabella said cheerfully. "I suppose you want to go back to kissing Nan. Don't you think it's a bit too busy for things like that?"

"Absolutely not. We've hit a lull, which is exactly the time for kissing."

Ignoring that, Isabella asked Annabel, "Shall you pursue Lady Selma, Nan?"

"Her, and all the others who escaped," Annabel said, rather grimly. "The bicycle girls, too, if I can get them. I won't have people like that running around in New Civet. They'll just make trouble."

"Very good!" said Isabella approvingly, and wafted away toward the stairwell. "I shall assist Mr. Pennicott in securing this end of the secret tunnel, in that case."

Melchior seemed to sigh. "I'll add that to the list of things that need to be fixed before the school can reopen."

"I don't know why you're looking at me when you say that," said Annabel, as Isabella slipped back down the stairs. "That bit wasn't my fault, after all. I only erased a few parts of the school, and that was only to stop the Old Parrasians taking over."

Melchior's lips curled. "A little sensitive, are we, Nan?"

"Yes," said Annabel, putting her nose in the air. "And it's no good kissing me, either. I'm annoyed."

"Is it not?" asked Melchior, kissing her below the ear. "What a shame! I feel like I ought to put forward my best efforts, in that case."

Certainly by the time Isabella came flitting briefly back up to inform them that there was some species of dinner available in the ruined dining hall, Annabel wasn't feeling particularly annoyed. She wasn't sure if that was from Melchior's really undeniable pleasantness as a kisser, or because it was simply so nice to sit down for a little while without anyone trying to kill her.

At any rate, she was pleased to stroll down the hallway with him, avoiding the blunderbuss-made holes in the floor and the fallen plaster, and not pick any fights. Even when one of Mr. Pennicott's men met them partway through the hall and said rather delicately, "Mr. Pennicott hopes he can speak to you shortly regarding a certain, er *acquaintance* and that acquaintance's disappearance, with regards to today's events," Annabel only blinked at him and smiled vaguely. She had always been annoyed when Luck smiled vaguely at her, and now she felt that she understood the urge.

"You could be wondering, Nan," said Melchior, when he had sent off the man, "exactly when I mean to tell you about—"

"I'm not."

Melchior's hazel eyes glowed with instant amusement, his lips curving. "Is that so?"

"And you can stop being mysterious about it, too," Annabel told him. "Peter has been playing with time, hasn't he? Ever since he found out it's definitely possible, he's been wanting to do experiments with his tickerboxes. I suppose something went wrong."

"Wrong, or right," said Melchior, shrugging. "I'm never sure when it comes to Rorkin and Peter."

"And I suppose he's the one who has been leaving clues in books," Annabel said, unsurprised. "It sounds just like what he would do. Things about Poly, and me, and the castle—oh, and that top hat of yours—"

Melchior laughed aloud. "I yield, Nan; I yield! Do try to leave me with some shreds of mysteriousness, won't you?"

"No," Annabel said. "I've had enough of mysteriousness. I'm going to make it a royal edict when I'm crowned. No More Mysteriousness. I won't let it slide for you, either."

"Won't you?" murmured Melchior, lifting her over a missing floorboard. He swung her lightly back to the floor, and curled close in against the wall with one arm around her waist. "Then shall I have to persuade you?"

"Yes," said Annabel, finding Melchior's coat collar a pleasant way to cling to him. "Try. But I think you ought to know that I'll need to be persuaded again and again."